Agnes Smith Lewis

The brides of Ardmore

a story of Irish life

Agnes Smith Lewis

The brides of Ardmore
a story of Irish life

ISBN/EAN: 9783744739696

Printed in Europe, USA, Canada, Australia, Japan

Cover: Foto ©Raphael Reischuk / pixelio.de

More available books at **www.hansebooks.com**

ROUND TOWER AND RUINS AT ARDMORE, COUNTY WATERFORD, WITH DÉCLAN'S ORATORY.

THE
BRIDES OF ARDMORE.

A STORY OF IRISH LIFE.

BY

AGNES SMITH,

Author of "Effie Maxwell," "Glenmavis," etc.

London:

ELLIOT STOCK, 62, PATERNOSTER ROW.

1880.

PREFACE.

The notes which form the basis of this story were found amongst the records of the nunnery at Kilcheechan, on the banks of the Suir, opposite the city of Waterford. They are in the handwriting of Grainné Ni-Carthy; only a few additions being from the pen of another. Considering the opportunities enjoyed by that fair matron for studying the characters and motives of her young companions, as well as indirectly through them, of their husbands, the Editress thinks herself fortunate in having become possessed of the record of a state of things now so completely passed away. She trusts that it will not be less welcome to the reader because of the historical and local descriptions with which she has sought to illustrate its meaning.

It may be as well to say, however, that by the word "bishop" is here meant, not the magnificent dignitary who now bears that title, but a member of the class to which it was applied by the Irish of the first eleven centuries. St. Patrick is stated to have ordained seven hundred of them. (See Appendix p. 379.)

THE BRIDES OF ARDMORE.

CHAPTER I.

It was summer-time at Ardmore. The sunbeams rested lovingly on the wide tract of woods surrounding the promontory, and on the still wider expanse of ocean which lay sleeping at its base. They had woven a tissue of rich colours about the picturesque dwellings which nestled close to the church and lofty Round Tower, and lent their deepest tints to the clustering foliage which blended these somewhat incongruous buildings into one harmonious whole.

The pine woods had been cleared away from Ardmore Hill. On its northern slope rose that slender, massive, solitary beacon, which has withstood the storms of centuries, and still hides in the silent circle of its bosom the mystery of its origin.

Some twenty-five yards distant from it stood the double church, whose massive walls yet testify to the strength of early Irish piety. Against its southern side rested some solid wooden buildings, whilst others of similar construction were grouped around the little stone cell of Declan, to the southeast of the church, and likewise against the inner side of the broad, grassy rampart which enclosed, at some distance, church, cell, tower, and *plateola*, or park.

These dwellings were, as we have said, of wood. They were well fitted and finished, most of them having double walls; whilst over their thatched roofs a variety of creeping plants had been trained. Many were brilliant with yellow lime-wash, and stood under the shadow of lofty oaks, whose large trunks screened them partly from view. Others, again, retained their natural colour, and could hardly be discerned amidst the bloom of honeysuckle and the scarlet splendour of the mountain ash. A variety of flowers, planted amongst beds of common vegetables, gave sweet sustenance to the inhabitants of numerous bee-hives, who, not content with their legitimate dwellings, had burrowed likewise amongst the roots of the trees.

Ardmore was still, seven centuries ago, an ecclesiastical colony. The handsome wooden buildings which nestled against its church were the refectory, kitchen, pharmacy, guest-hall, and manuscript-room of a Culdee settlement, or family. The huts around Declan's sanctuary were the cells of unmarried brethren, bishops, or students; whilst those under the shadow of the rath were the private property of those members who preferred to live in holy wedlock.* Five smaller stone churches, with curious conical roofs, served as places of retirement and preparation for those of the bishops whose turn it would next be to officiate in public worship.

The vallum, or rath, was a solid embankment of earth some seven feet in height. It was protected on the outer side by a ditch, and strengthened by a casing of rough stone covered over with mossy turf. On its summit flourished a quick hedge of mingled blackthorn, crab-apple, and elder.

One single hut broke this line of verdure: this was the Grianan, or guest-chamber, directly above the abbot's house; a round cottage whose solitary window caught the first rays of the morning sun, and commanded a view second only to that from the summit of the Round Tower.

The rath had only one legitimate entrance, spanned by a massively built low arch, opposite the western end of the

* See Appendix.

church. But several gaps in the hedge, with slender ladders reaching downwards from them, and short planks over the ditch, gave tokens that other paths of exit had been well trodden by nimble feet.

At a short distance outside of this rampart were a few humble wooden houses, flanked by sheds formed of double walls of wattles filled in with clay. Here were all the cheerful sights of a farmyard—cows swinging their long tails, plough horses tended by stalwart youths, and fowls scraping about after golden grains.

The afternoon was growing apace. The sun shone with less fierceness, as if half exhausted with his long effort; the hum of voices began to rise as the sweet tones of a silver bell sounded from the top of the tower. Then the pharmacy door swung on its hinges, and a white-robed girl stepped on to the greensward, carrying in her delicate hands an exquisitely leaved water lily.

The girl was short of stature, but possessed one of those finely-moulded forms which still delight us in the statues of ancient Greece. Her flowing linen robe reached scarcely to her ankles, and was confined by an " inar," or jacket, of soft green wool, and a zone of yellow leather, fastened by two large hooks of silver. Her graceful head was surmounted by ringlets of very dark auburn hair, and her brown eyes flashed from beneath long eyelashes. There was an air of slightness and yet of rounded womanliness about her whole person, made the more attractive by the piquant vivacity of her face. The hand which held the tender flower stem was delicate, yet not small: it had taper fingers, coloured with the hues of lilies and roses, yet the lines across the wrist announced it to be the active tool of an energetic brain; and the eyes, which drank so deep a draught of pleasure from the creamy cup of the water blossom, were yet prompt to mark every circumstance which could affect their owner's life duties. It was but a moment that she paused in the bright sunshine; then, stepping briskly forward, she crossed the green and entered one of the leaf-embowered cottages within the shadow of the western rampart wall.

Sorcha, for such was the girl's name, stood at once in a circular wood-panelled apartment, in the centre of which a round fireplace of hewn stone contained a few smouldering embers. The room was hardly eight feet high; yet, though the smoke issued from a hole in its roof through an iron funnel, its furniture presented an appearance of taste in harmony with the carvings about its entrance. Two settees, or beds, with coverlets of red deerskin, stood with their lower ends towards the fire, and on one of these was seated a figure sufficiently striking to engross all attention to itself.

Amada, Sorcha's grandmother, was a sunny old lady. Although stoutly built, and habited in a garment of dark wool, there was about her that air of comfort which we are wont to associate with tidy hearths and hospitable receptions. No one could gaze on her cheerful face, colourless, yet not pale, framed in its kerchief of snowy linen, and crowned by a wealth of blonde hair, without feeling that it was an embodiment of domestic peace and felicity. Yet for many years Amada had enjoyed no great share of worldly prosperity.

She was the only daughter of a wealthy Bo-aire, or gentleman farmer, as he would be called in these days. But in the twelfth century men had not progressed far in the art of doing business by deputy, or of making those ingenious arrangements by which the owners of wealth are absolved from the toil of preserving it. Angus O'Carrol possessed more than three hundred cattle, with the right of pasturing it on as many acres of fine land. He had by seven years' payment of tribute acquired a prospective right of ownership in some splendid fields on the death of his chief. Yet he sowed and reaped his own harvests, whilst his wife and daughter distinguished themselves by the excellence of their dairy produce. But Eugenia and Amada did not accomplish this entirely with their own hands. Attached to the soil were several families of *Bothachs*, or serfs, who furnished a constant supply of domestic and farm servants. It was considered meritorious on the part of wealthy matrons in that age to train members of the half-heathen population around them to habits of diligence and order. And if the works so strongly insisted on by the Apostle James had any efficacy in the way of entitling their possessor to a place in the Church, then assuredly the wife and daughter of Angus should have been considered as two of its palatial corner-stones. But apostolic rules are apt to be wondrously overlooked. Eugenia and Amada belonged to the minor gentry of the country. They could boast no near connection by blood with any of its hereditary chiefs, and still less with that clerical caste which was then attaching to itself as much homage as had formerly been bestowed only on the descendants of Erin's princes.

They deserved higher honour, nevertheless, than any earthly relationship could have given them. They were surely evangelists in the best sense of the word, maintaining in their own household a high standard of morality and good conduct, whilst every year reclaiming from downright barbarism some member of the population around them. Many clerical families in the neighbourhood had been supplied with good servants through Eugenia's tuition, but such advantages were taken by them as a matter of course ; it never once occurring to the lady-members to place her labours on an equality of importance with their own. The good woman's character was too much tempered by humility for her to perceive this. But her daughter Amada cherished a more far-reaching ambition.

She was early married to Rossa O'Ahern, a Bo-aire of the same class as her father. She brought with her a small dowry of cattle, the bulk of the property going, as was customary in that age, to a brother. Her new home was situated in a distant part of the country. She thus on entering it found herself completely separated from the associations of her early life. She possessed her mother's energy of character and her mother's conception of the obligation to make her home a pattern one. She had also sufficient shrewdness to discern the tendencies of thought and feeling then current in society, and one consuming wish took possession of her breast—the desire to see her children ennobled by alliances with the servants of the Most High. For the Celtic Church had come to occupy a position unique in the annals of Christendom. It was still independent of foreign control,* whilst its married priesthood enabled it to retain a sympathetic hold on the affections of the people. The social *status* of a family could not fail to be raised by connection with the Church, and as noble birth had been for centuries the best of qualifications for entrance into its ministry, the reigning families, both in Church and State, had gradually become welded into a most despotic oligarchy.

It would be doing Amada an injustice to say that the idea of thus raising herself ever formed itself quite distinctly in her mind. Her daughters were well educated, because she had a talent for stimulating their minds. She loved the Church on account of its being the depository of the truth. She waited on the lips of its servants as the Queen of Sheba did on Solomon's. Her husband was of an affectionately simple disposition; and what more worthy use could they imagine for their worldly goods than to place them at the disposal of those messengers of light whose feet were so beautiful on the mountains of their native land? After a hard day's work in fretting over the stupidity of some untaught being whom she was transforming into something human, after superintending the operations of dairy and kitchen, Amada was wont to deck herself in becoming array, and play the part of hostess to any tonsured guest whose necessities or love of good cheer induced him to seek her hospitable roof.

Such guests soon came in swarms, with their families.

* Appendix.

Amada's suppers became celebrated, not only for their culinary excellence, but for the flow of wit with which the viands were seasoned. We may doubt if the great Co-arb of Patrick himself had a more sprightly circle around his hearth. Contact with highly-cultivated minds was an education by which Amada was not slow to profit. Her rich intellect was as loamy land which has lain far down in a valley, and which some gentle upheaval of the earth's surface raises at length to the kind influence of continuous sunlight. But her mental progress laid bare to her view the deficiencies of her early training. Though an authority in domestic economy, and immeasurably superior to the herd of peasant girls with whom she came into hourly contact, she had not received that refined artistic culture which was the exclusive privilege of ladies born into the ecclesiastical world. She could read fluently the two copies of the Sacred Scriptures which were heirlooms in her family ; but she lacked the ready gift of transferring these to fresh parchment. She could not cheer with song the winter evenings, and the embroidery stitch of the Normans was an accomplishment far above her comprehension.

The consciousness of these things made her anxious that her daughters should not only become skilled in household management, but should be able to take no inferior place beside the graceful maidens whom they could not rival in birth, but might possibly surpass in those talents by which birth is so fittingly adorned. Nor did Moriath and Grainné fall short of their mother's expectations.

They were separated in age by only eighteen months. Yet with every apparent likeness in outward conditions, the real education of the two had been essentially different. For Amada had one real weakness of which she was totally unconscious. Her native shrewdness did not enable her to see that children are more likely to be peaceable and affectionate if treated with rigid impartiality. There was something in

Grainné which early touched a hidden spring in the mother's heart, and made her most unreasonably accord an undue measure of love and honour to the younger of her children. Perhaps it was some subtle trait in the infant features which recalled a memory from the dim recesses of the past; perhaps it was the fact that Grainné really was a very consequential little person, arrogating to herself the first place on all occasions, and displaying a self reliance and self-respect which partly satisfied the mother's wish for male offspring. The place which Grainné assumed she kept. Her very faults became virtues when viewed through the medium of maternal love, whilst the tender-hearted and bashful little Moriath might display excellence unnoticed. Their father observed the mischief only to aggravate it. When he tried to balance matters by praising Moriath, this had only the effect of making the mother more confident in her own opinion, and more determined to exalt Grainné in every possible manner. Not that her elder girl was neglected. As far as physical well-being was concerned, no children could have been better tended; but the unequal treatment told on both with an effect which could hardly have been expected. Her father being seldom in the house, except when guests were present, or on winter evenings, Moriath derived little advantage from his partisanship, and she came at length to acquiesce in that view of things which placed her sister on a lofty and unapproachable pedestal. Yet, as Moriath grew older, she was the more demonstratively affectionate of the two; the more solicitous about her mother's comfort, the more eager to meet her parents' wishes in the fulfilment of every domestic or literary task. She felt no sense of injustice; she was proud of her sister's superiority; and took it as a matter of course that the stately Grainné should attract all the admiration of strangers. Grainné was unmistakably clever. She had, her mother thought, been born with a faculty for always thinking and doing the right thing. Her reputation for possessing such a faculty was perhaps heightened by the self-confidence with which she enunciated her opinions, whereas Moriath's habit of quoting the views of others for the purpose of strengthening her own was an unfailing subject of amusement in the family. Amada's partiality was much to be regretted. It weakened the natural bond of sympathy between the sisters, and prepared trials for Grainné in later life which she might otherwise have been spared. Yet it did not seriously detract from the girl's merits. In a less worthy family it might have done so, but the two sisters enjoyed such exceptional advantages both of inheritance and of example that it would have been difficult for either of them to stoop to anything savouring of aught but high principle. They had an unfeigned respect for both their parents, and it was not till a wider knowledge dawned on Moriath with advancing years that she came to perceive the one flaw in her mother's character.

Theirs was indeed a happy home. All that could ennoble their young lives was present in full measure. The work of superintending servants, of instructing the ignorant of their own sex, and of economising in a way which had no savour of niggardliness, was but the necessary foundation on which their parents reared a structure of unbounded generosity. Amada was of a lively temperament; her husband no less so; innocent mirth and frolic were encouraged in so far as they did not trespass on the seriousness of work, or of religious duties. A cynical critic might have whispered that kindness to strangers was being carried too far; that the goods so lavishly bestowed on distinguished pastors might have been laid up for the girls' marriage portions. But Moriath and Grainné were too ignorant to cavil at this. They profited by the opportunities within their reach, whilst their mother received a deferential respect from men who were her *beau-ideals* of goodness which could not fail to exalt her in her own estimation. A change was, however, rapidly approaching.

CHAPTER II.

Ireland had, from the earliest times, been cursed with a superfluity of princes. Each of her five kingdoms contained a couple of ruling clans, whose members claimed a right of supplying the throne in alternation. Those who were out of office spent their time in concocting the most dangerous plots.

Nor was the ambition of an Irish king limited to the regions of his own inheritance. The choice of his four peers might make him Ard-righ, or sovereign of the whole island. But in that case he would have to compel obedience by his own good sword. Only when the strongest sat on the throne could Erin hope to enjoy peace.

Nor could any worse plan of succession have well been devised than the law of tanistry. No office or property was strictly hereditary; it fell, on the death of the occupier, to the oldest and strongest male relative; to the one, in short, who was considered most capable of using it. And as no personal defect could be tolerated in a ruler, great chieftains sought to evade the decrees of the Senchus Mòr by blinding their rebellious kinsmen. Thus was the whole country torn by contending factions.

Munster had, since the reign of Brian Borumha, enjoyed comparative prosperity. But it was, in A.D. 1151, overwhelmed by one of those catastrophes from which nations are slow to recover.

For nine years its throne had been occupied by the restless Turlough O'Brien, a monarch who possessed all the ambition without the genius or the patriotism of his great ancestor. He was much given to the royal sport of cattle-lifting, a pastime not unknown to the contemporaries of Achilles, and which was at least as good as that of trying to move his neighbour's landmarks indulged in by a Duke of Aquitaine or of Austria.

Turlough had made raids into Leinster, with very varying success. Emboldened at length by a victory, he led a band of marauders into Connaught, and knocked down the fort of Galway. Turlough O'Connor, the monarch of that district, was king of all Ireland, with opposition. He was " a flood of glory and splendour, the Augustus of the West of Europe;" but yet, though "full of charity and mercy, hospitality and chivalry," he was by no means the man to leave an insult unavenged. Joining with the notorious Leinster king, Dermod Mac Murrough, he invaded Munster, plundering right and left, till he reached the field of Moin Mòr, near Cork.

Then ensued a slaughter which can only be compared to that of Flodden. Turlough O'Brien was vanquished, and seven thousand of his men, the flower of Dalecassian valour, lay dead upon the field.* Amongst them was the tanist, or royal heir of Munster (a nephew of Turlough), with many of the Roydama, or king-material, and the chieftains of almost every clan. But on few did the blow fall more heavily than on the O'Aherns.

The Flath, to whom Rossa owned allegiance, was amongst the slain. Amada's peaceful home was soon engulfed beneath the waves of lawlessness and rapine which broke over the land. Its walls were not actually pulled down, but the fields which Rossa had cultivated were given to another; and the cattle, his only riches, were swept away to swell the enormous spoil with which the two kings returned to their own provinces.

* Appendix.

Amada had, with her daughters, sought refuge in the religious house connected with her husband's clan. But its precincts soon became too strait for the crowds who flocked thither; and though its actual sanctuary remained inviolate, all its outlying property was engulfed in the general ruin. When the danger had passed, therefore, the three women were glad to leave it for the shelter of their dismantled home. They found themselves face to face with poverty.

Rossa was, however, of a sanguine temperament. He had an unfailing trust in Providence. Had he not been a faithful steward whilst his riches lasted? and though he could no longer give the prophets food and clothing, would they not now remember the unnumbered kindnesses he had shown them? He had made to himself friends of the mammon of unrighteousness, and had secured protectors for his children in the event of further misfortune befalling them. At the worst, they might end their days in one of those women's monasteries now become so common throughout Ireland. Some of his former guests would surely have influence sufficient to procure for Moriath and Grainné a favourable reception at Cluain-Credhail, or at Killcbree.

Rossa found, however, that he had reckoned too rashly. His clerical friends, who had professed such a warm attachment to him, who had flattered him for virtues he was hardly conscious of possessing, seemed now to have a strange dislike to visiting him without express invitation. And Amada's pride would have been keenly wounded had she been obliged to receive any one without placing suitable cheer before them. The few whose friendship was as effusive as of yore were all of the poorer sort—men without influence, bishops certainly, but unconnected with any of those families whose members alone were supposed eligible for the office of presbyter-abbot. Amongst those few was a bishop named Maidoc O'Bric.

Maidoc was a middle-aged man, who had long enjoyed the

pastoral care of a neighbouring village. Its people were devotedly attached to him, yet neither his name nor his voice were ever heard more than a few miles beyond it. The poor became accustomed to him as they did to any common gift of Providence. Yet he had acquired a degree of learning which might have made him a conspicuous figure in any of the great centres of intelligence. His sermons were extremely impressive. He possessed a ripeness of thought which melted into mild words, and made hearers hang on his lips with the confidence of those who need fear no disappointment.

There was something sterling about Maidoc. You could see that at a glance, although you might never have listened to the equable flow of his eloquence in the pulpit. He was stout, with a massive figure. His dark eyes were small and unimpressive, and he was of so taciturn a disposition that you might possibly have passed him over as a man of only ordinary ability. But a careful scrutiny would have dispelled the illusion. The small eyes were intensely observant; the full lips were quivering with expression, as if responsive to every movement of their owner's soul.

Would that he had possessed more energy! So thought Amada when, in the day of her prosperity, she indulged in a secret laugh at him. "There is no one I like better to hear in the pulpit," she would say. "Yet his wife and he seem as if they shared a single voice between them. He uses it in public, she in private, and certainly with discretion."

"Yes," Grainné would answer; "it is provoking to see him listen so often to disputations which he could settle with a single word."

"Maidoc is not in his right place," her mother would respond; "preaching to poor people, when he might be in a lector's chair. He will have to wait all his life if he expects others to speak for him. He has been kept in the background only because the great men know him not. I tried to make him talk when some of them were here. He will never have such an opportunity again. But it was of no use. The man sat and listened as if he had been one of the stone heads on King Cormac's new church at Caisel."

But Amada's wit spared Maidoc in the time of her adversity. Then he came, noiseless as the fall of a dew-drop, but with a movement of lip and hand that spoke more eloquently than words could have done. Roused from the habitual torpor which only seemed to master him when he was in society, he was all eagerness, all attention, and sat imbibing the story of the family's hardships as if it were an aliment necessary to the growth of a stronger affection for them.

"I cannot pretend to sit at your board," he said, " any more than I can ask you to do so at mine. I am poor as you are. If I can make you any return for the great kindness you have shown me, let it be in the way of instruction. Your daughters may come and read with me on any evening they like to fix."

From that moment Bishop Maidoc held the most honoured place in Rossa's household. It was felt that he had redeemed the character of his brethren. But for him Amada's faith would have been sorely shaken in the excellence of a divinely ordained institution. Her late experiences had not, however, altogether opened her eyes to the earthy nature of the vessels in which world-blessing treasures were deposited. She had an ardent Celtic temperament, much given to hero-worship. Her hero was Blathmac O'Flannahan, and though now little gratified by sight of him, it was wonderful how ingenious she was in excuses for his lack of friendliness.

"He has the care of all the churches on his shoulders," she said. "I must say I wonder at the O'Mullaneys and others. But Blathmac! The very touch of his garment is an honour, without his giving up his time to us. He belongs to the Church ; not to one nor to another."

Grainné could not help thinking that Blathmac had once

looked as if he belonged to them, and had time enough to spare when there were mead and milk flowing. She was wise enough, however, not to contradict her mother.

Maidoc was not quite justified in calling himself poor. If a man's wealth were to be measured by his chains of the metal rings which represented the currency of that day, the good bishop assuredly could lay no claim to any amount of it. But he was rich in what money seldom gives. His wants never exceeded what could be furnished by his modest pittance. The only luxury he indulged in was books, and, as he had free access to the library at Lismore, there was little necessity for his turning spendthrift to gratify his tastes. The confraternity of Ardmore, to which he was attached, would see justice done to him in the matter of a retreat for his old age, whilst both his office and character ensured him a full meed of respect and honour. He had, moreover, made the best of all acquisitions in a helpmeet who was more than the exact complement of himself. She was one of those women whom to look at is to love. Her features were not strictly faultless, but they were the translucent covering of a soul whose brightness seemed to glorify their every outline. She was devotedly attached to her husband, and all the more so that Providence had not blessed their union with children. Her wifely and maternal instincts were alike gratified by her incessant care for his welfare; and whilst he leant on her in all practical matters, she reverenced him for the learning which she was sufficiently well instructed to appreciate. Their souls had become so much blended into one that it was difficult to imagine how they had ever lived apart.

Yet another bishop remained true to Rossa. He was, however, cast in a very different mould. The first look of him would have repelled you. His harsh features, dark complexion, and stern, brown eye told of a spirit as unbending as it was rigidly virtuous. Yet he knew how to make himself agreeable. You would feel flattered, my fair reader, were the fierce lion of the desert to crouch submissive at your feet; so you need not wonder that Amada and her daughters were gratified to see the harshest critic of their acquaintance unbending grimly to the enjoyment of jokes at their table.

Olrud MacCarthy's motives for coming there were twofold. His movements were, I grieve to state, governed in the first place by self-interest. He was connected with the religious foundation of Inisfallen, and at Rossa's house some of the more distinguished members of that confraternity were to be found; not engaged in the fulfilment of duty, but in that state of leisurely enjoyment so favourable to the growth of mutual goodwill. It was possible that some of those whose voices were all-powerful in council, might get a better insight into Olrud's worth and capabilities than they were likely to do in the wilds of Kerry. Of the worth there could be no question, and as for the capabilities, they were, in their owner's opinion, of no common order. He belonged to an obscure family. It was not without a hard struggle that he had obtained entrance into the clerical profession. His father had been Erenach, or hereditary bailiff, over the termon-lands of Inisfallen, and it was therefore considered that the son had stepped out of his sphere by becoming a student of theology. He was also, on his mother's side, descended from a so-called water-hound, or Dane who had acquired the rights of an Irishman by marriage. Olrud felt himself looked upon as an outsider by men of less ability who could count their ministerial ancestors. He had a notion that he might possibly triumph over these disadvantages by attracting some great man's notice. Nor did any constitutional timidity stand in the way of his doing this. No matter who might be present, Olrud's voice was always the first in prayer or exhortation. To have a sense of one's own superiority is a great step towards impressing it on others, and one result of Olrud's efforts was that a vivid conception formed itself in his mind of the intensity of admiration with which every one regarded him. Another was that, whilst some looked up to his stalwart figure with venerating awe, many of his brethren entertained towards him a dislike which they would have found it difficult to account for.

Other motives soon allied themselves to this one in prompting Olrud's visits. He derived real enjoyment from the society he met with, and felt a lively sense of gratitude for opportunities already vouchsafed to him. For Olrud was much given to self-examination, being one of those regular, well-conducted men who must shape their thoughts into definite words before putting them into action. He could no more act from impulse than he could be guilty of calling himself a fool. He had a high standard of rectitude, and was unmeasured in his condemnation of those who failed to conform to it in any one particular. Conscious of no frailty himself, he could make little allowance for it in others.

His second motive took root and developed itself at a much later period. A superficial observer would have found it no easy task to discover whether or not Olrud possessed a heart; yet a closer examination might have convinced him that such an organ actually existed. It was not capable of great expansion, but there it was, making up for what it lacked in the way of bulk by exceeding tenacity of fibre. And it was altogether an ill-used member. It was not allowed to utter a word until its intellectual colleague had decided on several interesting points, viz., that matrimony was an honourable estate; that it was distinctly enjoined on bishops in the Epistle to Timothy; that thirty-seven was an age when a man ought to be competent to make a wise selection; that a Christian young woman would be a help rather than a hindrance to the growth of spiritual life; and that he, Olrud, would be neglecting his plain duty were he not to admit such an one to the valuable example and instruction to be derived from his society.

Another set of points required more anxious deliberation;

but after a careful scrutiny they were at length determined, and it was resolved by all his faculties in solemn council, that Grainné Ni-Ahern was likely to fulfil all the requisite conditions. Any want of gravity on her part would doubtless disappear when she had become sufficiently impressed with his solemn teachings ; and though there was an element of liveliness about her and her mother, which was perhaps of less consequence in a layman's family, he had never noticed in either of them the least approach to a love of slander. As for sobriety, faithfulness, and ability to rule over her dependents, no one could look Grainné fairly in the face and harbour a suspicion that she would be found wanting in them. She was comely too, she had a goodly presence, and was indeed of an appearance which must command attention. She had been well brought up, and had doubtless inherited from her parents that esteem for good men which is a great help towards being good ourselves.

It would be doing Olrud more than justice to say that he did not count on Grainné's portion. But before we can determine whether he was really in love with her, we must reflect that there were few others who would have suited him. The daughters of his brethren were not without proper ambition, and he had too great a horror of being refused on account of his want of birth to apply where he had no sure hope of success. Amongst the lay families he knew there were none so well educated or so worthy of being raised to the clerical caste as the children of his friend Rossa. Olrud was unfeignedly thankful that it had pleased Providence to bestow on the object of his choice the worthless gift of personal comeliness.

He was keenly disappointed when Rossa's circumstances changed. But it did not turn him from his purpose. His resolutions, once formed, were like well-feathered arrows that must fly straight at the mark to which they are pointed; whether that mark be the quivering side of a victim, or the misleading glimmer of a rock amongst the copsewood. So in the day of Rossa's deepest distress he came forward with his proposal.

Amada did not receive it favourably. Olrud had never been a favourite of hers. She had more than once been provoked by his forwardness in the way of taking up the word when cleverer men were present. She had often resented his dictatorial manners and unreasoning condemnation of others. She would have said " no," with poverty staring her daughter in the face. Rossa, however, insisted that Grainné should have the opportunity of deciding for herself.

To the surprise of her parents, Grainné hesitated. She claimed a night to think over it, and in the morning requested them to accept for her the offered position.

" I know that he is peculiar," she said. " He likes his own way, and is much too severe in his judgments. But recollect that he has had no female companions. His mother died when he was a baby. It says a great deal for him that he asks for me now. He is a man of thorough integrity, and will perhaps bear to be told that he sometimes encroaches on other people's right to converse. I have no wish to have my own way. In fact, I should rather like to be ruled. It would be a variety," she continued, with an affectionate glance at her mother.

" Thou knowest not of what thou speakest," exclaimed Amada.

" I do, mother," replied the self-willed girl. " I have thought well over it. I should like a firm hand over me."

Rossa shrugged his shoulders. He glanced meaningly at his wife. It probably occurred to both that Grainné was not so far wrong in preferring wedded life, of whatever sort, to the monotony of the cloister which threatened soon to be their only refuge.

Rossa had been obliged to form a definite plan. There were two ways open before him. He might rent other land,

and stock it; but he would have to do so on borrowed money, and the only dealer in that commodity he could think of was an Israelite in Waterford, upon whose greed there existed no check except an outbreak of anger on the part of the populace which could only be counted on once in ten years, and was even then likely to be vicariously applied. It seemed far better that he should give up farming, and seek a post in the permanent military retinue of King Tadg O'Brien, brother of the vanquished Turlough. No other career was open to a gentleman who had lost his connection with the soil. And loyal soldiers could always look forward to a share in the fruits of pillage. For the sovereign of Ireland maintained his authority only by a ceaseless struggle with hydra-headed rebellion, strengthening himself not a little by fomenting feuds between the more powerful clans who were nominally subject to him. Turlough O'Connor had divided Munster betwixt Tadg O'Brien and Cormac MacCarthy, after banishing his own formidable namesake. Those who were in the service of either chieftain need never suffer from lack of victual. Rossa had no alternative. He shrank from the idea of dragging his family down to the condition of Bothachs, and allowing the culture they had so laboriously acquired to disappear in the next generation. The money he would get by selling his house would be sufficient to procure admission for Amada and Moriath to Killchree, and if fortune so far favoured him as to place distinction or affluence within his reach, there would be no difficulty about their rejoining him—the Celtic Church not having yet discovered that vows of perpetual celibacy were pleasing to the Creator.* For was not the royal heir of Ireland, Roderick O'Connor, himself, descended from a twice-wedded Cailleach Dé, or nun of Glendalough ?

It was long before Rossa's resolution took definite shape. Nothing but the actual pinch of want could have ripened it, for the house which he proposed selling had belonged to his

* Appendix.

family for a period beyond the memory of any one living. Yet he bore it with more resignation than did Amada. She did not share his buoyant hopes as to the future.

" They would have been natural enough in a young man," she said, " but in him they were simply preposterous. Neither King Tadg nor King Cormac would be on the throne an hour after Turlough came back from Tyrone. It would be safer to wait and see who *was* their sovereign. And the world was much rougher than Rossa expected. She would not murmur at her own lot, as far as creature comforts were concerned; but the constant anxiety she would feel about him would be sure to shorten her days."

There were yet other hearts who sympathised with the family's distress. The poor faithful servants whom Amada had instructed; the labourers who had ploughed their lands; the peasant families who had looked on Rossa as both kinsman and master, showed a depth of feeling which could hardly have been expected from such half-tutored men and women. But their own households had lately been invaded by famine and by epidemic disease, and many of them had emigrated to Leinster; and thus a wail for their own sorrows mingled with the groans of those who wept over the threatened departure of their kind benefactors.

CHAPTER III.

Rossa was not, however, permitted to carry out his plans. Ere the preparations for Grainné's marriage were completed, he fell a victim to the prevailing pestilence. This event threw his family into a double dilemma. It at once deprived them of their best earthly stay, and the means for procuring an asylum for themselves. The house could not now be sold. By the Brehon law it passed to the next of kin, females being excluded from the succession. The sons of Rossa's only cousin were not slow in putting in their claim. Amada was at first too much stunned for action. But Moriath showed the spirit of a heroine. She told her sister's bridegroom that he was at liberty to withdraw his offer if he felt so inclined. This Olrud had no thought of doing. But he certainly looked black enough at the possibility of having two additional females on his hands.

"Give thyself no concern," said Moriath ; "I will take service in some noble house, and I will work until I can repay thee what thou expendest on my mother."

"Where wilt thou gain admittance ? " asked Olrud.

"I shall go to each one who has eaten at our table," replied Moriath. "I shall tell our story, and say that it is not for myself I beg, but because I know thou art too poor to have such a burden thrown on thee. Thou wouldst be happier with Grainné alone. There is no reason why I should not work for our maintenance ; I shall find a friend somewhere."

So Moriath went from one religious settlement to another, inquiring for women whose fathers or husbands had been wont to make much of her. I grieve to say that she was for the most part very coldly received. The families to whom she applied had taken her parent's kindness as a matter of course. It had indeed been a condescension on their part to accept of it. They had received it as an humble recognition of the greatness and sacredness of their hereditary vocation.

"Amada has benefited her own soul," was their tacit rejoinder. "She has no right to expect a reward on this side of the grave."

Moriath at length, mounted on Olrud's pony, and accompanied by a peasant and his sister, journeyed towards Ardmore. Her youthful face wore an expression of unutterable sadness. There were blue circles round her dark eyes, and her pale lips were firmly pressed together. She could think of no friend in the settlement save the chief Lector, and with him her acquaintance was slighter than with many of those who had refused to aid her.

Leaving her humble companions outside the arched gateway of the rath, she inquired timidly for Mael-Patrick's cell. She was immediately conducted towards the simple stone hut now known as Declau's dormitory. Entering by the low, narrow doorway, she found herself in an apartment whose bare walls, scarce ten feet high, were hung round with leathern book-satchels, and pierced by a solitary round-headed window. The Prue-lector was a young man, she knew not if he were wedded. And Moriath trembled to stand in the presence of one whose fame had spread far beyond the bounds of his native land. A handsome, golden-haired form rose from a wooden table as she entered.

Moriath could never tell what she said. Her tears flowed fast, and she sobbed; for Mael-Patrick's brotherly tones touched all the aching chords in her heart. She told him of her weary journeys, of the coldness of her former friends. "I want nothing but work," she said; "I seek the favour of some one who will speak for me to a chieftain's or an abbot's wife."

Very lovely Moriath looked in her mantle of dark wool, bordered with green, and fastened on her breast by a small silver clasp. Her large brown eyes were flashing with eagerness.

Mael-Patrick placed his hands behind his head, and stepped to the door. He stood for a few minutes inhaling the fresh sea breezes ; then turned and seated himself at her side.

"I think that Providence showeth me something else," he said, fixing his thoughtful eyes tenderly on her. "My mother was taken from me some months ago, and I have felt lonely. My work has taken hold upon me, and I cannot leave it to go in search of a wife. I have prayed that God would send me one ; and lo! when thou didst enter my cell, it seemed as if an angel touched me, saying, ' Arise, and take what the Lord giveth.' "

The calm, gentle voice assured Moriath that the good bishop was not jesting. She looked up in his face ; there was a seraphic sweetness in it. He continued,—

"Think not that I speak as a fool. The little that I saw of thy father impressed me deeply with his worth. And thy mother is one with whom the bishops' wives here cannot be compared. All speak her praises, so that it passes my comprehension how they fly not to her help. Thy young heart has been wounded ; let mine be the hand to bind it up."

Mael-Patrick hardly spoke with the diffidence of a lover. And yet he was of a modest nature. But he was too simple-minded not to expect Moriath's acquiescence. He was famed for his learning and piety ; he knew that his wife would share his honours. She would feel herself sanctified by union with him.

Moriath was unspeakably thankful ; but she dared not think entirely of herself. "And my mother ? " she asked humbly.

" Thy mother may dwell with us," replied Mael-Patrick ; " but if it please her to dwell with thy sister, let me bear the half of her maintenance. She will be to me in the place of her who is gone."

Moriath kissed his hand gratefully. How he responded to that demonstration of affection she never disclosed ; but she left Declan's cell with flushed cheeks and sparkling eyes.

Grainné received the news with bewildered astonishment, and undertook to communicate it to her mother. But it produced an effect on Amada the very contrary of what might have been expected. Whilst her children's hearts beat high at this sudden deliverance from a crushing anxiety, she deemed their looks of contentment slightly unbecoming.

" It was not the way that people courted in my young days," she said. "I cannot say that I think Mael-Patrick has behaved handsomely. A man of his standing ought to have known better than take advantage of a girl's simplicity. The proper way would have been to have paid me a visit, and asked my consent first."

Amada was not altogether wrong in her judgment. Mael-Patrick had been quite irregular in his mode of proceeding, according to the manners of that age ; nothing but his entire singleness of purpose could have excused him. Well-trained maidens never expected to hear the accents of love till after the suitor had sought and obtained the consent of their natural guardians ; and it may be questioned if they were in aught less happy in consequence.

"I know it was wrong, mother," said the kind-hearted Grainné, noticing how perplexed and abashed her sister was. " I mean that it would have been wrong in any one but Mael-Patrick. He has very little time for his own affairs. He will come and ask thee properly as soon as he can make it convenient."

" Then I shall let him know my mind," replied Amada.

"I hope, mother, that thou art not going to refuse him,"

persisted Grainné, who was accustomed to a boldness of language which would have been considered impertinence from Moriath. "It would be madness for thee to do so. He offers Moriath a home, and that is a great thing in the present circumstances. Bethink thee, too, who Mael-Patrick is. Thou must be very wicked if thou dost not expect to get benefit from his sermons, thou who art always troubling thyself about thy soul."

Grainné was the more noble in her advocacy of her sister's interests, because she felt a slight touch of chagrin at the prospect of that sister's lot being more brilliant than her own. But she had a strong love of justice, and had been deeply touched by Moriath's heroism. She was also acute enough to perceive that her mother's very virtues made her incapable of appreciating the ordeal through which Moriath had passed.

What could Amada know of the world? She could claim to have been longer in it than Grainné had, and her trials had been severe enough; but she had never herself known what it was to seek help from strangers. She had no conception of the coldness which the prosperous so often show to those who have the smallest favour to ask from them. Moriath had tried to spare her feelings and keep up her spirits by studiously concealing the depth of the unkindness she had met with; and she had done so the more willingly, perhaps, that she had found her mother inclined to charge her with an uncharitable exaggeration when she had endeavoured to depict the scenes through which she had passed. Amada had by far too favourable an opinion of human nature in general, and of the human natures in particular which had been developed under the influence of habits and beliefs which she held sacred. She was actually disposed to blame Moriath's pride and want of tact for the ill-success of her efforts.

"And it was bold in thee to go to Ardmore," she said. "I could not have done such a thing; no, not for worlds."

"I daresay thou wouldest not," muttered Grainné to herself, hardly able to control her rising anger.

But the soft touch of her sister's hand silenced her. "Let her alone," said the weeping Moriath. "She will see her mistake in another world, if not here. If thou canst persuade her to be kind to Mael-Patrick, that is all I want."

Two days later the good bishop presented himself. Amada showed herself more agreeable than her daughters could have anticipated; and as he very gracefully apologised for the irregularity he had committed, she soon looked, as Grainné said, "almost as if she were in love with him herself." Nor would it have been quite impossible for a man to reciprocate such a feeling. Amada had now reached the age of fifty-five; but much of the charm of her youth was perpetuated in the graceful vivacity of her manners. Her regular features, fair complexion, and wealth of soft light hair formed as pretty a picture as one could wish to gaze on. And her conversation was adorned by a play of wit which seemed to afford as much diversion to herself as to any of her hearers. Moriath was intensely happy at seeing that the two beings she loved so much completely understood each other. A hallowed influence spread itself around, for even Olrud's harsh voice became subdued in the presence of one whom he held in unfeigned honour.

The wedding ceremony was as simple as could be. It took place in Bishop Maidoc's little church. As his mild voice spoke the irrevocable words which united the two couples to each other, Amada hardly felt as if she were giving her girls away; but thought with thankfulness of how the Lord had led her by a path which she knew not, and that she was now indeed a mother in Israel, having Mael-Patrick for a son-in-law. She blamed herself because she could not feel quite the same towards Olrud. He was a bishop also; there was no fault to be found with his orthodoxy, nor with his integrity either. Yet she could not help wishing that her darling

Grainné had waited a little longer. Amada readily forgot the past, and the straits she had been in when Olrud came forward. After the marriage the brides thought of departing to their respective homes.

"Thou must get ready to go," remarked Grainné to her mother. "Our cousin has let us stay here only till after the wedding. We must not trespass more on his good nature. Olrud thinks thou canst ride on his pillion."

"But I have been considering about it," said Amada slowly, "and I have made up my mind now. Though I shall always think of thee, and would like to visit thee in summer, I would like—after all, I think I would like better to stay at Ardmore."

Amada hardly dared to look at her daughter's face as she said this. Grainné was not, however, so much disconcerted as she had anticipated. She replied in a cheerful tone—

"Well, in sooth, mother, I think it would be better. Mael-Patrick is richer than Olrud, and Moriath will take good care of thee. Of course, I should have liked thee, and when thou tirest of them, I shall only be too glad to have thee. But then, Ardmore is such a pleasant place, full of everything thou canst desire, and has such good society. I can hardly expect thee to prefer Killague.

Amada's words formed an era in Moriath's life. They were a revelation to her, more precious even than the one which she had heard from Mael-Patrick's lips in Declan's cell. The affectionate self-denial of years now found an unexpected reward. She could imagine no greater bliss than the consciousness that her mother appreciated her loving care so much as to prefer her roof to that of the idolised Grainné.

CHAPTER IV.

Thus it came to pass that the pretty circular-roofed wooden cottage was built under the oak trees within the grassy rath which enclosed the monastic settlement of Ardmore. There Moriath enjoyed for years a social position second only to that of the abbot's wife.

It would be a mistake, however, to suppose that these were years of unclouded happiness. Earth is not now an Eden, and the breezes of Paradise have long ceased to ripen for us the fruits of contentment. For as the harmony of the planets' movements is disturbed by outward and sometimes unsuspected causes, so the members of Mael-Patrick's family could not fail to be influenced in their relations to one another by the state of affairs in a far-off household.

Grainné was not happy. Her mother's foreboding of evil had not been quite unfounded. She possessed an excellent husband. But integrity, though a very desirable quality in itself, does not form the sum total of what makes life tolerable for us. It is like the framework of bones which gives strength and shape to our figures, but when brought into undue prominence without a sufficient covering of softer substances, is apt, notwithstanding its wondrous perfection, to appear ungainly. Grainné had not been mistaken in saying she would like to be ruled. She could have submitted to power of will matched with power of intellect, but she was not long enamoured of it when separate from such companionship. Her natural spirits were high, and she made a heroic effort to curb them in deference to her husband's wishes. But the habit grew irksome. Her active mind worked with the more vigour by reason of its being thrown so much on its own resources, and she at length made the fatal discovery that her husband was much her inferior; in fact, that he was often wrong in the very moment when he most took credit to himself for being right. When her eyes had once been opened in this way, and a closer observation confirmed their testimony, the reverence with which she had regarded him was gone. The memory of her marriage vows was terribly strained by being so constantly used to support her in the duty of submission. Nor was Olrud altogether to blame for this. It lay in the constitution of his mind. He could no more help taking harsh and narrow views of things than he could help the darkness of his complexion. Grainné was not altogether what he had expected. She knew rather less of housekeeping than he had given her credit for; in fact, she must have taken more than her share of praise when under her parents' roof. She was accustomed to state her views much too readily, and with a decision altogether unbecoming a Christian matron in presence of her husband. It required a great deal of firmness and patience on his part to break her off this, and more than once his dream of success in having accomplished it was rudely broken through by a display of temper on her part. He was not himself the meekest of men; in fact, he was in the habit of comparing his character more with that of Elijah than with Moses. Grainné ought to have seen it to be an aggravation of her faults that they undoubtedly hindered him in the work of testifying against the corruptions of the Church and of society. He was even provoked into retorting sometimes with more vigour than was necessary, as if he wanted to crush the evil for ever. And he was much irritated at perceiving that the medicine had acted too strongly; that his wife was now lacking in the cheerfulness which had distinguished her; in fact, that her handsome face might rather have belonged to a martyr than to a happy mother in Israel. But before we blame him for this state of things we are bound in all candour to examine if he was responsible for it.

Grainné and he had been most unequally mated. She was not only remarkably clever, but her natural gifts had been cultivated to a degree which would have fitted a member of the rougher sex for the highest functions of government. Her mind was like a full flowing stream, which in a well-directed channel might have been a source of unspeakable blessing and comfort to all around it; but which, after the freedom of its wild youth is past, finds itself hemmed in and crushed together by the resistance of stern, unyielding rocks. Her misfortune was not simply her husband's inferiority to herself; it lay rather in the fact that he was quite incapable of appreciating her. His idea of what a woman should be was founded partly on literary descriptions, but still more on the productions of his own inner consciousness; for, unknown to himself, Olrud possessed some grains of a faculty he professed to despise, and was more indebted to imagination than to revelation in this very matter. The age had long passed when women had been slaves. That was a relic of heathenism, which the spirit of Christianity had so far banished as to give to a Bridget and a Cera the highest of places in Celtic hagiology. But every woman could not be a Bridget, and the near approach to equality which the working of liberal ecclesiastical institutions had procured for her was not as yet quite realised or acknowledged. Grainné, moreover, had been spoiled by her mother. She had never been accustomed to put the rein on her rebellious spirit, and the lesson of submission was now doubly hard. All honour to her for learning it as she did. No ascetic who lies on the bare ground and scourges himself has half so hard a battle with the flesh. But there were ugly scars remaining from the conflict, and it needed all the balm of Christian principle to make the two hearts forget their soreness,

And no conflict can happen quite unobserved. Strangers might not notice it; indeed, many thought that Grainné must be either very good or very blind to get on so well with Olrud. But her altered appearance when she first visited Ardmore gave both Amada and Moriath a sad shock. Her features were the same, there could be no doubt of that, and when alone with them she sometimes enjoyed a laugh in her old merry way. But her opinions were advanced, even to Mael-Patrick, with an unwonted timidity, and the look of chastened fear she cast on her husband when asking his consent to anything had something strikingly painful in it. She was changed—changed beyond the hope of recovery. A sadness had stamped itself on her handsome features, and quenched the bright, keen sparkle of her dark eyes. It was the same face, with the freshness of youth for ever gone, and the cares of middle life written on it far too closely.

Can we wonder if a feeling of bitterness arose in the minds of both mother and sister ? Grainné never complained ; only once when Moriath, throwing her arms around her neck, asked if she were not happy, she burst into a copious flood of tears. She never said that her husband was unkind; it was touching, indeed, to hear her identifying herself with him. But nothing can deceive loving eyes, and even Mael-Patrick shook his head when he spoke of her appearance in former days. The memory of that visit left a gloom in the peaceful cottage.

Moriath felt that her mother's heart was elsewhere. Amada had indeed too many resources to allow of her constantly brooding. Her time during the bright hours was mostly given to reading. The Sacred Scriptures, the Confessions of Augustine, the Commentaries of Sedulius, and the stories of the martyrs were never-failing treasuries of interest for her. But during the long hours of semi-darkness by her daughter's fireside, or meditating on her fur-covered couch, she passed many watches in groaning and tears. She felt herself afflicted beyond measure, all the more so that it was by a grief whose extent was hidden from her.

" I saw it all at a glance," she said ; " I looked at his hard face, and I knew how it was. Grainné was never accustomed to dictation from any one. She was not a girl it was good for. Thou wouldst have borne it better, Moriath ; 'tis in thy nature."

" Indeed I would not, mother," replied Moriath ; " I never would have placed myself in the way of it ; but I would not have covered it up as she does ; I would have cleared the air by a storm."

" Thou couldst not have had a storm with Olrud," replied Amada ; " thou wouldst soon have been wrecked."

In vain did Moriath try to divert her mother's mind by assiduous attentions. Amada was nursed and tended like a princess. The best seat in church was kept for her ; and the most able men were encouraged to come and converse with her on the long winter evenings. Her every want was anticipated. But her thoughts were far away with the child of her heart.

There was indeed a striking contrast in the lot of the two sisters. Mael-Patrick was reported rich, not in the way that we understand the word, nor in the way that it would have been understood by an Irish chieftain. But he had more than most bishops, much more than was sufficient for his humble wants. The heads of the Ardmore community lived in a style that was almost luxurious, their principal meal being taken in the great refectory, whilst Amada's were supplied from the college kitchen. Her simple mind could scarcely grasp the idea that it was possible to wish for better. And Moriath had only one child, whilst the poorer Grainné had to struggle through the task of providing for six. From no point of view did the contrast present itself more vividly to Amada's mind than from that of education. She saw clearly how it would be. Sorcha would have every advantage which that age could offer. No Norman nor Irish princess could be nurtured with more care, or have her eyes and fingers better trained in all feminine arts. She would be entitled to a place amongst the noblest and most distinguished ; and she was being reared on a soil which had nourished worse seeds into forms of enduring beauty. The other little ones, some of whom had inherited Amada's own features, and about whom she could trace signs of their descent from beloved ones now in glory, would have need of all their native vigour to push upwards from the common level of their countrymen. Amada would have liked all her grandchildren to be distinguished ; indeed, she would scarce wish to own them for hers if they were not. She had a very keen sense of the value of a thorough training to prepare them for becoming so. " The very carrots need the husbandman's hand," she would say to Moriath. " Our children's characters are greatly our own work. I know well I have not done my duty by thee, but that is no reason why thou and Grainné should not do yours."

Thus the years wore on, Amada fretting more and more over her inability to help her younger daughter. But a more terrible trial was in store for her. Mael-Patrick was stricken with deadly fever; Moriath caught the infection whilst nursing him, and both were consigned to an untimely tomb.

Sorcha was then fifteen years of age. Her father, with wise foresight, had evaded the working of the Brehon laws by purchasing from the abbot a right for his daughter to reside in the old cottage. She had a claim on the college for maintenance and education, and no objection could possibly be made to her grandmother's sharing the humble roof with her. There need be no anxiety about Sorcha's future. Within the rath of Ardmore she would be well sheltered from the storms which were then rending the nation into fragments; and by right of birth alone she was entitled to have her interests furthered in every way. Her father's labours had thrown such a lustre over Ardmore that the family of its pastors would have considered themselves disgraced if she had been suffered to lack anything. If troublous times came, if Danish pirates were to scatter the learned community, or if unholy hands were again to rifle the treasury of Declan, why then Sorcha would be no worse off than other maidens. She would be sure to acquire those aptitudes which would make her an honoured guest at any European court.

Mael-Patrick's death was sincerely mourned. He had been beloved as few of his colleagues or predecessors had ever been. No great demonstration of esteem had gladdened him in his lifetime; but over his mouldering bones men began to realise that a great man had passed away. He had been made of the same stuff as the olden saints; as the men who had attended on Patrick's footsteps; as those who had sailed with Columba to bestow a new baptism and a new name on the wild Caledonians, or those others who had founded amongst the snowy Alps communities which were an everlasting praise to the Western Church. Projects which his loving voice would never have succeeded in recommending, now became quite feasible, because he had formed them. Amongst these was the transplantation of Bishop Maidoc to a congenial soil. This excellent man was called to Ardmore, to fill Mael-Patrick's place as theological lector and custodian of parchments. In this Amada greatly rejoiced. It was like the return of old times, she said. And she had been partly the means of it. Mael-Patrick had known Maidoc all the better by reason of her descriptions; and she had lost no time in telling the abbot how much her son-in-law had set his heart on it. It was a great benefit to the Church to have a man like Maidoc drawn out of obscurity; and it was a gratification for Amada to see his kindness to her and hers repaid to him tenfold.

Maidoc proved himself worthy of the honour. His powers

in the pulpit were beginning to fail ; and teaching was a work for which he had a special aptitude. His worth was soon recognised, and his unassuming manners awakened no jealousy amongst his brethren. He and his wife felt a special obligation to act the part of parents towards Sorcha. Thus the widow and orphan found counsellors provided for them at the time when they were most in need.

CHAPTER V.

AMADA soon became alive to her new responsibilities. Her daughter's sudden death was a rude awakening from the dream which had carried her away from the realities of her present surroundings. It was very painful for her aged eyes to adjust themselves to their new relations, but she possessed too much native vigour to shrink from the ordeal. The blow that would have crushed a meaner spirit only stimulated her to take a fresh hold on life. She was now responsible for something, and that something stood before her in the shape of a very lovely girl, whose features recalled memories of one whom all Erin almost worshipped, and whose flashing dark eyes were the image of Moriath's. Sorcha's tones never fell unheeded on her ears; Sorcha's gentle touch thrilled her aged frame with new life, like the soft spring rain falling on some brown, knotted trunk. Amada was indeed little able to attend to household affairs, but there was no need for her doing so. The warm-hearted peasant girl who had accompanied Moriath in her memorable journey had been retained in their service. She did the rougher work, whilst the culinary skill which Sorcha acquired in the college kitchen supplied the rest. Amada felt herself gliding very gently downwards towards the ocean of eternity, but she was glad to linger on the broadening river of time and catch a glimpse of what was likely to come after her.

She was seated on that July afternoon with an open parchment on her knee. But her eyes had long ceased to dwell on it. They had wandered from the glorious imagery of Isaiah to view the heavenly city, amidst whose ineffable brightness she hoped soon to see the faces so dear to her, and to hear the burst of music which should herald her own arrival amongst them. She mused on that wondrous prospect till the Uncreated Love seemed to cover her round as with a veil, and her wrinkled face glowed with a happiness which no object in that picturesquely-furnished room could have accounted for. The stillness was intense, but her increasing deafness made her unaware that it was at length broken. She shrank back as Sorcha's light hand came suddenly on her shoulder.

"Is it thou, child?" she exclaimed. "Thou hast made me start. I thought I was away with thy father and mother, and that they brought me flowers from the banks of the river of life."

"Then they did something like what I have done," replied Sorcha, as she placed an exquisite blossom on her grandmother's knee.

"It is beautiful," said Amada. "How camest thou to pluck it?"

"I sought one of these lilies at the pond," replied Sorcha. "There is a pool where they grow very thickly, but it was impossible to reach it; all the buds grew so far out, and there was nothing but leaves near the edge. Who, thinkest thou, helped me?"

"How should I know?" asked Amada.

"A young man named Fergus O' Flannahan," continued Sorcha. "He is one of the travellers who are to speak on Declan's birthday. Ita Ni-Bric says she used to meet him in thy house."

"Oh! Fergus, to be sure," exclaimed Amada, with the little laugh which did duty for her smile. "Said he aught of moment to thee?"

Sorcha's face showed the slightest suspicion of a blush. "Yea," she answered. "He asked how thou farest, and said he hoped to see thee soon. And he said I was very like my mother, as like as the rosebud is to the rose."

Amada let go the parchment. Leaning backwards in her chair, she laughed heartily.

"He is a poet,'" she said at length, "a second Cairbré. But I shall be glad to see him. Is that all thy news?"

"The two messengers have given their report," replied Sorcha. "Ita says it is considered weighty. And the abbot came to me whilst I was working in Maidoc's cell. He asked if thou wouldst be at home this afternoon."

"Did he?" exclaimed Amada. "He has not seen me in church for a long time."

"I doubt if he has noticed it," said Sorcha. "Though indeed he might, seeing thou art wont to sit in the front row. His wife never troubles herself to ask for thee."

"Poor woman!" said Amada with a slight shake of her head. "But they all mean to be kind; they cannot be expected to think of an old creature like me. But he cometh!"

A dark form was then passing the window. Sorcha rose from the low stool on which she had seated herself, and opening the door, curtseyed reverently to the figure who stood before it.

He was a massively-built man, with heavy shoulders and a large head, crowned with iron-grey locks. His brow was slightly flat on the temples, and was rendered unnaturally prominent by a band of baldness which extended above it, and was continued over the ears : this was the tonsure which the Culdee bishops so long retained as a distinguishing feature of their communion. The abbot's face was much marked by lines of studious thought. His deep-set eyes, his straight nose, with its wide nostrils, and his firm lips, showed him to be a man whose sphere was not likely to be bounded by his library walls. Amada rose at his approach.

"Sit thee down, sit thee down; the Lord bless thee!" said the abbot.

Amada obeyed, having caught his meaning from the

motion of his lips. Sorcha placed a chair by her grand-mother's side. The abbot thanked her with a slight nod, but seated himself on the end of the other couch.

This was very tantalising to Amada. The abbot's visits were so rare, that it was doubly hard for her to lose any of his conversation. Increasing infirmities had long debarred her from the privilege of attending public worship, and she understood that the abbot had come to visit *her*, not Sorcha.

He looked critically at the room, with its walls of polished pine, and the quaintly-carved rafters of its ceiling; then at the round stone fireplace, where a single log of wood smouldered, and at the silver-tipped crosier suspended near the head of the couch where he had seated himself.

" Thy grandmother must find it quiet here," he remarked at length.

"No, I believe she does not," replied Sorcha. " She is extremely fond of reading. She has the Bible, with Augustine and Sedulius in Irish translations, besides the books that Bishop Maidoc lends her. Not to speak of Duns Scotus."

Amada disliked extremely to see lips moving when the sounds that issued from them were unintelligible to her. She drew the end of her couch nearer to that of the abbot, and leaning forward, recalled him to a sense of her presence by inquiring—

"I hope thy wife is well? 'Tis long since I saw her."

"Indeed!" exclaimed the abbot. " She is well. Wouldst thou wish her to visit thee?"

" I should," replied Amada.

Sorcha turned away to hide her dissatisfaction.

" I hear of thy family sometimes from my grand-daughter," continued the old lady. " She spends half the day in the college. She goes there in the morning to learn cooking and medicine from Ita Ni-Bric.

"Indeed!" responded the abbot, with a slight elevation of his eyebrows. " Ita Ni-Bric is a worthy woman."

"And Maidoc himself," continued Amada, " is so kind as to let Sorcha have the use of Declan's cell when he teaches in the church. She has nearly finished copying the Gospels. Thy daughter has the most skill in that, they say."

" Yea," replied the abbot, with a gratified smile. " Some of Mòr's work has been sent to England."

" The messengers have returned from Rome ? " asked Amada, eagerly.

" They have," replied her visitor. " We are satisfied with their report. It was wise to send two, for one corrects the errors of the other. The public meeting will be on Declan's birthday. Thou wilt be there ? "

Amada shook her head. " No ! " she exclaimed. " If I were ten years younger I should not be the one to stay away. I must be content to hear of it."

The abbot now rose to go. Amada looked dissatisfied. She laid her hand on his arm.

" Thou knowest that I never hear thy ministrations," she pleaded.

The three knelt together on the rush-covered floor. A voice rose in prayer, but only two hearts went in unison with it. The third felt herself shut out from the blessing, and was forced to seek, with a strong inward groaning, for something special to herself.

Amada received the abbot's benediction with a grave sadness. There was silence for a few minutes after the door had closed behind him. The two women looked at each other, and Sorcha perceived a tear rolling down her grandmother's cheek : stepping forward she kissed it away.

" I trust thou art pleased with the visit," she said.

" Alas, my child ! " exclaimed the old lady, " I could not hear one word he said. Couldst thou not tell him to raise his voice ? "

" I dared not interrupt him," replied Sorcha. " It is strange how he cannot remember, for I told him when he spoke to me this afternoon that thou couldest hear very well when people came close enough."

"I fear he cares not for it," said Amada. "I would have been just as well not to have seen him. And a man that could tell me the very things I would fain hear. But old people are of no use in the world."

"Say not so, grandmother!" cried Sorcha, throwing herself down again on the stool, and laying both her hands on the old lady's. "How could I do without thee? And I am sure thy mind is as good as his, though he knows it not."

"As good as the abbot's!" exclaimed Amada, forced to laugh in spite of herself. "Child, thou art presumptuous!"

"Indeed I am not, grandmother," persisted the beautiful girl, her brown eyes filling with tears of vexation. "Maidoc and his wife think thou hast a very clear view of things. Maidoc says if thou hadst been Queen of Ireland, church affairs would never have come to the pass they have done."

"Thou flatterest," said the old lady, looking tenderly at her. "But I return the compliment, and say if Maidoc had been king— No, I shall not. A higher hand turneth men's hearts."

Sorcha had a deep cause for dissatisfaction. She was now old enough to be aware that the estimation in which her grandmother was held amongst the Ardmore family was not quite consonant to what her mother's had been. Amada was entitled to respect, not only on account of her age, but because she was a living example of Culdee training, and had a grasp of intellect which would have made her opinion worth seeking by responsible leaders. But there were some who did not care to discover this. Amada was indeed the mother-in-law of Mael-Patrick, but she could claim no cousinship with any of the ruling families in church or state. Sorcha had not failed to mark the condescending tone with which women who had not a tithe of her education spoke of her grandmother; and of late she had been particularly aggrieved by the haughty airs which the abbot's wife had assumed towards herself. This lady was of royal descent : she was daughter to the deceased Nigel MacAid, presbyter abbot of Armagh, co-arb of Patrick, who, though dispossessed by Romish innovators of a heritage which his family had enjoyed for fifteen generations,* had been acknowledged as their *ard-episcop* by the majority of Irishmen. Uailsi was a woman of high talent and of high pretension. She had made herself unpopular by her assumptions of superiority over the other bishops' wives. These would have thought themselves honoured in giving precedence to a daughter of the Ua-Breasail. But their courtesy had been met by such an utter want of sympathy, that they groaned under a moral yoke which it was impossible to shake off. Things were not as they had been in the family. Envy and smothered resentment now reigned in hearts which had formerly thrown themselves unreservedly into every good work. And many minds were not strong enough to bear this social cross without the gratification of manufacturing a similar one for others. The abbot's wife kept her head high above theirs ; they took pains, therefore, to keep the more lowly-born Amada in her proper place.

The abbot himself was not unpopular, though holding his office by no hereditary right. Ardmore was the chief religious foundation of the Deisi, one of whose families, the O'Brics, had centuries ago been overpowered and driven into a corner by the O'Faolains. The O'Faolains had for some time claimed the right of supplying an abbot, but the O'Brics recovering strength, each new election became the occasion of such bitter feuds that both parties at length agreed to be ruled by a stranger ; and they accordingly applied to the abbot of Durrow, co-arb of Columba, to appoint over them one of his own kin. Erc O'Conaill had long been looked on as one of the rising stars of the Church. He had now reached the zenith of his fame, and shone with a light which

* Appendix.

was steady, if somewhat chill, so that men reproved themselves for not feeling more warmed by it. His face was a picture of calm benevolence. Many loved him, but those who did so were none of the younger generation. Some who knew he wished them well were profane enough to whisper that his part was played out; that his mind was in his parchments; or that it was like a used-up field from which no new sympathies could be expected to spring. Yet Sorcha could not thus account for his coldness to Amada. She had observed that there were people in whose presence he could exert himself. She therefore suspected that he was incapable of realising the growth of any intellectual blossoms outside of clerical circles. "Those who are not the cousins of bishops," she said bitterly, "are not worthy to talk with him on serious subjects."

Amada had a dim inkling of this; but she was much too charitable to express it. She was, moreover, well sheltered in the cottage walls. Her perception of social inequalities was not sharpened, like Sorcha's, by the daily contact of mutually irritating forces. Her disappointment was, however, too great on the present occasion to be altogether hidden.

"And I admired him so much!" she continued, in a sort of soliloquy; "there was no one I liked better to hear. I could always be sure that his explanation of a passage was the correct one."

"The abbot is a man of erudition," said Sorcha; "but not more so than Maidoc. Thy daughter Grainné hath taught me to observe, when the two have been speaking on the same subject, that it has taken the abbot a hundred words to express what Maidoc has made perfectly clear in ten."

"I understand that," said Amada; "though I should not have thought it."

"Grainné thinks the abbot learned," continued Sorcha,

"but she will not allow that he is gifted. He has a wonderful faculty for collecting facts, and arranging them in valuable forms. He is like a bee who knows how to extract the essence of flowers. Some men's minds, however, are like the flowers themselves—they distil honey. These are the highest order, and Grainné says the abbot is not one of them."

"I suppose Fergus O'Flannahan is," said Amada, with a laugh, which Sorcha could in no way account for.

"Yes," she answered; "but he is apt to give us a surfeit. Now the best kind of talent is partly of the bee and partly of the flower class. Those who are altogether bees suck so greedily that they get heavy, they can't fly; and those who are nothing but flowers, sometimes try to satisfy us with scent. Maidoc is a good deal of the bee, with a little of the flower; that is what makes him so pleasant to hear. You get fed without being aware of it. There is something a-wanting in the abbot's sermons. The energy and earnestness of his youth may have once made up for it; but we feel the deficiency now, when we compare him with others."

"It would take thy father's child to do it," said Amada. "Is it not wonderful that Maidoc has got no further on in the world?"

"He would make an excellent abbot," replied Sorcha. "He is as calm and judicious as Erc O'Conaill, and much warmer-hearted."

"It is his own fault," said Amada.

"Yea," replied Sorcha, "Maidoc is over-modest. But that is a fault, too, grandmother, most of all in a man. He and Ita live in a little world of their own, as far as the expression of their feelings is concerned."

"True," replied Amada. "But those who think them ciphers make a great mistake. They appear to see nothing when they are in company, yet everything is being written on their memories for future use. Ita has a difficult post to fill."

"She certainly has," replied Sorcha. "She has been appointed to superintend the training of the girls in both kitchen and pharmacy. It is a great responsibility. But the fathers would not have given it to her if they had not thought her equal to it. Her patience is marvellous; she never loses her temper, and looks fearlessly, yet humbly, at the abbot's wife. Nor less so at the chief cook, with whom she never interferes. Now, grandmother, how couldest thou be so foolish as to ask the Lady Uailsi to visit thee?"

"I did not think, child," replied Amada. "I can hardly believe she is so proud as thou sayest. She is very clever, and perhaps the people here do not understand her."

"Dost thou mean that the men of Armagh are a higher race, or have more learning?" asked Sorcha.

"No," replied Amada; "but I thought it was best to try and be friendly."

"Indeed," muttered Sorcha to herself. "Well, grandmother," she said aloud, "the best I can wish for thee is that she will not come. I shall not say that either of you is superior to the other, but you are different, and about as well matched as the bluebell would be with the rose leaf. And there is no need for thee to praise her daughter's work. Thou knowest quite well that when a copy of the Gospels was to be sent to the English king, every one thought, and I knew myself, that mine was the best. Yet hers was sent, because it had a few extra red spirals. The Lady Uailsi came to me this very afternoon, when I was working in Declan's cell. She asked me to show her what I had done, and she looked closely at every page, as if she were trying to get ideas for Mòr.

"Say not so, child!" said Amada. "I cannot bear when thou thinkest so hardly of people."

"I would fain not have done so," replied Sorcha. "I was very happy, and quite ready to show her everything that she was pleased to take an interest in. But the look on her face struck me—it was as if she were mortified at my success."

"Well, well!" said Amada, "Mòr and she cannot deny it thee, poor things! They will have plenty of trials if they do not bend a little. The high horse is a troublesome beast to ride. I venture to say that the people on the back of it are far worse off than those who have to journey on foot."

"To be sure," said Sorcha, laugbing. "I wish I could be content to look up from a safe level, like Ita and thou. But thou knowest I am ambitious?"

"Thou art!" exclaimed Amada, looking at her with gratified pride. "Just bring me one of thy pictured Psalters, I wish to look at it myself."

CHAPTER VI.

Whilst Amada discussed with her grand-daughter the reasons for the abbot's unpopularity, a solitary bishop sat in Declan's cell poring over the dim tracings of a mouldering parchment. The massive wooden chair on which he was seated had lately borne a fairer burden, relics of whose presence remained in the crimson-feathered quill, and elegantly-carved black oak inkstand which stood on the desk before him. It was a little chamber with low roof and bare walls. The door when open commanded a magnificent view over the sea, now glowing in the warm hues of sunset. But to this Maidoc was completely oblivious. He had a keen eye for the beauties of nature, but he was at this moment overpowered with the thought of what immense riches were contained in the two massive chests which stood on either side of him, and of which he carried the keys concealed beneath the folds of the black woollen mantle which covered his ample breast.

The fragrance of many lives, the golden stores of wisdom amassed by centuries of labour, were all embalmed and preserved for him in a small compass; and he felt awed and humbled at his own presumptuousness in venturing to commit to paper any thoughts of his own in the unseen presence of those spirits who were perhaps permitted to watch over the preservation and garnering of their own harvests. His eye at length fell on Sorcha's pen.

" 'Tis wonderful to live in such a time," he reflected, " when even a slight girl may wield that mighty instrument. She has genius, if a quick intelligence and a sense of the beautiful may be called so. Many may have regretted that Mael-Patrick had not a son, but it was not the way of Providence. Erin is in need of such a one. Had his great abilities, his meek and loving spirit, been united to the fire of youth in a man whose position would have commanded attention, there would have been a force potent enough to have drawn the whole nation from those temptations to foreign innovation which will prove its ruin. But the dove nestles where one would hear the roar of the lion. O God, Thou knowest what is best for us, Thou must have other means of working! Chasten us not according to our deserts."

Maidoc's head had sunk forward on his hands. A sound now startled him—it was the creaking of the door. He looked up slightly bewildered.

But a sunny face greeted him, and a step crossed his threshold whose presence he never regarded as an intrusion. Ita Ni-Bric was, like himself, of massive build, but with more alacrity and decision in her movements. Her hair, prematurely grey, was smoothly braided and covered by a black-edged white kerchief, whilst her blue eyes beamed with an expression of intense benevolence. Her chequered black and green tunic was confined by a black inar and a girdle of leather; and her feet were encased in dark sandals. She came forward with affectionate meekness, and laid her hand on Maidoc's shoulder.

"It groweth late," she said. "Thou hast read more than enough this day. I come to beg for thy company."

"Wherefore, wife?" asked Maidoc, with the petulant submission of a well-trained child disturbed amidst its favourite playthings.

"Thou wilt not deny me," said Ita, with more confidence. "I think it would be well for thee to visit Amada this night. Sorcha told me to-day that she often longs to see thee. And

I fear the maiden has been made unhappy by a visit from the Lady Uailsi."

" Ah ! " exclaimed Maidoc, laying down his parchment. " She must not lose heart."

" And a youth waiteth without for speech of thee," added Ita, an amused smile hovering about the corners of her mouth.

" Who is it ? " asked her husband, in a faint whisper.

" Ardal O'Brien, the prince-bishop, foster-son to our late abbot," replied Ita, her mild eyes glowing with pleasure.

" Thou shouldest not have let him wait," said Maidoc, anxiously drawing himself up as if apprehensive of some trial. " Wilt thou bid him enter ? "

Ita stepped noiselessly out. She soon returned, followed by a young man of some thirty summers.

Ardal had a tall and handsome figure, and an air of distinction which set it off to full advantage. His high intellectual brow was the more striking by reason of the Celtic tonsure which surmounted it. He had regular features, brown eyes, and abundance of light clustering hair. There was a gravity and sweetness in his countenance which could not fail to propitiate the beholder.

He came forward deferentially and grasped Maidoc's hand. There was something candid and decided in his manner of doing so. But this expression of good-will was apparently lost. Maidoc's arm seemed almost inanimate, and instead of returning the pressure, he allowed the hand to drop from his visitor's hold and sink helplessly at his side. The words that had apparently risen to his lips lacked courage to find their way out.

" I should like to have some talk alone with thee," said Ardal, looking earnestly at the reverend lector. " I trust thou wert satisfied with our report this morning ? "

" The twelve brethren have expressed themselves to that effect," replied Maidoc, cautiously.

Ita now stood at the window, watching her husband and the stranger very closely. An expression of glowing contentment animated her whole person as she heard them interchange words. She immediately offered a chair to her guest; then, seating herself near the door, she waited with folded hands in anticipation of their further converse.

But a pause followed. Maidoc was looking upwards, as if waiting for inspiration to come to him. Ardal did not interrupt his meditation. The lector at length spoke.

"It will need further discussion," he said. "Thou and thy friend have been approved by us. But the questions which we have sought your help in solving are too momentous to be fully treated in a morning sitting."

"I feel that strongly," replied Ardal. "Nor is the family of Ardmore alone competent to decide. The Romans had a proverb, 'Vox populi, vox Dei.' I would not go so far myself, yet I feel that the educated laity are as likely to arrive at wise decisions as are the fathers. The matters touch them nearly. Therefore I look forward to Thursday's gathering with fear and trembling."

"I share thy views," replied Maidoc. "Thy stay in foreign lands has, I presume, made thee all the more sensible to the vital nature of our differences with other churches."

"Say rather with another Church," replied Ardal. "The Bishop of Rome claims that the community under his control is alone entitled to that name. And there are various degrees of submission to his authority, even within its fold."

"I agree with thee," said Maidoc. "The time has now come when we must decide to go either back or forward: back to the simple faith of Patrick and Bridget; or forwards to the impressive ceremonies which are held in so much esteem by the rest of Christendom."

"By the rest truly," said Ardal, sighing. "That makes a painful impression on me. If we take the separate points which distinguish us, such as the adoration of the Virgin, I must truly say I think we are more of the mind of the apostles. But Paul himself says that the Church is one. How, then, should we differ from all the Lord's people?"

"The Church has had its errors and its schisms," replied Maidoc. "They troubled the earliest congregations of Asia. It seems to me as if the devil were at work even here in our midst. Each heart is a battle-field between him and the Holy Spirit. And why should the Church as a whole not be open to his attacks? Where the good seed falleth, there are the tares. It will be a conflict between the new man and the old until the last"

"But has not the Saviour promised to be with us?" said Ardal. "The Almighty cannot surely let His own Church fall into ruin."

"He permitted the Hebrew nation to go astray," replied Maidoc. "Why may not the Church yield to like temptations? I see it working amongst ourselves. Men in high places trust in the sacredness of their office, instead of in the living God."

"I see thy meaning," said Ardal. "But is that not a sign of our consecration not being perfect?"

"I will ask thee this," said Maidoc. "Hast thou observed aught of the kind elsewhere?"

"In truth I have," replied Ardal. "Pride and selfishness, the love of applause, and other vanities of the flesh are not unknown in Italy. My counsel will be that we stand fast by the old paths, even as Patrick and Columba have taught us."

"There thou art in error, my son," said Maidoc. "Thou art taking the first step that will lead us into temptation. It is ours to hold a record before whose ineffable splendour the highest glory of the classic Muses is but as glimmering moonlight. Let us not, then, go back to the history of our own island for anything more brilliant."

"Truly thou speakest well," said Ardal. "The Romans

may say Jerome as we say Patrick, or even Peter as we say John. The spring of knowledge should be purest at the fountain-head."

"My husband," said Ita, rising, "thy supper awaits thee in our dwelling. If thou wilt deign to share it," she added, turning to Ardal, "thou mayest continue to converse by our hearth."

"Willingly," said the young man, rising. "By the way, I would ask thee if that fair maiden, Mael-Patrick's daughter, dwelleth within this rath?"

"She dwells in her father's cottage," replied Ita, "with none but her aged grandmother."

"Thou hast seen her passing through the wood," said Maidoc; "and, if I mistake not, thou hast studied other tongues than that of Hellas. Thou hast even become acquainted with ditties which savour not of the cathedral."

The young man blushed deeply. His downcast eyes had a half guilty look.

"Thou shouldst tell the grounds of thy suspicion, Maidoc," said Ita.

Maidoc did not answer, but rolled up the parchment he had been studying, and, grasping it firmly in his hand, walked slowly out of the hut.

Ita and Ardal followed. The former paused to lock the door, and took the opportunity of laying her hand kindly on the young man's arm.

"My husband was seated in the forest," she whispered, "last evening, unperceived. He heard thee chanting to thyself a Provençal ditty. I fancy he knew the sense of it."

Ardal laughed, and blushed still more deeply. "That was hardly fair," he said. "But I thank thee for the warning. The sounds rose unbidden to my lips, wedded as I have heard them to entrancing music. Another might have thought me giddy, but I trust thou wilt not do so."

"No, no. I am too wise," whispered Ita.

CHAPTER VII.

Amada and Sorcha, having finished their frugal supper, had
kindled a fresh pine log in the round hearth. An oil-lamp,
suspended from the rafters overhead, supplied light sufficient
for Sorcha to ply her busy wheel, whilst the strapping Cacht
wielded a distaff in a corner near the door. Sorcha paused
occasionally to direct some remark to her grandmother, who
was trying, by the help of the red glow, to decipher the
writing on a bulky parchment.

Some one knocked loudly at the door. Sorcha rose and
opened it. " Is Amada within ? " asked a cheerful voice.

Sorcha recognised the young bishop to whom she had
been that morning indebted for the flower.

He was a man of short stature and peculiar appearance.
He wore no beard, and the Celtic tonsure on his forehead
was concealed by the manner in which his locks of auburn
hair were allowed to fall forward. They hung likewise down
his back, and this, combined with his smooth shaven face,
gave him at first a somewhat feminine appearance. But
feminine grace was altogether lacking. His figure was erect,
rather inclined to bend backwards, and the slight wriggle in
it was repeated in his mobile features, giving the impression
of eccentricity or of genius, not unmingled with affectation.
A bad habit, or possibly weakness of vision, made his blue
eyes appear half closed.

" Welcome," said Sorcha, motioning to him to enter.

Amada looked up. The stranger's hand was in hers.

"I could not be here without visiting thee," he said.

" Thy memory hath been dear to me as the words of an olden song. For thine eye still glittereth with a heaven-borrowed splendour."

" Alas ! " said Amada, sadly ; " I have had many a severe trial since I last saw thee."

" I know, I know," said the young man, throwing himself down on the foot of a couch. " But thou art like our native holly, or rather, like the southern myrtle, green in spite of the winter."

" This land must seem bleak to thee after Italy," said Amada. " But I have heard that it is not the worst in the world."

" There are more tempests around Caledonia," replied her visitor. " This sea-washed island is fair. The gentle rains array her turf in a brighter green, though the sun spreads not his gold-tipped locks over so vivid an expanse of blue. Besides," he continued, glancing at the polished walls, " I have not, in all my wanderings, seen a dwelling so beautiful as this, whose inhabitants, too, look like the spirits of the wood."

" Thou wert ever a flatterer," said Amada, looking half amused and half pleased.

A somewhat timid knock was now heard at the door. Sorcha again opened it.

" A troop cometh," exclaimed the young bishop, as three figures successively appeared.

First came Ita, her mild face glowing with friendly warmth; then her husband, looking unusually cheerful, although his person seemed almost too large for the little doorway ; last of all, the young bishop Ardal, who looked rather timid, whilst Ita embraced her female friends.

" This young man," she said to Amada, " claims an old acquaintance with thee. He was often in this house when a boy. Ardal, son of the royal Turlough, and foster-child to Abbot O'Faolain."

"He is welcome," said Amada, a bright smile coming over her face. "Bring more seats, Sorcha; the place is narrow for so many."

Fergus O'Flannahan had started on seeing his colleague. A cloud of displeasure crossed his face; he pressed his upper lip with the under one. This was, however, unnoticed, and disappeared in the alacrity with which he rose to offer his seat to Maidoc.

Sorcha returned from an inner chamber carrying three chairs. The hand with which Ardal relieved her of two of them trembled just a little. All were soon seated round the fire, Fergus manœuvring in a manner which placed Sorcha betwixt Ita and himself.

"We thought not to find thee here," said Maidoc, who *could* speak upon occasion.

"I am like a crow in a dove's nest," replied Fergus, shifting about restlessly in his chair.

"Our sister Amada," continued Maidoc, "would fain learn of your journey. We hoped to give her that pleasure by bringing Ardal, but it seems we have been forestalled."

Maidoc seemed in a very communicative humour. His whole broad person was aglow with contentment, and diffused over the company the sort of pleasure felt by lovers of nature when the cactus flowers.

"That was partly my object in coming," said Fergus. "I know she will hear little on Declan's birthday, and there is none more interested in the object of our mission."

"Then we may have a little council," said Ita; "and speak the more freely that we are all friends."

Amada had been meditating for a few minutes. She now turned to Fergus and asked: "What impression does home make on thee?"

"Well," answered Fergus, tossing back his hair, "it is not so grand as Rome or Aix. Here at Ardmore much is changed. There is a new abbot."

"He had just been appointed when we left," said Ardal, keeping his eyes resolutely away from Sorcha. "It was too soon then to foretell the effects of his rule."

Maidoc and Ita both looked grave. Ita's gravity was a thing worth studying; it was so striking in its quiet solemnity.

"Think you that we are changed for the better?" asked Amada.

"I should hardly say so," replied Ardal. "The warm-hearted O'Faolain, my foster-father, made the place livelier. But he was not considered so learned as Erc O'Conaill."

Fergus's eyes twinkled. "Erc O'Conaill has a wife!" he exclaimed.

There was a burst of merriment, in which Maidoc was forced to join. His laugh was an unusual convulsion, and looked as if it might shake him asunder. Ita's and Ardal's were unrestrained, like the laugh of children. Ardal at length recovered himself.

"It would be unfair to blame her altogether," he said. "She must have some effect on him; yet the driest winds will not parch a soil that has water beneath its surface. The roots of family pride have grown there for generations, and they swallow up much of the sap that should go to nourish the Christian graces."

"He takes the Scottish side in the dispute with Rome," said Maidoc.

"True," replied Fergus. "But he treats much with foreign prelates."

"You would not have him narrow-minded," said Maidoc. "Conference with strangers cannot be hurtful."

"No; but he makes too much of them," said Fergus. "Hast thou heard him boast about an Irish bishop as he does about Gillachrist, about O'Toole, and about Gelasius, the very man who has displaced his wife's cousin at Armagh?"

"For my part," said Amada, "I think the Lady Uailsi is to blame. She is doubtless of high rank, but she should not have come here if she did not mean to show courtesy."

"That is precisely our weakness," said Ardal. "Our pastors have sought for great alliances. Since the time of Patrick they have wielded a tremendous power, even without that. Our chiefs sought to share that power; and both together have been conspiring not to let it pass out of their hands. The consequence is that we are divided into patricians and plebeians, and the line of separation is as distinct as it ever was in ancient Rome. Those who are not of gentle birth by both parents are held to stand lower in the social scale. It savours of heathendom."

Sorcha's heart warmed towards the speaker, who, though a prince, perceived so clearly what had long been to her a concealed source of trouble.

Ardal caught the influence of her look, though his eyes were directed towards her grandmother. He gathered courage to continue.

"The pride of our pastors," he said, "is no match for that of the Roman ones. Their armour will give way at the first blow. They are alienating the sympathy of the very men they have educated. The Romans, on the contrary, manage to keep any scholar on whom they have bestowed real pains within the Church. We have come to such a pass in Erin that people will welcome the sway of the Roman prelates as a deliverance from that of their own."

"There be too many of us who fold our souls in pride," said Fergus. "The Lady Uailsi may be a palpable incarnation of it, but it rioteth everywhere, as the Philistines rioted in the land of Israel. It hath laid its hand on the ark of the covenant."

"Is it not revolting!" said Ardal. "Men glory in the possession of a vice. Pride is the peculiar temptation of the rich, as dishonesty is of the poor. It is a theft from our neighbours; a theft of their right to respect. The rich have no disposition towards material robbery, so they commit a moral one."

Thus Amada's hearth became the scene of a discussion on the momentous questions which were then agitating the religious communities of Ireland; questions relating not only to home discipline, but to the relations of the Celtic bishops with those of other lands. The chief topic which now perplexed men's minds was the claim of the Bishop of Rome to the undisputed sovereignty of Christendom. It was no new claim, the men of Erin well knew, and eighty years previously it had been formulated by Pope Gregory with special reference to them. Half a century had elapsed since the Synod of Rathbresail, summoned under royal auspices, had given a most reluctant consent to the subdivision of the country into prelatic dioceses. The decrees of this Synod had been received with such disfavour that thirty years later a fresh attempt had been made by the Synod of Kells to reduce them to practice. Those who loved the old ways now felt that the flood was upon them. They could afford to look on in silence while a Lanfranc or an Anselm consecrated bishops over the Danish communities of Limerick and Waterford; it was another thing altogether when the Romish Gelasius had forced his way into Armagh, and the Pope's own legate, Christian, ruled not merely in Lismore, but had the effrontery to claim jurisdiction over an independent community like that of Ardmore. The Romish claims were, in truth, as old as the days of Patrick. For had not Pope Celestine sent Palladius with orders to bring the churches of the West to a state of canonical obedience? And had not Palladius come?* Had he not sailed round these shores? and, though received with courtesy, had not Patrick and the bishops of those days informed him that, like the mother church of Brittany, they owned no head but the crucified Redeemer? They had felt His presence with

* Appendix.

them. They had seen His finger guiding them as plainly as the pagan emperor could possibly have discerned the flaming cross in the sky. In vain did Palladius tell them that their ways were different from those of Catholic Christendom. Their teachers had not been sent by the Roman bishops; why, then, should strangers reap what Patrick had sown? And the Irish had been strengthened in their resistance by the remarkable success of their missionaries in Europe. Two Celtic pastors had given material help to the great Charles when he founded the University of Paris. Another had assisted the Saxon Alfred with the same work at Oxford; and whether at Luxenil or at Bobbio, at Regensburg or at Seckingen, the communities founded by the Scots were distinguished above all others by the purity of their morals, and the high standard of learning which they were able to maintain. The story of Ardmore itself had been a story of battle with Romish pretensions, as well as with the darkness of ignorance.

For some time after the departure of Palladius the Roman bishop had not troubled them. But things were now wearing a different aspect. The native churches of Wales were one by one giving in to the superior power of English prelates. In Caledonia the backbone of resistance had been broken, not only by the banishment of the Iona family beyond the Grampians, but also by the overpowering influence of the Saxon Queen Margaret. For the Roman hierarchy were steadily aggressive. They had brought to perfection the art of entering into other men's labours; and were more than suspected of having re-written ancient records with the view of showing that the early Celtic saint belonged to their order. And the Irish camp was divided. Some men were for purity of doctrine and independence, some for unity and Catholic submission. Little did Amada and her friends dream that whilst they debated, a sword was being sharpened which should cut the knot of their difficulties in a manner as unexpected as it was disastrous!

CHAPTER VIII.

The moonbeams streamed through the narrow window of a hut close to the sanctuary of Declan. They seemed almost like celestial visitants hardly welcomed, for they had not only a thickness of ivy to pierce, but were mocked by the flicker of a feeble rushlight hanging from the rafters of the low roof. In a corner was a fresh bundle of straw covered by a single yellow blanket. The only other furniture consisted of a wooden tub, with a pitcher of water, a small deal table, and two chairs. One of these latter was occupied by the form of the young bishop, Ardal.

The rushlight was burning low, but he did not heed it. He was bending forward, his clear, thoughtful brow supported in his delicately-shaped hand. His dark woollen garment was partly unfastened, and you could trace in the heaving of his throat the symptoms of strong agitation. Of what was the young bishop thinking?

He was surely not present altogether in that narrow chamber. There was that within him which, freeing itself from the fetters of time and sense, could wander away to regions which were nevertheless connected in a strange way with the objects around him. It seemed but yesterday since he had played in these pathless forests and climbed the tallest pine-stems in search of eggs or squirrels, distinguished only from his young companions by the scarlet inar and brass-ringed hurling-stick which marked him out as the son of a king.

For Ardal was the only child of Turlough O'Brien's marriage with Tualath, daughter of O'Faolain, prince of the Deisi. Turlough had many sons by two former wives, and after the disaster at Moin Mòr, he had consented to his young wife placing Ardal under the fostering care of his uncle, the co-arb of Declan. Tualath did not long survive her husband's misfortunes. She had renounced for Ardal all claim to the succession of Munster, and had thus rescued him from a horrible fate. Her husband recovered his throne within a year, but his family seemed to have received the brand of Cain. The few notices which contemporary chroniclers have bestowed on them are enough to make the blood run cold. Tadg's usurpation was the beginning of a series of mutual blood-sheddings amongst the Ua-Brien which can only be excused by the necessity under which Irish kings lay of protecting themselves from the fear of assassination. And as the ard-righ Roderick had signalised his accession to the throne of Ireland by blinding some of his brothers, what wonder if Turlough's son, Domnall O'Brien of Munster, followed his liege's example? It was well for Ardal, therefore, that he had been reared as one of the Ua-Faolain. Yet was he allied in blood to the rightful sovereigns of England through the marriage of his ancestor Donough with a sister of the Saxon Harold.

And it seemed but yesterday when he had first seen the University of Lismore,* whither he had been sent to complete his studies. He had ridden towards it more slowly than was his wont, overpowered by a feeling which made its venerable walls seem to his boyish fancy as solemn as those of the Temple could possibly have done to an Israelitish pilgrim. There was there no Shekinah, no visible presence of the Deity, but not the less truly had a supernatural influence been felt within them, hallowed as they were by having been the dwelling of many heaven-sent teachers. Songs of praise

* Appendix.

ascended daily like incense by the grave of the sainted Carthagh; the sound of pleading was never hushed; and daylight seldom broke without disturbing some scene of wrestling
with the Covenant Angel. Down the shining Blackwater had
hastened thousands, bearing, not in little silver tabernacles,
but in the more precious caskets of sanctified hearts, the
holy bread of a Living Word to far-off climes—to the hills of
Northumbria, to the islands of Caledonia—till the Tree of Life
seemed to grow on the earth of Erin, and to scatter its leaves
in no stinted measure for the healing of Europe. A two
years' familiarity with the life of Lismore had not dispelled
these visions. The holy traditions of bygone days were not
quite renewed in the habits of the youth who thronged to the
feet of its lectors; still there were some amongst them who
felt the solemnity of their calling, and waited with trembling
humility until their lips should be unsealed and they should be
permitted to go forth and preach the unsearchable riches of
Christ. "God can save by few as well as by many," had Ardal
thought. "He has not quite forsaken Erin when a man like
Mael-Patrick is left to it. May I be one of a band of conquerors! May I win the victory over myself, and thus be
qualified to tread in the steps of Patrick and of Columba!"

He had gone forth from Lismore prepared for the fight.
Crowds had waited on his ministrations, and the seal of
popularity had been added to the seals of a more real success.
The ancient lineage which was his family's boast had seemed
to him but a trifle in comparison.

Then in the first vigour of manhood a not less honourable
work had been made ready for his hand.

Irritated by a message from their would-be diocesan, the
twelve brethren who ruled over the family of Ardmore had
held a council. Some were for temporising, but Mael-Patrick
rebuked them. "Our real foe is disunion," he said. "When
the Milesian invader set his foot on our soil, what did he
find? Three princes quarrelling for the sovereignty. Let us

stand shoulder to shoulder, and no foreign invader shall touch our civil or our ecclesiastical rights. Men say that the best policy in the leader of an army is to strike. Those who stand merely on the defensive are lost. But we must proceed with caution. We must know the situation. So before we come to a decision let us send forth two of our ablest men— young men—whose minds are pure from thought of evil. Let them go to Rome, to Burgundy, to Provence. Let them tell us how the Latin system works in cloister and in court. Let them have speech of Greek priests if they can, and learn the reason of the great schism. For, just as when you build a house you must take into consideration all the conditions— the way the winds will blow on it, the foundation on which it will rest, and the state of society in the country—so you can-not judge of an institution without looking all around it. By its effects on prince, on chieftain, and on slave would I esti-mate the value of any teaching which claims to be Divine."

Mael-Patrick's counsel was followed. The choice of the twelve brethren fell on two of the young bishops subject to their own jurisdiction—Ardal and Fergus. After much earnest prayer these two were set aside and appointed to this important duty. " Ye will be to us as feet and eyes," said the Abbot O'Faolain. " What ye see, write it on the tablets of your hearts; treasure it up, that it may be to us as a library of knowledge. Presume not to tell our affairs to strangers. Yours will be the task to observe; ours to judge."

This had been Ardal's second consecration. His mission had lasted three years. It was now at an end. What a variety of life and manners had been presented for his inspec-tion ! He had striven to enter into other men's feelings so as to probe the secret spring of their motives. He had been a courtier at Paris and at Aix, a reverent pilgrim at the shrine of Peter. Winds of strange doctrine had played around him, but he had not felt them so keenly as the breezes of worldly passion. This earth was more than a place of preparation for heaven. And the heart of a man beats very audibly beneath the robes of pastor or of priest.

The question now agitating him as he sat in his lonely chamber was not the outcome of his spiritual labours. It related to something more directly personal, even to that vexed question of marriage which some even amongst the Culdees were beginning to think unlawful. But Ardal's intellect had long been satisfied. A man of his warm temperament could not live on ethereal comforts. The balance of his judgment had therefore dipped to the side of a reasonable liberty.

He was fully persuaded in his own mind that matrimony would not only be a check to his roving fancy, but a material help in his spiritual labours. There were saintly women in Erin, he well knew. Had not many pastors' wives rivalled their husbands in all good report? The great Master had sent out His disciples by two and two; what was to hinder the same plan being carried out with that difference of sex which would render their union permanent, and make the qualities of the one supplement those of the other?

Ardal had looked narrowly into the workings of celibacy It had given birth to some very beautiful plants, but he questioned if they were of a fibre which would have withstood the small frictions of daily domestic life. Wickedness flourished in the world around them, quite unchecked by their touching simplicity. Indeed, it seemed as if some men made the very existence of these holy anchorites an excuse for their own continuance in wrong-doing. The doctrine of vicarious merit was gaining ground everywhere. Ardal had seen in southern climes men whom he would have been proud to claim as countrymen, men on whose countenances the peace of God had set its visible seal. But they formed no part of the great world; they were bound to it by none of those strong temporal cords which twine into the very roots of our being. Knights and ladies looked on them only to think that they were formed of other flesh. Wicked men sought the benefit of their prayers, and trusted to the ease with which they could obtain this. The burden of intercession for human iniquity would surely prove too heavy for a few poor mortal lips.

There were some, again, to whom the utmost stretch of Ardal's charity could not assign the merit of being better than worldlings. What did celibacy do for them? It only marked them out as partakers of an office to which they had been consecrated with solemn rites. Society esteemed them as they deserved. Ardal was well aware that there might be a few black sheep amongst the Scottish brethren. But these must at least hide their natural colour. They had not the unblushing effrontery of some highly-placed Italian ecclesiastics, nor were they invested with such awful authority.

Ardal was very susceptible to female influence. He had been exposed to its utmost power at the Provençal court. He had, in truth, been glad to seek safety in the austere solitude of Citeaux. He wondered with what eyes the ladies had looked on him. He was no knight, although of princely blood, and the opinions of these dark-eyed southerners had been divided as to his real *status*. Was he a priest, or was he not one? No gentleman of France or of Italy would have given him his daughter whilst there was a doubt on the subject; yet fair maidens had blushed when he looked at them. He had summoned all his stoicism to make him bear their glances, for he had resolved to look elsewhere for a helpmeet; to choose a daughter of the Green Isle, who would not think it strange that he wooed her. He had not felt at liberty to meditate on the subject till his return to Erin.

Ardal would not have allowed that he was superstitious; but a presentiment had laid hold of him that he would meet his fate at Ardmore. He came there with eyes wide open, and a heart ready to receive the first impression of love.

He did not need to wait for it. On the first night of his

arrival he was introduced to the abbot's family. The Lady Uailsi was particularly gracious; and there is something very charming in the condescension of a proud woman. Ardal was not blinded by it, but he could not help being struck by the perfections of her daughter. Mòr Ni-Conaill was not lovely, but she was elegant, and her face had a look of inquiring intelligence that gave to it an expression of child-like simplicity. She knew that she was talented, and she was better without the mock-humility which might have made her affect to stand on the level of others. She had a round face, with blue, earnest eyes that looked straight at you, and seemed in their deep sincerity to plead for fair dealing. Any little trace of haughtiness about her was evidently a parasitic growth, which would fade and drop off under a more healthy influence than her mother's.

Thus Ardal had thought seriously of her. There was a frigidity about the family, but he trusted to the sunshine of his own sociability to thaw it. There was something flattering to his vanity in the idea that he might aspire where others did not even venture to contemplate, and a child of the Cinell Conaill and the Ua-Bresail would indeed be a fitting match for one of the Ua-Brian.

But a fairer vision soon passed before him. Looking from a window of the Round Tower in the early morning, he had discerned a wondrous picture on the shining turf beneath. The rosy hues of sunrise were on the dark expanse of forest, on the gleaming billows, and on the little ivy-covered cottage which he had once revered as Mael-Patrick's dwelling. From the cottage door issued a form of exquisite loveliness — a young girl, robed in greenish-red tartan, with a cluster of dark brown locks falling on her shoulders, a finely-moulded little head, and features so wondrously chiselled that they would have won for their owner the first place at a Provençal tournament. Ardal could not withdraw his eyes from her. She seemed a child of nature; the hue of her robe harmonised so well with the blush of the landscape; and yet there was something that spoke of refinement in her elastic step, as if the beauty of intellect had robed itself in the beauty of humanity. The snowdrop of the forest is often fairer than the snowdrop of the palace garden, and it awakens in us a more devout thankfulness for the lavishness of the Creator's gifts. Here, untouched by the dust of worldliness, unscorched by the sunbeams of flattery, bloomed a flower as delicate as any that could be culled from the *parterres* of princes.

Ardal never forgot that moment, and his heart throbbed with an intensity of eagerness when he heard that the beautiful maiden was indeed Mael-Patrick's daughter, the Sorcha whom he remembered as a chubby child at her father's knee. He rejoiced that his intimacy with Mòr had gone no further, and he waited impatiently till the descending sun gave token that the hours of study would be over. Then he sought Maidoc's cell.

He had two objects in doing so: one was to ask for counsel as to his public line of action, the other to seek a more particular introduction to Sorcha. He did not distinctly avow the latter; but Ita's eyes were quick to notice the signs of deep feeling, and she invited him to accompany her to the cottage with a frank delicacy which went to his heart. She understood him, he saw; for young love is a plant which shoots best when shaded from the fierce rays of publicity. It must be touched with a respectful tenderness, for it will not bear a curious finger at its root. Ardal trembled as he accompanied his friends to the cottage. He could have faced ten thousand auditors; how was this? Surely he must be losing strength! Was his the same form that had ridden so unweariedly over thousands of miles? He had stood in the presence of princes and of scholars, why should he shrink from encountering a pair of brown eyes?

He scarcely saw the smile with which Sorcha greeted him. He was only conscious of a presence—disagreeably conscious, too—that there were adverse influences in the room. For the first time he felt that he hated. Another form was by Sorcha's side, other lips were daring to whisper in her ear. And she seemed pleased; she laughed. Ardal felt miserable. That exquisite beauty had dawned on his vision in order to madden him. The devil had him now. Whom did he hate? His own colleague, the sharer of his mission, the man who had been consecrated with him to the same service. There he sat, bold, confident, leaning backwards on his chair, looking at Sorcha with the air of an accepted lover. What chance had Ardal by the side of Fergus?

For Fergus was irresistibly charming. Ardal had seen it when moving with him in far other scenes. He had marked the proudest ladies of Provence simper at his compliments —flatteries, Ardal would have called them—but there was always an element of truth in them which saved them from the imputation. Ardal had heard Fergus's praises everywhere—amongst the common people, amongst the votaries of learning, amongst the giddy and the thoughtless, and most of all from the lips of women. His sermons were heavenly; they made men fancy themselves already in Paradise. He had an insinuating skill which enabled him to play on every fibre of the human heart. And the hearts which he touched were as harps which sounded forth his praises. Ardal had tried to analyse his companion's mind, but it was a task which baffled him. There was a deep spirituality in it that was distinctly perceptible in his sermons; there was an appreciation of solemn truths which often made him impressively grand. But in the lonely hours which they had spent together, Ardal had missed the refreshment of sympathetic converse. Fergus was delightfully confidential on any subject that did not touch too closely on the inner life. Ardal had sometimes been startled to see that any remark about their common responsibilities would make his companion grave and melancholy. Fergus seemed to begin his study of all subjects from the picturesque side. Religion? Yes, even religion. But Ardal suppressed the uncharitable thought that Fergus's conception of this was solely artistic. No man could be hypocritical enough to preach as he did without having felt its power.

But where was charity, when a rival was seated beside Sorcha? Ardal was ashamed of his own thoughts. Fergus's genius appeared to his colleague to be a doubtful quantity. Had he not often been applauded for his clever appropriation of the thoughts of others? Had he not even made use of Ardal's own? No mind can be entirely original. The greatest ones must have the most power of assimilation, but one ought at least to put such borrowed thoughts in a new dress. Whole passages of the fathers came unchanged from Fergus's lips. Not in Erin—there the ancient writings were too much studied—but in France and in Italy, where the audience had no sprinkling of scholars. And the compliments which this sort of talent evoked were sometimes received with a very complacent smile. Was this self-deception? Ardal devoutly hoped that it was. He could excuse Fergus the less for it because he had great powers of his own. Fergus had an off-hand way of speaking which was not exactly falsehood, but led people to give him credit for knowing much more than he did. Only a very close and prolonged intimacy could have given Ardal opportunities for finding this out.

And was Fergus always to be the most favoured? Was he, with little anxiety and trouble to himself, to receive a meed of popularity equal to Ardal's own, and at the same time to rob him of the sweetest flower of love? Ardal did not care for popularity, but he did value influence. He had a consciousness that he would give as good an account of that influence as Fergus would do. The use Fergus made of his talents seemed to have a recoil of blessing on himself. The worker was never lost sight of in the results of his work.

It was very uncharitable in Ardal to cherish these feelings at such a moment. But he had given way to Fergus in many things. It had become, in fact, a habit with him to remain in the background when one speaker would suffice. But too much was now being asked of him. Did Fergus suspect the reason of his visit? His look of triumph had seemed to imply this. Should Ardal resolve to give up thoughts of Sorcha?

He had been able to think all this whilst taking part in the conversation. For man is a complex animal. He can speak calmly of things—ay, of deep things—when his emotions are at war in the little sanctuary within. And Sorcha gave him once a look—it was when he spoke of family pride—which made him almost lose his self-possession. He could fancy himself standing beside the forbidden tree in Eden; and just as he had resolved to turn away without tasting, an apple had fallen unbidden on his lips. Its delicious taste would never be forgotten. It made him long for more.

He left the cottage in a state of extreme misery. Should he yield to his love, or should he not yield? Sorcha would not be won without a battle, a battle with himself as well as with his rival. But he must not become unworthy of her by cherishing bad feelings.

Strange, that two nights ago he had made this a subject of deliberation. He had acted with no impulse when under Uailsi's roof. The match with Mòr commended itself to his judgment. He had weighed well every aspect of it. Now the rush of emotion came with a force which almost excluded thought. He retired to his humble cell, not to meditate, but to pray.

It is very hard to submit to the Divine will when our own disagrees with it. The designs of Providence are mercifully hidden from us; but our uncertainty about the future makes us on the whole less rebellious. So it was with Ardal. He groaned about the possibility of losing Sorcha. And for a long time his blood was too feverish for his thoughts to settle into words. He did not know even if words were permissible. At last a light dawned on him. It was as if an angel had carried it. The lantern which showed him something was surely not lit on earth. And Ardal fell on his knees.

He had now a warrant for praying. He had a sudden conviction that Fergus could not possibly love Sorcha as he did. His nature was by far too shallow. Ardal knew not the language of gallantry. That tongue, unspoken in Erin, had come to Fergus when in Provence, as melody comes to a bird. Sorcha might, perhaps, listen to it. Then Ardal must seek strength to resign himself, but till then he would not give up hope.

CHAPTER IX.

Amada was in high spirits after her visitors had departed. Sorcha felt rather ashamed of her discontent. They had both spent a delightful evening. What did the coolness of some people matter when they were able to enjoy the society of sympathising friends? "I can't be such an old, useless creature after all," remarked Amada. "No less than three bishops! and they not the meanest for learning! But it was not me alone." And her aged face assumed a wonderful look of beauty as it rippled over in sunny laughter. Her eyes literally sparkled with merriment.

Even Sorcha, though well accustomed to her grandmother's ways, could not help staring in much surprise.

"Thou art like a child's ball," she said; "one moment it is on the ground, the next leaping up to the sky. It is pleasant, though, to have people talking to us as if we were rational beings."

"Is that all?" asked Amada, pausing in the midst of her laugh, and fixing on her grand-daughter a very curious gaze. "What was Fergus saying to thee, might I ask, round in that corner?"

"Nothing, grandmother," replied Sorcha, colouring slightly, whilst her voice sank just a little.

"We shall pluck rosemary for thee in spring, child," said Amada. "Give me my lamp now, and pleasant dreams."

She retired into one of the small apartments which jutted out like wings on either side of the cottage, leaving her grand-daughter in a state of some bewilderment. Sorcha had more than once heard quiet jokes about the power of her own attractions from Maidoc and Ita, but this was the first time that any such hint had dropped from her grandmother's lips. Could it possibly be true ? Sorcha was too simple-minded, and had too lowly an opinion of herself, for the idea to have easily found entrance. It was indeed a very flattering one. Her father's reputation had been as great as Fergus's was ever likely to become. But he had lived in comparative obscurity, and the respect which people had felt for him was perhaps too deep to be readily expressed to her. Fergus's genius was of another kind. It was brilliant, dazzling ; it was as the effulgence of a comet, which, spreading over great part of the sky, attracts the gaze of men, who see in its light a deeper significance than in that of the more steadily-shining stars. Fergus's praise was on every tongue. He was not only magnificent in the pulpit, he was the cynosure of all eyes in social life, his wit being supported by a warmth of manner that could only spring from real and deep sympathies. That such a man should bend in homage before her seemed to Sorcha impossible. Yet had not her grandmother said it ? Sorcha reflected on the events of that night. Fergus had not come there with Maidoc ; no, he had expected to find her and her grandmother alone. And was it not his hand that had plucked for her the beautiful lily ? Sorcha was weak enough to rise from her couch and step round the prostrate form of Cacht, who lay amongst the rushes, to have another look at the lily. She wished to make sure that it was not all a dream. Then she went to sleep, lulled by hopes that were delicious in their strangeness.

She awoke with the sense that some sort of change had come over her. It required an effort to recall what the change exactly was. Sorcha was surprised at the glow of pleasure she had felt. Somehow or other things did not seem quite the same when viewed in daylight. The magic of

Fergus's presence was gone, and she thought of him with admiration, it is true, but without any strong wish for the fulfilment of her grandmother's words. Why was this? Sorcha could give no account of it. She thought it right, in so important a matter, to subject herself to a rigid examination. Fergus was indeed eminent. Wiser heads than hers agreed to think him so. He was engaged in the noblest of all callings; and he was fitted for it both by his irreproachable character and by the variety of the gifts which Providence had showered on him. Her own ears had been ravished by his burning eloquence. Women worship power, and what power can be equal to that of the orator, before whom multitudes of men bow their heads like so many reeds? Why did she not care more to have that priceless jewel within her grasp? Its possession would make her grandmother's life so happy. Sorcha sighed. Had she discerned a flaw in the diamond?

No, reader, its lustre was too great to allow of her seeing one. And she did not even suspect the presence of any. She took blame to herself for her want of appreciation. She felt as if she were a cracked mirror which cannot help showing distorted images. Sorcha was a hero-worshipper, but her hero must be modelled after her own taste. Her conception of manliness was not exactly Fergus. Was there any one who fulfilled it? Yes, there was, but he was not for her. Would she throw away a betrothal ring because of the gems in King Roderick's crown?

The glow of sunrise had hardly died away when, after attending morning prayers in the church, she clambered to the summit of the rath and hastened down an outside ladder in quest of her usual supply of milk. She was returning with it, and looking at the glitter of the dewdrops on the unshorn turf, when a figure advanced to her from beneath a tree. Sorcha started; her fingers could scarcely retain their hold of the milk-can. In a moment Fergus was beside her, touching her so closely as to make the colour rush to her face. He looked at her with a peculiar tenderness.

"Let me take that from thy hand," he said.

Sorcha resigned her can and walked by Fergus's side towards the great gate of the rath.

"Thou hast a step like Venus," he said, "when she vanished from her perplexed son. Thy ringlets, too, scatter ambrosial fragrance on the breeze."

"I have no wish to resemble a heathen goddess," replied Sorcha, turning her dark liquid eyes full on the speaker, as if to read into the depths of his soul. But the earnest gaze which she encountered made her look to the ground.

"Thou art early abroad," she remarked.

"Yea," replied her companion. "I love to see the sun on his first awaking, and the flowers opening their eyes, whether beneath a veil of grass or of broidered linen."

They had now reached the cottage door. "I cannot ask thee to break thy fast with us," said Sorcha, "as we take our first meal in my grandmother's chamber."

Fergus looked disappointed. "The abbot was kind enough to ask me," he said. "Yet I would rather have been with you. What doest thou all the day?"

"I shall be in the pharmacy, preparing medicine," replied Sorcha. "At ten or eleven I visit sick people when it is my turn to do so. At noon I come back for dinner, and I have to see that my grandmother's is taken to her first. I dine, of course, in the refectory."

"And after noon?" asked Fergus.

"I am generally in Declan's cell, reading or copying," replied Sorcha. "Sometimes I pay visits after four o'clock; sometimes visitors come to us."

"Is home, then, bright with thy presence at eve?" asked Fergus.

"I then remain with my grandmother," replied Sorcha, "unless there is some special service in the church."

" Wilt thou not come with me on the river ? " asked Fergus. " I have a sweet little coracle, which will be to thee as the green cup is to the lily."

" Will any one accompany us ? " asked Sorcha.

" No one whom I know of," answered Fergus. " We can glide down ere darkness falls on the forest."

Sorcha meditated for a moment. There could be nothing wrong in entrusting herself to Fergus's guidance, yet somehow she did not like it. Such a proceeding, even when the parties were betrothed, was, to say the least, unusual.

" I will think of it," she replied.

Fergus took her hand. He fixed his blue eyes on her very earnestly. " I dreamed last night," he said, " that I was being wafted along the water by an angel, and it seemed as if the vision might become true."

" Nonsense," said Sorcha, disengaging her hand not without a struggle. She raised the latch of the door.

" I shall see thee soon," said Fergus, as she disappeared with a graceful curtsey.

Sorcha was not quite pleased. She had sometimes imagined that she would like a lover, but hardly one so pressing as this one. A few honeyed words could not repay her for the loss of her free choice. Fergus had tried to make her decide on the instant that she would break through all rules of conventional propriety for the sake of spending an hour or two alone with him. Was this not a foretaste of what would happen when she was away in the boat ? Would he not take advantage of her weakmindedness to make her utter some irrevocable vow ? Her very going with him would be irrevocable in the world's eyes. She might as well string half a coin round her neck in token of her betrothal.

She lost no time in consulting her grandmother. Amada listened patiently, and in a tone of eager interest inquired, " Why wilt thou not go ? "

" I am not his spouse," replied Sorcha. " Even if I were,

is it customary ? Wouldst thou have done so when thou
wert my age ? "

"That is no fair question," replied Amada. "I cannot
say what I would have done had I been courted by a man
like Fergus. If it were any one else I would say no at
once. But he is a bishop ; thou canst go where thou wilt
with him. It would be a pity to lose him for that."

Sorcha looked thoughtful. Her grandmother might be
right from one point of view ; but she had not made up her
mind about taking Fergus, and she instinctively shrank from
committing herself in an irretrievable way. The more she
tried to realise what it would be, the more did she feel that
she owed something to her own self-respect.

In the meantime other eyes had not been indifferent to her
movements. She had been watched. Ardal had, in fact,
clambered up the steep ladders in the interior of the Round
Tower a little before sunrise, and, looking out from a window,
had lost not a detail of her doings. He had seen the bold
frankness with which Fergus had accosted her ; he had observed her downcast eyes, and her sudden glance of critical
inquiry had been transfused by his heated fancy into one of
trustful affection. He saw Fergus hold her hand for several
minutes at the cottage door ; he saw that he was pleading—
pleading for what ? A wild storm arose in Ardal's heart.
He crumpled in his hands the precious parchment which had
cost him days of labour, and which he had meant to deposit
in a box on one of the shelves of the tower. He had seen
Fergus chatting familiarly with other women ; but that was
in a foreign land, in circumstances when both parties must
have been well aware that it could issue in nothing. And to
none of them had he spoken exactly as he was now doing to
Sorcha. What had given him this advantage? Oh for a
tithe of such boldness !

Ardal's first impulse was to hasten down and waylay Sorcha
in her walk towards the college pharmacy. He wished to

hear his fate from her own lips. But what presumption! He had only been introduced to her on the previous night; Fergus had had a few days' start of him. But Fergus seemed to have been previously intimate with some of her relatives, and had no doubt been favoured by them. Some men, moreover, had a faculty of putting their feelings into words. He would only make a fool of himself if he tried to imitate them. The reverence with which he regarded Sorcha made it impossible for him to step rashly into her presence.

Was all hope, then, gone? Ardal feared so. At the same time, the struggle need not be given up. He could only consider himself quite defeated when Sorcha showed herself fairly beyond his reach. He would watch her more narrowly than ever; and if he saw that she cared for his rival, he would submit. But she must appear to do so with her whole heart before Ardal could be satisfied.

He stepped down to the foot of the tower. He lingered in the shadow of the church with the intention of speaking a friendly word to her on her passage to the pharmacy. He tried to picture to himself her beautiful eyes glancing up at him just as they had done last night, and as he was sure they had done also to Fergus that morning. He needed such an encouragement. It might, if it came, make the task of renunciation more difficult; but the momentary pleasure would be worth all the prospect of future suffering. But what if she would not look at him? What if she were annoyed? At length she came out of the cottage, carrying a small basket.

Ardal turned from his apparent study of a rude sculpture commemorating the conversion of his own ancestors. He stepped a few paces forward, hesitating.

Just then Sorcha gave a faint smile, which was not for him. Another form issued from behind the great yew tree which stood in front of the abbot's dwelling. Fergus stepped along the smooth turf, carrying a bunch of violets. Ardal could hear what he said :—

"I have gathered these for thee, or rather for thy grandmother. Shall I take them to her whilst thou art in the kitchen ? We may find more gorgeous flowers this afternoon. Thou thyself wilt be a blossom bright among thousands."

"They will be a joy to my grandmother," replied Sorcha. "Good morning."

She bowed gracefully, and disappeared within the door of the pharmacy. Fergus stood looking after her for a moment. Then he turned towards the cottage, humming a well-known Provençal air—the same, in fact, which Maidoc had surprised on Ardal's lips. It ran thus :—

> "Roussignoau que cantes sans cesso,
> Dins moun jardin,
> Vai veire ma bello mestresso
> De bouen matin ;
> Vai, digo li, dins toun lengagi
> Tant amourous,
> Que siou un bargie doou villagi
> Ben malhurous.
>
> "Digo-li que toujour souspiri ;
> Mai se voou ben,
> Mougras qu'a touto houro n'en plouri
> Serai counten.
> Mespresai tout : bouenhur, richesso,
> Scienço, favour ;
> Moun soulet ben es la tendresso.
> De seis amour.
>
> "Eme ta vouas tendro et poulido
> Et toun dous chant,
> Ss ma mestresso es endourmido
> Canto li plan ;
> Du'n ton que la tendresso esvillo
> Sanso estre fouar,
> Noun toques gaire soun courillo
> Mai ben soun couar."

Sorcha was soon busy in her work of compounding. It was a responsible duty, for the sick and the suffering over a large extent of country looked to the college pharmacy for help. The stores on its shelves were by no means of a despicable kind. They included all the remedies known to Hippocrates, and therefore almost all which were used by our grandfathers. There were barley-meal and rice-flour for fever potions, oxide of zinc for feeble eyes, with cantharides, mustard, foxglove, bryony, iris, wild celery, and other herbs, whose virtues could only be extracted by subtle processes. All Sorcha's faculties, bodily and mental, were engrossed in the work of preparation. She knew that the welfare of some fellow-creature depended on her dexterity.

There was a pause shortly before the dinner-hour. Sorcha slipped quietly up to Ita.

"There is something I wish to ask of thee," she whispered. Her eyes were downcast, and there was a tell-tale colour on her cheek.

"What is it, child?" said the kind matron, passing her arm round the girl's waist.

"Thinkest thou it would be quite right," stammered Sorcha, "for me to go on the river this afternoon? Fergus has asked me to do so."

Sorcha did not see the anxious look which came, like a cloud, over her friend's beaming face. She did, however, notice a significant ring in the voice.

"With him alone?" asked Ita. "Has he asked no one to accompany thee?"

"I believe not," replied Sorcha. "I cannot tell why he asks me, but my grandmother would fain have me go."

"I should advise thee otherwise," said Ita. "Thou couldst hardly do so if thou wert betrothed, and I suppose thou art not so?"

"No," replied Sorcha, pressing her friend's hand, but not daring to look up. "I thank thee for thy candour."

She went into the refectory hall. There were two large dining apartments, one of which was reserved for the families of the resident bishops and visitors.   Sorcha had a right to sit there, but she did not like the constraint which governed everything said or done in the abbot's presence.   She preferred to share a humbler meal in the larger refectory, where four tables gave accommodation to a number of young boys and to the under teachers.   A few of the bishops, with their wives, had a similar taste, and amongst these were Maidoc and Ita.

Sorcha, who always sat next her friends, noticed that they looked at her with peculiar gravity.   She felt uncomfortable. Did they disapprove of her conduct in entertaining any thought of the proposed excursion, or was it perhaps that they saw her approaching a momentous crisis in her life? Sorcha was quite at home amongst the boys, who were arranged in classes of twelve.   It was a pleasant sight to watch their fresh young faces, and she had become acquainted with many things which never reached the lectors' ears. But to-day it seemed as if they were nowhere.   She was too ill at ease to enjoy anything.

On issuing from the refectory, she encountered Mòr.   That young lady had always been friendly to her ; and though her parents had encouraged a hurtful rivalry, there was still a kind of comradeship between the two girls, which sprang from their fresh and sincere natures.   Mòr was looking unusually cheerful.

" Why dost thou not dine with us ? " she said.   " It has been dull sometimes, but we have had quite a treat to-day. The conversation was brilliant.   Fergus knoweth well how to interest every one.   I never spent such a delightful hour in my life.   I wish much that thou shouldst have the same pleasure.   Wilt thou not come to-morrow ? "

Sorcha knew that Mòr was speaking truth.   For the abbot's daughter was not quite in harmony with her mother. Uailsi prided herself on the official position of her husband no less than on the princely blood which ran in her veins.

It would have been a hopeless task to persuade her that she was similarly constituted to the herd of common mortals. The spirit of Christianity has overturned many things; but in that age it had hardly begun to fight against aristocratic privileges. The very colour of the fluid that issued from the veins of princes and nobles seemed of a peculiar hue; they bore the same relation to the rest of their fellow-men as the gold of their coronets to the iron of the plough. Religion was, in Uailsi's eyes, so much the more valuable that it taught men to know their place.

Mòr had been initiated into all this; but somehow it did not make her perfectly happy. She was the image of her mother in many things—in personal appearance, in natural gifts, and in aptitude for learning. It may be doubted if her heart were really warmer; but there had dawned on it a something which was not in keeping with the rest of its adjustments; a ray of that light, in short, which is apt to show the dust in our moral atmosphere. A quick throb of life had passed through her; a seed had sprouted which had been sown by no earthly hand. It grew into a plant, tender indeed, but eager in its striving after sunlight. It was this that made her so child-like, even in her acquired haughtiness; it added to her nature a sensitive element which her mother lacked; she could enter into other people's feelings in a way that superficial observers would not have given her credit for. Mòr became dissatisfied with some of her surroundings. Why could she not enjoy free converse with the young of her own sex? Pride is a sorry substitute for sympathy, and Mòr fancied that her life would have been happier had she been less highly born. Her father might well be proud of her. Her natural talents had been diligently cultivated; she accomplished with ease any literary or feminine task. His heart was gladdened above all by her display of the Christian graces. She would do no dishonour to her ancestry, princely or clerical. For Mòr strove to still her heart-hunger by abounding in all good works. She was incessant in her visiting of the poor. None was so energetic as she in the laboratory, none so skilful in ministering at a sick bed. The abbot pointed to her with pride as the pattern maiden of the family. There was a ring of complaisance in his voice when he preached from the text, "That our daughters may be as corner-stones, polished after the similitude of a palace."

But Mòr had very penetrating eyes. She had at length discerned that her mother was on no good footing with the bishops' wives. Why this should be was not at first apparent, but nevertheless it was so. Mòr began to suspect that high birth was not so much to be coveted. She had heard of happy gatherings where she was not present; she had even marked the shadow of constraint gather over faces that had looked bright just before she approached them. People threw something formal into their mode of addressing her, and Mòr fancied herself not of the family, though in it. She watched her parents' conduct; she compared it with that of others. Did the consciousness of their superiority chill people? Maidoc was as learned as her father; he was reserved and taciturn; yet a laugh was never hushed on account of him. She saw a warmth in the mutual glances of others which was never turned on herself.

Mòr was much given to meditation. It was not long before the whole state of the case revealed itself. She saw that her father's teachings were not quite at one with her mother's. And a course of patient observation made her aware that the abbot's hospitable intentions were often thwarted; that he, in fact, had long ago resigned much of his liberty in deference to his wife's tastes. Mòr threw the small weight of her influence into the balance whenever there was a discussion between her parents; but her mother's foot was too heavy in the opposite scale. The abbot's wife was indisputably the head of the house. She would, indeed, have resented any one affirming this. She yielded to her husband all outward honour ; but both took it as a matter of course that their dignity must be maintained ; Uailsi being the natural judge of the means to accomplish this. Mòr discovered that her mother was proceeding on a wrong principle. Not thus had the followers of Patrick changed the face of their island world. " Before honour is humility," a wise king had once said, and Mòr strongly suspected that her father's rule would have had a surer foundation if it had been reared on the fact that all the baptized are equally entitled to be the objects of a pastor's solicitude. She could not, however, break through the charmed circle. Her filial duty forbade it. She had, nevertheless, a wish to fashion things in her own way, and she longed for the chance of attempting it. She might aspire to be the wife of an abbot herself ; and she would then have the opportunity of showing how a Culdee family ought to live. She at least hoped that a wise marriage might deliver her from an intolerable restraint, even though by it her lot might be cast in a sphere very different to the one she coveted.

Her words to Sorcha only did Fergus justice. It was a virtue which no one could deny to him, the faculty of making others happy, by drawing out their powers of mutual entertainment. He was emphatically a society man. And he did it so easily that men did not attribute the whole of their enjoyment to him till they had a taste of his absence. But his own wit was ever the sprightliest. It was like a never-failing stream, running, bubbling over every obstacle, shining in the sunlight of an ever-present popularity, and refreshing the whole face of nature around it. Sorcha regretted that she had not been there.

She was accustomed to pay her grandmother a short visit before settling to her afternoon work, that she might see if the old lady's dinner had been properly served, and convey to her any piece of news which might modify their plans for the afternoon. On passing the corner of the church she again met Fergus.

"Thou art always astir," he said, "like one of the elves who go the same round. Whither away?"

"Homewards," replied Sorcha.

"Thou wilt come with me an hour hence?"

Sorcha looked at him. "Not to-day," she replied.

She gave him no time for remonstrance, but hastened into the cottage.

"Art thou come to get ready?" asked Amada, who was arranging her violets.

"I am not going," replied Sorcha. "Hast thou had a visit from Fergus?"

"Just for a moment," replied Amada. "He brought me these, and said he would call again."

Sorcha hastened back to her afternoon duties, in the hope of avoiding her lover. Why this was she did not know, but she had a dim consciousness that he was too pressing; that he was giving her no opportunity for reflection.

There was no denying that she enjoyed his society; but she would rather that his visits had been confined to the hours when her work was done. To call in the expectation of sharing their breakfast seemed to her an unwarrantable intrusion, even on the bounteousness of Celtic hospitality. She felt safe in Declan's cell, however. She had successfully resisted the temptation of going with him on the river, and it had been to her no slight one. She was, therefore, able to give herself calmly to the task of transcribing the sacred letters. Perhaps there was something stimulating in Fergus's friendship. It nerved her to higher achievements. Was it possible that the hope of his approbation had inspired her gentle fingers? The page which she illuminated that afternoon seemed, even to her, a miracle of art.

There are men in the nineteenth century who would give much to know with what materials Sorcha worked. We shall not gratify their curiosity; we will not withdraw the ever-thickening veil which hides her little box of brilliant colours; nor will we tell by what subtle processes she had extracted them from the rich juices of our mother earth. Sorcha never attempted those ambitious designs where much exquisite work has been expended on a perspective less advanced than that of China, and where the specimens of moving life are more grotesque than those of the Assyrians. But her spirals were executed with a precision which even a Poynter might envy; nor would any of our modern lady artists have alto-gether despised the delicate tints of her flowers.

She worked for some time in silence, without looking up. Then, pausing at the foot of a page, she surveyed its gorgeous outlines.

An indefinable something crept over her, akin to the sen-sation of a closed blossom, which feels the presence of the sunlight, without discerning it. She glanced mechanically round the cell as if to make sure that she was alone.

But in a moment she started up, uttering a low cry. For there, leaning against the bare stone wall behind her, was the object which she had been trying to banish from her thoughts. How had it ventured to intrude on her privacy? How had it dared to enter Maidoc's cell? But she had no time for questioning. The object was a living, breathing one, and it at once spoke.

"Thou art diligent, Sorcha. I have stood here for an hour. Thou hast not once raised thine eyes. May I see thy work?"

Fergus sat down without further ceremony, and began examining the precious pages.

"Beautiful, exquisite!" he exclaimed, his blue eyes glitter-ing with pride. "Thou makest our country worthy of her renown. She is still the Isle of Saints."

He laid his hand tenderly on Sorcha's arm. She shrank back.

"When I am alone with thee," he said, "I hardly know what I am doing. Thou art like one of those glorious images in the Roman churches. All that is great and true in womanhood finds its expression in the Madonna, just as of old it did in the bright-eyed Virgin of the Parthenon. Thou wert born to make us understand the meaning of higher things."

"Yes," replied Sorcha, hardly understanding him. "It is worth doing, is it not? copying these beautiful texts. They may be a treasury to some one whom I shall never see."

"I spoke not of thy work," said Fergus rising, and trying to take her hand. "I meant thyself. The lily needs not to work. She is beautiful because God made her so. But I hope thou hast a warmer heart than the lily has. Else it will be sad for me."

Sorcha wished to cut short this talk. It seemed meant to lead to nothing, except to draw from her an avowal of feelings which she had not quite given herself permission to entertain. She was quite ready to be won, but it must be in a straightforward, open manner. She dreaded to give some sign of capitulation before being formally besieged. Any crafty means were with her likely to defeat their own ends.

She did not half know her mind. When Fergus was present, she felt willing to take him, but upon the condition that something which she had not yet seen was there. She had the capability of loving him, but the music of her nature would respond only to a firm touch. He must distinctly say, "I love thee," looking frankly and sincerely out of those blue eyes of his. She already loved her own ideal of what he ought to be; in fact, she adored him, *plus* an element of straightforward manliness that had not yet contrived to show itself. She knew that he was eccentric, and she preferred to trust her feet on solid ground rather than on the glossy quaking of the bog.

For Sorcha, like many humble-minded people, had a very exacting nature. It was difficult for her to believe that

Fergus loved her so much as to make him want her for a wife. He was so brilliant, so gifted ; and she was only one of hundreds who might feel themselves honoured by his notice. She would not humour a passing fancy ; she must hear it more than once from his own lips before she could bring herself to believe it.

She did not wish to remain there with him, so she asked him to accompany her home. It would be a gratification to her grandmother, she knew, and would be only anticipating the visit he had already promised. They crossed the park together, and soon stood at the door of the little cottage.

CHAPTER X.

Amada was seated, as usual, on the foot of her couch. Her aged face glowed with pleasure as she saw Fergus enter.

"I feared thou wouldst not come," she said. "Thou mightest find something better to do on a bright day than visit me."

"The place where thou art is always bright," he answered gaily, standing beside her in the attitude that a son might have taken. "And I congratulate thee on Sorcha's work. It is beautiful as those flower tapestries which the sunbeams weave upon the meadow."

"Yea, and look at her spinning," said Amada. "Show us the sheeting, child, that thou hast finished last week."

Sorcha obeyed somewhat reluctantly. Opening one of the large chests which stood against the wall, she displayed several rolls of fine linen.

"These are spun from the flax, and woven in our own house," said Amada. "Sorcha's mother learnt it from me, and she is not a step behind any of us. The days are past when weaving was thought to be menial."

"A truly Irish idea," said Fergus. "We have learnt something more from the Saxons than this new fashion of curled hair. Though we might, indeed, have held the loom in more honour, knowing by whose hands it was plied in the palace of Priam."

"Then there is the Norman tapestry work," continued Amada. "Sorcha, show it."

Opening another chest, Sorcha displayed a small picture in coloured wool. It represented Ruth, the gleaner.

"An emblem of herself," said Fergus. "And of thee too in bygone days. You have gathered golden grain, both of you, and there is blessing in the house of the righteous."

This last remark struck a chord in Sorcha's heart, because of its truth, not because of the lips that uttered it. There was a blessing in that humble cottage; not the sum of her own acquirements, but the never-failing store of love which exhaled its clouds of fragrance around. God had blessed her in every way; in giving her trusted friends, and in surrounding her with much that was tasteful and ennobling. He had blessed her not least in the gift of this aged grandmother. But her very thankfulness made her the more alive to her grandmother's weaknesses.

Amada was talking very familiarly to Fergus. She had a right to do so, if she had confined herself to her own concerns. But during the whole of that evening the name of Sorcha was seldom absent from her lips. It was as if she had taken their betrothal as an accomplished fact, and was bent on gratifying Fergus by showing him how great a treasure he possessed. Why should he appreciate the wheaten cakes more because she had made them? He might surely be left to find things out for himself. Sorcha was uncomfortably conscious that she could not succeed in being as dignified as she wished.

And she felt unhappy after Fergus left. It ought not to have been so had she really loved him. She sat thoughtfully by the hearth whilst her grandmother looked to the fastenings of the door.

"What aileth thee, child?" asked the latter.

Sorcha did not reply for a few minutes. Her grandmother was not usually quick to notice her humours. They were not, in truth, of a troublesome character. Amada's own variations of temperament were worth the study of younger people, and it was a new sensation to both to have their relations in this respect reversed.

Yet it would have been stranger still had Amada not noticed her. Her lustrous dark eyes were fixed on vacancy. The corners of her coral lips were drawn very far down, and she sat immovable, as one who sees too deep into the heart of things.

"What aileth thee, child?" repeated Amada, in a somewhat louder tone. Sorcha rose. Her face took on a more natural expression, but she looked less of a child than of a woman who felt the power of her own will.

"Grandmother," she said, laying her hand caressingly on the old lady's soft hair, and gazing straight into her eyes. "Knowest thou that I am not pleased with thee?"

"Why?" asked Amada, staring back at her in perplexed amazement.

"Because," replied Sorcha in a clear but very firm voice—"just because thou art so kind-hearted that thou hast compromised me a little."

"How?" asked Amada, looking more perplexed than ever.

"Thou sayest that Fergus comes here for my sake," said Sorcha. "Perhaps he does, but he has not told thee so. And thou hast talked of nought but me to him all this evening, just as if I belonged to him. Thou knowest it well."

"But he seemed to like it," replied Amada. "He could have spoken of something else if he wished."

"But thou didst not ask if I would like it," persisted Sorcha. "I am no packman's ware that thou wouldest fain be rid of."

"Ah!" exclaimed Amada, as if a light were dawning on her. "I thought not of that. It seemed so natural to do it. I would not have any one think that I held thee lightly. I shall be more cautious. I shall not do it again, I promise thee."

Sorcha laughed till the tears came. "Dear, naughty grandmother," she said. "I know well that thou wilt do it again. Thou canst not help it."

"Thou shalt see," said Amada. "Aye, and Fergus shall see it too. I am not such an old fool."

Sorcha kissed her affectionately ere they parted for the night. But events were marching too quickly: she was losing control over them. She had faith in her grandmother's promises, for the old lady was now on her honour. But the effects of that night's doings could not be so easily obliterated. It would be more difficult now for Sorcha to appear indifferent; she must do all that Fergus wanted, or she must lose her temper. She was amidst rapids through which she lacked courage to pilot herself. Was there any friend to whom she could turn for counsel ?

There was one who stood to her in a peculiar relation. Confession was not practised in the ancient Church of Ireland,* but intimate confidences were recommended between pious young people and their spiritual guides.

It was customary for any one who was much concerned about the momentous questions which determine our destinies to choose some one as a "soul-friend." This one might be of either sex, and need not necessarily be a pastor, but was simply one who had more experience in the Divine life, and sufficient human sympathy to make him enter readily into the difficulties of others. Those who needed such a support were free to choose it; but when once chosen the relationship was as public and as willingly recognised as that of foster-parent. Sorcha's "soul-friend" was the good Bishop Maidoc.

She had never found him unsympathetic. He had stood beside her in those dark days when she had failed to catch a ray of light from the Divine promises, when the rainbow of redemption seemed to have altogether vanished from the clouds which obscured her vision. She had not troubled him

* Appendix.

with every little detail of duty, but she knew that his heart was glad when he saw her walking consistently with her profession, and he had more than once counselled her to submission under the very justifiable provocation she received from the jealous haughtiness of the Lady Uailsi. Maidoc was always kind, patient, fatherly, and would pause in his most important studies to listen to her, as a gardener will turn from some interesting occupation to note the drooping of a favourite flower. Once, when she had indulged in a passion of discontent, and had afterwards expressed her sorrow for having wasted his valuable time, he had replied:

"Say not so, my daughter; the seal of my ministry are ye in the Lord."

Then he had continued, his face suffused with a heavenly radiance:

"What is my hope or crown of rejoicing? Art not even thou in the presence of our Lord at His coming?"

Sorcha knew, therefore, that she could go to Maidoc for disinterested counsel. But she felt a strong reluctance to do so. If it had been about any other matter, he would have been sure to comprehend her, and perhaps would have even been gratified by a fresh proof of her confidence. But how could she even manage to tell him? She fancied herself slipping into his cell in the early morning, leaving her breakfast untasted till she had delivered her errand. But it would not do. Her cheeks tingled too violently at the notion.

Fearful of encountering Fergus, she sent Cacht for the milk. Amada attributed this unwonted indolence to the exhaustion produced by excitement. But Sorcha was of too hardy a fibre to experience any such feeling. She could spend half a night in thought, and next morning move about with her usual briskness.

It was as she had expected. Her lover accosted her on her way to the village kitchen.

"Thou art late," he said. "Like the morning star, thou

hast had a cloud over thee. I shall be absent all day, for I have to preach at Youghal. I have been looking for some Provençal poetry. I should like to know what thou thinkest of it, for I copied it only for thee."

"Is it thine own?" asked Sorcha.

"No," replied Fergus. "I wish I could translate it, for the verses have been running in my head. Thou canst fancy that thou hast inspired them."

Sorcha took the tablet. Her curiosity was piqued. There was quite a world of romance sealed to her by her ignorance of the language of "oc," and a world of learning too, she fancied Mòr knew something of the "gaya sciencia," and spoke rapturously. This tablet might give her a glimpse into that world. It would also give her a glimpse into Fergus's meaning. It would at least be something tangible should she summon up courage to consult Maidoc.

She had several opportunities for doing so in the course of the day; but she shrank back. At length an idea occurred to her.

It would be easier to break the ice through Ita. There was to be a meeting for prayer that evening in the church. Maidoc was to preside at it. There was a great ferment in men's minds, and possibly some one might detain him after it was over. She would lead Ita out of doors; darkness would favour her disclosure.

The church of Ardmore consisted of two parts, forming a large choir and a nave. The choir was the ancient building, and the nave had been added to it fifty years previously. At the junction between the two was a beautiful pointed arch, some thirty feet high, resting on pillars, whose capitals were sculptured in the form of lotus flowers. This arch was the pride of the Ardmore community, and was considered by them as great a triumph of skill as the Menai tubular bridge appeared to the men of the last generation. The round-topped windows and doorways of both churches were splayed inwards, and had the characteristic ornaments of Celtic ecclesiastical architecture, besides the conventional habit of getting narrower as they receded from the ground. The roof was formed of well-polished wood, whilst a small library of books was stored in the row of ornamental niches in one of the walls. An octagonal stone font, richly carved, and a table covered with fair white linen, were the only ornaments of the choir.

Evening came, and the wooden benches were gradually filled, chiefly by members of the college family, and by the dwellers on the termon - lands. Many of these stood in groups before the door, discussing with much eagerness the preparations for Thursday's assembly. The younger people were glad that the monotony of their lives was to be broken by some excitement ; but the older ones felt that they were in the midst of a crisis. The time was coming when each community must finally determine whether it would or would not carry out the decrees of the Synod of Kells. The tide of Anglo-Romanism was sweeping onwards, ceaseless, irresistible; it was obliterating ancient landmarks ; it carried the monarch of Munster on its crest, and it had invaded even the time-honoured sanctuary of Lismore. A barrier must be set to its advance, and a stout barrier too. For through every little hole it would insinuate itself; it was subtle and elastic ; yet it had a might that could sweep nations into its current. A few years hence the ancient polity might be gone for ever. There would only be a few ruins to mark where it had once stood, like the stones of Calabrian cities engulfed beneath the wave. What could hold the ocean in check? What but almighty power ? And the strongest weapon of Erin's sons lay in an appeal to heaven.

Therefore the prayer-meeting was convened. Many were attracted from curiosity. They knew that Ardal would be present, and they expected that he would give an account of his travels, or at least favour them with some definite state-. ment of the views he had formed. Others there were who in solitude had wrestled with the Angel of the Covenant, and desired to collect the separate units of their strength into one prevailing effort. These foresaw that the ancient church polity would have to struggle for its life. The coils of superstition were around it, and none knew but that their gentle pressure might soon be tightened.

It was an impressive sight to see these faces upturned beneath the smoky lamplight, and still more so when all, rising to their feet, sang the glorious hymn of Patrick, to the accompaniment of two harps, one of which was played by Ardal, the other by a professional minstrel. Then every knee was bent while Maidoc's soft voice rolled forth in earnest entreaty.

Sorcha was deeply moved. She, too, felt the magnitude of the crisis, and she was much ashamed that her concern about it should be so much mingled with the thought of her own personal interests.

Those who had come for the purpose of hearing Ardal were disappointed. He spoke, indeed, but it was only on the necessity for self-abasement. There were none of those glowing descriptions on his tongue which it could so easily have uttered. He is reserving himself for Declan's birthday, they all thought. And a few lingered after the benediction, as if they scarcely believed the meeting was over.

Yet somehow these spiritual exercises inspired Sorcha with courage to unbosom herself. "It is self-love which stands in my way," she thought. "If a thing is right, it ought to be done, whether my friends think better or worse of me for it." So she led Ita out into the darkness.

She passed her arm softly within her friend's. "I would fain learn thy husband's mind," she said, "about something that troubles me. Yet it is what I dare not speak of."

"What is it, child?" asked Ita.

"It is about Fergus O'Flannahan," replied Sorcha. "My

grandmother thinks—well, thinks he loves me ; and he always comes where I am ; and I know not if he is worthy."

" I will tell Maidoc, then," said Ita. " Wait thou till we go into our dwelling, then follow us thither. I know he will give thee good counsel."

Sorcha obeyed. She walked slowly towards her own cottage, and then returned to the church door in time to see the figures of Maidoc and Ita disappear into their own house.

She went slowly in their steps. It was not without much trembling that she knocked.

Ita opened the door. Her mild face was unusually grave. Maidoc rose and welcomed her with solemn kindness. He motioned her to be seated at his side. Sorcha kept her eyes fixed on the ground.

" My daughter," he began, in a voice low from fatigue, " Ita has told me what troubleth thee. Thou wouldst fain learn what I think of Fergus. Hast thou looked closely into thine own heart ? "

" Yes," replied Sorcha, demurely, but without the faintest semblance of a blush. " I feel so differently at different times, that I cannot tell what to think."

" Has he told thee that he loves thee ? " asked Maidoc.

Sorcha felt that the black, bead-like eyes were fastened on her.

" Not in so many words," she replied. " But he is always saying that I am pretty, and comparing me to flowers and fairies." Sorcha's face began to burn. " And he gave me this," she added, holding out the Provençal tablets.

Maidoc laid them on the table. " I trust thou wilt allow me to peruse this," he said. " I would fain have a night to ponder over it. Thou knowest that the first stroke of the bell findeth me at work. Visit me after sunrise, and thou wilt hear what I have to say."

Sorcha bade him a grateful good-night. Ita insisted on accompanying her home.

What was Sorcha's surprise to find Fergus with her grand-mother!

"Why hast thou tarried?" exclaimed Amada. "Fergus would not believe that thou wert at the prayer-meeting."

"I returned from Youghal two hours ago," said the young bishop. "Thy grandmother and I have had a long talk about the state of the Church, from Polycarp downwards. She is well read in the Fathers."

"Aye," responded Amada, "and about the state of the Church within the rath of Ardmore. We are a little epitome of the world without. We have our good sides and our bad sides."

"It groweth late," said Sorcha, "and it were well for my grandmother that her rest be not disturbed."

"Then I must say farewell," said Fergus.

"Thou hast no look of weariness," said Amada, "though thou hast preached twice to-day."

"I often work till after midnight," he replied. "I would never retire to rest sometimes if the lamp did not go out, when I do not happen to have a flint, or cannot find the oil-bottle in the darkness."

"Thou burnest the lamp of thine own life too quickly," said Amada. "I like those that wear themselves steadily out, not a great flare-up, and then it is dark."

Fergus looked reproachfully at Sorcha whilst shaking hands, and then disappeared.

The girl was up betimes. There was, indeed, scarcely sufficient light for a scholar's needs when she sought Maidoc's cell. It had, nevertheless, been strewn with clean rushes, and he was there with a pile of manuscripts neatly arranged before him. He welcomed Sorcha with his usual calm kindness.

"I have thought over it," he said, "and I must confess my own inability to give thee substantial help. In matters relating to the spiritual life I am at home, but this lieth somewhat out of the range of my observation. Hast thou ever formed in thine own imaginings any idea of what a husband should be?"

"I cannot tell," replied Sorcha. "But thou hast often told me we must take facts as they are in this world. What thinkest thou of Fergus?"

"He is a man whom I regard with the highest esteem," replied Maidoc; "and I have a warm friendship for him, both on account of his office and character. But the truth is that women look at men with very different eyes from what we do. It is just as thou findest in thy illuminating work. Art thou not sometimes satisfied with the form of a letter, and yet wish the shade of colour had been different?"

Sorcha smiled. "Often, if it be yellow," she replied. "There would be no difficulty if I knew my own mind."

"That makes counsel exceedingly difficult," said Maidoc. "But thou needest not doubt now if he loves thee. I have read these verses carefully. Thy knowledge of Latin should help thee to decipher them. Listen, while I read them plainly—

> "Domna, oimais vos en cre ben—
> Vos est cella qu'ai encobida,
> Vos est ma mortz, vos est m'a vida;
> Vos est cella que a delivre
> Me podetz far morir o vivre;
> Vos est cella que, ses enjan,
> Am et tem et cre a reclam;
> Vos est mos gaugs, mos alegriers,
> Et vos est totz mes consirers."

"Could he not have said it in Irish," said Sorcha, "instead of looking it up in a strange tongue?"

"Fergus is not like other men," said Maidoc. "His mind is essentially poetical. But let us take facts as they are, for though God has promised to guide those who ask Him in faith, He has long ceased to answer by tokens. He means us to make use of the perceptive faculties He has given us. There is only one plan I can think of."

" What is that ? " asked Sorcha.

" That thou watch thyself yet more closely," said Maidoc, " and note especially thine impressions on Thursday, for the full sunlight of publicity sometimes shows our friends in new aspects. Observe Fergus, and observe the other speakers. Then ask thyself, Do I reverence him more than them all ? For that, I think, is the foundation of wedded happiness, especially when the husband is a bishop."

"I will do so," said Sorcha, rising. " Perhaps I shall learn more by comparing him with others. And perhaps I have done him injustice. If he had not tried to be so constantly near me, I might have thought more of him."

" That may be," said Maidoc. " It is as when we view a mountain—we must neither be too near nor too distant to take in its just proportions. All I will say, in conclusion, is, deal fairly with Fergus as with thyself. It were no kindness to say, ' Yea,' if thou canst not truly return his love."

CHAPTER XI.

ARDAL had in the meantime been no passive observer of
Fergus's actions. This was the greatest trial which he had
ever undergone, and he could not, by the subtlest process of
reasoning, account for the effect it had on him. Eight days
previously he had been master of himself; his whole thoughts
and hopes concentrated on his sublime vocation. He had
been able to reflect on his own destiny, to survey dispas-
sionately the prospect around him, and to judge in what
quarter the sweets of domestic happiness might be most
readily culled. Now a mist had come over his eyes, and the
cause that produced it could not well be explained. He knew
very little of Sorcha's character, save from the accounts of
others.   But she was exquisitely beautiful; she seemed to
him the harmonious realisation of all that was true and of
good report.   To look at her was to feel ennobled; she was,
to outward resemblance, the highest expression of the Divine
idea in the creation of man. He watched the ever-changing
play of her features with reverent wonder that such transcendent loveliness should be embodied in breathing flesh.
Earth would have a taste of heaven for him, and heaven
itself would be doubly glorious were such a product of the
Divine goodness to wander henceforth by his side.

And the vision had appeared but to baffle him. He was
like a mariner who has pursued some phantom ship. Nor
could he easily regain his lost course. He must make a
great effort. The manliness, the energy which was needed

for his country's service must not be carried away by a resistless current, to be sucked into a whirlpool of feeling out of which he would soon be powerless to withdraw it. Fergus, he saw, was constantly in Sorcha's cottage. He could not well be so without her favour. And she could be under no illusion. For the last few days his rival's every gesture had been that of a lover. There was no reason why she should dislike Fergus. Was Ardal unselfish enough to wish that she might enjoy happiness without him?

Ah no! The lamp which he let down into the depths of his heart revealed spots in it which had hitherto escaped his scrutiny. Perhaps this was a visitation of Providence, a process by which he was to be made more meet for accomplishing the task to which he had devoted himself. Ardal had little faith in the virtue of ascetic practices. He often said that it were easier to scourge one's flesh than to subdue one's inborn pride. He held to the notion that a bishop had better form the same ties as other men; that if he needed chastisement it would come to him, and would be laid on more effectively by the Almighty's hand than by his own, and that the occurrences of common life supplied more opportunities for self-renunciation than any we could seek out for ourselves. He was only beginning to taste of the cup he had dreamed about. Was not its very bitterness, therefore, to be prized all the more that it must be drunk in secret, and that he could imbibe with it no temptation to spiritual pride?

His struggle was long and sharp, but he had not to rely on his own power. Spiritual faculties grow by such exercise. The breath of doubt can have little influence on a mind which is conscious of having received help from the Unseen. Ardal rose from his knees with his wicked passions not merely conquered, but transformed into a hearty love towards his rival. He himself marvelled at the change; but he was not proud of it, he was only deeply humbled at having felt the opposite. He was unconscious of having achieved a victory greater far than that for which many a Romish saint has been canonised.

His love for Sorcha was not quenched. He had not done violence to his nature, but he had come to see the possibility of loving and yet resigning her. He was a sanctified man, and not the faint imitation of an angel.

As he preached on Sunday in Ardmore Church none could detect the havoc that earthly affection had wrought within him. His hearers were only conscious that an exceedingly beautiful spirit was before them, pointing the way in which they too might walk. Thus in the bosom of Erin's mountains we may behold some moss-covered crag over which the heaven-dropped waters trickle merrily, and be totally unmindful that its contrasted loveliness of furrowed rock and clustering greenery is the result of desolating storms as well as of sunshine. The greater part of our earth would be a desert without the howling but rain-laden winds, and none of our friends smile so sweetly as those who have often shed wholesome tears.

Monday brought little change to Sorcha. She was kept in a continual flutter by Fergus's visits, and she managed with consummate skill to avoid being again alone with him. Her grandmother acted with more prudence than she had expected. Amada put a restraint on her feelings. Much as she enjoyed Fergus's society, she maintained towards him a dignity which made her look handsomer than ever, and had the effect of rendering Fergus more deferential than he had been.

On Tuesday afternoon, as Sorcha sat working in Maidoc's cell, she heard a very timid knock. Opening the door she encountered the blooming face of her servant Cacht.

"May it please thee," said the panting woman, "thy grandmother bade me fetch thee. Thy mother's sister hath come, with her husband."

Sorcha folded up her parchments and hastened towards the cottage.

The sound of a gruff voice proceeding from it confirmed the servant's statement. Seated on the end of the couch opposite to that of her grandmother was the angular form of Olrud, his swarthy face lighted by a friendly smile, whilst the statuesque figure of Grainné stood in an observant attitude. The former welcomed her with the effusion which has the unmistakeable stamp of sincerity in stern natures. The latter surveyed her with motherly fondness.

" We have come for to-morrow's meeting," she said, "and have already visited the church to render thanks for our safe arrival. My husband felt loth to let such an opportunity slip. He is anxious to learn what the men of Ardmore think. It is duty and pleasure for me both at once.

Amada looked the picture of happiness. But though she talked with Olrud, her gaze was soon wandering over the room, attracted by the erratic movements of Grainné. She was not long in satisfying herself that there was a change for the better. A placid contentment had begun to take the place of suffering resignation.

Olrud and Grainné had at length shaken themselves together. Constant friction had rubbed down the roughnesses of both of them, leaving a smooth polish on the surface of their mutual intercourse ; and the grain of both being of a peculiarly hard quality, they had lost nothing valuable in the process. The influence of time and the growth of paternal cares had brought them into a kind of harmony, just as the worst arrangement of bricks and mortar will become mellowed by weather stains, or so covered by creeping plants as to be artistically beautiful. Providence sometimes compensates us in this manner for the irrevocable character of our mistakes.

Another figure soon emerged from Amada's chamber. This was Sigurda, Olrud's sister, who resembled her brother only in the swarthiness of her complexion. Fifty-five summers had left their memento of wrinkles on her face. Yet her cheek was ruddy withal, and the warmth of her manner quite concealed any angularity which she might have inherited. She presented a strong contrast to the fair and queenly Grainné.

The party had just sat down to their evening meal, over which an elaborate grace had been pronounced by Olrud, when the inevitable Fergus appeared.

He started at sight of so many faces. But he soon recovered himself, and returned Grainné's somewhat critical glance with an air of easy assurance. He recollected Olrud, although it was long since the two had met under Rossa's roof.

"There is quite a covey of rooks swarming here," said Fergus. "Each house is filling with friends and relatives. Hast thou come officially," he continued, turning to Olrud, "or in the way of private friendship? "

"Neither," replied Olrud. "But the Inisfallen brethren are interested in to-morrow's gathering. It is the duty of every man, and above all of every bishop, to note, as much as in him lies, the signs of the times. As Ardmore pronounces itself, so will a hundred other clerical communities."

Sigurda sat with mouth half open, as if wishing to drink in the stream of her brother's wisdom. Her eyes were now turned towards Fergus.

"True," replied the latter. "Thou mayest feel how a nation breathes by the throb at one of its extremities. And a nation seldom pronounces wrongly—*Vox populi, vox Dei.*"

"I differ from thee," remarked Grainné. "There was once a cry, 'Not this man, but Barabbas.' "

Sigurda at once made the sign of the cross, fearing that her sister-in-law's speech might be blasphemy. She was reassured, however, by remarking that the two bishops received it with a smile, and that Amada shook with quiet laughter.

"And Demosthenes was fined by the Athenians," said Olrud. "Had we lived in the days of Patrick, or of Columba,

I should have had no fear for the issue. But we no longer hold strictly to the inspired canon. We have framed earthen vessels for ourselves, and we resort seldomer to the golden pitchers."

"Thou speakest of the Book of Armagh,"* said Fergus. "It is a singular thing that, notwithstanding its promulgation, the office of Co-arb of Patrick should have passed away from its hereditary guardians. If thou lookest well at it, it seeks to place the Abbot of Armagh in the same relation to us as that in which the Bishop of Rome stands to those who acknowledge him."

"Yea," replied Olrud. "What else could these abbots expect? They pretended to have received a power by Divine revelation to which they were in no way entitled. Then comes Malachy O'Morgan, and says, 'You must yield to me. I have a better claim, for I have received a mandate from Rome.'"

"Malachy was a great man," said Fergus, "and he was the son of an Irish presbyter; yet hath he done more to denationalise us than any other. For my own part, I was not sorry to see the family of Armagh humbled. If we must offer our sandals to a superior, let it be to him who wears the purple."

Olrud started. A frown crossed his warthy face, making it look like a sculptured anger. "Wilt thou risk," he said, "any departure from the simplicity that is in Christ?"

"If thou meanest episcopal parity, no," replied Fergus. "I only said, if I had to yield to one of two evils, I should prefer to acknowledge the pretensions of Rome before those of Armagh. Rome would at least give us an equivalent for our loss. She has the glory of royalty about her. There was something infinitely mean in the way that the Abbot Celsus travelled over the country, sweeping away all the tithe cattle in his train."

* Appendix.

"There I agree with thee," said Olrud; "but I quite differ on the point that one evil may be cured by another. Thou knowest that Peter's pence have been claimed already. We have only felt the touch of the little finger; by-and-by we shall feel the weight of the iron glove. Those wonderful cathedrals, those vestments broidered with gold—who pays for them? Is it not one of the notes of a true bishop that he should not be greedy of filthy lucre?"

"Aye," replied Fergus; "but it is not for themselves, it is for the service of God."

"That may be," said Olrud; "but was God any the worse served when there were none of these things? There may be times of persecution coming; but better, I say, that we should suffer hunger and nakedness than allow the true light to flicker for a moment."

Fergus looked unusually grave. He remained silent for a few moments, patting gently the arm of his chair.

Amada took up the thread of conversation.

"Think you it will come to that?" she said. "I know that the Synod, the Synod of Kells, took on themselves to put bishops over us, just like the Roman ones, and to tell the old tale about our bishops not being rightly ordained, and that when each one died there should no one but a simple presbyter—priest, as they call it—be put in his place. But I thought every one was determined to resist this. They have not managed it yet."

"True," replied Olrud. "But other causes may be at work which will upset all our calculations; just as the men of Marseilles were startled by the falling of their tower, when Cæsar's legion had approached it under cover of a shed, and had picked out all the small stones at the foundation. The mischief comes from our loose hold on Scripture."

"And on Christ," replied Amada. "He is the sure foundation. There is too much talk about Patrick and Columba for my taste. It is like 'I am of Paul, and I of Apollos.'"

"Aye; and if we only *were* of Paul!" exclaimed Fergus, rousing himself from his reverie.

He now said good-night, shaking hands with each of the company. Few could help noticing that Olrud's manner towards him had lost its friendly warmth. Both bishops looked grave, apparently from different causes; but the glance of unfeigned admiration which Sigurda cast on Fergus quite atoned for her brother's coldness. All eyes were directed to Olrud after the door had been closed.

He shook his head ominously. "Unstable as water," he said. "'Tis sad—sad."

"But yet he excels," exclaimed Sigurda. "How dost thou explain that?"

Her brother looked darkly at her. "Sigurda," he answered, "beware lest thou be found to have itching ears. Fergus O'Flannahan is but a tinkling cymbal when a true note has to be struck."

Sirgurda's eyes were downcast at her brother's reproof. But Amada felt that he had gone too far.

"Thou must not call him that," she exclaimed. "If he be but a cymbal, he is at least a good one. There are some that would be the better of making more music themselves. I did not agree with what he said about Rome making up for anything it took away, but I am sure he did not mean to favour it. No one could be more strict than Fergus if it came to the point."

"I hope so, I hope so," answered Olrud. "Hath he been much in thy company of late?"

Amada's eyes twinkled. "He is after an orthodox business," she replied. "He will not yield to Rome for Sorcha's sake."

There was a burst of merriment. Sorcha's cheeks were tingling with shame and vexation. She sought refuge in her grandmother's apartment.

"Is it so?" said Olrud. "Then I shall forgive him;

for, as thou sayest, a wife would bind him to the Irish Church. But I cannot allow such utterances to pass unreproved."

" Sorcha is to be congratulated," said Sigurda. " I suppose it is all settled ? "

" No, in truth it is not," exclaimed Amada in alarm. " He has never said so in words.   It is only my sharp old eyes that see through a chestnut husk."

" Then, mother," said Grainné, quietly, " I advise thee to wait till the husk breaks. Thou wilt hurt thy teeth if thou try to crack it. I am glad of the hint, though, however it came."

It was now arranged that Amada should resign her room to Sigurda, and occupy one of the couches ; the one, in fact, which had belonged to Moriath, and into which she had a great dislike to see a stranger enter. Olrud was to seek accommodation in one of the neighbouring cottages.

CHAPTER XII.

THE silver bell of Ardmore Tower began ringing before sunrise. It announced to all within earshot that the children of Declan had resolved to mark, by something unusual, the birthday of their spiritual father. This day was reckoned, by a beautiful Irish custom, to be, not that of his entrance into this mortal life, but that of his reception into glory. And many eyes peered anxiously forth from door and window-slit, seeking to discern from the face of the sky what hopes they might entertain of fair weather; for the sun which illumineth the Emerald Isle hath ever had much to contend with in the way of vapours. Yet were his beams then so beneficent as to relieve the husbandman from all duty in the way of haymaking, they likewise imparted to the region about Ardmore a climate which still in summer recalls to us somewhat of the balmy air of Sorrento.

As the light grew stronger, a multitude of figures flitted about, pursuing the usual avocations of kitchen, stable, and dairy. Ardmore was in a flutter of excitement, and few of its inhabitants had broken their fast ere the tramp of hoofs and roll of wheels announced that some of the expected visitors had arrived.

Towards nine o'clock several groups might be seen wending their way along the face of the hill fronting the sea. Fishermen who had left their tiny skiffs in the safe shelter of Ardmore Channel, Bothachs, or farm-labourers on the termon-lands, had all donned their holiday attire, and hastened, in company with men of superior station, towards the group of huge boulders which then surrounded the fountain of Declan. All were much occupied in discussing the nature of the report which they hoped to hear from the lips of Ardal and Fergus.

"Hast thou seen aught of the young bishops?" asked a countryman of Cacht, adjusting over his stalwart shoulders the plaid of saffron-coloured wool, which did duty with him both by day and night.

"Aye," she answered; "but thou needest not to look for marvels. Their stay abroad hath not nourished a silver moon behind their heads, such as I have shown to thee in Mael-Patrick's foreign gospel, nor even a pair of long ears, like thine own are apt to come to."

"And have they no sacred bits of wood to show us?" asked the labourer, unabashed by her ready wit. "Methinks mine eyes would fain rest on that which hath borne the weight of the Crucified One."

"Hast thou seen Declan's treasures?" inquired a stalwart blacksmith, whose forge stood on the inner side of the entrance to Ardmore rath. "There is amongst them a rag of the swaddling clothes, brought thither by a pilgrim of the last generation. Yet have I heard Bishop Ardal say that the words of Paul are more precious than his bones."

"Which of the two thinkest thou will be the man of fairest tongue?" asked the labourer. "Hath their speech not grown thick with the utterance of strange sounds?"

"Nay, that may I not tell," replied the smith. "But thine eyes should have a feast. For is not Bishop Ardal the grandson of our own chieftain, besides being the very image of great King Brian?"

"God bless him!" exclaimed several of the bystanders. Over the rocks, near the fountain, a small wooden platform had been erected, supporting some thirty benches, one of which had been covered with a scarlet cloth for the use of the abbot.

The crowd here soon rapidly increased, men, women, and children flocking over the daisied turf to range themselves on the hill-slope directly above the gushing spring, in whose waters they and their forefathers had been baptized. They were for the most part habited in saffron-coloured mantles, those of the wealthier being bordered with brilliant chequers. The women wore no other head-dress than a simple kerchief of white linen.

Other men soon began to ascend the platform, whose tunics of white wool were covered over with cloaks of undyed black. They were all distinguished by the shaven coronal, and were the bishops of surrounding villages, together with those resident in Ardmore itself. As if by instinct, the male part of the audience gathered on the space immediately before the platform, whilst the women and girls squatted on rugs around the outside.

Amongst these latter were Amada, Grainné, and Sorcha. The Lady Uailsi, who sat with her daughter at a little distance, acknowledged their civilities by a gracious bow.

The Lady Uailsi was in unusual spirits; for beside her on the smooth turf stood a group of men whose chequered trews, silver-fringed crimson mantles, golden bracelets, and jewel-hilted swords marked them out as nobles. Chief of these was a man of stately mien, whose haughty glance seemed to claim the homage of the whole assembly. This was Prince Malachy O'Faolin, chief of the Deisi, who had been attracted thither principally by a desire to see how his young kinsman, Ardal, would comport himself.

Amada had insisted on being present in the assembly, in spite of Grainné's remonstrances. "Thou wilt not deny me," she had said. "I shall hear nothing; but who would miss the sight of so many good men? One can guess much from people's faces. I shall know which side they are taking. I should be uneasy at home, and would fain know the result before the meeting separates."

Sorcha's spirits had sunk very low. She felt as if on the course of this day's proceedings not only the purity of Erin's Church, but her own individual destiny, would depend. Her eyes sought the centre of the black-robed group. There Fergus sat. He had noticed her; he had darted a friendly smile across the intervening throng. Sorcha could not well examine him, but she had an impression that he was much excited, and that his restlessness made him the most prominent figure in the assembly.

No ceremony attended the abbot's entrance. He stepped forward simply and sat down, throwing back the hooded cape from his massive head. He bowed an instant in silent prayer, then, rising, made signs to the minstrels to strike up Patrick's hymn.

It was a solemn moment when its measured notes rose into the quivering air. Deep, sonorous voices blended with the music of harps, trumpets, and cymbals, whilst some sweet and tender ones, and even Amada's low quaver, added their strength to the sound. It rose like a cloud of incense from the altar of free and devout hearts, and seemed to come echoing back from the clear blue sky, unfettered by any roof of human rearing.

After a few minutes of earnest prayer, the abbot spoke. His clear handsome features were, as usual, composed and pleasant. As he surveyed his audience all traces of anxiety soon disappeared in a glance of satisfaction that his summons had been so well responded to.

"My friends," he began, "the elders of Ardmore have called you together to help them in deciding on a point which will affect the welfare of your children's children. Sixteen years have passed since the Synod of Kells confirmed the decree of that of Rathbresail, imposing on the free community of Ardmore an ecclesiastical superior. But, like other Irishmen, we have been loth to obey laws which transgressed the traditions of centuries. Four years ago the Abbot Christianus, of Lismore, addressed to my lamented predecessor, the Abbot O'Faolain, a most touching remonstrance. 'Why will ye not return to the true fold?' he said. 'God hath suffered the churches of Ireland to go on their own way for a time, but He calleth on them now to repent. Ye make a schism in the body of Christ.'

"And Abbot O'Faolin replied: 'We cannot return where we have never been. The truth has been handed down to us through an unbroken line of bishops and presbyters, who were none the less truly ordained of God although their names have not been tabled on earth. From the apostles, through Irenæus and through many others, the Word was conveyed to Brittany, and thence the noble Patrick bore to our shores that imperishable seed, whose sprouting has made our island a bright spot of verdure in the eyes of Christendom. But Patrick received his first ministry by no imposition of hands. The Spirit of God spoke as directly to him in the wood of Foclud as He did to Paul on the road to Damascus. We have felt His presence ourselves, felt it in our inmost being, and have therefore no need to seek for other credentials. But we wish not to seem wise in our own conceit. Give us four years to learn what ye seek of us. We will do what our forefathers did half a century ago, when the Pope wrote to them about the Easter controversy; we will send messengers to Rome, to Antioch and Jerusalem, if need be, that we may know whether your system be better than that of Declan, better than that of Columba, of Aidan, and of the other holy men into whose labours ye seek to enter.'

"Brethren, the four years are past. The messengers are before us. From their lips ye shall learn what are the fruits of that unity which yearneth to embrace us. Bear with me whilst I say a few words of my own.

"This struggle, as you well know, has lasted for seven hundred years. Rome has been victorious everywhere, even in regions where the tramp of her imperial legions was never heard. The wild mountaineers of Caledonia and the elders of our beloved Iona have been coaxed or forced into submission. Lindisfarne has long ago been forsaken by those of its sons who would not adopt a foreign ritual. The hearths of a pure faith have in the Cambrian valleys been quenched in the blood of the saints of Bangor.* The foundations of Columbanus,† of Fridolin, of Gallus, have conformed to the rule of Benedict. Nowhere but in Erin do the Celtic Britons hold their own against the power of the Romanised Saxons. Brethren, we are strong in our isolation, strong in our union, stronger still in the memory of victories won by the sword of the living Word. Yet the foe is amongst ourselves. The antipathies of race have been skilfully used by him. Those Danish settlements on our shores, near the mouths of our great rivers, have sought consecration for their pastors from Canterbury; and the men whose fathers ruthlessly plundered our shrines now lend themselves as handles to the foes of our spiritual freedom. And our kings, the sovereigns of Munster, have they not consented to the partition of our country into prelatical districts? Whither shall we look for help under this dire oppression? Where but to that Divine Comforter who hath never yet forsaken us?

"But whilst I advocate resistance, and advocate union, there is one point on which I desire searchings of heart. Romans and Saxons have treated us badly, cruelly, I may say, when I think of the martyred Britons of Cambria. But have we been careful to show them the charity that is not easily provoked? Have we never shut ourselves up in the haughtiness of our superior purity? What meaneth that old tale of our ancestors not eating with Romanists, of casting the leavings of their meals to the swine, and of scouring with sand every vessel polluted by the stranger's use? Brethren, let us feel that, notwithstanding diversities of doctrine, we are yet one in Christ. We may refuse to acknowledge a human head

---

* Appendix.　　　　　　　　　† Columbanus of Luxeuil.

below the Divine one, just as we may decline to place a screen between our eyes and the sun. Let those who prefer the screen keep to it, if they will ; but they have not yet shut themselves out from some enjoyment of the light. Let us be careful to exercise hospitality even towards those prelates whose claims we resist. Let us show them that ours is the better way by the purity of our lives, and by the love that is ready to pardon a multitude of sins. So shall we gain a victory ten times more enduring than if we had overcome them by the valour of our right arms. Let us pray that God may change their hearts towards us ; then may we unite with them in the warfare against ignorance and vice."

All eyes were now turned on Fergus O'Flannahan, who, flushed with pleasure and excitement, stretched his slender figure to its utmost height, and smiled in a way which sent a thrill of expectation through the assembly. There was a gleam of triumph in his blue eye ; he felt and looked like the bright particular star whom the multitude had come forth to be dazzled by. Sorcha's eyes were rivetted on him as by enchantment. She felt her heart heave to that state of transcendent emotion which made it ready to receive deep and lasting impressions.

" Sons of Declan," began Fergus, in a voice whose silvery ripple ran to the utmost limit of his audience, " inheritors of a faith pure as the translucent gems of your own mountains, I feel that the choice of our fathers might have fallen on a better man than I am ; yet I cannot stifle the gladness that kindles in my heart at sight of hearers so well fitted to use any crumbs of information I may have gathered for them. The last three years have been very eventful ; they have seen the flight of one king from green-valleyed Erin, and quarrels amongst the others which have made the Isle of Saints like a gathering-place of clouds replete with noisy fire. Whatever may be our ecclesiastical state, there is no doubt that we need a strong hand to roll the storms from our country. I yield to no ancient bard in my admiration of the Celtic character. We have been to our friends as the grateful sunbeams are to budding boughs, but as the very fire-winged lightnings of the skies to our enemies. Our love of fighting springs from an innate sense of valour, and from an originality of thought, which, when sanctified, has borne the sounding eagle wings of our renown throughout Christendom. I have crossed the foamy paths of ocean to a land where the name of Scot was no transient beam of fame. High and low, rich and poor, priest and layman, vied with each other in showing honour to the countrymen of Maelmuire and of Duus Erigena. Yet there was an impression amongst them that we are deficient in artistic culture. 'How is this?' I asked of an Italian priest. 'Have ye no esteem for our Bibles, the work of our recluses, as well as of our white-handed maidens? Can anything surpass the faultless regularity of their letters; the brilliance or the ingenuity of their colouring?' 'True,' he replied, 'the eagle eye of the sun looks down on no richer storehouse of sacred or classical learning than Erin. But your taste goes no further than these Scriptures; you scorn to apply it to your sanctuaries, or to the implements of common life.' Then I told him of the Ardmore bell, whose voice is tuneful as the airy murmurs of the harp, and I said that I would challenge any Italian artificer to fashion a more wondrous instrument than the trumpet of the O'Faolain. Yet I felt there was truth in his words. We are gifted above other races in our love of beauty —why not apply this to the service of God? Would our worship be less acceptable because offered amongst gracefully sculptured columns, instead of between those bare walls which argue a meanness of intellect? Erin hath ever been noted for the melodiousness of her clerics; yet doth the music of our native hymns bear the same relation to the tones of the Gregorian chant that the notes of our early spring warblers do to the whirling blasts that burst at night from our cloud-capped mountains, their awful thunder broken only by the noise of purling torrents. Our prayers and liturgies need not come the less from the heart if we make them more solemnly impressive. Thus might we defeat our opponents with their own weapons. Let us acknowledge wherein they excel us by trying to give to our pure faith a grander expression. The king's daughter was to be brought to her royal spouse in raiment of needlework; her clothing was to be of wrought gold. Believe me, my brethren, in these things we have erred. Let us have lofty, towering walls to our churches, framed after those Grecian models whose exquisite proportions charm the eye even in ruin. Let us deck our altars with whatever is precious; let us welcome all forms of adoration which worthily set forth the praises of our God; so shall Erin, clothed with the fame of the mighty, be again a beacon of light to other lands, and our children shall find in the burnished gold of our sanctuaries that which shall attract them from the glitter of strange shrines.

" And though the Gaelic race be the finest in the world, we have yet much to learn socially from others.. We are naturally chivalrous, and we live under laws which embody more than any others a sense of respect for the fair sex. Could it even have entered into the mind of a Cæsar or of a Justinian to decree that all presents given by a married man to a strange woman should belong by right to his wife? But, nevertheless, we have no code of honour to regulate the minor courtesies. Even in battle the knights of Normandy —men who have dyed a thousand fields with their enemies' blood—throw over the haughty faces of their wrath the blooming rainbow of politeness. Our chieftains behave as if they, like Achilles, had a heaven-given warrant for railing. In place of these endless bickerings about cattle, the Franks have their splendid tournaments, where the proudest has to win his spurs in the soft sunshine of ladies' smiles, and re-ceive his prize from hands fairer than the drifted foam. The art of wooing has been reduced to an exact science. The princesses of Provence do not think themselves demeaned by sitting in judgment on affairs of the heart. Might we not engraft all this on our social polity without detracting from our manliness? So shall we gather the flowers and fruits of our own virtues, sending them down to far succeeding times, instead of letting them be scattered like the white showers from our hardy thorn-trees."

A murmur of assent went round the audience whilst Fergus spoke. Many smiled sympathetically, but Sorcha noticed that a few grew graver as he proceeded. One of these was Olrud, who had slipped from Amada's side and managed to edge his way into the centre of the crowd. Another was Ardal. As Fergus sat down, he rose very deliberately.

It is always trying to speak after a brilliant orator. When men have just inhaled the perfume of the rose, the fragrance of other flowers must appear to them insipid. There had been a magic in Fergus's manner which it is impossible to portray, and which acted on Sorcha and others like a sudden sunbeam on wet flower-buds. The spell lasted for a few minutes after he had sat down; yet, as Ardal's handsome figure and massive head stood out clear against the group of dark forms behind him, there was something in his bold features and yellow locks that recalled traditional memories of Erin's national hero, and made men draw their breath more softly whilst he spoke.

"Brethren," he said, "and sisters in Christ, I, like the last speaker, stand before you to give an account of my impressions, and to offer a few suggestions which may help you to decide on your line of action. Our Church has been emphatically a missionary one. My researches have convinced me that the larger half of Europe has been evangelised by it. The great Saxon nation, which now stands foremost in the ranks of our rivals, owes much of its intelligence and knowledge of the Scriptures to the poor Irish bishops. Our very humility has helped to conceal this fact. We have sown the fields where the emissaries of Rome have reaped such abundant harvests. What saw we in Caledonia, whither we first directed our steps? Iona, where for nigh two centuries the lamp of truth burnt so steadily—Iona, the home of Columba, is now occupied by a Romish confraternity. Vainly did successive monarchs try to maintain its ancient authority. Since the decree of King Nectan* banished its true sons beyond the Grampians, those who had ousted them received but a hollow homage, and were powerless to summon Scottish swords to their help when the wild sea-pirates rifled their shrines. Dunkeld obtained the supremacy which Iona had lost—Dunkeld, whose abbot was held worthy to mate with royalty and to become the ancestor of Caledonia's kings. I must not harrow your feelings by dwelling much on the events of the last ninety years, nor tell too minutely how a sovereign, himself the near descendant of pious bishops,† set himself to the task of reconciling Scotland with Rome. The work was only half begun in the days of Malcolm and Margaret. It has been carried on most vigorously by their sons. Prelatic seats have been established; and though no native Scot has been persuaded to fill them, though a Turgot and a Robert have had to forbear exercising their functions at St. Andrew's, the power of these foreign offices is at length becoming consolidated. You wish, doubtless, to learn how the ecclesiastical colleges have been treated. The new bishopric was invariably offered first to the abbot, and invariably declined. To the twelve resident brethren was given the choice of becoming canons-regular, or of renouncing all their rights in the next election, and submitting to a reduction of their incomes to the extent of three-fourths of all funeral oblations. The two communities continue to live side by side. At St. Andrew's we saw its rightful owners offering their simple prayers in a very small corner, whilst the body of the church was kept for the pomp and circum-

* Appendix.   † Ibid.

stance of a foreign ritual.   Does not this foreshadow our own fate should we give our assent to the decrees of Rathbresail ?

" In England * the disastrous change has gone further. The nation has been crushed under a despot's heel. The story of Lindisfarne has been too often repeated.   Other abbots besides Colman, other brethren besides the spiritual sons of Hilda, have sought shelter in the wilderness rather than conform to unscriptural rites. The lapse of time has justified their conduct, for the proud representatives of the Roman bishop have become a byword for their worldliness. Men who professed themselves celibates have procured the appointment of their sons to the highest functions of government.   Cruelty and rapine reign in episcopal palaces.

" Yet from quarters undreamed of has a purifying, rain-laden wind come, rousing into life and beauty those seeds of pious feeling which lie dormant in every human heart.   The preaching of the new Cistercian monks has met with currents of thought springing from the utter despair of Englishmen at the fearful havoc caused by the late civil war. Streams of blessing now flow where, in church or in hedgerow,. men meet for social prayer. But will not these soon run shallow, if their force be directed to the glaring sunshine of cathedral building, rather than to the secret but eager study of the sacred Scriptures ?

The struggle has begun in Cambria. The massacre at Bangor only made the love of their native clergy sink deeper into Gaelic hearts. Here we found churches as pure as our own ; but the married bishops † cannot always succeed in keeping their benefices. Too often the choice of the communicants has been overruled by some Norman baron, a Romish stranger being introduced by force of arms.

" In Brittany it is the same story. The days are past when its children could keep aloof from the Franks. During the last forty years it has been a penal offence for a son to

* Appendix.   † Ibid.

succeed to his father in the ministry, and every effort is being made to have ecclesiastical offices filled by celibates.

"I come now to speak of lands which are more directly under the rule of Rome. My colleague has given you a glowing description of the courts of love, and of the influence of chivalrous laws on polite society. I would fain utter a few words of dissent. The ruling of these feminine tribunals is almost never in accordance with the morals of Scripture. Words would fail me to tell of the corruption and the disorganisation of social life which they have produced. It would be a libel on the Romish Church to say that she looks on these courts with a favourable eye. Nevertheless, they have sprung up under her teaching. But I say, give me the wild lawlessness of our heathen ancestors, rather than these refined specimens of impure casuistry. There is the less need for me to dwell on them, since they are so utterly foreign to our Irish nature.

"'And what is the Church doing, then?' you will ask. She is as a voice crying in the wilderness. Whether it be that the strength of religious zeal has been expended on the effort to rescue Palestine from the infidel, or whether the pomp of ritual diverteth men's minds altogether from the Scriptures, I know not; but certain it is that nowhere did I meet with so much blasphemy, so much reliance on human reason, and so much utter rejection of inspired truth as in that very Provence which has so recently been the honoured residence of a pontiff, and in Champagne, where the bold thinker Abelard was condemned to burn his writings. Yet are there living communities in Southern France. The Word of God was translated several years ago, and widely scattered through the efforts of a rich merchant. I have stood in the squares of the great cities, under the rays of a broiling sun, and heard Peter Waldo announce, in language simple but impassioned, the wondrous message which earth's kings have been trying to smother since the hour when it was

first proclaimed on Bethlehem's hills. Waldo speaks of the
Church in no measured terms. He calls it the barren fig-
tree, the mystical Babylon, and other terms which our
ancestors would hardly have dared apply to it. The congregations founded by him must at length come into conflict
with the Roman bishops. God alone knows what the issue
may be.

"Let me next say a word about Scandinavia. We visited
it not, but one of its sons whom we met in Rome told us
some things you may wish to know. There men struggle
fiercely about a question which interests ourselves — the
question whether better missionary work be done by celibates
or by married men. No Swedish or Danish priest doubted
his own right to marry before the Council of Rheims * met
fifty years ago. Twelve years later Pope Innocent sent his
legate, Cardinal Cibo, to Denmark, with orders to enforce
obedience. Then deeds of violence were done. Those who
refused to dismiss their wives were even punished with death.
But it has been in vain. Archbishops, priests, and people
still hold firmly to their ancient customs. The Archbishop
Peter, of Upsala, hath even suffered deposition at the hands
of the proud prelate Absalom for his persistence in consecrating priests' sons. The lower clergy are now in despair,
and all alike appeal to a general council. And in Iceland,
whither the gospel was first carried by our own Cormac, the
custom of pastors' sons being trained for the ministry is so
firmly rooted that I cannot believe it will ever perish.

"But what hope is there now of a general council? You
may judge from what I have told you what is the measure
of real unity in the Romish fold. Milan and Florence have
seen their altars deserted for want of ministers,† no one
being willing to take the place of those disciples of St. Ambrose who had become a proverb for sanctity, and who chose
rather to resign their offices than their wives. And what

* Appendix.   † Ibid.

shall I say of Rome? Shall I say with Bernard of Clair-vaux, that for their very enemies the Lombards can find no more contumelious name than that of Roman, and that the district so long governed by God's vicar hath become a pasture of demons rather than of sheep? Shall I say, with the Romans themselves, that the blood of Arnold is on the Church? I will say none of these things, but I will merely state that the vaunted home of peace and unity is now torn to pieces by civil war; that the Pope cannot enter his own city, where a prefect now rules in name of antipope and emperor, and that pontifical service has been performed in St. Peter's whilst the pavement up to the high altar was reeking in blood.

"Brethren, can we wonder at the vengeance of God? Can we wonder at that mysterious sickness which in one night destroyed two thousand nobles and prelates, sending the German army to retrace its laborious steps across the Alps? Brethren, I will say no more. We have seen shameful things in Ireland, but they were not done in the name of religion, and God grant that the day may be far distant when our endless bickerings, bloody as they are, shall be exchanged for the gigantic contentions that have turned Italy into a desert.

"We, too, suffer from the separation of the Church from the world. We, too, have not succeeded in leavening the whole nation with our teachings. Are we not feeling the touch of decay? Whence, then, the proverb that the saints of Patrick's age were as if robed in flame, those of Columba's were as burning mountains, and those who have come after but as the glimmer of lamps in the valley? Some of us, I fear, are but as smoky torches. Why is this? Because we neglect to rekindle ourselves at the true altar; because we allow the pride of birth and the pride of office to obscure the brilliance of the beacon that should guide the feet of our fellow-mortals. We have not so far perverted the gospel as to burn incense to the queen of heaven, but we have too often made it of none effect by allying it with the pride of this world. If we would maintain our ecclesiastical, or even our national independence, we must lay aside carnal weapons, and, like Sedulius or Columba, furnish the slings of our natural abilities with pebbles from the clear running brook of inspired truth."

As Ardal sat down, Olrud strode quickly to the front. He had been very restless for some minutes, his dark eyes fixed on the sea of heads before him. He shouted out just as the abbot had risen—

"Men and brethren, one word. It is the word of a stranger, but it cometh from lips well practised in preaching. Reference has been made to Patrick. He lent not to clerical matrimony the force of his example. The pioneers of truth must, like soldiers, deny themselves many things. But he never discouraged it by precept. He could not thus proclaim himself to be doubly the child of sacrilege. Yet did he make it one of the qualifications which he desired to find in a candidate for a settled episcopate, that he should be the husband of one wife. Our great Master honoured the wedded clergy when He gave us Patrick. Have not our very best rulers and teachers been the children of bishops? And there was conjugal love in Eden before the Fall.

"We in this island have had abundant experience of ascetics. There are few of our religious settlements which have not been crowded with them. The rule of our Columbanus, travestied as it hath been,* was surely not inferior in strictness to that of Basil or of Benedict. Yet, never at Durrow, nor at Bangor, at Clonmacnois, nor at Ardmore, have men been permitted to bind themselves by irrevocable vows. Our most enthusiastic ascetics usually settle down into married bishops. Doth not the whole worth of self-renunciation consist in its being practised by willing hearts? Why, then, force men to continue in its paths by hedging

<hr>

* Appendix.

them round with oaths ?   Those who are truly called to such
a life need no such safeguards, and I object to have another
man's conscience made the rule for mine.".

Olrud was collecting himself for a further effort, when
another bishop deliberately cut short what he feared might
be the beginning of an interminable harangue.

A variety of speeches followed, indicating various shades
of opinion, but almost all concurring in the resolve to offer
a determined opposition to the claims of the Abbot of Lismore.   The Synod of Rathbresail, they argued, did not
truly represent the Irish Church.   Not one-third of the
Munster bishops were present at it.   It was largely packed
with monks, Danes, and others who had no settled flocks ;
those who were not influenced by royal persuasions being
many of them opposed to the obnoxious measures.   The
Synod of Kells had numbered still fewer recognised pastors.
Its decisions were well known to have been foregone con-
clusions, and the very fact of its having been presided over
by the Romish Cardinal, Paparo, showed that it was an
assembly altogether outside of the native Irish communion.
Few, excepting the Abbot Gelasius of Armagh had been satisfied with the way in which its business had been conducted ;
and even he must have experienced a secret smart at the
manner in which the ancient authority of his abbacy had
been encroached on.   The old Irish argument for not obeying the decrees of the four Catholic councils held good likewise
in this case—that those who had been unrepresented could
not be expected to tender their submission.

At one o'clock the speeches were still going on, although
the abbot had made an effort to close the meeting in order
that the Eucharistic, or thanksgiving service, might be begun
in the church.   Maidoc and several of the elder bishops now
retired.   They wended their way to the church, and began
the chanting of Psalm cxvi. in honour of Declan's translation,
preparatory to dispensing the emblems of the Saviour's death.

They were followed thither only by the few who wished to reach their distant homes before sunset. Amongst these was the O Faolain. On leaving the church he pressed his nephew's hand.

"Would that this held the sceptre of Brian Borumha," he said eagerly. "There is a wisdom behind it which might pilot us safely past these perilous rocks. Why hide thy talents under that shaven brow? Other Irish princes have wielded both the crosier and the white wand of sovereignty. Come with me to Roderick's court; I have done him such service that a word from me would procure thy advancement."

"I have a yet greater Master," replied Ardal, "and much as I love thee, thou must pardon me for saying that were I co-arb of Declan, thy services to Roderick should make thee be held unworthy of touching the sacred cup. My brother Domnall," he continued with a shudder, "may not be what thou wouldst have him, but we might well change his rule for a worse one. And I will never wade to power through a stream of kindred blood."

"Thy speech is rough," said the O'Faolain, sighing. "Thou thinkest that the sword of my justice hath been a gory one. Would that I had drawn it for thee, and not for Domnall!"

Amada also had left the assembly, accompanied by Sigurda, Grainné, and Sorcha. They wandered by a winding path towards the brow of the hill, Amada leaning on Sigurda's arm, and pausing every few moments to inhale the fresh sea breeze. Sorcha gave her a brief account of the arguments that had been used.

"Thou seest," remarked Sigurda, "that the abbot is very anxious for charity. But I think he is not wiser than his fathers. These Romanists are just such as the Corinthians were told not to eat with—they are idolators."

"What hath been thy thought of Fergus's speech?" asked Amada.

"Excellent!" exclaimed Sigurda.

"For my part," said Grainné, "I was disappointed. I have always looked on Fergus as one of our first men. He never seemed to touch the core of the matter."

Sorcha looked fixedly at her. These words deepened an impression of which she was half ashamed.

Grainné continued: "For my part I would trust Ardal O'Brien more."

CHAPTER XIII.

THE assembly came to its decision at a late hour. This was declared by a show of hands, a fashion as prevalent among the men of Ireland as it had been amongst those of Argos three thousand years previously. Olrud returned to the cottage after sunset. He had indeed been the efficient cause of the crowd's dispersion, having had both the longest and the last word. Yet his stalwart frame showed no sign of exhaustion.

"What hath been the result?" asked Amada, her eyes sparkling with excitement.

"The children of Declan will keep to the old paths," replied Olrud. "It is like a game of chess. We have lost a crowned head and a couple of knights, perhaps, but we have an unbroken phalanx of pawns."

"And a great king who cannot be checkmated," said Amada. "They can never come within a dozen squares of him."

"Is that not irreverent? said Grainné. "I, for my part, cannot see what all the lamentation is about. If all the rest of Christendom hath gone the wrong road, it will not hurt Erin so much to be in company with others."

"Thou art wrong," said Amada. "Her fall will be greater because it will be from a greater height; and she will take longer to recover herself than will the others."

"Assuredly!" said Olrud. "I had an hour's talk with Ardal this morning. He thinks that we will need all our strength to maintain our political as well as our spiritual liberty. He has a strong suspicion that since a handful of our clergy swore fealty to the Bishop of Rome at Rathbresail the said bishop has made a gift of the whole island to the English king." *

"Nonsense," said Grainné; "the man must be dreaming."

"Ardal is no dreamer," replied her husband. "He is not likely to believe anything without sufficient ground. You know that the Roman bishop claims the right of deposing sovereigns. Ours have not been pattern ones by any means. He says that it is well known in France how a bull to that effect was issued thirteen years ago, and that though it be kept secret, the new prelates are all aware of it. What think you that our colleges are called in this bull? 'Nurseries of vice.'"

The cheeks of all flushed with anger.

"That is too much!" exclaimed Sigurda. "The whole world knows what the Culdee families are. What was Iona? what Bangor? what is Lismore? Nurseries of Scripture truth and of Scripture manuscripts."

"And of science and literature," said Sorcha. "Have not our forefathers seen their colleges crowded with Saxon students eager to learn at the feet of Irish lectors those tongues in which the sacred books were first committed to writing? The Roman bishop must surely have been referring to something else."

"Not at all," said Olrud. "Yet methinks the term would have been more fitly applied to those courts of love over which Queen Eleanora presides. But see ye not what is vice in *his* eyes? It is to seek baptism from persons unauthorised by him; to give the cup, as the apostles did, to the laity; and to let bishops lead about their wives, like Peter."

"But is there any real danger?" asked Amada.

"The danger lies in disunion," replied Olrud. "If we keep

* Appendix.

firmly to our faith we are safe for this generation. Our children must look after themselves. But there is a glamour over men's minds. That Fergus, now, is doing the enemy's work. He helps to darken the issue."

"Pray leave Fergus alone," said Amada. "He is not responsible to thee."

Olrud shrugged his shoulders. "Another source of mischief is," he said, "that men will not believe in the existence of the bull. Ardal, it seems, has tried to mention it to our friend Maidoc and his wife. They were both very indignant, and said it must be a libel. No Christian pastor, they insisted, could be guilty of such a scandal. Ardal thought it better not to speak of it in public since he had met with so little credit when he disclosed it to one or two."

"Dost thou believe it thyself?" asked Sigurda.

"I do," replied Olrud; "but I see not how it can be carried into effect. The King of France would help us by attacking Aquitaine."

"But there is another point," said Amada. "We are told to notice in the Old Testament how the Israelites were left to be defeated by the Philistines whenever they wandered from God. Perhaps that is His meaning about us. We have wandered very far from Him, there is no mistake in that."

"Thou sayest truly," said Olrud. "Look at the Lady Uailsi. If all I hear about her be true, she is a specimen of the spirit that has been at work. As long as our bishops were poor and had nothing to trust to but the power of the Word, they made converts by thousands. Tribes, if not nations, were born in a day. They carried the laity along with them at first, and both together made progress in secular learning as well as in wisdom. But the pride of office soon began to show itself—the gifts of the Spirit came to be thought of as a monopoly. Men remain within our ranks because they find there an honoured career; and now that the colleges are rich, there is no longer the same simplicity of life.   There is actual luxury; and it helps to separate us still more from the people."

"Thou dost not object to honey in thy pottage," remarked Sorcha; "although the Senchus Mòr says it is only for kings' sons."

"And thou needest not to speak of the Lady Uailsi," said Amada. "We might look nearer home. Each of us is proud in our own conceit; and we think ourselves fitted to judge others. Hast thou not broken bread in our church this day?"

"That I shall never do in Ardmore," replied Olrud. "Yonder sculptured arch savours only of the things that be of man."

Maidoc and Ita called at a late hour; but Fergus failed to appear, perhaps because he feared to encounter Olrud, with whom he had already had a slight war of words. Maidoc and Ita both looked curiously at Sorcha. It was impossible for them to discover what impression the day's events had made on her.

Sorcha was, in truth, ill at ease. She meditated about it during the night, longing to be satisfied. The effort to compare Fergus with others had been altogether vain. There was no doubt that he had been a distinguished figure, and that, had the sense of the meeting been taken, it would have been found that Sigurda was not alone in considering him to be by far the most talented of the assembled bishops. There was a spell in his presence from which no one could escape, unless, like Olrud, they dwelt in an exceptionally hard shell. Sorcha felt this spell, and would willingly have yielded to it, had she been well assured that its strongest potency was for her alone. Yet why should she doubt this? Was not Fergus a Christian minister, pledged by his profession to the strictest integrity in both love and friendship? Was he not placed on a moral pinnacle from which no earthly temptation was likely to induce him to throw himself? Had he not given her tokens of his regard enough to have satisfied an ordinary maiden? Sorcha was vexed with herself. She was capable of love in the abstract, why, then, did she fail to trace any concrete form of it amidst her present sensations ?

Fergus had never plainly said, " I love thee." But there are more ways of speaking than that with the lips, nature having furnished us with organs which transmit our inner meaning often in spite of our wishes. In a man of Fergus's culture these must be completely under control. He was no poor unlettered fisherman, who keeps his eyes fixed on some fair one till his neighbours begin to laugh at him. All that Fergus did must have a meaning. Was it not her fault, perhaps, that the decisive words had never passed his lips ? Had she not been in haste to withdraw when he clasped her hand ; had she not avoided looking into the liquid blue of his eyes ? His confident self-assurance had displeased her ; but perhaps it was a quality natural to genius. The modest fearfulness which accompanies love might even show itself in this lack of direct speech. She must not judge him as she would other men. Perhaps a greater degree of encouragement would lead him to show himself in a new light.

Sorcha felt keenly the discomfort of her position. She had blamed Fergus for it, and now she was beginning to blame herself. It must be evident to those near her that she was being courted ; she was no longer free to move about in her own way ; yet she could not lift her head boldly and say, " I am a spouse." Fergus was taking some of a lover's privileges without any valid warrant for doing so.

" Why so restless, Sorcha ? " asked Grainné, who occupied with her one of the couches. " Thou art so quiet in the daytime, that we can hardly get a word of thee ; yet now, when one would fain sleep, thou art lively. What aileth thee ? "

" Nothing," replied Sorcha ; then, half conscious of having uttered a falsehood, she said—

" Grainné, did any one ever ask for thee before Bishop Olrud ? "

Grainné laughed. " The question is curious," she said. " Dost thou wish to know how he asked me ? "

It is always a sweet surprise when a young heart finds an older one capable of true sympathy, when the difference of years vanishes in the similarity of sisterly experiences. Sorcha's eyes beamed in the flickering firelight.

"I should not tell thee," said Grainné, "but that I think thou hast a reason for asking. There is not much to tell after all. It was at the very darkest period of our family life, when we felt as if we might become peasants. Olrud did it very respectfully, and all in order. He spoke to thy grandfather first."

A ray of light flashed on Sorcha's mind. Her aunt was perhaps the very one, not only to give her counsel, but to ascertain the state of Fergus's mind. None could be endowed with a finer tact.

"Supposing he had come to thee first," she said, "what wouldst thou have said?"

"Just the same," replied Grainné. "Thy father tried the opposite way, and of course he succeeded. But few parents would have approved of it, and neither would thy grandmother, if it had not been such an exceptional case. I sometimes wonder what a man would do about thee. My mother, with all her excellent qualities, is not quite an efficient guardian. But I must speak lower."

"There is no need," said Sorcha. "She could not hear us at this distance, even if she were awake. As for Cacht, she is like the brown-haired Oscar; we might roll a stone against her head without making her rise."

"Hast thou been troubled in that way?" asked Grainné.

"Yea," replied Sorcha. "I have had hints more than once from Ita and other women, that some of their young friends cared for me. The abbot is my proper guardian; and I know not if any of them ever asked me of him. I doubt much, though, if he feels any responsibility on my account. So when I have heard anything of the kind, I have taken care to answer very decidedly."

"Thou art wise," said Grainné. "If it were not for Maidoc and Ita, thou wouldst be rather unprotected. Men will speak to thyself sooner because thou art an orphan. But what is the case with Fergus?"

Sorcha felt her cheeks burning. It was a few minutes before she answered—

"Well, aunt, I can hardly tell what to say. He has visited us three times a day for the last week; and I never go out of the house without meeting him. And he sometimes speaks to me as if he were in love. Yet he has never said so."

Grainné made some inarticulate sound. "Dost thou esteem him much?" she asked.

"Every one does," replied Sorcha. "I think him wonderfully gifted, but I had rather he had said more on the right side to-day, in place of speaking about ornaments. Bishop Olrud is not wrong in that."

"Then thou dost not think him perfect?" asked Grainné.

"No one is so," replied Sorcha. "Speaking of him as a bishop, I have often been impressed with his sermons. I recollect that when I was a child he preached here sometimes, and I have trembled at his descriptions of the miseries of the lost. No doubt it was good for me to tremble. But now that my mind has become more settled, and he has come back from such a long journey, I seem to see him in a different light. There is not the same spiritual savour in his expositions that there is in Maidoc's, or in Ardal's. They are often sublime, but it is as if, after hearing the thunder and the whirlwind, one listened in vain for the still small voice."

"Thou hast a keen discernment, child," said Grainné. "May I whisper to thee my real belief? Fergus O'Flannahan is not a Christian!"

Sorcha started. A cold shudder passed through her.

"It is a serious thing to say," continued Grainné, "and an awful thing, when I think of his profession. But I have good grounds for my judgment, Sorcha. When my father was ruined, we felt that there were none who owed more to us than did the O'Flannahans. We had shown them kindness and hospitality without end. The elder brother, Blathmac, who is now dead, was introduced to the family of Lismore through my father's influence. They were poor, and we furnished them with the means to carry on their studies. My mother did as much for the sisters as if they had been her own children. Yet from the day that we became poor, we never saw any of them in our house. I have heard both brothers preach, but have never spoken to either again as to a friend till I came here."

"That is most strange," said Sorcha. "But knowest thou aught worse of Fergus?"

"My child," replied Grainné, "he hath learnt too well the language of gallantry. Some men, who are quite scrupulous in their dealings with their own sex, have no sense of honour when they are trifling with women's feelings. And that is what I fear he doth with thee."

Sorcha groaned. She had suspected this, but yet she suffered when it was spoken aloud. "But suppose," she said, "that he were really in earnest. What motive can he have for deceit?"

"Vanity, child!" replied Grainné. "He loveth admiration so much as to court it. I say not that the man is without feeling. He hath a quick eye for the beautiful, and I flatter thee not when I say thou dost gratify it. Fergus would fain have it said that thou hast remained unmarried because of him. And he might, perhaps, like thee for his wife. But thou seest he hath been too cautious to commit himself."

"But how could he like me," inquired Sorcha, "and yet not seek me?"

"There is strong self-interest at work," replied Grainné. "He will look for some one of high birth. He doubtless knows many such. Should he fail in this, he can fall back on thee. And he may possibly never marry at all; for if the new prelacy gain ground, some high office may be open to him."

" Art thou sure of this ? " asked Sorcha.

" I am sure of nothing," replied Grainné. " My impressions may be uncharitable ones. But a man who can flatter so well can also amuse himself by a little love-making. Thou must not act altogether by my advice. I may be swayed by my recollection of the family's conduct to us. Those who have known sudden poverty have their eyes too much opened. And I will say this for him, I believe he would make a good husband if he ever did marry. He is flighty, he is eccentric ; and his wife would have her trials ; but he is nevertheless not without a certain kindliness of disposition."

" How knowest thou this ? " asked Sorcha.

" Because I know his sisters," replied Grainné. "They are devoutedly attached to him ; they admire him as much as Sigurda does. But somehow or other he has extinguished them. They are tame household drudges, without much mind and with little will of their own. They are content to be mirrors reflecting their brother's excellences. Some women seem to have been brought up in a school which treats them more as shadows than as helpmeets to the other sex. Sigurda is one of them ; only her will asserts itself in spite of her, and Olrud is not quite Fergus O'Flannahan."

Sorcha laughed. There was certainly a difference between the brilliant Fergus and the hard, cold, dry, dogmatical Olrud.

" I only speak of talents," said Grainné. " Morally, I consider my husband the superior of the two. He never looks or hints a thing he does not feel. His word is to be relied on more than many another man's oath."

" That is true," said Sorcha.

" As for Sigurda," continued Grainné, " I might get angry if she did not make me laugh. The woman has a good enough mind if she would only exercise it. She takes credit to herself for great humility in declining to hold an opinion till she knows what some bishop thinks of it. If she has a good man's name to tack to her ideas, there is no getting her to look at the other side of them. Now, is that not what we blame in the Anglo-Roman system? It transfers the responsibility of using our reason to ecclesiastical shoulders. How angry Sigurda would be, could she hear how I have spoken of Fergus! It is my honest opinion, though, that even if he means honourably, thou canst never have any real love for him."

"Why not?" asked Sorcha.

"Thou wouldst be incapable of criticising his sermons," replied Grainné. "Thou hast penetrated the truth of them; and that is a sure sign that the golden mist hath never blinded thee."

"But there are other things besides intellect," said Sorcha. "A man may have lovable qualities which one can think about quite apart from his literary attainments."

"True," replied Grainné. "Yet it was not of his talents thou spakest. It was of something that affects his moral nature much more closely. Well, Sorcha, all I shall say is, if he proposes outright, and looks as if he meant it, take him for better for worse; but beware lest his attentions keep thee from any one else."

"There is little fear of that," said Sorcha. "I can think of no one else who seeketh me now."

Grainné was silent. She knew that her niece was extremely beautiful, but was at the same time apparently unconscious of being so. She did not wish to break the charm which surrounded her as with a halo. "Hast thou spoken with my mother?" she asked.

"Once or twice," replied Sorcha. "But she cannot give me disinterested advice. Fergus is a man quite after her own heart. There is one from whom I did seek counsel—Bishop Maidoc."

Grainné laughed. "Maidoc!" she exclaimed. "My child,

he knows as much about these things as a little linnet that has just broken its shell. Maidoc, indeed ! "

Sorcha felt rather vexed. She had been much influenced by Maidoc's expressions of esteem for Fergus.

" Maidoc has done very well for himself," she suggested.

" He truly has," said Grainné ; " he was guided by a right instinct. But that does not make him better qualified to advise thee. He is himself too simple-minded to perceive any want of uprightness in others, and the very cleverest men never get the insight into character that a woman does. In proof of this, I ask thee to notice how many worthless and cunning women make the other sex believe them to be angels. There may be some who think Queen Devorgilla * one, not to speak of Eleanora. I see it with Olrud. He has a power of very minute observation, and has a most practical turn of mind. And he is not disposed in general to be lenient to people's faults. Yet most women can make him believe a plausible story. Times without number have I had to inter- fere for his enlightenment. He always acknowledges it, sooner or later. He considers that this is one advantage of matrimony to a bishop. Believe me, we judge the other sex more truly than they ever do us."

A few minutes' silence followed.

" I see thou art not convinced about Fergus," said Grainné. " Be not swayed too much either by Maidoc or by me. Thou hast faculties of thine own ; thou canst not go wrong by trusting entirely to them. There is a gratitude for being loved which most women feel, and it is often quite sufficient to marry on. Thou mayest be capable of that, although thou art quick to detect faults in thy lover. There are some men, too, whom we esteem more than we like ; others whom we like more than we esteem. I should say Fergus belonged to the latter class ; and I have no right to say that he is not sincere."

* Appendix.

CHAPTER XIV.

Sorcha had quite relinquished her habit of going out in the early morning, perhaps from an unconscious wish to avoid encountering Fergus. She had the intention of spending the forenoon of the next day in a village about six miles distant, a little girl having accosted her on the previous evening with the message that an invalid grandmother would be glad of a visit. She accordingly slipped out after breakfast, and, climbing nimbly over the rath, disappeared into the thick forest in such a manner, that few could have observed her. She needed time for thought; she wished to weigh well her answer to the momentous question which would decide the happiness or the misery of her life.

The track which Sorcha followed was passable for small chariots, being subject to a periodical clearing of brushwood and other impediments. It was diversified by long stretches of grass and deep, irregular ruts. The lofty pine-trees on either side formed a pleasant shelter from the burning sunshine.

Nor was there danger even in that rude age for a lonely girl in following such a track.* The forest with its clearances for miles around was part of the termon-lands of Ardmore, whose sanctuary none but the heathen foreigner had as yet dared to contemn. Like many others throughout the island, it formed a peaceful oasis in the midst of a wilderness of disorder. Sorcha had therefore much leisure for reflection

* Appendix.

as she descended Ardmore hill towards the narrow strip of sea-water which then encircled it on the inland side, and which, being almost dry at the ebb, was crossed on stepping-stones.

It seemed a cruel thing to have the thread of her fate put into her own hands. With many a maiden of later days, she almost envied the lot of those who, like the daughter of the Roman Latius or of the Hebrew Caleb, were disposed of without the shadow of a choice being left them. We are all in part weavers of our own destiny. Although the warp of surrounding circumstances may be prepared for us, it is we who unquestionably form the pattern of it. The process is carried on, for the most part, unconsciously; we are not aware what important issues may depend on our most trifling actions. But certain times come when the pattern must be definitely chosen, when the shuttle of our desires stops a moment from its incessant darting, and we hesitate before we let it slip forth to form the first stitch of a fresh design. Well for us if we are persons of taste, if we have been trained to discern what is lovely; and not, like Sorcha, dim of vision as to the excellencies of the things that compete for our preference.

Sorcha felt the burden of existence. She ought not to have done so; she was a young thing, fashioned in a mould of un-common symmetry, full of the quick, throbbing life that seems too buoyant to be easily crushed. "Men have serious duties to fulfil," she thought; "but their shoulders are strong, their hearts are brave, their brains have a calibre which will stand many a rough pull on their energies. We poor women are sheltered from many anxieties; but our weak shoulders are unable to carry this one great one which is laid on a few of us. The happiness or misery of my whole life will depend on a resolution which I have to form in a few brief hours; and I have little scope for a survey of the scenes where my lot will be fixed by it. Fergus may be leaving in a few days; he may offer to break a coin with me; shall I do it ?"

Sorcha's walk had become slower. Standing on the brink of a small brook, she stamped her foot impatiently on the ground, whilst her coral lips pressed themselves together in anger.

"It is mean of him," she exclaimed, "to keep me in suspense. He is quietly entangling me, whilst he keeps himself free from the meshes of a promise. It is not noble thus to take advantage of my weakness."

Her heart swelled almost to bursting. "I could love him," she murmured, "if he would only give me a definite assurance. It is, perhaps, thoughtlessness; he imagines that my composed manner shows me incapable of suffering. But can the love be very strong that does not impel to some utterance?"

As Sorcha continued her walk, her thoughts wandered back to her aunt's experiences. Grainné had not talked like an unhappy woman. Why, then, was her grandmother always lamenting? Her aunt might have suffered, for Olrud did not look like the man she would have chosen. True sympathy must have been a late flower with both of them. Sorcha thought of them as of two mountain streams: the one clear, pellucid, sparkling; the other dark with the grit it had accumulated in many a conflict with impeding rocks. Their channels had met; they had rushed together in a series of wildly leaping waves; the shock had been tremendous, and for a long stretch of way they had not wholly commingled, though their efforts to do so had produced a succession of small but dangerous whirlpools. The union, however, had been at length accomplished; they were flowing onwards in a broad, cheerful stream; the grit was ground into fine sand, and deposited on the swelling banks. The keenest eye could not detect that they had ever been imbued with mutual repulsions. Their lives were fuller and richer than if they had remained separate. Was it, then, so absolutely necessary that a woman must have her true affinity?

Our mental constitutions have a strange texture, Sorcha thought. Yet she little knew how strange are those of the physical world. Modern science has taught us that substances are capable of very unexpected combinations; a component part of one material being sometimes inexplicably attracted by some component part of a neighbouring one. Human beings, perchance, have the same capabilities of adjustment. One part of Grainné's nature had been pushed incessantly forward; it was the part that suited Olrud. The rest was kept somewhere in the background. She had a wider range of sympathies than he had; so no doubt the process of change had been going on more actively in her.

But Grainné knew how to adjust herself. Had the instinct been stronger in her than in other women? The object to be attained had been placed quite clearly before her, Sorcha reflected. The worst of Fergus was that one would never be quite sure of his wants. Ah! if he were insincere!

The thought cost Sorcha a real pang. Was this a proof that she had begun to love him? He was going away, and she would be left with nothing but remembrances. She would, perhaps, learn to read her own heart in his absence.

She had already traversed a wooden bridge spanning the deep, broad stream of the Lickey, which the clearing away of the forests has since so much reduced in volume. She now reached the village of Clashmore, situated in the depths of a romantic dell. It consisted of some thirty hovels, built of wattles with a picturesque variety of shape that was suggestive of much resource on the part of the architects. Each hut, in fact, looked as if it had rolled downwards from the rim of the dell and been tumbled into shape by the rubs which it got in its descent. A sprinkling of growing grass lent colouring to roof and wall, and from the apertures in some of them issued thin blue columns of smoke. Other columns arose from other quarters, but these were caused by the open-air fire, where dark-robed women squatted as they watched their simmering pots. The whole was surrounded by a hedge of blackthorn, sprinkled with the red rowan-berries, and flanked on the outside by a narrow ditch.

Sorcha stopped at one of these abodes. She dived into it in spite of its stifling atmosphere.

There was just sufficient light to disclose a recumbent figure, stretched on a heap of rushes in the furthest corner. An old woman raised herself as Sorcha approached.

"Is it thou, Sorcha Ni-Faolain?" she exclaimed. "I have longed for the sight of thee. My bones ache worse than ever. I can do nought but think of the kingdom."

Opening a small leather satchel, Sorcha took from it various liniments with rolls of cloth; then turning to the woman's daughter, she gave directions how these were to be applied. She then took out a book, whose leaves of vellum were protected by polished wooden covers.

"I shall read to thee," she said; "but I would fain sit in the doorway for the sake of the light."

The invalid's eyes glittered at these words. A small three-legged stool was placed for Sorcha's accommodation, and a little company soon collected outside the house, composed chiefly of women and boys. Sorcha opened the volume, whilst a number of tangled shocks, representing heads, were pressed eagerly over her shoulders to catch a glimpse of it.

It seemed to these simple souls like a work of magic that those clear beautiful signs, traced by the maiden's own hand, should reveal to her their hidden meaning so easily. They could have bent their knees to her in worship; she seemed to possess the endowments of another sphere.

Sorcha's sweet tones were soon heard, lending deep pathos to the predictions of Isaiah, and from these gliding easily to the wondrous story of the Crucifixion. All held their breath, and the woman within groaned and sighed whilst Sorcha repeated one after another those warm invitations which a loving God addresses to the repentant sinner.

Her eyes closed as she uttered the language of prayer. A deep peace fell on all around her, and a deep solemnity too, for it seemed as if the gracious Being who had uttered these promises were Himself standing in the midst of them. When Sorcha had finished, she approached the invalid.

The woman held her hand. "Come again soon," she murmured. "It seems as if the Lord had sent His angel, as He once did to Peter. I, too, have come out of a prison house. Thou hast given me a glimpse of the home beyond this darkness."

Sorcha pressed her hand warmly. "Thou art perhaps more to be envied than I am," she said. "Thou art nearer the Great City—the road is shorter for thee."

"And wherever thou art," said the woman, "my blessing will follow thee. For how should I have known His words if thou hadst not read them? The young ones go to the preaching, but what they tell me is always at second-hand; thou hast let me hear His own very words."

Sorcha left the hovel. The women curtseyed, the small children stood back respectfully, gazing at her with finger in mouth, and a world of wondering awe in their blue eyes. But for a moment only was this demeanour maintained. Pressing forward, they assailed her at once with a hundred questions, and some actually laid their brown hands on her arm as if to detain her.

"I will return to-morrow afternoon," said Sorcha. "I must hasten homewards, for work awaits me. Your husband's dinner will be spoiled if you linger."

The women fell back at once. Some few children continued, however, to hang about Sorcha's skirts, running a few yards before her, and hovering like gnats round a hazel bush. Sorcha walked forward quickly, smiling in spite of herself.

A tall figure suddenly emerged from behind the projecting eave of a cottage.

Sorcha shrank back. She at once recognised Ardal, who had been a silent listener to her reading.

The young bishop had come there on a similar errand. He had visited a sick man, and had made arrangements to hold an open-air meeting on the following evening, if the weather should prove fine. Not wishing to disturb the women in their morning duties, he had been on the point of returning to Ardmore, when his attention had been arrested by the sound of Sorcha's voice. He had crept stealthily near, so as to avoid disturbing her audience, and had stood hidden behind a mud wall in a position where he could see everything without being observed.

It was a striking picture which met his eye. The fair young girl in her black mantle bordered with blue and green tartan, her sweet face flushed with intense enthusiasm, and the yearnings of her spiritual nature shining forth in a tender pity from her dark lustrous eyes, seated against the dingy wall amidst a flock of unwashed savages, might well have seemed to a duller fancy than Ardal's like a visitant from another sphere. Ardal had seen holy maidens in other lands. He had watched them closely, where, shrouded in sepulchral black, the charm of their countenances toned away by ghastly linen bands, they had glided about silently ministering to the wretched and the depraved. He knew that their feet were blessed on such errands; he had read whole histories of self-renunciation and devotion in their pale faces. But theirs had been a ministry which claimed recognition; there was a humility in it, no doubt, but it lacked the charm of unconsciounsess; and though he had heard many sweet things from their lips, he had never before witnessed that utter oblivion of self which comes to all who strive to utter fully the sublime language of Scripture. Sorcha was simply, naturally graceful; she did not try to hide her beauty. Whatever attraction was in it was made subservient to the work of saving souls. She was a ambassador from heaven as much as was the archangel Gabriel; yet she was a very real woman withal, and the dew of her message seemed to gather added sweetness by being distilled through the fragrance of her very being.

CHAPTER XV.

Whilst Sorcha visited Clashmore, Grainné sat in loving consultation with her mother at the cottage door. There was a parchment on the old lady's knee, but it had rolled itself up, and the sunshine drew an actual glitter from the smooth braids of her hair. The fire of a youthful spirit sparkled in her aged eyes, and her face was overspread by a sweet peacefulness that made it really beautiful.

Grainné was looking serious, but not sad. Her manner to her mother was marked by a tender affection, very different from the air of calm dignity which she maintained to the rest of her fellow creatures. There were depths of love in Grainné's nature, but the outlet to these was often concealed, as is the surface of some riverine lake by the wealth of vegetation which seems to choke it. Grainné had many other qualities wherewith to attract admiration. Thus it was only at moments like the present that the full richness of her nature could be detected. She looked queenly, yet she looked womanly, as she sat beside Amada on that calm July morning.

"Where are thy grey hairs, mother?" she asked playfully. "Sorcha says thou hast a few, but thou art fain to brush them below the brown ones. I fear lest thou give us a lesson in vanity."

Amada laughed. "Cacht says," she replied, "that I shall see a hundred summers."

"Then I hope thou wilt not spend them here," said Grainné.

"Thou must know my boys; I would fain have brought the two elder ones with me, but Olrud would not hear of their leaving school. Unless thou try to visit us, thou and they must remain strangers."

"I should like nothing better," replied Amada. "But I am frailer than thou thinkest. I feel the worse of being at that meeting yesterday. And what should we do with Sorcha?"

"She might stay with Ita till thy return," said Grainné. "She would consider it a waste of time to visit us for as long as we should like to have thee."

"But suppose I were to take ill," persisted Amada. "The poor girl would be much distressed, and she could not well travel to us alone."

"We must trust in Providence somewhat," replied Grainné. "Moriath used to lecture thee, mother, for looking so much at the dark side of things. Thy face always bewrayeth thy speech."

"Alas, my child!" replied Amada; "it is well to talk thus when thy limbs are supple. Poor Moriath! Sorcha is growing liker her every day, and I am troublesome, and she is used with me. No, Grainné, much as I would like to see the dear children, I must never be away from Sorcha."

"Thou art perhaps right," said Grainné, sighing. "We think of sending the elder boys to Lismore next year, and that was partly the reason of our coming here. We thought thou mightest have influence with some one who would procure them admittance."

Amada looked grave. "I will speak frankly," she said. "The abbot has not been quite so friendly as he might have been, considering that he is Sorcha's natural guardian. I believe he is a good man, but I would as soon eat a crab apple as ask him for a favour."

"Olrud will never manage it," said Grainné. "There is a prejudice against him for his Danish birth. And it would scarcely be fair to make use of Sorcha. Many who might do it for the sake of Mael-Patrick's daughter would wish that the favour had been more personal to herself. Could Maidoc not help us?"

"I fear he hath not much influence," replied Amada. "The abbot has the right of naming some scholars, but he will wish to keep it for those connected with Ardmore."

"Naturally," said Grainné. "My children would have a different stamp if they studied at Lismore; for though the place is now overrun with Romish rites, the teaching of the new doctrines has not yet penetrated into the class-rooms. And my boys are not fools; Rossa is sure to win anything he sets his mind on—no one need be ashamed to recommend him. I am amazed to see how little their father can do for them at Inisfallen."

Amada was silent. She knew the reason, but was too prudent to mention it.

"Olrud hath had a hard struggle lately," continued Grainné, "because of his interference with the observance of Beltain. He saith that the bonfires which are kindled before dawn on every hill-top are but a remnant of the old sun-worship. And he fought hard about a poor bull which his cousin, the Erenach, was about to drive through the flames. I know not if it was so much on account of the animal's suffering as because of the insult offered to its Creator."

The great silver bell gave several peals.

"I must leave thee now," said Grainné, "as it is dinner-time. Sorcha is surely late in coming. But if thou wilt send Cacht to the refectory I shall look to thy wants."

The noon-day meal was finished, yet there were no tidings of Sorcha. Grainné thought it very imprudent in her to stay away so long; but Amada was not in the least distressed.

"There may be some one ill at Clashmore," she said. "Sorcha would not for the world leave if she could be of any use. She will easily get some rye bread and milk. I would not trouble myself about her."

" Where is Fergus to-day ? " asked Grainné. " We missed him in the refectory."

" He is preaching at Youghal," replied Amada. " He hovers about here in the mornings after Sorcha, I fancy."

" Wouldst thou give her to him ? " asked Grainné.

" I would," replied Amada. " He would make a kind husband, for all he's so restless. It would give Sorcha a settled position, and she is just the wife to suit him."

Grainné shrugged her shoulders. " I have no wish to interfere," she said ; " but I trust thou wilt not say much to influence her. Let the girl have leisure to make up her own mind."

" And who says she will not have it ? " inquired Amada, rather nettled.

" No one," replied the politic Grainné. " But if thou wishest it, thou shouldst say as little as thou canst. Thy doing so might set her against him. A girl brought up as Sorcha has been is apt to prize her freedom."

" I might have learnt that from thee," replied Amada, looking archly at her. " Thou wouldst take neither hint nor guidance."

Grainné's eyelids fell for a moment, whilst the faintest suspicion of a sigh shook her breast. It was happily inaudible to her mother.

" Now as things have turned out," continued Amada, " I cannot wish them otherwise. I have got reconciled to—— *him*," she whispered. " He's a sterling man, there's no doubt of that, and thou mightest have done worse."

" Let us speak of something else," said the cautious Grainné. " I see Olrud coming through the gate."

Her husband advanced with long strides. His brow was darker than usual.

" Hath Sorcha returned ? " he inquired.

" Not yet," replied Grainné. " My mother says we need not be anxious, as the maiden is in great request at Clashmore.

The poor people hang on her lips more than on many a bishop's. I don't mean anything personal of course."

"That may be," said Olrud. "But it is a long way for her to walk home. I highly approve of her reading the Word to those who have not the key of it, and who may by such means be initiated into the mystery of godliness. I would encourage her to attend to the sick, if she have the skill of a wise physician ; but I would hardly let her go so far alone. We have our Blessed Lord's sanction for His messengers working in couples."

"It might be more prudent," said Amada. "The abbot's daughter goes also on missions of mercy. I have often wondered that the two could not work together."

"I shall set forth to meet her," said Olrud. "And perchance a door of utterance may be opened to me ; so that her visit may bring a double blessing to the village. I may thus also show that her conduct has the seal of my approval."

"Thou speakest wisely," said Grainné. "I counsel thee, therefore, not to be too slow of movement. I would fain touch Sorcha's harp," she continued, turning to Amada, "and raise for thee Olrud's favourite lay. It is a gem from the Welsh bard Taliessin, and has kept its worth for more than five hundred years."

Grainné's deep voice soon rung out :

> " Woe be to that priest yborn,
> That will not cleanly weed his corn,
> And preach his charge among.

> " Woe be to that shepherd, I say,
> That will not watch his flock alway,
> As to his office doth belong :

> "Woe be' to him that doth not keep
> From Romish wolves his sheep,
> With staff and weapon strong."*

---

* Appendix.

CHAPTER XVI.

Ardal O'Brien was the more ready to appreciate the excellence of Sorcha's character, that he was conscious of no selfish wishes whilst watching her. He had gained a thorough mastery over himself.

Sorcha received his greeting timidly. She was somewhat in awe of him, his superior sanctity and learning making him appear to her unapproachable. She esteemed it an honour even to attract his notice.

" Thou art going homewards," he said. " I have heard thee say so ; I, too, am bound for Ardmore."

Sorcha smiled. They had struck into the forest path, and he was walking quietly by her side. The children had disappeared.

Ardal was now ready to blame himself. He began to fear for his newly-found peace. Why could he not have turned into another path ? This maiden was about to become the spouse of another, and it was a transparent fiction that he owed her the slight civility of an escort.

His presence had no disturbing effect on Sorcha. Her mind had been calmed and soothed by religious exercises ; the all-engrossing image of Fergus was obliterated for the moment. She thought only of her high privilege in being permitted to associate with an eminent scholar.

" I trust thy grandmother is well," said Ardal. " I have seen less of her than I could wish, but I have feared to intrude, seeing she hath so many friends. She is a lady who is much beloved."

" In truth she is," replied Sorcha. " Many of us wish that our old age may be like hers. She was at the assembly on Declan's birthday, and though she could not hear the discussion, she was deeply interested in it."

" The little I have heard her say on Church matters," said Ardal, " proved to me that she understood them. She would have no compromise with the new prelates, I think."

" No," replied Sorcha, with an amused smile. " If she had her way, not one of them should ever plant his foot on Irish ground."

" That is somewhat my own feeling," said Ardal. " There are good men amongst them, whose very virtues give a sanction to the covetous ones. England owes much to Archbishop Theobald ; but the most of her bishops are less like him than like Roger of Salisbury. The system encourages clerical pride, and we have enough of that without it."

" No Church has ever been free from it," remarked Sorcha.

" No," said Ardal. " The sword of truth which our Saviour brought must ever struggle against indwelling corruption, even in the hearts of believers. When there is no conflict, truth must be slumbering. And the very ripest fruit is in most danger of rottenness."

" True," replied Sorcha ; " but in this case the difficulty seems to be to determine on which side the corruption lies. My uncle, Bishop Olrud, is very angry at the view taken by Bishop O'Flannahan."

Ardal started. He gazed at Sorcha ; but could not detect the faintest trace of a blush on her cheek. Yet she avoided encountering his glance, and went on speaking rapidly.

" Bishop Olrud thinks there is danger in too much seeking after beauty in worship. He is not sure of Bishop O'Flannahan's soundness. What sayest thou ? "

Sorcha looked up this time half timidly, half inquiringly. She was groping in the dark for some answer to a question which she dare not put directly to her companion. Ardal might well be puzzled. His sense of honour made him shrink from saying anything that would shake her faith in his rival.

"I am not sure that I understand thy meaning," he said, evasively.

"Well," said Sorcha, "I cannot tell if Olrud quarrels with Fergus' creed; but he thinks that his tastes have placed him on a slippery incline. If we are to copy anything at all from the Roman ritual—finer music, Latin prayers, or a higher style of church architecture—we might be led to substitute these for true heart-worship. Our teachers till now have tried to make us realise the unseen, and he fears that Fergus wishes us to walk more by sight."

"One might have gathered that from his speech," replied Ardal. "Olrud and Fergus belong by nature to two very different schools of thought. One could wish that they might make a little exchange of attributes. Olrud generally reasons correctly, but he has a dry forbidding way of stating his views; and Fergus is wonderfully eloquent—dost thou not think so?"

"He is," replied Sorcha; "but if he has taken up wrong opinions, will they not be the more dangerous?"

Ardal gave a deep sigh, as if trying to relieve himself of an oppressive burden. Sorcha interpreted this sigh as an expression of grief at his colleague's deficiencies; whereas it was, in truth, a rolling away of something which had lain very heavily on his spirits. Had she ventured to look up, she would have seen that his eyes were sparkling with joyful hope.

They were now stepping on to the bridge over the gleaming river. To Sorcha, as she crossed it, came the satisfaction of a decision. All exertions of our will are invigorating to the moral nature, and Sorcha felt both braver and happier as she resolved to shake herself free from a tormenting delusion.

Fergus might possibly be sincere in regard to herself, but she would never place herself in a position where she would be closely connected with possible error. Her companion had said little; but he had not uttered one word in depreciation of Olrud's judgment.

The two were soon far into the depths of the wood. Not a sound could be heard save the occasional rustle of a bough beneath the squirrel's tread, or the faint trickle of some unseen brooklet. Their very footfalls were noiseless on the soft turf.

The tide of feeling was rising in Ardal's breast. There was nothing to check it, no sense of honour towards a brother bishop, no constraint from the presence of spectators. She was walking by his side, she whose form had mingled with his day-dreams of earthly felicity. The enchanting vision had come close to him, more dazzling even than in his loneliness. It seemed within his grasp; should he put out his hand to take it?

Yet he feared to do so. There was something so immaculate in her unconsciousness; it seemed like crushing a rose to feel the scent more keenly. The rose had thorns all around it; and in the very act of coming nearer he might be banished to a distance. Might not the palace which his fancy had erected crumble at the first touch of reality?

He walked on silently, struggling with his hesitation. Sorcha's spirits were, however, rising. "I think," she said, "that we are very fortunate in having been born at this epoch. The study of the inspired record is, thou sayest, dying out over Europe. How happy it has made us! giving us a treasure in this life, with the means of helping others to share it. Will it not be a privilege, too, if we have to fight for the liberty of thinking? There would have been no need for us to have done so had we been born earlier."

Ardal felt grateful to her for suggesting some topic of speech. Yet he answered almost mechanically, for, dear as the topic was, there was something almost dearer which he could not touch on.

"If many thought as thou dost," he answered, "it would be a privilege; but yet I fear we are on the losing side."

Sorcha started, and looked at him in vacant wonder.

"I do not mean," he said, quietly, "that the right will not one day prevail. God's decrees cannot be altered, and thou knowest that He has told us of a time when we shall not need even to teach each other. But hast thou watched the ebb and flow of the ocean? There are times when the advancing tide appears to recede with some large retiring billow. God's providence moves in cycles which we cannot measure; and I believe that the Christian world is just now on the receding wave. Erin will go with it, and will awake just when she is sucked down into a whirlpool."

" Why thinkest thou so ? " asked Sorcha.

" The force against us is so strong," replied Ardal; " and we are divided both in heart and mind. Hast thou read about the early ' takings ' of Erin ? Each set of invaders found the natives at war with each other. That lies in the Celtic character, and Rome is skilful to take advantage of this weakness."

" That is true," replied Sorcha, thoughtfully. " Still I cannot imagine how, with the Bible so much studied amongst us, it can be possible for us to agree to the worship of images. Might we not say, with King Cormac, that it were more reasonable to reverence the mechanic who made them ? "

" Foreign help may be called in," replied Ardal.

" I know it," said Sorcha ; " Olrud told us that thou hadst mentioned to him about the Pope having given us to the King of England. My grandmother thinks it nonsense.

" Would that it were so ! " replied Ardal. " I was told of it by a French prelate. He and I had waxed hot in argument, and had perhaps lost our tempers. So, as a farewell comfort, he told me that the Papal Curia were counting on a sure victory over us by this means."

"How dreadful!" exclaimed Sorcha. "But will not all Irishmen rise in defence of their chiefs?"

Ardal shrugged his shoulders. "Have the chiefs ever united in defence of anything," he asked, "save when my ancestor Brian welded them together by sheer force? Methinks that civil liberty hath no lasting existence unless liberty of conscience come first, and thou knowest how these new prelates have worked on some of our bishops to vote our liberties away. That was done at Rathbresail."

"But when they see what use is being made of their compliance, will they not be roused?" asked Sorcha.

"I fear not," replied Ardal. "Our system of Church government hath been too long an oligarchy. Men become bishops as a matter of secular wisdom, not because they have heard the Spirit's call. Such will always yield to temptation when an increase of power or wealth is offered them. Rome knows how to bait her hooks. The doctrine of purgatory is to her priests a mine of wealth.

"It is no easy thing to be a bishop," he continued. "Self-seeking comes to us in a thousand shapes. Methinks we ought to be like the transparent crystals of our own mountains; having no colour in ourselves, always ready to reflect the light of heaven, and shining all the more brightly for every hard rub we get in the world."

A thought flashed on the young man's mind as he spoke these words. Should he not put an end to this state of uncertainty? If he did get a rebuff, would it not come as one of the rubs he had spoken of? Without being aware of it, he walked a little closer to Sorcha.

She stood suddenly still. The path before them ran downwards; and presented a monotonous vista of tree-stems, and dark foliage, relieved only by the thin green line of turf which formed the foot-track. Sorcha turned half round. Her companion moved further off. He feared he had offended her.

Yet he could not withdraw his eyes. She was grand in her

loveliness, like a spreading tree which ravishes our eyes in its graceful dignity. She placed her finger upon her lip, and her brown eyes seemed to grow larger. Ardal felt relieved when she broke silence.

"I fear we have mistaken our path," she said. "I see no sign of the brook."

"Is that possible!" he replied with a smile. "I was trusting to thy guidance. Is there no mark by which thou canst discover the way back?"

"Let us turn," said Sorcha, "and perhaps I may see some familiar object. I have been very stupid, but methought thou knewest the way."

"The fault was mine," replied Ardal. "It is awkward to get into the depths of these forests. If we can only recollect something we have passed, we may at length perceive an outlet."

He saw little prospect of this, even while he spoke. He had been far too much engrossed in seeking an outlet to his feelings.

Sorcha now walked more rapidly, scanning every mossy stem as she passed it. She was soon obliged, however, to moderate her pace. Her companion had no motive for haste.

"Thou hast spoken frankly about Fergus," he said at length. "I hardly thought thou wouldst have noticed his mental tendencies. Thou dost not consider him a model bishop?"

"Who is?" asked Sorcha, naïvely.

"No one," replied Ardal, "can well lay claim to the title. Yet some, methinks, are more conscious of their responsibilities than others."

"Maidoc, for instance," suggested Sorcha.

"Yes, Maidoc," replied Ardal. "I esteem his friendship one of the greatest privileges of my life. And Ita's too. But Maidoc has not the opportunities for leading that Fergus has. I must confess I did not think thee so penetrating, more especially as I have reason to believe that Fergus cherishes a warm regard for thee."

Sorcha's step slackened. She felt the colour mounting to her temples.

"I am perhaps intrusive," continued Ardal, "but I fancied that Fergus stood in a relation to thee which would prevent thy judging of his pastoral influence."

Ardal's voice was soft and penetrating: it was like the voice of conscience. Sorcha had a sense of guilt in her heart: she dared not look up.

"Hath he spoken to thee of love?" inquired Ardal, relentlessly.

Sorcha covered her eyes with her hand, which was, like her cheek, overspread with a delicate pink colour. This was far worse than confessing to Maidoc. She stood in great awe of Ardal, and somehow or other she fancied that his office gave him a right to probe her secret purposes. The native sincerity of her character forced her to an avowal.

"He has, but not definitely," she answered. "At least," she continued, stammering, "I mean——"

Ardal was too noble to profit by her confusion. "I have no right to ask any questions," he said, "save one, and that is simple. Dost thou return his love?"

Sorcha half turned away. She was not aware that they had come to a stand. "I cannot tell," she replied, in a clear, low voice. "If I do, it is not warmly."

The young bishop seized her left hand so impetuously that she shrunk back in surprise. "Then listen to me," he said, "ere thou decidest. I love thee too, Sorcha!"

He let go her hand, for he feared to frighten her. She turned pale, and leant against a tree-stem for support.

But it was only for an instant. The colour rushed back to her cheek and neck; yet the long-fringed eyelids still drooped. There was a wild throbbing at her heart; she needed time to collect herself. Ardal retired a few paces, and then stole noiselessly back.

Sorcha was indeed overwhelmed with surprise. The disclosure had come very suddenly, with the force of a long dammed-up cataract. A few hours ago she had longed to hear such words from Fergus; now they had been spoken by other lips with an intensity which left no doubt of their significance. Her mind almost failed to grasp the magnitude of the prize now placed before her. Not merely the love of a strong, true man, but the warm, self-denying devotion of one whom she had imagined far above her. She trembled at the thought of her own unworthiness.

Then she glanced timidly up. Her eyes had the dark beauty of the fawn's, seeking to shrink from the sunlight. Her right hand moved slightly forward. Ardal was not slow to touch it.

"I will not press for an answer," he said. "Forgive me for being so sudden. I would never have breathed it did I believe thou hadst any love for Fergus."

Sorcha looked up again : this time straight at him. The whole force of her soul seemed to go out in the glance of those clear, brown eyes. But again they drooped, and she blushed deeply.

"It is unfair of me," said Ardal, "to take this advantage when we are alone. Something impelled me to utter it; the thought, perhaps, that I may soon be sent to some distant town. Wilt thou walk on ?"

He offered his arm, and Sorcha took it. There was something in her manner of doing so that implied trust. She looked like a slender rosebush clinging to the stem of a sturdy oak.

And Ardal was supremely happy in supporting her gentle weight. They did not speak for many minutes. Each was oppressed with a new consciousness—he with the bliss of her presence, a bliss that might prove all too fleeting; she with

an intensity of happiness which she was really making an
effort to conceal.

Ardal knew that these . moments would be a cherished
remembrance all his lifetime, a remembrance which would
nerve him to new effort. He felt that he had won her esteem,
even if she should will to be another's. She seemed a treasure
too great for his deserts. He must enjoy this moment, for
it might never again recur. And the strong man's arm
trembled.

Whither were they going? Sorcha could not have told.
Her feet hardly seemed to touch the ground. Her body
might have been hovering, as well as her spirit, in those high
regions which extend somewhere above this lower scene, and
have no necessary connection with the trodden turf of a wild
forest. She was in a new world. All the instincts and long-
ings of her heart were being satisfied in a way that she could
never have dreamed of. He was walking by her side, the one
who fulfilled her high ideal of manliness, and whom it would
be an honour to help in the most blessed of all vocations;
one to whom, without hurting her conscience, she might well
be subject in everything. The very depth of her affectionate
reverence made her fear to express it. She did not doubt
that he knew it, and never once fancied that her silence
could be construed into hesitation.

So they walked on. Sorcha released her hold a little; she
thought herself too much of a burden. Ardal was surely not
so strong as he looked. She stole a half glance at his hand.
It trembled, too.

"Is there anything wrong?" she asked in a low, soft
whisper.

"Have I offended thee?" he said in return, not without a
quiver.

Sorcha looked straight up, and this time Ardal understood her.

It was sunset ere they reached Ardmore. There are some

days so bright as to efface all recollection of a hundred cloudy ones that have gone before. It is a happy instinct of our nature to be impressed by these, and to treasure them up so as to extract sunshine from their images in the midst of after darkness. Such a day had been this one.

CHAPTER XVII.

THE lovers were walking slowly homeward, having at length discovered the right path. They were making devious ways for themselves in order to prolong the sweet interchange of thought and feeling which had followed the mutual disclosure. They heeded not that the sun was now near the horizon; indeed, the first tints of his setting were hidden by the leafy canopy overhead. The straight towering pine-stems were, however, touched by a yellow radiance, and the foxglove bells were drooping and closing as if preparing for a long rest. Sorcha was looking up, replying to some playful remark of her lover's, when she noticed his eyebrows suddenly drawn together. Glancing forward, she beheld a singular spectacle.

They were approaching the brink of a well-known pond, a few yards removed from the direct road betwixt Ardmore and Clashmore.

Its surface seemed to heave as they drew near, and from beneath a mass of yellow floating vegetation emerged a figure of uncouth aspect.

Its form was human, though bent and twisted in so many ways as to be scarcely discernible. It rather appeared like a bundle of dripping cow-skins, loosely tied together, above which gleamed a visage encircled by grey masses of tangled, shaggy hair. Its wildly rolling eyes glittered as with unearthly brightness.

Sorcha, shuddering, clung closely to the arm of her lover.

The figure shook itself; then lifting a bony finger, furnished with bird-like claws, pealed out in a deep, sepulchral voice—

"Let the butterfly sport in the morning-beam; but beware lest the water-drop strike it. The cloud gathereth in the east; it draweth nigh. I, even I, feel the wind that heraldeth its approach. The maiden leaneth on a rotten branch; it will break, and leave her wounded."

Sorcha recovered her spirits while the man spoke. She recognised Phelim O'Bric, one of that race of hermits who were revered by the common people as saints.

His history had been a strange one. Trained at Ardmore for the episcopal office, he had, through the study of Jerome's writings, become violently enamoured of the ascetic life. Fired with the ambition of obtaining in the other world a glory superior to that of his fellows, he had left untried no means of subduing his unhappy body, and of bringing it into subjection to its more ethereal partner. The story of his nightly vigils, when a mere boy, was never related to mortal man. He had made great progress in sanctification, if not in learning, at the time when the fair Moriath settled at Ardmore. Then a form stepped between his mental eye and the sun of his self-attributed holiness. It was that of Cacht, the comely girl, who had left her kinsfolk to wait upon Amada. He would wake from his dreams of her to plunge into the cold waters of the Bric, and torture his poor brains to do impossible tasks in the way of learning. But, like the devil, came the pictured image of the maiden across his meditations. She seemed present with him even when she was effectually screened from view in the scullery outside of the little cottage. The conflict with her apparition, or perhaps the effect of so many adverse influences on his physical organisation, unhinged his mind, and drove him forth from the society of his fellow-men.

He had now for years dwelt in a cave on the face of a cliff overlooking the sea, impossible of approach save by a basket let down from above. Here, by the abbot's order, he was supplied with provisions; but unless these were of a kind which others would have deemed only fit for swine, he had a persistent habit of pitching them into the waves, and starving until a supply of commoner victuals was provided for him. It was one of the chief pleasures of the Ardmore schoolboys to be present at the letting down of his basket.

Only one man had ever entered his cave. There were sights in it, indeed, which few could have seen with a calm pulse. Driven, through the effect of mortification, from its bent towards heavenly things, his mind had turned aside to seek communion with the hidden powers of nature; not simply as they exist in a thousand beneficent forms, but as they have throughout all ages been fabled as in partial league with the powers of darkness. For him a pulse beat in every tree; the spirit of a Tuath-de-Danaan rode on every wind; and round every oak the fallen Druids circled in moonlight revel. Phelim became skilled in tracking the noiseless step of disease to some devilish plotting; and he actually longed to hold communion with that dark prince whose mighty heart seemed to vibrate under the ground, in order to coax from him secrets whose unveiling might teach mortals to avoid his snares. He, Phelim, had been commissioned by heaven to this work.

Cacht was quite aware of the influence she had exercised over him. Nevertheless she had considered it no part of her duty to retire from his view. On the contrary, she was as often as not commissioned by the fathers of Ardmore to convey to him his daily provender. They, as well as the country people, were proud of Phelim. The abbot, Maidoc, and the more enlightened bishops might well doubt if the example were a profitable one. But even they could scarcely shake off the universal feeling that he had some secret access into the world of spirits. They desired his sanctification, and only followed out an ancient Irish tradition in endeavouring to promote it by forcing on him a sight of some of the temptations from which he had escaped.

Phelim had learnt to climb up his own cliff. How he did so no mortal knew, but it must have been at the risk of his life. The neglect of years had, however, made him so repulsive an object that, however much of a saint he was held to be when in his cave, his appearance out of it was felt to bode no good to the beholder. Ardal and Sorcha therefore hastened away, and were even thankful when, on reaching the gate of the rath, they perceived the dark figure of Olrud advancing towards them with long strides.

Sorcha's head drooped as the foxglove's had done. She felt her cheeks flushing as she clung closer to Ardal's arm. She did not see the smile which illumined her uncle's face as he came nearer.

"What is this?" he cried. "I must scold thee, Bishop Ardal, for stealing my niece."

"Thou, too, hast committed theft in thy time," replied Ardal, laying his left hand affectionately on Sorcha's.

She, however, immediately slipped away, not liking the scrutiny of her uncle's gaze. She escaped into the cottage, where her rosy cheeks and dilated eyes told their own tale. She threw herself kneeling on the little stool, and hid her face on her grandmother's knee.

The old lady laughed; but Grainné looked anxious. "Is it settled now?" she asked. "Has Fergus spoken?"

"It is not Fergus," replied Sorcha. Her face now resembled a pink flower trying vainly to hide its loveliness behind its native screen of green leaves. They formed a striking picture. The old lady was bending forwards with curiosity and affection on her speaking face; the girl crouching at her knee, an emblem of innocent purity, as if the shining crystals had lingered on a fruit-laden bough to witness the budding of the summer blossoms. When Olrud and Ardal entered, they could not help pausing to gaze on it.

Grainné looked at the young bishop and so did Amada. They were far from connecting his appearance with Sorcha's, yet they wondered at Olrud's unusual cheerfulness. No one spoke for a few minutes; then Ardal stepped forward, and placing his hand on Sorcha's shoulder, knelt beside her at Amada's feet.

She comprehended in an instant. The rush of emotion was almost too strong for her; it recalled such vivid memories of the day when Mael-Patrick had claimed another of her heart treasures. But she laid her withered hands on their heads, and said in a trembling voice:

" The Lord of your fathers, the God of Patrick, of Bridget, and of Declan, bless you both, and make your house like the house of Rachel."

Sorcha kissed her cheek, and so did Ardal. " Thou dost not grudge her to me," said the latter. " Olrud has called me a thief, and I mean to be doubly so—I mean to steal thee."

Grainné laughed. "That is hardly allowable," she said. " Paul, I believe, limits the number to one."

" But our house must have a head," said Ardal. " I can hardly feel where mine is at present, and I fear we shall both come to grief if we have not some one over us. But has Sorcha no other guardian ?"

" There is the abbot," suggested Grainné.

" I would not take him into account," said Amada. " He has not been much of a father to Sorcha."

" Thou art wrong, mother," said Grainné. " It is an ancient custom to ask an abbot's blessing when the maidens of his family become spouses. It would be a very proper way to make it public."

" My own feeling," said Ardal, " would be to acknowledge the abbot's authority, but to present the matter to him as an accomplished fact, for which his sanction is a mere form. I would give neither to him nor the Lady Uailsi a right of interference."

" I see not why the match should not please them," said

Olrud. "It is most suitable in every respect. And I being her uncle, her nearest male connection, who else dare venture to judge it ? "

Amada and Grainné both smiled. "I will confess," said the former, "as it is best to be truthful, that I had set my mind on some one else."

Grainné tried in vain to look her disapproval.

"Because," continued the old lady, "there is no use in claiming merit where I have none. I wished Sorcha to marry Fergus, and I fear this will be a sore grief to him. But I am just as well satisfied ; nay, I am fully more so."

"As thou shouldst be," interrupted Olrud.

"Stay ! " said Ardal, interrupting in his turn. "I would fain hear it all."

"I am the more so," continued Amada, "because I believe thou hast more conscience about making her happy. I have not the shadow of a fear in giving her to thee. But it is a surprise, and you must pardon me if I regret Fergus just a little."

Grainné was now looking excessively annoyed. Ardal noticed it, and taking Amada's hand, he said :

"I don't wonder, for he is a fine fellow in his way. But thou seest that we must needs please Sorcha, and I have no doubt of his finding some one to console him. With all his quickness he was not quick enough. I have no doubt but that thou wilt like me the better of the two in time."

"Thou art conceited," replied Amada, shaking her head playfully. "And thou art just about as great a coax as Sorcha is. I understand how thou hast got round her."

There was a general laugh, in which even Grainné had to join. Sigurda now entered. Amada's eyes turned towards her.

"Come here," she said, " and give a welcome to my new grandson. I shall not say if I am pleased with him, but he thinks he is the very best I could possibly have got."

"I hope," said Olrud, "that you have both weighed well the responsibilities you are about to undertake."

"And I hope," said Grainné, "that Sorcha has an unbroken cake for us."

Grainné presided at the supper table. Amada was in unusually high spirits, and indeed so was every one. Olrud alone tried to put a restraint on their mirth. He was afraid of its appearing too boisterous.

The lovers' health having been drunk in red ale, they all gathered in a circle round the hearth. Olrud took one of Sorcha's beautiful manuscripts and began to read all Saint Paul's injunctions to married couples. This would have been felt to be appropriate had he confined himself to the inspired words ; but the pure stream of apostolic utterance was made not a little cloudy by the remarks which he threw into it. He turned the most sublime truths inside out, and transposed them in such a manner that his audience was only saved from weariness by glancing at the happy faces of the lovers.

Amada at length bestirred herself. "That is doubtless very improving," she said, "but it is somewhat dull for me. I would fain hear a prayer, and as I get so much benefit from thee every night, I wish Ardal to come quite near me."

Amada's wishes were obeyed ; and all felt as if Ardal's ministrations lifted them into a higher sphere. "Oh if *he* were only like that," thought Grainné to herself ; "but it is my cross, and I must bear it."

CHAPTER XVIII.

Sorcha awoke next morning free from care. She felt as if few could be so favoured as herself in the blessings of Providence. "I have a good hope for both worlds," she thought; "a rich treasure of human affection besides the prospect of an incorruptible inheritance. I shall be protected from life's storms. My grandmother cannot be with me always in the course of nature, yet I need not look forward with so much dread to the day of her birth into glory. The parting can only be for a short time at the longest, and my life will be full of interest. Ardal will prove a better support in her declining years than any one she could have dreamt of. I almost feel as if my parents were rejoicing in heaven over my happiness.

She dressed with alacrity, as if quickness of movement would bring her nearer to the time when the one face which floated before her mental vision would again appear. She went out for the milk herself, the sleepy Cacht not being yet stirring.

She flew like a fawn over the greensward. The very cows turned round their sleek heads, as if they saw something new about her, and the dairymaid chanted one of Columba's Irish hymns whilst the milk went splashing into the pail. All nature seemed to her pervaded with devout thankfulness, as if the winds from Eden were again blowing, and man were on the best of terms with his Maker. These feelings set a stamp on Sorcha's happiness. Her love was not incompatible with a deep spirituality; it rather added new intensity to her appreciation of the Creator's gifts. The sky had never looked bluer, nor had the fleeting grey clouds which speckled it assumed a more exquisite *contour*, than on the first morning when she counted the minutes before meeting with her lover.

And it had been so unexpected! Only yesterday she had been murmuring at the hardness of the task imposed on her in being obliged to decide whether she could love or not. The cup of joy had been prepared for her, and had been withheld so long from her lips only that its taste might become sweeter. It had surely been mixed by no careless hand. She knew that the vows which awaited her were solemn ones, but were they not symbolical of the mysteriously sublime union between the Heavenly Bridegroom and His ransomed people? " My own marriage feast will be but a faint foretaste of the joy that awaits us beyond the grave," she thought. "I am indeed thrice happy in having both the symbol and the reality of such bliss."

Her eye fell on some withered branches that were lying prone on the turf. " Dost thou not anticipate storms ? " they seemed to say. " O ye branches ! " replied Sorcha, " ye do indeed look desolate with your yellow-spiked leaves and your broken twigs. But if I am better than a sparrow, I am certainly better than you. Troubles will come to me as the curtain of darkness drops over the brightest sky; but I shall have a strong arm to lean on, I shall have a true heart to share life's griefs. The wind may blow bitterly, but I shall have a refuge in my husband's love."

The thought of this possibility made her slacken her step. She carried the heavy milk-can with an easy grace, yet it almost dropped from her hand when she suddenly perceived a pair of blue eyes peering very closely at her. She had forgotten that it was necessary to avoid encountering Fergus.

"At length," he said, "my eyes are refreshed. The fairies have returned to their wonted circuit. I was blaming myself for having broken their ring."

Sorcha drew herself back with dignity. She bade him a courteous good morning. Her eyelids did not droop.

He offered to share her burden, smiling confidently as he did so. "Thou hast no right to be so beautiful," he said; "thou hast taken more than thy share from others."

The words were lightly spoken, but they were accompanied by an expressive glance. She had been flattered by such compliments before. Now her spirit met them with a strange repulsion.

"I am something more than a fairy," she said, tartly. "They are supposed to be useless beings."

"Thou art cruel," replied Fergus; "but perhaps I deserve it. There have been princesses guarded by an ogre; and I have lacked boldness to venture near thee."

Sorcha understood that he was referring to Olrud. "My grandmother may have wished to see more of thee," she replied. "Otherwise we know that thou hast been better engaged. We are not lonely with our three visitors."

She bowed gracefully, and taking up the can, which he had for a moment set down, she placed it on her shoulder, and hastened over the rath.

Fergus was startled. There was something which he had not before observed in her manner towards him. "It must be that wretched Olrud," he thought. "A man cannot fight against prejudice. But if she is cold, it is only for a time. The ogre will go, and she will be easily won."

He whistled gaily as he mounted the ladder. Perhaps a little wholesome reserve on his own part would do good. He would make her long for his company. Only for a short time, however. He would run no real risk of losing her.

Fergus had a great belief in his own powers. He did not think himself handsome, but he knew that educated women were strongly attracted by talent. He had never heard of any one who could be compared with himself in this respect. The abbot and Maidoc were more learned, but they had no

power to awaken the deep sympathies of an audience. Or if
Maidoc had it, it was of a kind that did little good to himself.
Then there was Ardal. But he would never be a rival; not,
at least, in regard to Sorcha. He had never concerned himself much about the fair sex. If he married at all, it would
be some quiet woman who would manage his housekeeping.
One of Fergus's own sisters, perhaps. They were both slightly
older, but that need not matter so much. He would try to
bring it about. Ardal was of royal blood, so the match
would reflect lustre on himself. He was so engrossed by his
pastoral duties that it would be a real kindness to seek out a
wife for him.

Fergus did not quite keep to the plan of withdrawing himself. He waited for Sorcha towards noon, but somehow she
failed to appear. She had, in truth, left the pharmacy at an
earlier hour.

It was difficult to keep her secret from Ita. But Grainné
had enjoined on her to do so. "We must pay respect to the
abbot," she said; "and he will consider that we are doing so
if we make the disclosure first to him."

As the silver bell of the tower rang out its noonday peal, a
little party emerged from the cottage. First came Amada,
guided by Olrud, and crowned by a snowy linen kerchief;
then Ardal, with Sorcha on his arm; and lastly, Grainné,
with Sigurda. The old lady looked extremely happy, and
diverted attention from Sorcha's blushes by the fuss she
made about herself.

"I am presentable, I think," she said. "We do right to
acknowledge the powers that be. Now, Olrud, thou must
speak first, for thou seest I am fluttered."

A smile hovered about Grainné's mouth. She doubtless
thought the injunction needless.

They walked slowly on account of Amada. Fergus caught
sight of them from his station behind the corner of the church.

"What is that?" he thought. "Amada going to the refectory. Some of Olrud's stupid ideas. And there is Sorcha: she is walking with Ardal."

His brow grew dark as he watched them. Sorcha was robed in a lena of white linen, with an inar embroidered in gold. Her dark locks were half concealed beneath a veil of delicate texture.

" I see how it is," thought Fergus ; " Olrud has made Ardal his friend. They hold the same views, and Olrud knows where to push his advantage. But I would rather that Ardal did not walk with Sorcha. I must hasten in, lest they find places together at the table."

The abbot was seated with his family in the chief refectory. It was a spacious apartment, whose polished wooden walls bore shelves supporting a goodly array of cold meats and condiments, platters and cups of yew. Around its table were the faces of several venerable men, who, having fulfilled a lifelong episcopate had come to spend their declining years in the college which had been the nursery of their minds. These were eligible for filling up vacancies in the great council. The rest of the company consisted of the families of those whose educational duties obliged them to be permanent residents ; with others, who, like Sorcha, had an inherited claim for maintenance.

A smile crossed the abbot's face as he espied Fergus. The Lady Uailsi advanced with a gesture of welcome.

" You will have a visitor to-day," said the young bishop, carelessly. " Amada Ni-Ahern is, I believe, on her way hither."

" Is it possible ?" responded Uailsi, with an air of indifference. " There are several vacant seats at the other table."

" Perhaps," suggested Mòr, " she is going to dine with Sorcha."

" I wonder at her taste," said the abbot. " Our viands are more choice than those of the students."

At this moment Amada's bright face appeared, looking most picturesque in its contrast to the grim visage of her companion. Those who had already seated themselves near the door rose with instinctive respect. Mòr would have followed their example, had not a glance from her mother prevented her.

There was much bewilderment, however, when, following close on Amada, came the tall figure of Ardal and the graceful one of Sorcha. The abbot took in the situation at a glance; so did Maidoc and Ita, who, catching a glimpse of what was going on, had hastened hither from the large refectory.

None, however, had time for reflection. The little procession swept rapidly forward, and stood within two paces of the abbot.

"We have come to announce to thee," said Olrud, "that Bishop Ardal and Sorcha have given and received a promise of marriage. We ask thy sanction for their espousal."

The abbot grasped Sorcha's hand. "Let us ask God's blessing," he said.

All knelt whilst he did so. Then, bestowing a kiss on the maiden's cheek, he congratulated her with a kindliness which encouraged her to glance upwards as she received the same token of good-will from Uailsi. But she was startled at the expression on the lady's face; there was mortification written there, for the corners of the mouth were rigidly drawn down, whilst the eyes were hard and glassy. Sorcha's hot lips touched an icicle.

There was a tinge of the same thing in Mòr, only it was softened by the warm pressure of her grasp. Sorcha could see that she was conquering her vexation with an effort; indeed the tears were almost welling to her eyes. But any eccentricity of these ladies was thrown completely into the shade by that of Fergus.

He had not heard a word of the abbot's prayer. He had

knelt, indeed, along with the rest, but his brow was feverish and his auburn hair much disarranged when he rose from his knees. His face flushed to the hue of a cherry as he came forward with his felicitations. Then, when all had seated themselves at table, and he had taken his wonted place beside Uailsi, his restlessness was something remarkable. He had never been more witty, never more ready with his repartees. Amada, who was seated next him, divined the cause.

It was well that she did so. She was extremely nervous at having to dine in company, after having been so long accustomed to the privacy of home; but all sense of fear was lost in that of pity. Fergus had always been a favourite of hers; his mind was like a finely-strung harp, which, though it sometimes gave out wild music, might be expected to vibrate audibly to every breath. Amada could not bear to think of his suffering.

And Grainné found a subject for study in the affectionate solicitude of her mother's manner towards the lively young bishop, whose wit came forth in such wondrous flashes.

Sorcha bore her honours with a gentle humility. She was so unassuming that no one could well grudge them to her. She was, however, not quite at ease. She had heard how brilliant Fergus usually was when at dinner, but she could not help thinking that there was an extra sparkle caused by unusual agitation. Perhaps he had loved her, after all. Perhaps she had not acted fairly by him; she had listened to his compliments. Would it not have been more considerate had she devised some means of acquainting him earlier in the day with an unwelcome truth?

The repast being finished, all moved away to their respective business. Ardal led Sorcha out, followed closely by Amada and Olrud. Maidoc and Ita stood outside the door of the other refectory as they passed it; their faces actually shone with unfeigned happiness. Sorcha needed no further testimony to the wisdom of her choice.

A few quiet jokes were exchanged ere they found themselves on the greensward. Here they were joined by Fergus.
He looked wilder than ever. He walked by Sorcha's side, as
if he had the right to claim part of her. She pressed her
lover's arm gently, and her tone in replying to his rival had a
slight touch of compassion.

But it was no compassion that Fergus wanted. He was
fearfully excited, though he was making a bold effort to conceal it. He spoke with Ardal of things indifferent.

But in parting he took a long look at Sorcha. There was
a fierceness in his eye like that of some hunted animal. His
face flushed again, and he started abruptly away.

Sorcha gave a sigh when he was gone. She looked at
Ardal, half fearing that he might be displeased. But his
brown eyes had a roguish twinkle in them.

"Thou art worse than a Saracen," he said. "Thou hast
borrowed Cupid's arrows, and none can suck the poison from
their wound."

"It is no matter for jesting," replied Sorcha. "I should
have let him know of it sooner, but I never dreamt of his
taking it in this way."

"I esteem him the more for it," said Ardal. "A little
poison may be a good medicine, if it be taken with discretion."

Fergus was not the only one whose mind was disturbed by
Sorcha's betrothal. The Lady Uailsi saw her most cherished
project shattered. She had longed to have Ardal as a son-
in-law, not for days, but for years. When her daughter was
only seven she had looked about for the most promising scion
of a princely family with whom she was likely to come into
contact. She had kept all other maidens at a distance that
they might not interfere with Mòr's chances. She had
lavished the wealth of her own intellect, and had for the last
week been profuse in her hospitality, in order to keep Ardal
in her social circle. She saw that Mòr had made an impres-

sion on him at first. True, he had been afterwards more reserved, but that was perhaps to be accounted for by the serious matters which were weighing on his spirits. It never once occurred to her that a guest whom she and the abbot delighted to honour could dream of seeking pleasure in the society of others.

And she had had absolutely no hint of this! It had come on her like a thunderbolt out of a clear sky. She felt doubly thwarted, because she had taken pains to instil into her daughter's mind the idea that the young bishop cared for her. She had done Mòr a wrong in this. The girl was so affectionate, so dutiful, that she was but too ready to believe her mother's word. And Mòr would be so much hurt by a slight!

The two hastened to the upper chamber of their own dwelling—the only one where they might converse quite unheard. Uailsi's hands were clenched, and her face expressive of much bitterness. Mòr burst into a flood of tears.

Her mother waited till the paroxysm had subsided. She then spoke with vehemence:

"Is it not base conduct?" she exclaimed. "But he will be punished for trifling with thee."

Mòr's blue eyes looked more transparent than ever through her tears.

"Call him not base, mother," she said. "It is we who have been mistaken. Thou hast praised me overmuch; and thou hast fancied that others would do the same. I should feel humbled were it any one but Sorcha. She is as accomplished as I am, and more worthy of Ardal's love."

"Thou art good in saying so," said her mother. "But no one who knows you both would agree with thee. Who is Sorcha? Her father was a learned man, doubtless, but her mother's family is not quite so distinguished. In truth, they were very poor at one time, and they have not the least pretension to birth. It is impossible that their culture can be equal to thine."

"I cannot see it, mother," replied Mòr. "Sorcha is as good a Latin scholar, for I have read her translations. And as for her penwork, thou hast thyself said that I would have to labour if I hoped to have my gospel sent to England."

"That may be," said Uailsi. "Let us grant that she equals thee in some things; but there must be others in which she is inferior. Culture does not mean a few accomplishments. It is something that cannot be defined; it is a sweet odour that pervades our every action. It must be of a finer kind where it has been valued for threescore generations. Then consider the connection which the son of O'Brien is forming. Instead of allying himself with a family who for centuries have given abbots to Armagh, who are the rightful custodians of the Staff of Jesus, the co-arbs of Patrick, in short, and of the race of Hy-Niall—he gets a wife whose nearest male relative is a *Bo-aire*, and whose mother's sister is married to that disagreeable Danish fellow, Olrud. I wonder that Bishop Ardal did not blush when the man ushered him in."

"But where did we get these notions about birth?" said Mòr. "Was it not from the bards of heathendom, who imagined their rulers to be of the race of gods? I would rather have in my veins the red blood of which Paul spoke at Athens, than any mixture of ichor from that questionable Olympus. And Sorcha's face is excuse enough for a king's son. She will never disgrace her new rank. Perhaps we should be happier if we did not think so much of our great kinsfolk."

Uailsi laughed.

"What amuses thee, mother?" inquired Mòr.

"I see Ardal O'Brien," she replied, "in the company of his new friends. Sigurda is a very refined person, and the old lady is in her second childhood; then Olrud."

"If Ardal is a bishop at all," replied Mòr, "he should suit himself to all conditions of men. They are quite worthy people in their way, and Sorcha says her grandmother is not failing in the very least. Bishop Maidoc, indeed, thinks her quite superior."

"My child," replied Uailsi, "it hath been a misfortune for thee to have been reared so far out of the great world. Thou shouldst have seen the men and women at Turlough O'Connor's court. Thou wouldst have known what superior people were. Maidoc never spoke with one of them in his life. Turlough himself was called the Western Augustus, and they say that the lays of Gilla Enos O'Clowen would sound like those of Horace, if they had been framed in the measures of a less barbarous tongue."

"It is a pity that he did not commit them to parchment," said Mòr. "His monument would then have been more lasting than a pillar of mountain-mist, reared by the wind of foolish praise. I cannot say I have been deceived," she continued. "I never felt as if Ardal cared for me. And he had a right to please himself."

"We must submit to it," said her mother, rising. "I am glad that thou art a philosopher. Sorcha would not have spoken thus in thy place."

"Speak not of Sorcha," said Mòr. "I will try to be more her friend since she will be my equal by her marriage. I thought Ardal the best and the handsomest man I had ever seen; but others may be good in a different way."

Mòr was, in truth, more vexed than she would willingly have allowed. The possibility of Sorcha's rivalry had never once crossed her mind. She had not permitted herself to fall in love; she was too well brought up to do so without sufficient encouragement. But she had her full share of natural vanity, and it was impossible to hear so much about her own unapproachable perfections without coming to believe in them. She felt slighted. In vain did reason say that there was no cause for her doing so. Mòr knew that the delightful little suppers they had enjoyed in the young bishop's society had been got up for her sake. She had done her best to please; not obtrusively, but with the open simplicity which marked her every action. Sorcha had never been present in the refectory, so that all the attentions of the two young travellers at the noonday meal had been to her. She should never forget the evening of their arrival. They had both looked at her very persistently, and she was conscious of being the most highly-placed maiden they were likely soon to meet. Ardal had been more reserved latterly, but she had attributed this to the natural diffidence which all young men must feel in regard to her. His image had mingled itself with her day-dreams; and it was a rude shock to find that the reality had removed itself for ever away from her.

Her heart had warmed to Ardal all the more that she had noticed how sociable he was. He was a born prince, the descendant of famous chieftains, yet his humility was beautiful. It was like the fragrant violet, making no effort to attract notice, and lying so near the soil as almost to seem a part of it. Others might talk of condescension; the young bishop seemed to have nowhere to descend from. And she could read in his eye a strength of will which might force even her mother to bend to his views.

She was, therefore, doubly disappointed at his defection. The rope which she had wished to grasp had seemed so firmly tied; it had given way, and she was afloat on the chill billows. This was perhaps sent as a rebuke to her pride. Mòr began to fear that she had been ill-educated; that with all her getting she had not got understanding. She had a nature as noble as Grainné's own; indeed, there was something much alike in the two women; only Mòr had grown up in such different circumstances that she had run into quite another mould.

Yet, whilst Sorcha's success was a blow to her vanity, she felt that it was a tribute to her power of discernment. It was a confirmation of the fact that she had formed a correct estimate of her mother's mistakes. "Sorcha must have something that I lack," she thought. "It need not necessarily be beauty. She has easy manners; men do not need to use ceremony in approaching her. The hedge which separates me from my fellow-creatures may be growing thorns. I will tear it up by the roots."

Alas! how could she do this? Pride makes us very lonely, and Mòr saw that she could not escape a penalty for having cherished it so long. She yearned for some heart-communion outside of her home. There was a sanctuary within her which neither of her parents could enter.

CHAPTER XIX

ANOTHER, besides Ardal, had spoken to Mòr in natural tones. Unawed by Uailsi's haughtiness, he had dared to associate with her on the footing of an equal. Genius had asserted its birthright when Fergus O'Flannahan's wit had disarmed all efforts to exclude him from the highest coterie of Ardmore. He brought into Mòr's experience the freshness of a new intellectual breeze. He breathed a few magic words, and lo ! all dulness disappeared. Her mother had come to think of him in the light of a privileged fool.

For Fergus, like Olrud, was supposed to be of lowly extraction ; to have risen, in fact, from a stratum of society beneath that of Rossa and Amada. Diamonds sometimes lie very deeply buried, but even they need a certain amount of washing and polishing before they are fit to clasp the robe of royalty. It remained to be determined whether Fergus O'Flannahan was a diamond. There are gradations in the value of precious stones which it needs a practised eye to mark. Opinions were divided about Fergus. He was no mediocrity, that was certain ; but the lustre that can force its way up from the bottom of a well must be both persistent and steady. If birth were everything, Fergus O'Flannahan had no right to approach a maiden of the Cinel Conaill ; but if talent ennoble all who are connected with it, then a princess herself might shine in the reflected radiance of a true-born poet.

Why was Mòr troubled by such musings ? Because Fergus

had already addressed to her the language of flattery. Mòr's simplicity was great. It exceeded even that of Sorcha. What wonder if she consoled herself for the loss of the man she might have won by thinking of one who seemed wishful to win her.

Mòr had shut her ears to the voice of the charmer. She had enjoyed his sallies of wit without apparently listening to the tender epithets which he secretly shot at her. Not by such artillery was a proud girl to be conquered. But now she was smarting under a defeat. Dissemble it as she would, she felt as if to-day she were scarcely so much worth as yesterday. "What is love?" Mòr thought to herself. "It is a tender flower which often blooms where we have not cultivated it. A passing frost may blight it; yet the rudest storms will only root it the firmer. It is sown and reared by the Creator's hand; we cannot regulate its up-springing any more than we can fix the courses of the seasons. There is nothing else on earth to compare with it. Love, the quint-essence of all delights, the flower and crown of human expe-riences—do we expect to make it for ourselves? or, having procured a plant of it, do we mark out the direction each leaf is expected to take, and then think that our production shall vie with Nature's? No, no! Far better to watch where it has already sprouted, and be thankful if we can cull its sweets, even at the risk of torn garments and wounded fingers."

Mòr observed Fergus more closely; but in truth she had little need to do so. His tender glances were quite fresh in her recollection. She had received them as offerings that she could never appropriate; they had lain untouched at her shrine. But now her spirit was more active. The pain it had just felt made it loth to inflict a similar grief. And she began to debate whether Fergus might not be preferable to Ardal.

In secret, however; her mother was no longer to be trusted. Uailsi had, in truth, shown little skill in her management. She had been too sure of her conquest to exercise much generalship; and any generalship was quite out of place, thought the maiden. It was repugnant to her whole nature.

She was not long kept in suspense. A very slight unbending, and her destiny would pass out of her own hands. Fergus was in a mood for resolving on something desperate. Had he loved Sorcha? The motives of such men are difficult to analyse; yet we think we have good grounds for saying that he had.

And in truth it was no wonder. He had seen queens of beauty; women chosen by the flower of Provençal chivalry to bear the twice royal title; but each and all would have had to yield the throne to Sorcha. He had called this a fancy at first; he had attributed half its strength to a natural prejudice in favour of a Celtic form; but in vain. Each day that he looked at her he became more convinced that his taste was unerring. It was no matter of fancy: Sorcha was fair as the summer morning; perfect as an exquisitely moulded peach; queenly as the moon riding in the nightly heavens. The reality always outstripped his last recollection of her.

And Fergus adored beauty. She was his goddess; the one thing that occupied a higher pedestal than the love of himself. Beauty incarnate; the loveliness of the natural and of the spiritual world blended into a woman's shape—should he not long to make it for ever his own? Yes, it seemed near him, it must be his potentially—actually also, if other things were meet. He might not find it convenient to be bound to Sorcha; but if he were forced to make an effort of self-denial, it must be by the exercise of his will alone.

For Fergus was also ambitious. This was the keynote of his character. He had trained his every faculty in an upward direction. His talents had doubtless raised him from a humble station to power; yet in the Isle of Saints there were other paths to eminence. He was very sensitive to his defects of birth; not that he would have allowed this; on the contrary, he professed to despise any advantages he might have got from a nobler parentage. Yet the more his pride tried to conceal it, the more was he conscious of a deep-seated chagrin at the want of high connections. There was only one way of supplying it, and that was by marriage.

Could he win a noble maiden, it would be evidence that others did not despise his family. Sorcha was well-born on her father's side, and not contemptibly low on her mother's. Indeed, had he and his brother not entered the clerical profession, they would have felt themselves immeasurably raised by an alliance with the children of Rossa. But that was past. Fergus was now on a higher step of the social ladder, and he would take the very longest stride that he could manage.

His intercourse with the abbot's family kept him alive to the fact of there being higher circles into which he might penetrate. By fixing your gaze steadily on the heavens, you may see a vista of clouds stretching upwards in thinner lines towards the sun. So it was with Fergus. Had there been no Mòr, he would have been quite dazzled by Sorcha; but the rarer atmosphere of Uailsi's household made him feel that a straighter path led from it to the goal of his wishes.

It was possible, however, that he might fail. Not with Sorcha. She was so simple, so humble, she blushed and drooped like a flower when he praised her. She was sensitive to his glances. He could imagine no more exquisite pleasure than to see her so much affected by them. Yes, there was one still in store for him. He had almost tasted it in Maidoc's cell. It was the bliss of the moment when, raising her clear lustrous eyes, she should give free play to the affection that was treasured in her soul. It needed but a word to bring this out. How often had that word trembled on his lip!

But its utterance might involve the destruction of another hope. The sweetness of beauty often disappears after several draughts of it. Fame aud honour never pall on the most satiated appetite.

Fergus wondered at his own foresight. It was almost superhuman how he put aside the cup of happiness. Only for a time, perhaps. It might be the best policy to drink it after all. He would see how he succeeded with Mòr. Her pride might be impregnable, and, if so, he would have all the more satisfaction in falling back upon Sorcha.

Not that he loved Mòr in the same way. He admired her intellect, which amongst its other attributes had the supreme one of rendering her capable of appreciating his. He was almost sick of undiscriminating flattery. He was formed to be woman's idol, but he would prefer that his worshippers should not be all of the common herd.

But Mòr was only a means to an end. It was for the sake of the ichor in her veins, and not for that of warm human affection, that he sought her. True, the maiden was comely, but her charms were not of the ravishing kind. There would be a wrench at his heart when she accepted him; nevertheless, he was nerving himself to bear it. The love of his own greatness was indeed excessive, when it would even have led him to renounce Sorcha.

We must not suppose, however, that his plans had been definitely formed. Any minute self-examination was an ordeal from which he had an instinctive shrinking. He was like a cork set afloat on the billows, constant in nothing but in keeping on the crest of every passing wave. He was fully aware of the discord between his several wishes, and considered that fortune had been somewhat unkind in failing to show him a way of harmonising them. The double dream was pleasant while it lasted, and he considered that there was sufficient cause in the wealth of his nature to account for his indulgence in it.

Sorcha's betrothal was a rude awakening. It startled him with a sense of falling akin to the experience of disturbed sleep. He felt dazed, bewildered. If the new trouble had sprung out of the ground, it could not more effectually have concealed its approach. A wild frenzy arose within him, whose manifestation was hard to repress. He could almost have slain Sorcha as she bent her lovely head before the unseen Presence whose blessing was sought for her. Fergus had what he feared might be a foretaste of hell.

But successful actors on life's stage must often pass the jest to conceal their own misery. Fergus scarcely felt that it was himself who spoke, even when the company were laughing at his sallies. Never had he so much over-mastered himself. He had a feeling of his own greatness. In that supreme moment, when most of what would have made his life worthy was slipping from him, he exercised a power of will that might suffice to enslave nations.

But the volcano was only slumbering. Its flames, driven back from their natural outlet, covered up with the hard crust of conventional decorum, made fearful havoc with his inner man. There was a gnawing pain at his heart; a pain that almost drove him to desperation. He walked to the cottage by Sorcha's side, as if he derived some assuagement from the fancy that he could yet snatch her away from his rival. Then he sought the solitude of the forest.

There he threw himself at full length upon the mossy turf. Had his friends cared to follow him, they would have been struck by his change of countenance. The bold brow was knitted with fierce suffering, the flushed cheeks were hollow; the lines about chin and mouth were expressive of the deepest dejection. He looked like the shattered wreck of himself.

"Why have I deserved this?" he thought. "Sorcha knew that I loved her. I have shown it to her in a thousand ways. I have never been forgetful of her presence; no, not when an appreciative audience was hanging on my lips. I have virtually worn her colours as her true knight. Why has she preferred Ardal? Some malice must have been at work."

Fergus's eye flashed. A cloud of intense bitterness over-spread his face.

"That wretch Olrud!" he exclaimed. "Yes, it must be he, the low, sneaking pharisee! enlarging his phylacteries, whilst he whispered distrust in her ear. My happiness has been sacrificed to these miserable church squabbles! Or stay," he thought again, "it may not be Olrud after all. It cannot be the old lady. Grainné? Yes, it may. She is so worldly-wise, and has no doubt been anxious to have Sorcha settled. She has looked for the best match, and Ardal is very simple. The girl has had no choice. I—did I give her anything to go upon? Perhaps I have dallied too long with uncertainties. Sorcha is unsophisticated; she doubt-less lacked courage to say to her aunt, 'Fergus loves me.'

"Yet I hate Olrud. He has been the black serpent in my garden. A cold, sneering, cynical hypocrite, without one spark of poetry or human sympathy. *He* venture to dispose of Sorcha! to protect her, perhaps, from one who has the taint of heresy! What right had he at Ardmore? An upstart fellow, who was born to be an *erenach*! who has no claim on a bishop's friendship but the barren one of office. The son of those black strangers whose impious hands once rifled our shrines. I shall raise a hue-and-cry after him. I shall have him cast out of the synagogue!"

This reference to a scriptural saying startled Fergus. His mobile mind at once took in the necessity for caution.

He was deluding himself into a belief of his own honesty. It never once occurred to him that he had for a moment hesitated about wooing Sorcha. No; with the retrospective light now cast upon it, his purpose had been altogether a single one. He had been guilty of delay, not dissimulation.

He considered himself a most ill-used man. If Sorcha had
given him the least hint, he would have tried to ward off the
approaching danger. He was sure that her kind heart had
not prepared this cruel surprise ; it was Grainné's management. She feared lest the disclosure should mar her scheme.
The maiden would surely have preferred her first wooer.
Perhaps she was even now regretting him.

The thought brought Fergus some consolation, yet it failed
to rouse him to any effort. Should he try to dispute with
Ardal ? He felt that the attempt would be hopeless. Sorcha
was now guarded by a dragon. She was perhaps ambitious.
The marriage would place her in the rank of princes ; for,
though Ardal had dropped his title at his ordination, he could
not divest himself of the honour of having once borne it. But
what was Ardal's genius compared with his ? Sorcha would
live to regret that she had forsaken him.

Fergus rose from his grassy couch. He spent the rest of
that day in aimless wanderings. They had no issue, so far as
his feet were concerned, but the whole force of his spirit was
thrown into the effort to immortalise its own workings. And
this he almost accomplished in a very beautiful poem, which,
like many other Celtic treasures, has perished in its voyage
down the ages. The labour brought with it sufficient exhaustion to make him at length seek his nightly pillow.

CHAPTER XX.

As the first rays of next morning's sun touched the pictu-resque cluster of huts that nestled round the tower and church of Ardmore, they found many of its inhabitants already astir; for the abbot had made known that he expected the visit of Tostius, Bishop of Waterford, a man of mark, who had long kept up a correspondence with him, and now wished to see with his own eyes the habits of the community which he deemed schismatical. The abbot had invited him most cordially to spend several days under his roof. News of the prelate's arrival at Dungarvan had come on the preceding night. He might be expected in the course of the afternoon.

There was unwonted agitation both inside and outside of the rath. Dairymaids were busy scouring their pails; the very scullery wenches polished and rubbed with a pardonable wish to make things look their best. Ita began an extra baking; whilst Uailsi, Mòr, and Sorcha were divided between the con-coction of some special dishes, and the elaboration of their own toilets. Sorcha found that her footing in the family had changed. The Lady Uailsi, having recovered from her fit of coldness, spoke to her for the first time as to a daughter; whilst Mòr's bright eye rested on her with peculiar satisfac-tion. She was now one of themselves. Sorcha was too happy to divine any selfish motive in this. She attributed it to the force of circumstances, and went about in serene un-consciousness of doing aught but her duty. Nevertheless, her overflowing heart sent out a new stream of sisterly affection towards Mòr.

The sun had fairly begun his descent to the west, and a

solemn stillness was falling on forest and meadow, when the space between the door of the church and the tower became sprinkled with picturesque groups. There were some fifty bishops, clothed in their black mantles, through the openings of which the edges of their white flannel lenas peeped forth. All carried their simple crosiers, and many of them had cases of wax tablets suspended by chains from their leathern girdles. Several women stood about, their dark robes relieved by bright tartans; whilst farm and house servants of both sexes wore their holiday attire of undyed saffron wool. Children mingled freely in the crowd, lending to it the charm of their rosy faces and innocent questioning little ways.

At length the abbot appeared, followed by Maidoc, Ardal, and Fergus. Then the bishops formed in procession three deep; and all, having descended the hill and crossed the channel on planks, set forth along the forest road to Dungarvan.

They had proceeded thus about half a mile, followed by a crowd of saffron-robed peasants, when the sound of music fell on their ears. Ardal glanced meaningly at Fergus, and the general pace became slower. The tones swelled to a rich volume of sound, and at length, at a turn of the well-trodden highway, appeared a banner, borne aloft by boys in white lace-edged surplices. There was a disposition amongst the abbot's followers to halt, but Ardal beckoned them forward.

"Let not that impose on you, my brethren," he said. "It savoureth of the pomp and glory of this world. We have nought but what cometh of our connection with the unseen."

The little company kept by Ardal's directions in the middle of the roadway, moving neither to the right nor to the left as the banner approached. Another was soon observed behind it; and the volume of sweet sound was evidently rising from the open mouths of a dozen boys, who walked bareheaded in front of a gorgeously-dressed old man; before whom rose a cloud of fragrant smoke, issuing from two silver censers swung by the white-robed youths. A priest walked on either side of him, with ample black and white garments, throwing into stronger relief the magnificence of his gold embroidery. His shining mitre was conspicuously adorned with a silver cross.

Ardal's eyes were quick to observe the effect of this splendour on his companions. He noticed that Fergus's lip was curled, as if in involuntary scorn, and that many of the other bishops looked troubled and anxious. Some of the peasants were staring in open-mouthed wonder, whilst others betrayed a disposition to smile.

The banners at length approached near enough for their meaning to be perceived. The first bore the conventional likeness of our Saviour's face, surrounded by a halo of silver spikes, and wearing the marks of intense suffering beneath the crown of thorns. Great crimson drops were sprinked all over it. The second bore a most touching image of the Virgin, placing her hand where the seven arrows stuck in her heart. Ardal noticed that, whilst some of the country folk seemed rather weak about the knees when they beheld the first picture, they straightened themselves up and looked defiant at the view of the second.

The abbot's party kept in the middle of the road. The young choristers arrived within a few paces of them, then ceasing their chanting, they ranged themselves in two rows on either side, whilst the bishop advanced between them with extended hands.

The abbot grasped them rather more warmly than was altogether pleasing to his followers. The two men looked into each other's eyes as if with an unspoken longing to realise their union in a common faith. Both groups meanwhile gazed curiously at each other. The prelate spoke first. "Dominus vobiscum, filii Declanis," he said, making the motion of benediction with his fingers, which, enigmatical to others, was well understood by Fergus and Ardal.

"Salve, frater, grate Ardmori," replied the abbot. "I trust that thou wilt find that we are indeed thy brethren, children of one Father."

The two walked on together. The priests following were escorted by Fergus, whilst Maidoc, whose duty it should have been to pilot them, fell back amongst the other bishops.

The choristers seemed at first puzzled what to do with themselves. Finding, however, that the grassy path was wide enough, they ranged themselves in double file, and walked by the side of the Irish ecclesiastics. Obeying a signal from one of the priests, they soon struck up Psalm cxii., "Laudate pueri Dominum." Ardal, who happened to be near them, at once joined in it.

The boys looked up in some amazement, for Ardal uttered it with an intensity of meaning to which they seemed utter strangers.

Planks had been laid across the shallow part of the narrow gulf which separated Ardmore from the mainland. The procession wound slowly up the hill, followed at a short distance by a troop of led horses and others carrying the visitors' baggage.

There was a crowd before the arched gateway of the rath, but a space had been cleared for the ecclesiastics to pass through it. On entering the blooming enclosure, they perceived a group of white-robed ladies standing before the church door. The abbot, however, seemed unmindful of their presence. Turning to his guests, he said :

"It hath ever been our custom, since the days of the blessed Patrick, that the stranger who entereth within our gates should first raise in our sanctuary the song of thanksgiving for his safe journey."

"A gracious custom," responded the prelate, gathering the edges of his rich mantle together, and crossing himself as he stepped over the threshold.

A singular spectacle met his eye. The double church was

decorated with festoons of green leaves and with Latin texts in floral devices all round the walls—the Ten Commandments and the Lord's Prayer being conspicuous on the eastern wall over the communion table. Ranged on either side of the outer chapel were about fifty boys and girls, with small parchment rolls in their hands.

The abbot led his guest forward. Together they knelt on a sealskin mat in the centre of the inner sanctuary, each remaining for a few moments in silent prayer.

But as the prelate rose, the swelling sounds of the Te Deum burst from a hundred youthful voices. The girls were led by Mòr and Sorcha—the one radiant in loveliness, the other with that noble seraphic look which hallowed her countenance when engaged in musical worship. The three priests, as well as the choristers listened and gazed in unfeigned admiration.

No one spoke till the anthem was finished. Then the abbot led his guest out of the chapel.

" I was not aware," remarked Tostius, " that you made any use of the sacred language."

" Of Latin, thou wouldst say," replied the abbot, smiling. " We hold it not sacred, but we study it for the sake of its classic literature, no less than for that of the apostolical Fathers. Our services, it is true, are conducted in the native tongue, for the benefit of our ignorant fellow-countrymen ; but amongst ourselves we sometimes sing the " Altus Prosator " of Columba, or the " Sancti venite," when we partake of the Eucharist. We have the Psalter in Erse measures, but we have deviated from our usage of it in order that we might have a point of understanding with thee."

The prelate bowed his acknowledgments. " I cannot wonder," he said, " at thy attachment to thine own ritual when the musical part of it is made so attractive."

The graceful figure of Uailsi now appeared, accompanied by several other matrons. The abbot spoke distinctly, and with a pardonable pride.

"My wife," he said, "bids thee welcome to our humble home."

Tostius took the fair lady's hand with the air of a courtier. He even made a motion as if he would raise it to his lips, but this Uailsi gently resisted.

Ita was presented, then Mòr and Sorcha.

"We have arranged," said the abbot, "that thou shalt be my special guest. We are simple people, and never change our ways of living. Thy two friends are invited to spend the evening with some of our bishops in the great refectory; the boys, we think, will be most at home with our young scholars. I hear from their tongue that they are natives of Erin. I must ask thee to accompany us to our dwelling, where thou wilt find some needed refreshment.

He led his guest to a house built against that part of the rath which was nearest to the Round Tower. It occupied the highest ground in the enclosure, and was half overshadowed by the gigantic yew-tree, in whose branches birds had built ever since the days of Declan. Two young men sat constantly at the door to await or to execute his orders. The dwelling assigned to the prelate was, however, that known as the Grianan, situated on the summit of the rath, and approached by turf-cut steps from the abbot's door.

Their guest having retired, Mòr turned toward Fergus with the question—

"Thinkest thou that he is pleased? Thou hast a critical ear; did our arrangement of to-day agree with thy wish?"

"Perfectly," he replied. "It was a delicate compliment to him to utter our worship in the cosmopolitan Latin. The more we study each other in these minor matters, the more firm shall we find it possible to be in essentials."

"There is no harm in it," said Mòr, "seeing that it is a tongue which our children are learning. But had there been a mixed audience, it would have been a dangerous precedent. Our services must be made intelligible to the worshippers."

" Flowers," replied Fergus, "speak a language that all can understand. Are they not emblametic of our hopes to bring forth the fruits of the Spirit ? "

" Call them not a part of worship," said Mòr. " Cain was not accepted, though he robbed the fields."

" Yet are there shrines where one may offer them," said Fergus, taking from his breast a bunch of violets. " These mean something, for their fragrance is everlasting."

Mòr gazed inquisitively at him as she took them. There was a penetration in her glance from which Fergus shrank. The prelate's return, however, put an end to their converse.

Uailsi had surpassed herself in the artistic arrangement of her supper-table. A superb bouquet of wild flowers stood in a silver-mounted ox-horn in the centre; whilst smaller horns, supported on feet carved out of their own material, and foaming with claret-coloured ale, rested lovingly on the snowy linen. The viands were simple, but exquisitely cooked. A lamb and a sucking-pig, roasted in honour of their guest, were flanked by loaves of wheaten bread, and balls of golden butter nestling amongst delicate water-cress. Nor was the usual fare awanting; and those who had no taste for luxuries might satisfy themselves with dishes of white curds and basins of oatmeal porridge flavoured with leeks. Half a dozen oil-lamps vied with the fire in throwing an air of cheerfulness over the fur-covered couches and benches of the homely apartment; the only one in Ardmore which could boast of a chimney in the side wall. Uailsi herself presided, in sober yet tasteful attire; her active movements and her bright intelligent face throwing an additional charm over all her belongings. She had invited a select company to meet the stranger. There were Maidoc and Ita, who both seemed determined to win the praise of gravity; Fergus, whose changeful expression gave token of a vivacious intellect; there was Ardal, whose heart happiness threw a warmth over his every movement; and Sorcha, more beautiful than ever amidst her blushes. The prelate's eyes rested with a curious interest on her and on Mòr.

These maidens were indeed fair specimens of a class which he had never yet had so good an opportunity of studying. It hardly needed a second glance to tell him that they were different from the other women he knew, different from his sisters, who had passed the flower of their youth within the walls of a convent; different from those courtly ladies whose grace was always accompanied by a shallow wit. Their white lenas and inars displayed to advantage the perfection of their forms, whilst the beauty of their countenances was enhanced by the sparkle of intellect by which they were illumined. Tostius thought that, had he been a worldling, he would have imagined nothing more winning than Mòr; yet in personal loveliness Sorcha appeared to surpass her.

He almost forgot his weariness in contemplating them. It was only by repeated pressing that he was induced to do any justice to the viands. An absorbing passion had taken possession of his soul. These flowers of Erin must be culled for the garland of the Redeemer. It was too sad that they should blossom outside of the true vineyard.

A few words of thanksgiving having been spoken by the abbot, the table was cleared and placed in a corner. Fresh logs were heaped on the glowing embers, and the company gathered in a wide circle round the hearth. The conversation soon took a practical turn.

" Ye have fine lands round the monastery," remarked Tostius. " I presume that they were the gift of some chieftain?"

" Of several," replied the abbot. " Such benefactions are common with us as with you. They are often given for the encouragement of learning. Our colleges are, in the first place, educational; and, in the second, they give to the studious the quiet so requisite for the transcribing of books. We do not neglect profane literature, though our principal employment is the multiplication of the Holy Scriptures."

"I know, I know," said the prelate. "You have done yourselves infinite honour in this. Your labours are appreciated all over Christendom. The Holy Father himself has derived benefit from them; and this, more than anything else, has made his heart yearn towards you. All who invoke the sacred Trinity are his children by virtue of their baptism."

"I fear he must think us wayward ones," said Fergus, glancing mischievously at the ladies.

"He is not a stern father," replied the prelate, imperturbably. "None, indeed, who considers how Erin has been separated, shut out, in a manner, from the rest of the world, can wonder that her paths are not the same as ours. But it cannot remain so. Our Lord has distinctly said that His Church shall be one."

"We think of that often," said the abbot. "We are not obstinate. In some things we have conformed, but only when our reason convinced us that Scripture was not against you. Our forefathers changed their time of keeping Easter; and as for the tonsure ——" Here he ran his fingers through the tuft overlaying his bald forehead.

"I have been surprised since coming here," said Tostius. "I thought that five centuries ago all Irish bishops had adopted the Roman tonsure."

"So they did," replied Ardal. "But the controversy hath waxed so warm of late that many of us have returned to the old fashion, which, in truth, had never quite died out. Those who have done so wish to mark the strength of their motives for disobedience."

A slight frown passed over the prelate's face. It was immediately banished, but not before he had darted at Ardal a glance of peculiar meaning. The young bishop became deadly pale and turned towards the narrow window.

"Is there anything wrong?" asked Sorcha, laying her hand affectionately on his arm.

" No," he replied, recovering his composure with an effort; whilst the prelate continued, smiling affably.

" I myself see few obstacles to our speedy union. There cannot, indeed, be any, seeing that we both draw our warrants from the same Book. You do not acknowledge the authority of the four councils, I presume, because you were unrepresented at them. Another œcumenical assembly might dispose of the difficulty."

" True," replied Ardal, with an utterance made rather thick by some inward agitation, " but there are rights, very dear to us, which a General Council might ask us to give up."

A smile passed over every face, whilst Sorcha's cheeks tingled painfully. Ardal had, for some strange reason, avoided encountering a second time the prelate's glance. Fergus gave a convulsive laugh, and Mòr bravely struck in—

" He means rights of marriage. Our bishops will never part with their wives."

The prelate's brows became more contracted. " Thou hast touched the kernel of the matter," he remarked. " All else might be left open questions ; but that is a decided bar to inter-communion. Nevertheless, I think too highly of you Irish pastors to suppose that you would prefer your personal comfort to the furtherance of the gospel. I will admit that you have a scriptural passage in your favour ; but the Church was left free to frame her own laws in these minor matters, and the structure of her canons is the result of experience. When you come to see that it is a question of practical utility, you will wonder how you could have quarrelled with her wisdom."

" We dispute the practical utility," said the abbot, glancing round with an air of complacency. " I shall lay everything open to thy inspection during thy stay ; and I shall make thee welcome to point out wherein we are inferior to our Roman brethren."

"That will not be hard," said the prelate, smiling. "I will be frank enough to say, however, that were I not under the roof of one who has received the sacrament of ordination, I could imagine nothing more perfect in the way of household management. Your women are, doubtless, patterns of virtue in every respect. But I say it is impossible for a married man to give himself to the task of winning souls so unreservedly as one who has given up family affection."

Ardal and Fergus both looked grave. The former, indeed, had not quite recovered from his strange agitation.

"I have tried both states," said Maidoc, quietly, "and I must give a decided preference to my present one."

The abbot seemed much amused. "It is quite possible," he said, "that your army of monks have achieved successes of which we cannot dream. Yet methinks they profess to retire from the world chiefly for the benefit of their own souls, whereas the leading aim of our religious institutions hath ever been the conversion of other men. And if report speak true, the foundations of our Culdee ancestors, whether in Germany, Helvetia, or Italy, have been distinguished above all others for their purity of life and doctrine. Where, even in Clairvaux, can we find instances of more burning zeal than among the early Irish missionaries?"

"True enough," replied the prelate. "But what a glorious effect there is on general society when a man or a maiden renounces the innocent pleasures of life for the sake of a more thorough consecration. The Church would surely be the poorer were she to miss such self-denial."

"I have my own views," said the abbot, "with regard to the effect on general society."

"What are they?" asked the visitor.

"The Almighty is a great husbandman," replied the abbot; "and the human race is the first object of His care. We know that by labour and intelligent skill we can make the various plants produce more superb forms. Is the same not true of human culture ?   I believe in the possibility of moral perfection ; but I do not think that it can be attained in one generation."

" I fail to perceive," said Tostius, " what bearing that has on the question we are discussing.

" I am coming to it," said his host.   " The highest ideal, either physical or intellectual, is not likely to be reached by man as we know him now ; I doubt even if he is quite capable of conceiving it.   Our first parents had it, perhaps, before they sinned ; but Christian perfection must be a higher type than even theirs was.   Now, though all believers are justified, they are not yet fully sanctified, nor yet instructed to the degree that they might be.   It is a hard pull upwards ; but the higher we ourselves attain, the better vantage-ground will our children have to start from.   Those who have inherited pure moral and great intellectual natures may produce a race such as the world has not yet seen, more conformed to the Divine image ; in short, you cut off the waters of progress very near the fountain head when you prevent the rearing of so many Christian families."

" Thou speakest truth," said Ardal.   " Our pastors' children are the most valuable element in this nation.   Had we not committed some grievous mistakes they would have leavened it much more than they have done."

Uailsi looked displeased.   She thought it impolitic to speak of mistakes at the present moment.

" What are these ? " asked the prelate.

" They are only less hurtful than those of thy communion," replied Ardal.   " We have found our bishops' children so valuable, that we have tried to make them all servants of the Church.   More would have been accomplished had we en-couraged a freer circulation between the clergy and the laity."

" That never struck me before," said the abbot.   "I have often wondered how it was that we are, as it were, divided into two camps."

" And I have wondered," said Tostius, " though I need scarcely have done so, why your termon-lands are so much more flourishing than those around them. There is waste and desolation everywhere, save when one steps on to religious property. Yet with all your good management, you have many squalid villages."

" I would have thee distinguish," said the abbot, " between the dwellings of our proper Daer Ceiles, or villeins, and those who have only settled by permission on our lands. Swarms of poor creatures fly to us every year for protection and shelter; and so frequent have been the raids of rival chieftains, that they are often loth to return to their homes. It was doubtless amongst these that thou hast perceived so much misery. Nor can we forget that we owe to the establishment of the new sees the causes of most of our civil broils."

" How so ? " asked the prelate, frowning.

" Because," replied the abbot, with a glance at his wife, " the lands of our old ecclesiastical settlements have been confiscated for the endowment of these new ones. Thou knowest well that the changes made by Malachy at Armagh have been the occasion of bloody wars."

" We had better drop that subject," said Uailsi. " Thou wilt allow," she continued, turning to the prelate, " that we have had sufficient experience of asceticism. Seven of our recluses once died of hunger in an island of Lough Erne. We have brethren who follow the primitive custom of standing up to their knees in a pond for several hours before they break their fast, repeating the Psalms by heart; yet they do not speak more to edification than do others."

" Our Church," said Ardal, " has allowed the widest liberty in this respect. With regard to matrimony, though it might be undesirable for men like Patrick and Columba, who were pioneers of the gospel to utterly heathen lands, we find it most beneficial to those who exercise a settled ministry. The feelings which grow out of marital and parental ties are the very same that we need to cultivate towards our flocks. We learn to rule our house well before we seek to rule the Church."

" We must have more talk of this to-morrow," said the prelate ; " for it groweth late."

He bade them all good-night, and was escorted to the Grianan by the abbot.

Ardal accompanied Sorcha to the cottage.

" We have heard an interesting discussion," she said ; "but I regretted that Grainné was not present. She might have thrown some light on the subject. I wonder the Lady Uailsi did not invite her."

" I regretted it too," replied Ardal. " And I wish much that Bishop Tostius could speak with thy grandmother. But yet it may be better as it is. Amada is too uncompromising."

" And she might have excited herself," said Sorcha, " without doing anything towards convincing him. But Grainné has more penetration than either Uailsi or Mòr. The company would just have suited her. I fear it is because they do not think her their equal."

" Then they deserve to lose her society," said Ardal. " But there is a consolation. She could hardly have been there without Olrud ; but perhaps thou dost regret him too ? "

" Oh no ! " replied Sorcha.

" He cannot see us now," said Ardal, as he laughingly imprinted a kiss upon her cheek.

Sorcha started back in sudden terror.

" What is it ? " asked her lover.

" Nothing," she replied, making an effort to regain her composure ; " it was only the shadow of yonder tree in the moonlight."

" Thou art safe," said Ardal, soothing her ; " and wilt be doubly so when thou art under Olrud's wing."

He lifted the door-latch, and, with a silent pressure of the hand, they parted.

But Sorcha's cheeks were tingling painfully, and Grainné noticed it.

"Why, child!" she said. "Hath a stranger's frown made thee ashamed of an honourable engagement?"

"No," replied Sorcha. "Ardal's love ennobles me more than his father's crown would do. But I have a foolish fear lest something should come to tear it from me."

"Lest something should try to do so, thou wouldst say," replied Grainné. "True love is not a plant of earth. It has its roots in the unseen world, and these can never be reached by strangers, however much its leaves may be crushed, or its stalk broken."

Sorcha was silent. She felt that Grainné was right; yet she had the uneasy mind of one who has seen a vision. At the moment Ardal's lips had touched hers she had discerned a dim form close to the shadow of the church. A moonbeam had illumined its face, showing something like Fergus' blue eyes fixed reproachfully on her. She chid herself for the idle fancy, and thought that her brain had been doubtless heated by the excitement of listening to a discussion on topics which touched her nearly. But the vision returned in her dreams. Its appearance was heralded by flashes of vivid lightning amidst dark clouds, and there was a lurid light about it which made her flesh creep. Sorcha shook herself more than once from the horrible nightmare. She dare not again close her eyes, and lay awake till morning.

Ardal was also ill at ease. After leaving Sorcha he walked in the direction where he had noticed that her glance was turned, but a close inspection of the trees near the church wall disclosed nothing unusual. Ardal, like all Celts, had a tint of superstition in his nature. He could not help fancying that Sorcha's start might be an omen of coming ill. Yet the cause of his anxiety lay deeper. He had not forgotten the

prelate's glance.   Certain episodes of his life came crowding
on his recollection.   No, the two things were wholly distinct.   The past was buried and forgotten ; there could arise
no ghost from its grave.

But Bishop Tostius had a face which deserved study.   It
was a mild face, lighted by a pair of soft grey eyes.   Kind
eyes, Ardal thought ; but yet capable of emitting a beam which
went through your very soul. Did anything there shrink from
such scrutiny ?   Ardal feared not to confess to God.   Why
should he be thus sensitive to the eye of a fellow-mortal ?

CHAPTER XXI.

Bishop Tostius had also retired to rest. Weary in body, he soon fell asleep; yet awoke long before daylight to ponder over his strange surroundings. He had availed himself of all the dispensations which the Church allows to travellers, but he had now a trembling consciousness that such indulgence might be carried too far for his peace of mind. Rising from his comfortable bed, he knelt with bare knees on the cold rushes, repeating a few paters and aves till he became thoroughly awake.

He then threw himself again on his couch, clasping a small ivory crucifix to his breast. He sighed deeply as he thought of the sufferings it represented, and then of the hard impenitence which the sight of them failed to melt.

The experiences of the past day had made a strong impression on him—not a healthful one altogether. For the sunlight which brings vigour and refreshment to the green plant, fails to affect the one which is artificially dyed. Yet the false colouring had not as yet passed into the very core of Bishop Tostius' nature. Reason had not wholly yielded the victory to obedience. She sometimes struggled to get into a broader groove than that in which her tyrannical ruler confined her.

It was a strange position for a devotee of the Catholic Church. He had been sent to try his influence on a set of rebellious sectaries. He could not well hope to succeed without understanding his opponent's position, and that seemed to Tostius a most peculiar one.

"It must be true," he thought, "that the devil can transform himself into an angel of light. How can these men utter holy words whilst separating themselves from the Fountain of truth? My heart bleeds for these young maidens. They are too noble to be the prey of dangerous error. The daughters of Erin are a fine race. Their intellect has reached a higher development than that of their Saxon or Provençal sisters. Could I do aught to save these two? They have reason, but it would be hopeless to work on it amidst their present surroundings. I could beat any of these bishops singly in an argument, but the whole system is so cunningly framed that every joint of its armour will resist the entrance of truth. Our blessed Pontiff was right in naming these colleges nurseries of vice. I have thought the expression harsh, but now I have looked into the root of the matter. Ah, these maidens! The Church has surely set her seal on them when she has awakened such a longing for their welfare in my heart."

The prelate fell asleep again. He could not help wondering, when he awoke, why the fate of these lovely girls should concern him more than that of the other dwellers at Ardmore. The souls of all were surely precious.

"The abbot seems a learned man. Would that he could only taste the happiness of a sincere consecration! He is trying to serve God and the world," thought Tostius. "He has never really borne the Saviour's cross. He actually makes a merit of indulging his own inclinations. But God will have the whole heart from those who serve in His sanctuary."

The two priests now came to receive his morning benediction.

"How did ye spend the evening?" he asked.

"In truth, sorrily," replied the elder. "My cheeks grew hot at the pretensions of these low men who dare to puff each other up with the noblest of titles. I wonder that they tremble not to walk near their own cliffs. The rocks might fall on them."

" Did ye argue on those subjects whereon they are disobedient ? " asked the prelate.

" Aye, truly," replied the other priest. " But I am fain to stop my ears at blasphemy. The women speak with levity on sacred themes ; also a dark-visaged man, whom they say is a stranger, spoke very roughly of our gracious Mother, the Church."

" Ye bore yourselves with Christian meekness, I trust," said the bishop.

Both priests looked down.

" You are in fault," he continued. " You see much that is terrible here. But lay it to your hearts that ye answer no man until ye have silently repeated three aves. Then may the fire of honest indignation burn itself down to a gentle heat whilst ye think of Her whose servants ye are."

" We will," answered both the ecclesiastics, as they kissed his hand. " We are bidden to eat with the herd in the refectory. Thou, my lord, art expected at the abbot's table."

Tostius glanced for a few moments at the wide panorama of forest and green meadow which lay stretched out almost at his feet ; then at the white-crested waves beating in upon the rocky shore. " Erin," he murmured to himself, " thy bright emblem sparkles on the finger of a foreign monarch. When will the eastern breeze waft his ships over that briny expanse to claim thee for the breastplate of God's high priest ? "

He then descended by a flight of steps cut in the turfy side of the rath, and entered the door of the abbot's dwelling. He found the fair Uailsi presiding at a smaller board. Her husband and daughter sat round it, but none of the former guests save Fergus.

" I have arranged," said his host, " that thou and thy companions shall ride with me over our lands, that you may note our husbandry, and visiting some of the villages may see what order reigns in them. We ourselves do not hold them perfect, but Bishop Fergus tells me that he has seen worse on the domains of Clugny."

"We have a hard battle with ignorance," replied the prelate. "And there is a poverty which is permitted to exist for the manifestation of the Christian virtues. It is not by the outward semblance that we may judge of men's spiritual condition."

"Thou speakest truly," replied the abbot. "Yet our experience is that godliness, being in a manner profitable for this life, implants within the rudest breast a love of order which cannot fail to put forth visible blossoms. My wife has asked the friends who were here last night to grace our supper-table again with their presence. I have sought to introduce to thee chiefly those who are of reputation amongst us for their superior attainments."

"I judged as much," replied Tostius.

"I think I shall meet thy wishes," continued the abbot, "if I seek to make thee enter thoroughly into our daily life. We rise with the sun, aroused by the peal of our silver bell, and we begin the day with social worship. Those married men who have houses of their own conduct it in private. The others assemble in the church, where each of the twelve bishops who form our council takes it in turn to officiate. I would have conducted thee thither this morning had I been quite sure that it would be agreeable to thee. We have a short service before sunset, however, when thou wilt be welcome to witness or join in our devotions."

"Excuse me," replied Tostius, looking much embarrassed. "I shall be delighted to enter, as far as I may, into your daily avocations. But I am under vows of strict obedience to my ecclesiastical superiors, and I may not, without soiling my conscience, assist at any act of worship not conducted in an orthodox manner."

The abbot's countenance fell, whilst Uailsi's lip curled with a scornful smile.

"By orthodox," said Mòr, "I presume thou wouldst say whatever has not been sanctioned by the Bishop of Rome?"

"Not so," replied Tostius. "What is affirmed by the decrees of general councils, which ye do not acknowledge."

"For that reason," said Mòr, "we cannot argue the question of our differences with you on fair terms. Our friend here," she continued, glancing at Fergus, "and Bishop Ardal have told us that they frequently formed part of the audience at Catholic services during their travels. Our bishops place no restraint on our making ourselves acquainted with your ways, or entering into the spirit of them as far as our consciences will allow. It is impossible that you should understand us without penetrating into the sanctuaries of our devotion."

"Not so impossible as thou thinkest," replied the prelate. "Those on whom the Almighty has set the visible seal of consecration are gifted with the power of perceiving what others wot not of."

"This discussion is fruitless," said the abbot. "Our guest, perhaps, might like to see some of thy transcriptions."

Mòr stepped lightly to a coffer of black oak, and bringiug from it two volumes encased in embossed leather, opened them out before the prelate.

He crossed himself, and then turned over the leaves with reverence. Raising his eyes from the brilliant letters he fixed them inquiringly on her face.

"Who instructed thee?" he asked.

"My mother," replied Mòr. "It has long been an accomplishment in her family; but I have profited much by the lessons of an aged bishop."

"My daughter," said Uailsi, "is diligent in other good works. She visits the sick and aged, dispensing to them both bodily and spiritual comfort. None of our Daer Ceiles can read the Scriptures for themselves, though some of our bishops hope that the day may come when they will accomplish this. But thou canst not see her at this work."

" Why not ? " asked the prelate.

"Because," replied Mòr, " the essence of it is that it be done in secret. I should do violence to my nature were it otherwise. Besides," she added with a mischievous smile, " would that not be a breaking of thy vows ? "

"How so ? " exclaimed Tostius, starting. " Thou dost not take on thyself to officiate as a priest—to offer the body of our blessed Lord to the common people."

"I do more," replied the maiden. "I offer them Himself —spiritually of course. I do not dispense the sacraments, but yet I engage in religious services."

The prelate remained silent for a few minutes. It seemed as if an abyss of corruption were opening itself up to his view. The canker of error must have eaten very deep when a simple girl could dare to usurp functions that might well be envied by angels. He trembled at the prospect of new revelations.

The day passed away in active exercise. He saw many things of which he understood little, yet he returned to the college with a sense of having witnessed much worldly prosperity.

"I cannot quite comprehend thy position," he said to the abbot, when they were all gathered round the blazing fire. "Thou art not an ordained bishop."

"No," replied his host. "The early Fathers, I believe, made less distinction between the titles of bishop and presbyter than we do. The sainted Columba, to whose clan I belong, had, like Patrick, like Carthagh, Declan, and other founders of monasteries, no higher title than that of presbyter. In memory of him, those of the Cinel Conaill who aspire to the office of abbot neglect to take the episcopal ordination; although they take care to be well qualified for it. It is an anomaly, of course, that a simple presbyter should have rule over bishops ;* but yet it hath the advantage of showing them the rock from whence they were hewn."

"Dost thou dispense the sacraments?" asked Tostius.

"A presbyter may properly do so," replied the abbot. "Thou knowest it well, if thou hast studied the writings of Hilary and of Jerome. Yet our custom confineth the duty to bishops, save in the case of an abbot like myself. My kinsman, Columba, did not scruple to ordain a king."

"You have much liberty of action," said the prelate. "But suppose that the whole of Christendom were in the disjointed condition which your views would impose on it, how would it have been possible to drive the Saracens from the Holy Place?"

"That has sometimes occurred to me," said the abbot. "I must confess there is something glorious in the sight of a Peter and a Bernard summoning hosts of warriors to deliver the faithful from an oppressive bondage."

"Thou speakest well," said Ardal. "No power but that of the Roman bishop could have accomplished it. It is the one thing which reconciles me to the fact of so many having departed from the primitive simplicity of Church government. I would fain hope only for a time—until the great work of beating back the false prophet be accomplished."

"They that take the sword shall perish by the sword," said Maidoc, in a soft whisper.

"Thou hast spoken of primitive simplicity," said the prelate. "But Irenæus, whom you so often quote as one of your spiritual ancestors, was ever ready to show honour to the successor of Peter."

"He may have done so," replied Ardal, "though his homage fell far short of thine. We are far from placing him or any of the Fathers on a level with the Apostles. To me the Church is like an apple tree, whose fruit will have the

* Appendix.

finest flavour in its old age. Consider the matter for a moment. Her first converts came straight out of heathenism; they were habituated to its pernicious customs, and could not expect to equal in knowledge those who had been reared in the fear of God from their infancy. I firmly believe that we have had Irish missionaries who excelled some of the so-called Fathers. And it doth not yet appear what the saints shall be in the latter times."

"Yes," said Fergus. "The true Church is only building. We lay her foundations in the mud of this world; and it will be for after ages to add the polished top-stones. We become more delicate about the quality of our work as we proceed."

"But I have not observed," said Tostius, "that you excel so much in your sacred architecture. You, doubtless, my young friends, have seen the new cathedral on the Thames. Have you aught in Erin to compare with it ? "

" Nay, verily," said the abbot, "although I might point thee to the Rock of Cashel. But Bishop Fergus spoke in a figure. The stones which he would polish are the living ones, the men and women who break bread with us. The Church's foundations are laid very laboriously in our schools."

" And the work requires skill," said Mòr. " It is not so easy to assign to each stone its place, and the chiselling is done by the Almighty Architect. Our part lies in submitting to the process."

" These are beautiful ideas," said Tostius ; "but I fear ye will find that they are fanciful when reduced to practice. The plan of submission to a heaven-appointed Head is a more effectual one."

" Would that it were so ! " said Ardal. " We should not find the work quite so difficult. Your clergy are admirably organized for the end they have in view; but if that end be the raising of the masses, I fear that their success is not equal to their efforts."

" Thou must have faith in God," said the prelate.

"Certainly," replied Ardal, "else we might give in at once. But suppose for an instant that this organisation were a mistake. It will soon have swallowed up all other agencies and be like a huge battering-ram, which, if it be turned in the wrong direction, will work terrible mischief."

"It could not possibly be so," said the prelate.

"But, if it were," persisted Ardal, "it would crush the life out of whole peoples. The souls of men would lie shattered in the track of its wheels."

Bishop Tostius fixed his keen eyes on the speaker. "Take heed to thyself," he said, solemnly, "thou wilt have to answer for the fulfilment of thine own mission; thou hast taken the responsibility in a manner alone."

Ardal's cheek reddened. It was some minutes before he spoke.

"I have done so," he said, "and I have no wish to shift it on to others; but I should have had to answer for more had I refused it."

The prelate next morning bade his kind hosts farewell. The abbot, with a few of the bishops, accompanied him to one of the crosses which marked the verge of their territory; and Tostius grasped their hands with a consciousness that he was no nearer to the object of his mission. The very strains of his choristers, as they chanted their midday anthem, fell mournfully on his ear.

"It must be," he muttered to himself. "That family must be scattered. What chance had I against their united phalanx? Christianus told me that persuasion would fail. But these maidens must at least be snatched as brands from the burning."

"I wonder," said Ardal, as he sat at the cottage door with Amada, "what motive can have impelled that proud man hither. Meseemed as if a hawk were being nourished in our dovecot."

"I saw him once," replied Amada, "and methought he

had a hawk's eye. His coming bodes no good, for all so fair spoken as thou sayest he was. But thou hast doubtless seen many such in thy travels."

"Yea," replied Ardal. "He is a good specimen of an honest priest."

"Honest!" exclaimed Amada. "They know not what honesty is. The man must have been convinced, from what he saw, that our people are doing as much good as if they were walking in his way; yet thou sayest he would not admit it."

"Thou canst not see with his eyes," replied Ardal. "He is shut up, as it were, behind a network of minute rules. Anything that does not fit into the squares of these has no business to exist. There is, in the first place, a barrier to his understanding us in the prohibition to witness our social worship."

"Yea," replied Amada; "they shut their eyes to the light, but all the same they will be judged for not seeing. If I had been the abbot, I should not have been so ready to entertain him."

Ardal could not help smiling. "There are black sheep in every fold of the Saviour's flock," he answered; "but I will not allow that Tostius is one of them. I have a certain esteem for him. I should not wonder if he were nearer the kingdom of heaven than some of our bishops, who, if they hold more correct views, do so in such a cold way that you cannot think their heart is in their work. I admire zeal, though it be in a wrong cause. I would rather that Bishop Tostius tried to convert me. He shows that he thinks me worth something, and is more of a Christian in doing so than if he scorned us as some of his brethren do."

"Thou wilt come to grief with thy charity," said Amada. "I don't want to judge Bishop Tostius any more than I want him to judge me; but I am glad he is gone."

CHAPTER XXII.

Fergus had not formed part of the prelate's escort.   He had
remained at home on the plea of wishing an extra hour for
study.   He soon clambered over the rath, and found his way
into the forest, where he fancied that he would be likely to
meet either with Sorcha or with Mòr.

What was his motive for wishing to meet with Sorcha ?
It was an impulse of which he could give no account.   She
had for ever passed out of his reach ; yet somehow he thought
he might console himself with picturing to himself what
might have been.   He was in a strange humour.   He longed
for the painful bliss of gazing on the beauty he had lost, and
perhaps drawing from its lips a confession of regret, or of
seeing in its eyes a glance of pity.   He was trusting to a
chapter of accidents for the shaping of his resolves.

He walked quickly, devoured by a feverish anxiety.   Other
female forms met his gaze on the turfy highway ; but none
of them had any meaning for him.   Which of the two
beloved ones would present herself?   He almost wished that
fortune would give him the pleasure of troubling Ardal's
serenity.

At length he discerned the gleam of a white veil in the
distance, crowning a form remarkable for its straightness.   It
approached with a gliding motion, different from the heavy
lumbering swing of a peasant.   Fergus sat on a fallen pine
log, and fixed his eyes on a parchment scroll.

He could hear his own heart beat. The stillness seemed to grow more intense, and the soft earth failed to carry to his ear the sound of any footfall.

He at length ventured to look straight before him. No figure was there.

Fergus passed his hand over his eyes. The suspense was getting intolerable. To smother it he began repeating to himself the third canto of the Iliad.

He had only got as far as the descent of Iris, when a clear, cheerful voice exclaimed, " Bishop O'Flannahan ? "

He looked up, and was conscious of blushing painfully. The bright clear eyes of Mòr were fixed upon him. She came forward as he rose.

" The ground is damp," she observed. " There is little sunlight to dry the dews before midday. What readest thou ? "

" The Iliad !" she exclaimed. " Is that thy favourite book ? "

" It is for the present," replied Fergus. " No, I forgot; there is one that transcends it in beauty as much as a bunch of flowerets lifting their heads in the sunlit dew transcends one that is heavy with nightly showers ; but not always can I get a glimpse of the precious volume."

" What can that be ? " asked Mòr.

" Thou knowest," replied Fergus, looking up in her face with a meaning smile. " Thou canst, when thou wilt, place a seal on it hard as the fissured rock."

" I fear," said Mòr, " that thou hast studied too well the tongue of Provence, which is not altogether in accord with that in use amongst us."

" No, maiden," replied Fergus ; " the tongue that I use hath a tone soft and loud as the winds which sweep through the forest, and hath been in accord with man's soul since the days of Eden. It was spoken when the world was young ; for the sons of God learned to use it towards the daughters of men. It varies its accent in every age, but its grammar is substantially the same."

A faint colour overspread Mòr's cheek. Fergus was quick to detect it.

"Thou hast not gone with our guest this morning," she said. "Methinks he looked with longing eyes on thee and on Bishop Ardal. He would willingly have laid his consecrating hand on thee."

A slight shrinking was discernible in Fergus. "Doubtless," he replied, pursing out his lips in a manner peculiar to himself, "he thinks the young boughs will bend more readily to the south-eastern wind. Our Irish oaks are of a tougher fibre than it liketh him."

"He seemed much startled," continued Mòr, "at the notion of my visits to these villagers. Do the maidens of Italy never read the Holy Book to the unlearned?"

"No," replied Fergus; "their flashing eyes and their coral lips do duty only in discerning and praising the valour of those whose fame rises only in blood, and in urging them to turn their death-giving weapons against the infidel. There are those who delight in deeds of mercy, but these array themselves in dusky attire, withdrawing themselves from the love of man."

"Doth their faith not teach them," said Mòr, "that every Christian had his or her part to bear in the ministry of reconciliation; that we are consecrated priests by the blood which has saved ourselves; that we serve an unseen altar— though for the order of the Church, the dispensation of the sacraments as well as the duty of public teaching is confided to those specially appointed and set apart?"

"All is special in the Catholic system," replied Fergus. "God's gentle laws have been made to appear so hard by it, that most people are satisfied with vicarious merit. But I have reason to rejoice that thou wert born under brighter stars. It would undoubtedly have made a recluse of thee."

"Perhaps that is not such an unhappy life," replied Mòr. "I should have chosen it in preference to the other."

"Yet it is a wretched one in some respects," said Fergus. "Thou wouldst have done thy duty to God no better by being cruel to thy fellow-creatures."

"I hope I should have been cruel to no one," replied Mòr.

Fergus's blue eyes sparkled whilst he looked at her. "To me thou wouldst," he said.

"Why?" asked Mòr, simply.

"Seest thou yonder bush?" said Fergus. "It hath grown crooked, and whilst its leaves cluster thickly on one side, there is little but bare stalks on the other."

"Yea," replied Mòr. "It seeketh to get at the sunlight, and sendeth out its leaves in only one direction."

"Suppose that the golden beam marked it not," said Fergus, "or bent itself so as to fall a few inches aside, would that not be cruel?"

"It would, in sooth," replied Mòr. "But I see not what a hazel-bush hath to do with me."

"There are beams of light in thine eyes," replied Fergus. "Should they mistake the place of their falling, all the green within me must wither and die."

"Thou art a poet," said Mòr. "They who wear the feather robe are privileged. Their words must not be taken as the word of a Brehon."

Fergus stood suddenly still. "How shall I convince thee?" he said. "Mine is the fate of Cassandra, though I prophesy not evil. Wouldst thou have me speak plainly? Mòr, I love thee."

There was intense agitation in his voice. Mòr's eyes were cast down. It was a very sweet surprise to her; yet she feared that her dream might be a troubled one, even when it seemed possible for it to be realised.

"Hast thou asked me of my father?" she said, timidly.

Fergus took her hand. "Listen," he cried, passionately; "I know full well that I have raised my eyes to the downy hues of forbidden fruit. The world would think me no match for a daughter of the Cinel Conaill ; yet thou wilt never find a heart that beats more warmly than mine does."

"We need not ask the world," said Mòr, gently. "My parents' approval would be enough."

"Thou speakest rashly," cried Fergus, holding her hand against his arm. "If the lightest breath carry it to thy father's ears, I am banished from Ardmore."

"Thou doest him wrong," said Mòr. "I will break it to him. He will never cross my wishes, unless they are unreasonable."

"Thou thinkest so," said Fergus, "because he hath been ever kind. But yonder blue rolling sea which carries the fair coracle so lightly can form itself into white swelling billows, which will dash the frail skiff to pieces. I have heard thy father say, when he hath been in the company of one or two men, that he would have no meanly-born churl for a son-in-law, and that he had reared thee to bestow thee in good time on one who would transplant thee to a home as distinguished as that he would pluck thee from. Now," continued Fergus, drawing himself up, "I feel that I could win such a home, if I had the hope of thy blooming in it ; but at this moment thou knowest that it is yet to frame."

The hand which he held trembled. "But if I urge compliance on him," said Mòr, "I know he will not refuse. There is the heart of an humble Christian beneath the lordly one of the Hy-Nialls."

Fergus smiled with some bitterness. "Do it if thou wilt," he said ; "but thou wilt ruin me."

Mòr looked inexpressibly sad.

"Thy candour would cost thee nothing," he continued. "Thy father will say I have won thee with craft; that I have practised on thy ignorance of the world ; and that the honour

in my breast should have reined my tongue. I might bow to
his anger for a while, for we are young enough to wait; but
thy mother's influence would be persistent as the north-
eastern blast—the pride of race is as a blazing fire within
her."

"What dost thou counsel, then?" asked Mòr.

Fergus pressed her hand warmly. "Promise me," he
said, "that thou wilt never breathe a word of it to any one
till the moment that I allow thee."

Mòr looked much distressed. "I can scarcely think," she
said, "that it is lawful to give such a promise. I have never
yet done anything without my parents' knowledge."

"But there is scriptural authority," said Fergus, "for a
woman obeying her husband's wishes before those of her
parents. Has that no reflex effect? I ask thee to show
them no active disobedience. Thou art not called on to
account to them for the employment of every moment. Thy
father's displeasure, were it only temporary, would injure me
beyond hope of reparation. Though his power be nominally
curtailed by the council of the twelve fathers, thou knowest
that he is practically a despot with regard to those bishops
who have not yet received charges. And I have not, like
Ardal, powerful friends on whom I can fall back."

"But his opposition is only suspected," said Mòr. "We
have done nothing to find out if it exist. It hardly looks
like treating him fairly."

The tears were now rolling down her cheeks. Fergus
could not resist kissing them away.

"Beauteous one," he said; "be not so like to a rill-
washed rock. If thou love me thou must trust me. Thinkest
thou that I would ask thee to do it without urgent reason?"

"Thou wouldst not," replied Mòr. "But it seemeth
hard."

"Few people find their path otherwise," said Fergus.
"Our love is something worth suffering for."

Mòr walked on quietly by his side. The hour had come of which she had been foolishly dreaming; and there was a very bitter drop in the cup of nectar which was being held to her lips. She had expected some conflicts with her mother; but she could have better nerved herself to brave them than to carry out a plan of concealment. She had imagined herself a very Heloïse in self-denying constancy; now it seemed as if she were playing the part of a coward.

"But perhaps he is right," she thought. "I have no business to endanger his prospects by my scruples. It will be only for a short time, until he can offer me a settled home; and something may meanwhile occur to change the course of things. But I can never look either of my parents straight in the face. Would it not have been nobler in Fergus to have waited a few months? Ah! but then I might have lost him."

She returned home, happy, yet troubled. She started when her mother spoke to her, and replied in subdued accents. Had any one cared to notice her, they would have seen that there was a change in her manner when at the midday meal. She was no longer the fearless girl who seemed to have inherited the pride of a hundred generations; she had a gentle address, a demeanour which made her more womanly; yet her beaming eyes had lost half their brightness. There was a pathetic tenderness in them which appealed for sympathy. Her mother noticed it, but attributed it to her disappointment about Ardal.

"I wish thou wouldst try to be livelier, Mòr," she said. "Bishop Fergus was very witty to-day; thou mightest have laughed a little."

"Laughed I not, mother?" asked Mòr.

"In a most quiet way," replied Uailsi. "I love not to see thy face ripple with levity, but I wish thee not to appear less sprightly than Sorcha. She is getting more dignity than thou hast. She is only a spouse as yet, and thou art the abbot's daughter. Thou hast, perhaps, borne thyself too loftily in the past."

"I have no regrets about Ardal," replied Mòr. "Indeed, I feel not as if I could have loved him now, had he been my suitor. And if my dignity frightened him, is there no danger of its having the same effect on another?"

"Yea, my child," replied Uailsi. "I should like thy manner of to-day had a proper suitor been present, though thou mightest well exert thyself a little more in that case. Humility hath a charm which is too fine to throw away on our every-day company. Thou must not show it to the men of Ardmore."

"But thou knowest," said Mòr, "that I can only be what I am. I must be myself, whatever company I am in."

Uailsi sighed, and murmured more than ever against the fate which had fixed her daughter's lot so far from a royal court.

Days slipped past, but brought little change with them. Mòr felt herself enveloped in the incense-cloud of flattery. Her secret misgivings were amply compensated by her lover's ceaseless homage. From the time of her uprising until the shadows gathered over the evening sky, he managed to make her feel his presence in a thousand delicate ways, and oftentimes they met to hold sweet converse about their past and their future.

The whole current of Mòr's nature ran into a new channel. She counted the hours till she could be alone with the man to whom she had unwittingly surrendered her freedom of action; she hung on his glance as the opening rose watches for the unveiling of the sunshine. She wondered how, with him near her, she could ever have been induced to think of Ardal. As a closer intercourse made her better acquainted with his intellectual gifts, she found fresh cause for rejoicing that she had become a sharer in them. Ardal was accomplished, but he lacked the glitter and sparkle of Fergus. Mòr

was not aware that some men pay women a higher compliment by their esteem than others could possibly do by
their love.

Yet there were times in the loneliness of the night when
Mòr felt that all was not as it should be. She had intended
to be a submissive spouse, but she had never dreamed of
carrying her obedience to the length which Fergus exacted
from her. Had she been a convert to the Romish system,
having bowed to the power of the keys, whilst keenly alive to
the sin of Mariolatry, she could not have been more perplexed. It was hard for her to understand why people
should choose crooked ways for attaining their objects. Mòr
loved the straight road. It might be harder and less picturesque at times, but it had milestones which made it impossible for the stupidest to lose their way on it. "My
parents might have been in the wrong had they forbidden
our union," she thought; "but I cannot bear the idea of our
acting unjustly to them. I must have another talk with
Fergus about it."

"Thou hast known Amada long," she remarked, as they
were wandering in the woods together.

"Yea," replied her lover. "She had an hospitable house
while her husband lived, and we were their near neighbours."

"Were they not very poor," asked Mòr, "before her
daughter married Mael-Patrick?"

"Yes," replied Fergus. "They were like the mists that
lie at the bottom of yonder valley. The wind of fortune
hath raised them to sunnier slopes, or rather, I should have
said, Amada's own wit. She hath a scheming brain."

Mòr opened her eyes very wide. "I never heard that
Amada bore such a character," she replied.

"It may be that I speak too strongly," said Fergus;
"yet hath she known how to place herself before the breeze
of prosperity. Witness how well she hath managed for
Sorcha. Grainné is fashioned after her likeness, but she

hath a deeper tint of worldliness. I fancy it is she who hath arranged this match with Ardal."

"Then," said Mòr, smiling, "she hath done better for her sister's child than for herself. Olrud hath no admirere."

"She married him," replied Fergus, "at the moment when the blasts of misfortune threatened to drive them into ruin. They would never have come together under the soft gales of happiness. As it is, the heaven of their married life is as full of quarrels as was that of Olympus."

"Is it possible?" exclaimed Mòr, startled.

"In a bishop's household," said Fergus. "Thinkest thou that it would be possible for us?"

A warm pressure of the hand accompanied this question.

"I trust not," said Mòr. "But how knowest thou this?"

"It was on all tongues at Inisfallen," replied Fergus. "I have been told that they were as the struggling waves at the mouth of the Suir. They have blended together now, but thou canst trace the marks of the conflict on their faces, especially on Olrud's. He is like a cliff that has weathered many storms."

"He hath wrinkles enough," observed Mòr; "but I thought they were natural to him, his sister Sigurda having the same. But I had thought better of Grainné."

There was silence for a few minutes. Then Mòr spoke—

"Knowest thou that I am very unhappy sometimes?"

"Thou, my blooming one!" exclaimed Fergus.

"Because of my parents," continued Mòr. "Wilt thou not let me tell them of our love?"

Her eyes were streaming with tears. A dark frown gathered over Fergus's face. He let go her hand.

"Thou lovest me not," he said, sullenly.

"Thou art unkind to say so," replied Mòr. "Would I seek these lonely paths with thee if I did not? And have I not borne day after day the pain of feeling like a hypocrite, all for thy sake?"

"Then I will tell thee," said Fergus, "that thou mayest unbosom thyself this night, if thou wilt, and thou wilt be content, for thou shalt never see me again."

Mòr grasped his arm convulsively. He walked more quickly, as if seeking to get away from her.

"Listen," she said, panting for breath. "Fergus, thou usest me like a child. Thou wouldst have me obey thee—and thou knowest if I have done it—yet thou givest me no reason for anything."

There was a tone of keen reproach in her voice. Fergus felt it; he slackened his pace.

"Thou art not resolved to tell it?" he said.

"No," replied Mòr. "I but asked thee to think if we might not risk it."

"I am willing to give thee up," he said, "much as I love thee; for I know it were vain for thee to try and be happy without trusting me."

"I do trust thee," replied Mòr, drying her tears, "but I am weak and foolish sometimes. I cannot help asking for a reason."

"I must not tell thee everything," replied Fergus. "I am sure of its coming right soon, but thou must let me judge when and how to make the disclosure. Meanwhile, however, I will let thee try an experiment."

"What is it?" asked Mòr, eagerly.

"I would not tell thee of it," he said, "if I felt not sure of thy love. Speak of me before either of thy parents in the light of a suitor for some one else. Perhaps thou wilt learn something from what they say."

There was a shade of melancholy on his face. Mòr felt ashamed of herself.

"I will not try it," she said; "but I will cease murmuring."

Fergus replaced her hand on his arm, and they walked homewards.

CHAPTER XXIII.

It was a calm Sabbath afternoon, and the family of Ardmore were enjoying the season of quiet secured for them by the strict laws of their Church; for the Irish of that day understood the Fourth Commandment as literally as did the children of Israel. All unnecessary work was postponed, and wherever a man was on Saturday night, there must he remain until Monday morning. Strong arms, nimble fingers, and active brains were refreshed by full exposure to the breezes which thus periodically blew upon them from the spiritual Eden.

A few hours before sunset Sorcha enveloped herself in an ample *brat*, or mantle of dark wool bordered with green tartan, and fastened on the left shoulder by a silver, gem-studded brooch. Her brown locks peeped from beneath the gaudily-embroidered veil of white linen, which, falling on her neck, left her sweet face exposed.

" Whither goest thou, child ? " asked Amada.

" He waiteth for me outside," she replied, in a tone just loud enough to reach her grandmother's ear.

" Who ? Bishop Ardal ? " exclaimed the latter.

" Yes," replied Sorcha, with a blushing smile.

She had only been gone a few minutes when Olrud returned from a service which had been held amongst the fishermen on the beach.

He was followed by another figure, habited likewise in a

clerical mantle, but presenting as great a contrast to him as could well be imagined.

It was that of a round little man, with ruddy hair and bluish-grey eyes. His complexion had a tinge of pink in it, and his whole person was suggestive of genial good nature. His hands, which were soft and delicate, were constantly employed in adjusting some part of his apparel. He approached Amada.

"Dost thou recollect me?" he asked, with a peculiarly smooth roll in his voice.

"Yea," she answered, gazing at him for a few minutes, "I do—Bishop Heremon O'Mullaney."

"The same," he answered, shaking her hand warmly. "It is long since we have met. I had heard indeed that thou wert settled at Ardmore, but my duties have not led me hither. And this is Grainné. She is much changed, much improved, I should say, since I saw her under her father's roof. Poor Rossa!"

"I cannot return the compliment," said Grainné, with her usual dignity. "Thou art the same as thy image in my memory."

Bishop Heremon laughed in a soft, pleasant way. There was merriment, but no twinkle in his small eyes. "They tell me I wear well," he said, with complacency, sinking down on the end of one of the couches, whose height scarcely allowed of his little feet touching the ground.

"Thou hast had no heavy trials, I may hope," said Amada, "else thou wouldst look a little less fresh."

"Yea, but I have," said Heremon. "I have been married, and am now alone with nine children. Poor Monenna! she was indeed a treasure! It was well for thee that I saw her," he continued, glancing roguishly at Olrud. "I was on my way to Rossa's when it happened—indeed I was."

"Perhaps," remarked Grainné, with a slight smile, "I may think that it was well for me too."

"Thou art a wicked fairy," said Heremon, shrugging his dapper little shoulders. "I must confess that thou art unchanged in some respects."

"Thou art one of the Ardmore family," said Olrud. "Why, then, wert thou not here on Declan's birthday?"

"It was a long journey," replied Heremon; "and I thought it not worth my while. There are plenty of bishops to be seen any day, without travelling forty miles. As for hearing Fergus and Ardal, I expect to see them in my village ere long; and I can get more of any man's mind over a shell of ale than by listening to him for hours."

"Thou must know, Bishop Heremon," said Sigurda, "that Amada's grand-daughter is espoused to the princely Ardal."

"Is it possible?" exclaimed the stranger, with a burst of geniality. "I congratulate thee," he said, turning to Grainné.

"Sorcha is not my child," replied the matron, quietly; "she is my sister Moriath's."

"Alas!" exclaimed Heremon, with a sentimental inflection of the voice which was meant for condolence. Poor Moriath! I rejoice that she hath left a precious memento of herself."

".Now," said Olrud, "that we may spend our time to profit, let me read to you from one of the Gospels."

"I recollect," said Heremon, rising, "that I have arranged to study for an hour with a brother bishop. I must see thy grand-daughter another day. Farewell! God bless you all!"

Bowing to the company in a very consequential manner, he strutted out of the cottage.

"Where hast thou picked up that specimen?" asked Grainné, after her husband had closed the door.

"I met him wandering about," replied Olrud. "He accosted me, and seemed acquainted with my name. Then he asked me to bring him to thy mother."

"She is honoured by his thinking of her," said Grainné. "He came about us oftentimes when I was a child, and I never could behold him without laughing. I sometimes feared he would notice it."

"How doth he preach?" asked Olrud.

"I am hardly a fair judge," replied Grainné, "as I have heard him but once. But I recollect that I liked him not. He had an oiliness in his speech that made it sound unreal. Wouldst thou trust him as a spiritual guide, mother?"

"I would not listen to him for the world," replied Amada. "It would be worse than starvation; it would be the pretence of being fed. Nay, but I am not down to the husks yet."

The two lovers, meanwhile, had seated themselves on a fallen tree.

"I wonder where Bishop Tostius is to-day?" remarked Sorcha.

"Vexing his soul about us, perchance," said Ardal. "It is painful to think of the masses he will say for our conversion. With all his faults, he is thoroughly in earnest."

"Hast thou known many like him?" asked Sorcha.

Ardal rested his head for a moment on his hand, looking very thoughtful. "I would fain tell thee," he said, "some of the circumstances that have led me to a close acquaintance with Romish priests."

"They would naturally be objects of interest to thee," replied Sorcha, "during thy wanderings."

"Too much so," replied Ardal, in a tone of deep melancholy. "Yet is it surprising that when we come to live with people whom we have been accustomed to consider as opponents, we find them very like ourselves after all? It is not so much a difference of views, or of doctrines, that we have to fight against, as it is a whole atmosphere of thought which we have to change. Truly Satan hath been well named the prince of the power of the air. Transplant one of our hardy Dalecassian warriors to the vineyards of Sicily, and he will

soon become as lazy and luxurious as any to the manner
born.   There are things in my own experience that I much
regret, and some that seem to me now like a dream.   But
thou wilt understand me better when I have told thee of
them."

Ardal spoke thickly, not without a tremor. Sorcha listened
breathlessly.   She placed her hand within his, yet his eyes
were downcast as he continued—

" My stay in Paris did not impress me favourably with the
working of the Catholic system.   I saw too clearly what a
distinct line of demarcation it was drawing between the
Church and the world.   But I was in some doubt as to
whether I had attributed this effect to its true cause.   For
my intercourse with the Cistercians of England had taught
me that there are simple earnest men within the Romish
fold.   So I determined to study monasticism at its most
renowned centres.

" I spent but one night at Citeaux, for I was consumed by
a feverish desire to press forward into those solitudes where
it seemed as if nations had been born again by the preaching
of a simple monk.   ' Can these dry bones live ? ' one might
well have asked, looking at the spiritual state of Gaul before
Bernard entered Citeaux.   Yet within a year he had not only
covered Western Europe with his new foundations, but he had
stirred society to its centre. Kings, nobles, peasants, were crying out with one voice: ' What must we do to be saved ? '

"No sooner did I make known my intention of visiting
Clairvaux, than the Abbot Gillebertus gave me a letter of
recommendation to its newly-appointed abbot, Poncius.
Thou mayest have heard of him.   His highest praise is that
he hath caught some of the spirit of the noble Bernard. I felt
that under the roof of his monastery some of the chief ends
of my mission might be attained. After several days' journey,
I reached the valley of Wormwood. It was nightfall. I had
ridden for miles along the banks of the Aube, and the moon-

light was streaming peacefully through the tender foliage of the beech trees. The cloudless sky was aglow with stars, and as the low walls of the convent rose before me, bathed in a silvery splendour, I could not help imagining that the cloud of the Divine Presence had rested on them as once on Sinai. The first sight of them overawed me. For had they not been the home of something mightier than even the warm heart and great intellect of their founder, the whole of Europe could never have throbbed as it did to the sound of the words spoken there. A cross of flame flickered above the chapel tower; throwing a fitful light on the well-trodden turf before the chief entrance. The clank of our horses' hoofs seemed an intrusion as it resounded through the darkness. Our guide, after ringing a bell, led us through a dark passage into a courtyard flagged with stones; from the further end of which a flight of steps led up to the façade of a handsome church.

"'Salve, frater, in Jesu Cristo,' said the white-robed monk who laid hold of my bridle.

"'Salve, frater carissime!' answered I, delivering to him my commendatory letter. Seeing the superscription, he placed it to his lips, and, crossing himself, beckoned to me to follow. He led me through a smaller courtyard, surrounded by an open arcade, the wall of which, pierced by numerous cell windows, was adorned by bright pictures painted on fresco. I had no time to examine them, for I soon found myself in a high-roofed chamber, surrounded with benches of carved oak fixed into the whitened walls.

"The monk laid down the light he was carrying. 'Wilt thou wait a moment?' he said to me, in the common Frankish tongue. He disappeared through another door, by which some white-robed monks soon entered.

"There was an air of distinction about them which my guide had lacked. The pale massive features and grey hairs of the foremost made me guess before whom I stood. Making a low reverence, I announced in Latin my name and errand.

"'Thou art welcome,' he replied, in the speech of Provence. 'The countrymen of Marianus and of Columbanus are no strangers to us. We have appointed thee a dormitory, being apprised of thy coming; for we hope that thou wilt honour us by a long visit.'

"He had most beautiful black eyes, the finest I think I have ever seen. Thou must not smile, Sorcha, they were not unlike thine own brown ones, only they had not such long fringes; and could change very swiftly from a lustrous meekness to an eagle-like penetration. His head was bald, save for a close-cropped fringe of greyish hair at the back of the tonsure; and his whole countenance bespoke an intellectual force which might have made me think of Socrates, were it not for the traditional story that the sage of Athens was of grotesque visage. Not so the abbot Poncius. He had an arm which might have wielded the club of Hercules; yet his cheek was thin and sunken from the effect of long vigils. There was self-denial and determination written in its pinched *contour.*

"Tired as I was, I scarcely slept that night. The dormitory, situate in the roof, had a window from which I could behold the sunrise over the wide expanse of beech forest; not weird and mystic as our Irish ones often are, but clothed in a soft loveliness that seemed to speak of heavenly peace. Ever and anon would the chime of bells break in upon my musings. These were to call the monks to prayer, and to the singing of hymns in which the story of the Saviour's sufferings is most touchingly set forth. There was something sublime in such incessant devotion. The children of Bernard, as sentinels on the high places of Christendom, are never permitted to slumber at their posts.

"I stayed there three months. I need not describe to thee all the life I led. It is enough to say that I formed spiritual friendships. There was abundant opportunity for those who feared the Lord to converse together. For though silence was rigidly enforced in the refectory, the rule enjoying it was waived between vespers and compline. Then we wandered in couples through the cloisters. In the cool of the evening, after the dews had fallen, I often discussed the things of the Kingdom with Poncius, and with his deposed predecessor, the learned Gavfridus.

"It was sweet to feel that they were one with me in Christ. They thought that there might be some little value in our orders, such as springs from the recognition of good men ; but they regretted much that we could not be gathered into the Catholic fold. Their faith in the authority of Peter was so firm, so sincere, that it partly shook my incredulity. Perhaps it was the attraction of the abbot's strong will, perhaps it was real conviction ; but thou must know, Sorcha, that at times I felt ready to submit utterly to the claims of Rome.

"Thou must not blame me," continued Ardal, sighing. "Why, with the Scriptures in my hands, thou wilt say, could I hesitate? But God has other epistles, Sorcha, than those written of old with pen and ink. The impress of His finger is still to be seen on loving hearts. Such an one was Poncius. He was visibly stamped with the seal of consecration ; it was on his brow, and lent a dignity to every movement of his sinewy hands. When such men die, methinks their features will scarcely change in expression when touched by the light of heaven.

"There might not be such a fallacy in Peter's claim, after all. It had not been preferred by himself, for grace had at length made him modest ; but his immediate followers were inspired to see it with a clearer eye. At all events the claim was early acknowledged. Poncius and Gavfridus did not repel me as those do who say there cannot be salvation out of their Church. ' No,' they argued, ' thou art Catholic already by virtue of thy baptism into the Triune Name. The day will come when thou, as well as all God's other children, will receive grace to confess this publicly.'

"Then they had the love of literature. Gavfridus, though deposed on account of the dissensions which arose under his rule, is the author of a most beautiful work on the Song of Solomon, and is highly appreciated by the very men who would not submit to him as abbot. I had fortified myself with the thought that our system favoured the cultivation of the intellect, whilst the Catholic one tended to stunt it ; but I was informed that at Monte Cassino and at Clugny I should find libraries second to none in Ireland. Transcriptions were continually going on, even at Clairvaux; the Gospels in Jerome's translation were being multiplied by hundreds, and some of them were adorned with devices that are inferior in beauty only to our own."

"But were there Frankish ones ?" asked Sorcha.

"I doubt it," replied Ardal. "Heathen writers, historians, poets, were held in high esteem ; and I was myself permitted to copy some whose works are not generally known.

"There is a longing for union amongst all visible things. Living matter runs through the trees, percolating from root to twig, and finding its highest expression in foliage and in flower. But when the first frost of winter touches the leaves, snapping the tie which binds them to the stem, whither do these lovely children of the forest go ? Whither but to the bosom of the kind mother earth, from which they originally sprang, who has all along been nourishing them though they knew it not ? They mingle again with her common clay, they are part of herself. Not a brook that trickles through the forest, not a dewdrop that hangs from yonder grass-blades, but is working its way back to the waters of the mighty world-embracing ocean. The very vapours that float in the sky gather in ever-growing masses till they are ready to pour their blessing on us. If it be so in the natural world, shall it be otherwise with the trees of God's planting ; with the rills of heavenly grace which trickle through human hearts to the ocean of love around His throne ? They all seek to rest there ;

but as they wend their way over the rough stones or through the peaceful plains, is it so very wonderful that many of them would like to flow together? The solitary mountain streamlet may be beautiful, but it is neither so glorious nor so beneficent as the mighty river which bears the ships on its bosom. And when two waters approach each other nearly, both bound to the same bourne, their mutual attraction is almost irresistible.

"Day by day I felt this. It seemed like a sin, like a vexing of the Redeemer, this refusal to commemorate His death with those who I felt sure were His children. The corruptions of the Catholic Church became more faint as I looked at them; the more faint, perhaps, because at Clairvaux they were not obtruded on my view. Repeated arguments with Gavfridus made me think that our disputes are more about words than about things. We also have accustomed ourselves to language that is very misleading."

" I know not of what thou speakest," said Sorcha.

" For example," replied her lover, " after the prayer of thanksgiving over the sacred bread, do we not say that the officiating minister has made the body of Christ ? We mean it in a spiritual sense, as Sedulius and Duns Scotus have shown,* yet a stranger who heard it might marvel that we did not forthwith bend our knees in adoration."

" Thou speakest truly," said Sorcha.

"From this carelessness of speech many errors have arisen," continued Ardal. " I have met Irishmen who believed that Cuthbert was really succoured by angels, when we all know that the mistake arose from the custom of calling a helpful man by a celestial title. We speak of the cross of Christ saving us, although we believe that there is no healing efficacy in anything but in the touch of the great Sufferer Himself. Most Romish errors may be traced back to such negligences of speech. And the power of men like Poncius increases every day. They are the true salt of their com-

* Appendix.

munion. I believe they will be the means in God's hand of a great reform."

"But I wander from my tale. One day, walking through the cloisters in the cool of the evening, when the western sky was aflame with the glories of sunset, I could not help expressing my earnest longing to partake of the sacred cup with those good men. There was a craving within me for Christian fellowship. I had not known it since leaving England, for, compared to that of others, Fergus's love had seemed cold."

"Did he share thy views?" asked Sorcha.

"I had left him at Clugny," replied Ardal. "I felt myself very unworthy. I had done nothing towards the fulfilment of my high resolves. I had been puffed up with vanity, and had sought my own glory whilst I imagined that I was doing Christ's work. I even doubted whether I had received a true call. 'Perhaps the Catholics are right,' I thought; 'perhaps there is no valid ordination out of their Church.'

"'But how can the authorised dispensers of God's grace teach so many false doctrines?' thou wilt ask. I had been disarmed even of this weapon; for I found in Poncius and Gavfridus men who, like Bernard, were keenly alive to the presence of errors and of corruptions. 'The Church only bears with these for a time,' they said; 'they are no part of her real teaching. She has human clay to work with, and thou art well aware that whatever man touches bears the stain of his sins. If this is so in the natural world, if the crystal raindrop become impure by its contact with earth, if the sod which hath been pressed by a human foot be less fresh than that around it, shall we expect spiritual gifts to suffer no change by being housed in human hearts? Thine own Church hath erred in a thousand ways. The fire kindled by Patrick and Bridget hath been suffered to burn low. You have no longer the same missionary zeal; for your right arms are becoming palsied through your long separation from the heart of Christendom.

"'The Church makes no claim to perfection. Her authority is not bound up with the holiness of her rulers. She is but an earthly temple, but she hath the sure promise that in her, and in no other, the voice of God shall be heard—a voice that may shelter her chief pillars, but which shall always reach some ear sanctified for its reception. There are those within her, even now, who cry aloud day and night for her purification.'"

Ardal spoke with much emotion. "I cannot make thee appreciate my feelings, Sorcha," he said. "It was as if a family who had been my hereditary enemies had taken me into their counsel. Canst thou forgive me, Sorcha, for cherishing the wish to become one of them?

"It was thus that Poncius explained the Church's toleration of error. 'She hath employed,' he said, 'the wisdom of the serpent in her dealings with those false religions which she hath displaced. For even as the Milesian conquerors of thine own island incorporated amongst themselves the remnants of the vanquished Tuath-de-Danaans, so hath the Church embodied in her practice, though not in her teaching, many customs and ceremonies of heathenism.'

"'But hath she not erred in so doing?' I asked. 'Hath she not polluted the fountain of truth?'

"'Nay,' replied Poncius; 'these old faiths preserved in men's minds an element of reverence which it were not well to uproot with violence. Some of them had enshrined the precious remains of a primitive revelation; and God willeth not to quench the smoking flax. Thine own Church hath done the same; she too hath approved superstition.'

"'How so?' I asked.

"'Doth she not tolerate the fires of Beltain?' replied Poncius. 'And hath not the holy Bridget, with wise foresight, appointed her own nuns to watch over the virgin-guarded fire of the Druids at Kildare? * Hast thou not thyself

* Appendix.

17

told me how she fanned it into a national beacon symbolical of the new light that had arisen on the world ? In this she bowed to expediency, strengthening her empire over men's minds by laying hold of what was already precious in their sight. Yet these things, like the polygamy of the Hebrew patriarchs, are but for a time. A few more turns of the sand-glass and they will be swept from the temple.'"

" But how did he explain the sacrifice of the mass ? " asked Sorcha.

" In truth," replied Ardal, "my thoughts dwelt not on what I had been taught to loathe in it. The most repulsive object will lose its ugliness when we handle it daily. Even the snakes of other lands may become our familiar companions."

" Like the serpent sin," suggested Sorcha.

" Even so," replied Ardal. " I know not how it was," he continued. " I was very anxious about the validity of my own ministrations. If there were any truth in the Pope's claim, if he alone could give authority to dispense the sacraments, why should I not seek to obtain it from his servants ?

" ' The Church is tender to weak consciences,' suggested Poncius, when he found that I hesitated. ' She requireth implicit obedience from all who range themselves in her army ; yet are there times when the accomplishment of some great design sanctions some modification of her rules. She hath not scrupled to approve the sudden elevation of a layman to the rank of Archbishop of Canterbury. Thy aim, as well as hers, is the saving of immortal souls. If thou wouldst feel better equipped for this great work by receiving her mandate, I am ready to procure it for thee.'

" ' But I know not what price is to be paid for it,' I replied. ' I must submit to the discipline of the Church of Patrick, though that indeed hath been but loosely wielded. If I receive from one of your bishops the authority of a priest, you must ask me for no service that would tend to subvert the power of my native communion.'

"'It is for no political reason,' replied Poncius, 'that I offer thee this. It is merely in order that with a free con·science thou mayest again go forth to the conflict with evil. The Church of Erin is but a branch of the Catholic Church; we would fain effect her recognition, not her subversion. I have already written to Avignon on the subject. Thou knowest that I am in favour there, having been commissioned to carry the pallium to the royal Henry, Archbishop of Rheims, the brother of our King. As for the vows of celibacy, these are more a matter of expediency than of strict legality. They are even now waived in Sweden and Iceland. There is no formula for them in the service of consecration. If thou wilt, thou canst wear both tonsures.'

"The reply came from Rome. 'We have confidence in thy judgment,' it said to Poncius. 'The young man of whom thou speakest may be a chosen instrument for the bringing back of the Isle of Saints. Thou mayest leave it to his honour to make a fitting use of the gift which he will receive from us.'"

"And thou hast submitted to be re-ordained!" exclaimed Sorcha, with a look of melancholy surprise.

"I marvel not at thy amazement," replied Ardal, with a forced smile. "The mistakes are endless which we may fall into by looking more at ourselves than at the Saviour.

"I had not to pass through the minor orders. It was considered that I was already a deacon. The Bishop of Langres did not consecrate me, although Clairvaux lies in his diocese. Poncius preferred asking this service from the Archbishop of Rheims, who had begun his religious life as a monk of the monastery. 'It was meet,' he said, 'that the royalty of France should consecrate the royalty of Erin to a more humble submission to the Prince of Peace.'

"When Prince Henry's hand rested on my head, those of the other priests being outstretched above it, a something seemed to speak to me amidst the solemn silence—as if it were from no human lips that I was for the second time receiving authority to consecrate the mysterious elements of the Lord's Supper. This of course sprang from the satisfaction of the flesh. I now know that in taking up a human staff I was forsaking my true guide.

"My eyes were not opened whilst I remained at Clairvaux; but at Clugny I met with more worldly ecclesiastics. Poncius had promised that the fact of my reconsecration should not be revealed unless I myself found it expedient to allow it. During my stay in Provence I was much troubled in mind, and at Rome I met with a Greek priest.

"He was there to look after several members of his flock who had emigrated to the Eternal City. I was surprised to learn that the adherents of his communion far exceeded in numbers those of the Latin one. This fact deprives the latter of its claim to universality. He laughed at the notion of Peter's prerogative, and quoted the writings of Chrysostom in confutation of it. He also drew my attention to an explanation of Jerome, whom the Romans consider a great authority. Jerome says : 'Our Lord declares, " On *this* Rock I will found My Church," because Peter had said, " Thou art the Christ, the Son of the Living God. On this Rock, which thou hast confessed," He declares, "I will build My Church;" for Christ was the Rock on whose foundation Peter himself was built. For other foundation can no man lay than that which is laid, which is Christ Jesus.'

"Then it flashed on me that I had made a mistake. I would give worlds to undo it!" exclaimed the young bishop, pressing his hand to his forehead, where the blue veins were swollen with intense anxiety. "I had consented to wear a chain which is an unworthy fetter on Christ's freemen. I had sinned against the Holy Ghost by doubting the efficacy of His call."

"But there is forgiveness with Him," said Sorcha, softly. "Of course thou hast sought it ? "

Ardal heaved a deep sigh; then, taking her fair hand affectionately between his, he replied—

"Yea, but I have felt deeply humbled. In one only way can I retrieve my error; and that is by resisting the advance of the oppressor with my whole soul. Sorcha, art thou willing to aid me in the conflict?"

A flash of humour was darted from the brown eyes. "Am I not doing so," she answered, "in consenting to be thy wife?"

"I have taken no harsh vow," said her lover.

"Even hadst thou done so," said Sorcha, "it would have been thy duty to break it. Thinkest thou that what thou hast told me will have any effect on thy future career?"

"It would hurt me with my brethren were they to hear of it," replied Ardal. "I will make a public confession should it come to be bruited, explaining how deep my repentance has been."

"Doth Fergus know it?" said Sorcha.

"I feel sure that he doth not," replied Ardal. "He would have made a jest of it ere this, if he had. And he would be tempted to bring it forward now, if he thought it would be a means of separating us."

"Then think no more of it," said Sorcha, rising and gently kissing his troubled brow. "Let us go home and console my grandmother for our absence."

"My sweet one!" said Ardal, drawing her arm within his, "I visited Clairvaux on my return from Provence, that I might make known to Poncius the change in my views. And I have got rid of a burden since I have found courage to confess this to thee. It will never trouble me more."

"No," replied Sorcha, tripping lightly by his side. "Only the recollection of it will make us more indulgent in our judgment of others."

"It should make us see also," said Ardal, "how great is the influence of Christian character. Poncius won me first by

his consistent walk and by his genuine lovableness, before
he plied me with arguments."

"I wish Bishop Olrud could see that," said Sorcha.   "But
we fail so often ourselves, that we have little right to judge
him. Yet methinks that, if I had heard no teaching but his,
I should have been quite ready to imbibe error, if it came
to me in a cloud of sweet fragrance."

"The failings of good men," observed Ardal, "have done
more harm to the cause of truth than has all the malice
of wicked ones.' 'What are these wounds in Thy hands?'
we ask of the Redeemer. 'Those,' He answers, 'with which
I was wounded in the house of My friends.'"

On approaching the cottage they encountered Olrud, his
dark visage seeming longer than usual. Sorcha, on seeing
him, disengaged herself from Ardal, and passed swiftly into
the shelter of the doorway.

"I trust, brother," said Olrud, "that thou hast spent these
hours profitably."

"There is much to tempt the eye in God's universe," replied Ardal. "But our hearts are like harps which, if well
tuned, may be so kept in the right key that all outward
things may be worked up by them into pleasing harmonies.
Distractions present themselves to us in the very pulpit, as
thou very well knowest."

"Not I," said Olrud; "I regard not the face of man when
there."

"I, on the contrary," observed Ardal, "could not speak
well did I not study the looks of my audience. Shall an
archer avert his gaze from the quarry when he shoots?"

"It were well," said Olrud, "that in thy leisure hours
thou wouldst not remove thy thoughts so far from the quarry
as to blunt thine arrows."

"I am unconscious of doing so," replied Ardal.

"What conclusion," said Olrud, "will thy hearers of the
morning draw from thy conduct this afternoon? Pardon me,

I am a blunt man; I must needs be faithful, though risking the loss of thy friendship."

"My conscience is in this case satisfied," replied Ardal. "I have in no way transgressed against the spirit of the commandment."

Olrud shook his head portentously as they passed together into the cottage.

Amada gazed uneasily at her future grandson. She divined, however, from his troubled look that her intended reproof had been forestalled, and the instinctive reverence she bore to him made her loth to humble him before a man whom she considered his inferior: she therefore said nothing.

But her silence threw a constraint over the supper-table. Grainné alone seemed unaffected by it: she broached a delicate subject.

"You two," she said, "have had full time to form your plans. I should not be so presumptuous as to inquire about them, were it not that I would fain know if it be worth while for me to return home. Have you fixed the date of your wedding?"

Ardal's grave face broke into a sunny smile. Even Olrud's muscles relaxed themselves as he glanced inquiringly at the blushing Sorcha.

"In truth, we have not," replied Ardal. "But thou doest us a service by forcing us to be precise. Methinks thy mother's comfort should be first considered. The place of our abode will be determined by that of my future ministry. There are several vacant charges under the care of Ardmore, and methinks the men of Youghal may be ready to choose me as their bishop."

"Is Fergus not a rival candidate?" asked Grainné.

"He might be," replied Ardal, "if he seeketh not a wider field."

"Nay," said Grainné, "if the Ardmore fathers place him ot at Waterford, a little flock would suit him. They would be too humble to restrain his wanderings. He may make himself more talked of as a bishop at Youghal than at Waterford."

"Thou thinkest that he will visit many sheepfolds in place of tending his own flock," said Olrud.

"Yea," replied Grainné. "I grant that he is a star; but he is more like one of those which traverse the heavens with a trail of light, than of those that twinkle in their set place. His mind is a brilliant but not a fertile one. He would be in danger of repeating himself had he always the same audience."

Ardal darted a penetrating glance at the speaker. It was strange to hear from her woman's lips an opinion that had long floated indefinitely before his mental vision.

"Thou art perchance right," said Olrud. "I dispute it not, for thou hast been so in other instances. But I trust, for the good of the Church, that some law may be passed to keep him at home. For I fear lest the wandering star make people dance after it to their own destruction. Such orbs have been ever harbingers of ill."

"But thou hast not said," observed Amada, "when there is a prospect of thy settlement at Youghal."

"If all go well," replied Ardal, "it may be about the beginning of the year. I have looked at the last bishop's residence; it is small, but we can add a chamber to it. It might be made fit for our occupation about the end of spring."

"Then I must go home," said Grainné. "You will give me a few weeks' warning."

"Certainly," replied Ardal. "We could not well do without thy help in arranging for thy mother's removal."

CHAPTER XXIV.

It was the month of May, A.D. 1169. The trees wore their brightest green, and the white-thorns showered their blossoms over the primrose-studded banks. And on a memorable evening, within Mael-Patrick's cottage, Grainné and Mòr held a white care-cloth over Sorcha's head to determine the best way of adjusting it on the morrow.

Amada sat on the foot of a couch contemplating them with grave serenity. She did not feel very well, for her health was apt to be deranged by excitement. She had fidgetted much before Grainné's arrival, for the cottage had become the goal of so many visits that it was difficult for her to find time for repose.

Mòr had been attentive to Sorcha, though after a somewhat erratic fashion. Sorcha had indeed been occasionally hurt when, after receiving a full meed of sisterly sympathy, she found her friend colder than in former days towards her aged grandmother. This was more marked when Grainné came. Uailsi herself could not have looked more haughtily indifferent to the accomplished wife of Bishop Olrud than did this slender girl.

"We can never have real heart sympathy," thought Sorcha, with a sigh. "I was foolish in fancying that I had it. I might as well expect yonder pine tree to bend its branches as a woman who thinks herself highly born to be more than civil."

Grainné was not slow to notice this. She was too magnanimous, however, to underrate Mòr's real virtues.

" The abbot's daughter will never be friendly to me," she said, " but that is no reason why thou shouldst distrust her. Thou wilt, perchance, derive pleasure from her companionship in thy future life, and you may live to do each other good."

" I cannot welcome her in the same way," replied Sorcha, " when I see that her love for me is not strong enough to include my friends. I see not how so much littleness can dwell with such an amount of intelligence."

" Her eyes will one day be opened to her folly," replied Grainné. " We ought rather to pity the proud than to feel angry with them. They are the greatest sufferers, for they have real heart-loneliness."

" It is difficult for me," said Sorcha, " to feel any pity for such pangs, the more so when I know them to be self-inflicted. Yet methinks that Mòr may perhaps suffer from what thou speakest of. She often looks depressed. Sometimes I have wandered with her by the shore, and have felt as if she were wishing to tell me something, yet restraining herself in a very melancholy way. When we first became intimate, she rejoiced in my happiness, now it seems to awaken no responsive chord in her soul."

" Leave her alone," said Grainné. " Thou wilt not miss her, surely, when thou hast Ardal ? "

" She hath promised us an early visit," replied Sorcha. " It is sad to see a creature moving by my side whom I suspect to be harbouring some hidden grief. I have vainly striven to divine what it is."

" For my part," said Grainné, " I think thee a happy exception to thy fellow-mortals. Most women must give too much thought to the bearing of their own burdens, without spending time in guessing at what perhaps never existed. Thou wilt learn what troubles thy friend soon enough, if it be anything real."

There was some cause for Mòr's unhappiness. Fergus had for the last six months been placed over a congregation in

Waterford city, where his talent and eloquence had made
him a match for his Danish rival. His visits to Ardmore
had been short though frequent. They were for the osten-
sible purpose of asking the abbot's advice on points of church
discipline, as well as to the part which he himself ought to
take in the dissensions betwixt the Irish and Danish authorities.

"Fergus is more submissive than I had thought him,"
remarked Uailsi. "He looks so wild and independent that
none would have dreamed of his seeking ecclesiastical sanction for his every act. Ardal seems much more disposed to
rely on his own judgment."

Little did the proud matron imagine that this submissive-
ness was but a pretext to cover deep-seated rebellion! Had
she known of his secret meetings with her daughter, she
would have been less inclined to praise Fergus's loyalty.

"Meet me near Declan's well before sunrise," he had said
to Mòr on the eve of Sorcha's wedding. "Thou shalt then
learn the plan I have formed for our future."

And Mòr, whilst she held the care-cloth over Sorcha's
head, concealed in her breast an amount of agitation which
it was difficult to dissemble. Would that these exquisite
embroideries had been for her! She had as good a right
to wear them as the happy Sorcha.

The hour was approaching which would deliver her from
suspense. Mòr dreaded it, yet she could not wish things to
go on as they had done. The task of concealment had been
too protracted, and too distasteful. Whatever was in store
for her, an open avowal was the event she dreaded least.

Her health had suffered during the winter. Her cheek
was thinner, her step less elastic than its wont. She was
more than once visited by a sudden trembling, of which she
could give no account. As she gently stroked her father's
forehead to soothe him after a day of close study, she felt
as if her fingers had no right to come in contact with him.

They were guilty fingers; they had been pressed by a lover without his knowledge. She was pretending to belong to her parents after she had vowed herself away.

Other girls might have done this without feeling compunction for it; but Mòr was so loyal, so fearless, that she seemed as if forced into an attitude which did not suit her. She was as a young pine, whose instinct is to shoot straight, but which has been compelled by the hand of ignorance to outrage itself by trying to twine like the ivy. The cords with which she had been tied were too strong to allow of her rebound succeeding, but the effort injured her. Her youthful vivacity was gone, and in its stead came a feverish restlessness which tinged her cheek with the hues of health when in Fergus's presence, but left her a prey to exhaustion when he departed. Her parents had at length resolved to try change of air for her. After Sorcha's marriage should be over, Uailsi proposed to take her to the court of King Roderick.

" Cashel is out of the question," she said to her husband. " The O'Briens and O'Carthys are too much in league with the new prelates to welcome us. If thou hadst shown thyself a little less uncompromising, it might have been better for thee in a worldly sense."

" Ask what thou wilt of me," replied the abbot, " and I shall be willing to gratify thee ; but the interests of Ardmore and of the polity to which it adheres must come before all personal considerations."

" Dublin is even worse," continued Uailsi. " Its king is a poor fugitive, begging from foreigners what he cannot win with his own sword. Methinks the princes of our day would make but sorry figures on the page of a Tacitus."

" The flower of the land will gather round Roderick for that very reason," replied the abbot. " Besides, is he not ard-righ ? Thou must travel further, but thy advantage will be all the greater."

Uailsi therefore busied herself in the arrangement of her wardrobe. Her old court dresses were dragged out of heavy chests to be refurbished, and Mòr's listlessness began to disappear as she worked at them. Uailsi praised her own acuteness in having discovered a remedy.

"Thou seest that hope rouses her," she remarked to her husband. "The girl has blood in her veins which stagnates in obscurity. She needs a wider sphere for her development. We do not rear an eaglet to lock it up in a cavern."

But it was no prospect of court favour which quickened Mòr's fingers. Destiny seemed to beckon her as she plied the needle. Was not Sorcha doing the same? Providence had willed that all should be in readiness for her own bridal.

She scarcely closed her eyes on the eventful night. She remained talking with Sorcha till a late hour, whilst wreathing festoons of flowers for the decoration of the church. She had remarked how beautiful her friend appeared in the midst of her excitement, but there was no tremor in Sorcha's hand, no paleness on Sorcha's cheek; she was looking forward with confidence to the hour which would place her happiness in another's keeping. Her dark eyes were turned on Mòr with the sparkling assurance of a deep-seated peace.

"Thou hast no need to rouse me early," she said to Grainné. "I am quite sure to oversleep myself, and shall be all the better for so doing."

"But Ardal may visit us early," suggested her aunt.

"It matters not," said Sorcha. "We have a lifetime to spend together, and I have nothing to say to him that cannot wait."

The first faint sunbeam had scarcely tinged the eastern sky when a dark figure glided up the smooth turf of the rath by the steps close to the abbot's dwelling. The chill wind fanned its cheek, and blew its garments closer around it. It hurried rapidly downwards over the encircling ditch and past the farmyard, where a large watch-dog shook himself and opened his mouth for a bark.

The figure stood still, and displaying a small white tapering hand from beneath the folds of its mantle, threw out a morsel of wheaten cake. The dog's voice subsided into a low whine, whilst the figure glided onwards towards the summit of the hill.

Mòr—for it was she—walked leisurely as soon as the elevation of the ground she had traversed hid from her view the summit of the Round Tower.

"Shall I go on ?" she thought. "What I do this morning I never can recall. The way round by the shore is so wild and lonely. The very cliffs are dank with dew. Our fluttering hearts were never given us for such service. What if he should ask me to fly with him ?"

Then she thought of Sorcha. Was she, too, not venturing into the unknown ? Yet no shadow of fear had crossed her mind. Was the daughter of the Cinal Conaill but a poor coward ? Should she not now return to seek her pillow ? She would be safe there ; she would be under her parents' wing. Why, then, had she thought of love ? Did Fergus not deserve to be trusted as much as Ardal ?

She walked on more quickly. She dared not look behind, for the green roofs of Ardmore might call out that she was bidding them farewell. Mòr, pausing a second time, prayed that she might retain her self-possession.

At length she paused beneath the cliff which overlooked the gushing fountain. She sat down on a large rock, against which the bright sea-waves were rippling.

There was no sign of living thing along the shore. Mòr looked at the sombre sky, the vast stretch of grey water ruffled by an easterly breeze, at the fringe of pine trees on the near promontory, looming like so many ghosts in the darkness, and at the cold rocks against which she leaned. She began to fear that she was forsaken. The wind blew ominously on her slender frame, and, sinking down, she offered a humble prayer for help. It seemed as if she heard a low whisper.

"It waxeth day," said an unfamiliar voice.

"Had we not better return?"

"Hast thou left a couch of flowers," replied another, "whose scent lureth thee back? Thy rest will be the sweeter to thee for having been once broken."

The second voice thrilled through Mòr. Its deep tones were those of Fergus.

She raised her head timidly above a projecting rock, and discerned two figures with their backs turned to her.

"I know not that," said one of them. "Methinks, like the patriarchs, I could make a pillow of this stone."

"Thou wouldst look in vain for the angels," replied Fergus.

Mòr hesitated no longer, but gliding forward, came close to the well.

Her footfall was noiseless, yet Fergus felt it. He turned round.

"My sweet one!" he exclaimed, extending his arms. Mòr's head was in an instant pillowed on his shoulder. She trembled with fear and cold.

The stranger gave a few short coughs. When Mòr lifted her face, she recognised the plump figure of Heremon O'Mullaney. He stepped forward with much frankness.

"Thou art a brave girl," he said, "to come out in the darkness. But we must lose no time. Shall I begin?" he asked, turning his small eyes on Fergus.

Mòr's blue orbs were opened wide in perplexity. Fergus took her hand and spoke in a caressing voice—

"The time has come, my love, when we must act promptly. Our friend here has consented to say the words which will make us husband and wife."

Mòr drew slightly back, without, however, removing her

hand. "And then ?" she asked, fixing her clear eyes steadily on him.

"Then," said Fergus, "thou wilt join me at Waterford. Delay not, I beseech thee."

His brow was flushed, his hand feverish.

"I like not this concealment," said Mòr.

Heremon, placing his hands behind his back, moved away a few paces.

"It may not be what is due to thee," said Fergus, "but it is not a crowd of witnesses that makes a marriage. It is God's footstool on which we kneel; His presence is in yonder blue sky even more than beneath the church roof. And this is the only way in which we can ever hope to wed."

Mòr drew herself up to her full height as she calmly weighed the value of his words.

"I yield," she said, "but on one condition."

"What is that ?" asked Fergus, anxiously.

"That thou expect not blind obedience till after I shall have left my parents' roof," replied Mòr ; "and that I be permitted to stay there till such time as thou shalt make our union public."

There was a ring in her voice which warned Fergus not to overstretch his power over her.

"I agree," he said, pressing her hand more warmly than ever. "Bishop Heremon ! "

His friend strode leisurely back. "Have ye settled it ?" he asked, with a roguish look in his eye.

"Yea," replied Fergus, "we are both ready."

They knelt on the damp grass while Bishop Heremon offered an intercessory prayer. There was something peculiar in his voice. It was manly enough, but yet it seemed fitted to express thoughts that lay no deeper than the surface of his nature. Mòr felt as if she were listening to the panto-mime of a marriage service, and found it difficult to realise that she was going through the momentous reality. There was something flippant in the way that he presented the vows.

When they rose from their knees, it seemed to Mòr as if the knot were but loosely tied. Fergus covered her cheek with kisses. Seizing her hand, Heremon tried to snatch a kiss also.

"Thou must reward my pains," he cried. "I have encountered the cold of this morning."

"Thou hast obliged Fergus," replied Mòr, with dignity, "If thou seekest a reward, I trust thou wilt find it in the consciousness of having done him a favour."

"I have begun the day well," he said, gaily. "Let us walk back now, else the sun will be out to chide us."

They crossed the top of the hill, and dived by a devious way into the forest. Mòr hung on her husband's arm. She was silent, whilst the two men indulged in mutual jesting. She knew little of Heremon, but she did not esteem him. He seemed to be like some shallow brooklet, which has spread its waters over as huge a space as possible, but how shallow he was she had never suspected till that morning.

"Why had Fergus committed the blending of their destinies into such careless hands?" she could not help thinking. "Was there none other amongst his brother bishops from whom he could have begged such a service? If his reasons for secrecy were good ones, surely some more hallowed hands might have been found for the purpose. Heremon and he could not be intimate friends, she was sure. They were alike in nothing. Fergus, though so careless looking, was never flippant, whilst Heremon seemed to have no qualification for what he had done that morning, except his official position." Mòr felt less at ease than ever.

"Stay a moment," she said to Fergus, after Heremon had bade them farewell. They were under a convenient screen of trees.

"I would fain have thee tell me," she said, "how I am to act to-day?"

"As thou wouldst have done," replied Fergus, slowly, "had nothing unusual taken place."

"But it will be a deception," urged Mòr. "I shall have to appear as chief bridesmaiden, whilst I am a married woman."

"It will only be for a few hours," replied Fergus. "I promise thee solemnly, Mòr, that I will make the announcement before the company separate."

"If thou wilt do that," said Mòr, "I am content. But let me not play the hypocrite too long; thou knowest that I cannot bear it."

"Thou art brave as Minerva," replied Fergus, kissing her. "I am very grateful for thy patience; it shows the strength of thy love."

"As soon as may be," said Mòr, "I would have thee ask some one to offer a real earnest prayer for our happiness. I feel as if Bishop Heremon thought it was all a jest"

"No doubt he doth," replied Fergus, smiling. "He is not so bad, though, he is very good-natured."

"Not grave enough for a bishop," said Mòr. "He looks as if he had come into the world only to enjoy it."

"Thou wouldst do well to enjoy it a little more thyself," said Fergus. "But it will be all right to-morrow; thou hast no need to grieve."

He kissed her again, and they separated. Mòr hurried homewards, for she had much to do. Near the farmyard she met Ardal.

"Thou art early astir," he exclaimed.

Mòr was too much confused to answer him. She knew not how to regain her usual coolness. Ardal, happily, was in no mood for close observation.

"It is a sign of good luck for thee," he observed, "that thou hast met me. Thou wilt be married before the year is out."

"I wish thee happiness," replied Mòr, bowing gracefully, and hurrying towards the rude ladder which led up to the Grianan.

None of those who saw her cross the rath wondered. They knew the abbot's daughter to be an early riser, and had any one thought it worth while to venture a guess about her movements, it would probably have been that she had gone to seek wild-flowers for her dress. They were, however, too eager to finish their own business to bestow much solicitude on hers.

CHAPTER XXV.

Seldom had Ardmore presented a more cheerful appearance than on that bright May morning. The eastern breeze soon swept away the clouds that had darkened its dawn, and the first peal from the Round Tower awoke into unwonted activity the dwellers in the picturesque huts around it. Tall poles had been planted in a double row betwixt the door of Mael-Patrick's cottage and that of the church. These were now festooned by busy fingers with floral ropes of the creamy white-thorn blossom, whilst the path betwixt them was laid with rushes and sprinkled over with many a handful of wild-flowers. It was an universal holiday. The scholars gladly put aside their lesson tablets after early prayers, and the dairymaids hastened to drive their cows out to pasture that they might be in time to witness the bride's passage.

At another signal from the bell, a group of white-robed maidens assembled on the greensward, bearing in their hands bouquets of wheat-ears and brilliant blossoms, and on their bosoms sprigs of rosemary. Mòr was one of the last to join them.

She looked queenly in her rich array. Her hair, parted and turned back after the Saxon fashion, was coiled into a coronet and looped together with snowdrops. Her inar of fine white wool was embroidered with green, and her waist was encircled by a zone of twisted gold. Her feet, like those of her companions, were encased in white sandals.

But Mòr looked pale in spite of her stateliness. She gave but a cold welcome to the two youthful princes, sons of King Domnall O'Brien, who had come from Lismore to officiate as pages at the wedding of their kinsman.

It was her duty to knock at the bride's door. The other maidens became impatient.

"Sorcha waiteth for thee," said one; "I have seen Grainné's face at the window."

Mòr advanced, but knocked so gently as to be inaudible. Her hand trembled.

"Knock louder," said Prince Murtough.

Mòr tried to do so, but without effect.

The boy hesitated no longer. Stepping before her, he struck the door with his silver-mounted sword-handle. It opened, and Grainné appeared, leading Sorcha.

There was a buzz of admiration through the assembled throng. The bride was radiant in loveliness, her loosened hair flowing over her shoulders, the glow of her flushed cheeks and brown eyes being heightened by the glitter of white robes interweaved with threads of gold. Grainné looked beautiful also, as a full-blown summer rose overshadowing a delicately tinted bud.

The sun shone that morning on no fairer sight than the procession of sweet young faces that followed these two in their passage betwixt the wreathed poles. They were preceded by the young princes, clad in trews and plaids of scarlet tartan, one of them bearing in his hand a buffalo-horn cup filled with rosemary. But one amongst the maidens was pale, one voice joined but faintly in the psalm of thanksgiving that rose from their lips; and as the abbot came forth to meet them his eye rested uneasily on the form of her who followed nearest to the bride. Grainné was musing about that form with far different feelings.

"She is more haughty than ever," thought the matron. "It must be the excess of Sorcha's good-nature that finds aught to admire in her. Or perhaps pride is like a fungus in the heart, which has been there nourished till it has eaten all the sap out of a very sweet flower."

"Mòr is going to court soon," thought some of her companions; "but she might have waited till she got there before assuming such airs. She perchance thinks to make herself greater in the eyes of these boy princes and of the O'Faolain."

Mòr walked on, unconscious of the attention she was exciting. Her feet scarcely seemed to touch the ground; there was a tightness at her heart which threatened to stop her breath. She almost felt like a ghost that had come to revisit scenes which would have been fairer without her.

A burst of music heralded the bride's approach to the church. It came from a group of harpers, and from the mouth of a very long trumpet which, fashioned with curious skill, required the services of two men to keep it in position. Joy was depicted on every face, save on those of Mòr and her mother.

Ardal waited beside the O'Faolain and a group of his noble kinsmen. As Mòr approached he advanced towards her, holding out a purse of netted silk.

A merry laugh now arose amongst the younger brides-maidens. Darting forward, two of them seized his arm, endeavouring to draw him into the church. At the same time several young men approached Sorcha, taking her with gentle violence from the protecting clasp of Grainnè. They led her into the church, followed by peals of laughter from the girls who were vainly endeavouring to do the same to Ardal.

But the bridegroom at length yielding, suffered himself to be led under the narrow doorway; then over a carpet of fresh rosemary into the inner chapel, where all soon ranged themselves around the linen-draped communion table.

After a prayer and an exhortation, the solemn words were pronounced which bound two lives irrevocably together. Uttered as they were by Erc O'Conaill with deep pathos, they had the effect of making his daughter feel more than ever as if her own marriage had been but a mock one. Was it a nightmare through which she had passed ? No, for glancing timidly round the church, her eye met the amused stare of Heremon. Mòr felt a strange loathing at him, and even the face of Amada, though sparkling with unwonted joy, seemed to her as if enveloped in a strange mist.

When the last prayer had been uttered, the musicians were about to strike the first notes of the concluding hymn ; but Fergus, darting forward, seized Mòr's hand.

She was too much startled to resist. He led her in front of the throng, saying in a loud, commanding voice :

" Abbot Erc O'Conaill, I announce to thee that this morning thy daughter Mòr and I have been united in the bonds of holy matrimony. I ask thy benediction."

The abbot looked bewildered. His tongue at first refused utterance. The glances of all instinctively travelled from him towards Uailsi, who stood pale and motionless on the right of the bridesmaidens, looking more like an image of wax than like a breathing woman. Her head retained its haughty poise, but her eyes were fixed and glassy—all light seemed to have died out of them. There was something terrible in her self-command.

The abbot opened his mouth as if to speak ; but his attention was suddenly diverted by the address of a stranger.

Whilst the ceremony was going on, two dusty figures had slipped into the church. They were those of a handsome boy, in neat but travel-spotted garments; and of a grim warrior, whose shaggy beard and tunic of tanned cow-skin proclaimed him to be unacquainted with the refinements of life. The boy first stepped forward. He whispered something into the abbot's ear.

"What doest thou here?" asked the O'Faolain of the warrior.

"Thy sword will leap from its scabbard when I tell thee," replied the man. "Come out with me, lest thou affront the majesty of this place with its gleaming."

The abbot had become deadly pale. Grainné started; the travel-stained youth was her eldest boy Rossa.

The abbot, taking him aside, continued to speak rapidly. The O'Faolain meanwhile had left the church, but few except Grainné had noticed this; all being engaged in showering congratulations on Ardal and Sorcha.

The abbot at length stepped in front of the communion table. He grasped young Rossa's arm for support. It was a striking spectacle, if any one had been sufficiently calm to observe it—the massive form of the aged man, with the broad intellectual brow worn and wrinkled with study; and the bright angelic one of the vivacious youth who supported him. The boy's touch seemed to give the abbot strength, for, glancing at his pale wife, he nerved himself to speak.

All was hushed in an instant, the crowd of upturned faces hanging breathlessly on his lips.

"My children," he began, in a low but distinct voice, "I must put aside all personal matters to announce to you a national calamity. We are again threatened with invasion; nay, the foe has landed near the village of Bannow."

"The black strangers!" exclaimed Olrud, who looked very dark at the prospect of becoming acquainted with his kinsmen.

Amada now grasped the bride's arm. "Tell me," she said, tremblingly, "what is it?"

"Invasion," replied Ardal, speaking loudly in her ear.

"No, my children," said the abbot; "it is not the Danes we shall have to fight with. It is a company of freebooters, who may be the forerunners of many others. They are commanded by an Anglo-Norman knight named Fitz-Stephen.

Though numbering only four hundred, they are the flower of English chivalry. We have reason to tremble lest their coming has been sanctioned by King Henry."

"My counsel is," said Ardal, "that we be not soon shaken in mind. The men of Waterford will soon give a good account of them. The danger lies in their having followers, and that is not yet apparent. Let our Erenach lay up a store of corn in the Round Tower, against whatever peril may threaten us next year. Let some of our number be appointed to travel to all the chieftains of Munster, and obtain their promise to respect our rights of sanctuary; counselling them, at the same time, to sink their feuds in a league of national defence."

"We may take thee at thy word," said Fergus. "I would pray our revered abbot to send thee."

He had possession of Mòr's arm whilst he spoke. She was weeping, but she could not help wondering at his cool assurance. He was actually speaking in the tone of a man who had nought to crave pardon for.

Mòr felt a light touch on her head. Grainné's soft fingers were untying the coils of her hair. She darted a glance of grateful meaning from beneath her wet eyelashes. The matron's kind act made her feel that she had not forfeited all claim to honour.

"Let it be, then," said the abbot, replying to Fergus's proposal. He was too much stunned by the double blow he had received to be quite master of himself. Leaving the communion table, he passed out by a side door.

But many sorrowed at the sight of his bowed head. As he left the church a round soft hand was laid gently on his.

"Be of good comfort, brother," said the mild voice of Maidoc. "Thy daughter will give a good account of herself."

The abbot looked in his face. There was so touching a expression of sympathy in it, that he could only press the kind hand warmly in reply.

Uailsi's power of endurance at length failed. She had bestowed no glance on her husband as he passed, but now, heaving a deep sigh, she sank helplessly on the floor.

Many hands were outstretched to raise her. Mòr was too timid to approach.

"Let me not see the undutiful girl," she murmured.

"She is thy daughter," whispered Sorcha, "and the eyes of many are upon thee."

Uailsi controlled herself, and, bowing haughtily to the assembled throng, went out of the church.

Ardal led his bride over the flower-strewn pavement. All were too much excited to perform the ceremonies which had been arranged for her exit. Ita, however, had in the meantime stationed herself at the door, and as the newly-wedded couple passed out, she urged two young men to pour on their heads a copious shower of wheat ears.

The O'Faolain had meanwhile retired into Declan's cell with some of the ruling bishops. Grainné beckoned to her son.

"I cannot approach thee," he said, with a roguish twinkle in his eye. "I should spoil thy broidered lena."

He suffered himself, however, to be led out by his father. Seated beneath the great yew tree, he was made to repeat fifty times the story that he had told to the abbot.

The news had been brought to Lismore by a special messenger on the preceding evening. Rossa had undertaken to be the bearer of it to Ardmore before the Abbot Christian had time to indite a letter.

"I met the O'Faolain's henchman on the bridge," he said. "He hath come from Waterford, and hath seen the foe with his own eyes. They are not like the Black Strangers; their archers are men of skill whom none have yet been able to withstand; for the grey goose wings of Sherwood are now in the quiver of the Norman tyrant. Men say that this troop of Fitz-Stephen's is but the van of an expedition which hath been in preparation for years; and that the real head of it is the renowned Strongbow, Earl of Pembroke."

"Then the English king must be privy to it," said Olrud, darkly.

"I fear," said Ardal, who had left his bride for a few minutes beside her grandmother—"I greatly fear that he intends to subdue us. It will be but a light thing for him compared to what his great-grandsire's landing at Senlac was. The English will never respect our sanctuaries; for they are leagued with the men who contemn our orders."

"How so?" asked Maidoc.

"Perhaps thou wilt now be convinced," replied Ardal, "that there was something in what I told thee. Our country has been presented as a gift by the Pope to King Henry."

There was a murmur of horror throughout the assembled throng; even Maidoc turned pale.

"I could not have believed it," he said. "The heart of man imagineth only evil. But how comes the Roman bishop to claim power over us?"

"He hath received all islands as a gift to his predecessors from the Emperor Constantine," replied Ardal.

"That cannot be!" shouted the hereditary Erenach of Ardmore, a bluff red-bearded man in a tartan-fringed mantle. "Erin belonged to the Cæsars in no wise. The Roman bishop needs, methinks, as Columbanus said, to be instructed by his juniors. I might as well pretend to give thee the Rock of Cashel."

"Doth King Henry deserve the gift?" asked young Rossa.

"I trow not," replied Ardal. "Men say that he hath been known to jest in presence of the consecrated Host; and he hath sought to lord it over his Primate."

"But the Pope hath been his friend in that quarrel," remarked Fergus. "It is but a year since he issued against the archbishop a decree of suspension. Did the monks of Citeaux not tell thee how they had been forbidden to harbour

A'Becket, under penalty of losing their property in four kingdoms ?"

"That may be," said Ardal. "I would have you know, brethren, that I have not warned you without cause. The parchment exists on which the gift is declared."

"No, no!" cried a score of voices.

"And how hath Erin sinned, that she hath come to be made a chattel of?" asked the smith, who had been no inattentive listener.

"The Bull itself tells," replied Ardal. "We have been unwilling to obey their foreign laws, and to give the pence due to the fisherman's successor. We have amongst us, also, nurseries of vice which must be extirpated."

"Is the king, then, a Nathanael," asked the Erenach, "to whom this commission hath been given?"

"No more so than is his queen, the Amazon-Crusader,"* replied Ardal. "Men say that her wrists have borne chains, although she has brought him the fairer half of Gaul. Her mind hath been sorely chafed because of the love that he showeth to the sons of Rosamond."

"Then are we doubly insulted," remarked Olrud.

"I have heard better accounts of him," said Fergus. "Men say he is high-minded, and hath a fair tongue; also that to the courage of his great-grandsire he adds much warmth of heart."

"I grant him some kingly virtues," replied Ardal. "He may be a noble friend, and a dangerous enemy. He is sudden in anger, and pitiless as the bolt of the cloud. God grant that he be not launched at us."

"What wouldst thou have us do, then?" asked the Erenach.

"We have the weapon of prayer," replied Ardal. "Let us humble ourselves in God's sight, and it may be that He will yet avert His anger."

* Appendix.

"Thou speakest of the Almighty's justice," said Olrud; "but doth not England deserve punishment yet more at His hands? Where, even in the pages of heathen authors, can we read of more horrible doings than those of the Norman barons during the last reign?"

"True," replied Ardal. "Had it not been for Theobald of Canterbury, men say that life in England would have been as life in hell. These are the very men, too, who yearn to quench their thirst for blood on us. We, however, have nought to do with others. Our Church has fallen from the heights of her simplicity; she will be trampled under foot of men if she find not space for repentance."

As Ardal uttered these words, a weird mis-shapen form darted from behind the corner of the church. Phelim O'Bric stood amongst the crowd brandishing in his hand a withered oak-branch, its twigs and leaves half burnt away.

"See ye what the sparks have done?" he cried, wagging his grizzly beard. "The little firebrand hath been thrown over the dry forest, and as the tiny sparkles enkindle the small wood, so shall the same set the great wood ou fire. The red glow appeareth where the river windeth to the sea: it will break into a flame which turneth nations into ashes. Blasts of death go before it, and whither will ye hide from its scorching breath?"

All shrunk back as Phelim passed amongst them, none venturing to speak until his voice had become faint in the distance.

"Thinkest thou that he knoweth the issue?" asked the Erenach of Ardal.

"I cannot tell," replied the young bishop; "but let not his words frighten us. Men say that he hath held converse with the powers of darkness, and the secret of the Lord is not with such as he."

CHAPTER XXVI

Mòr had, in the meantime, withdrawn to hide her tears in Maidoc's cottage. She wept there for an hour before being discovered by its occupants, who had been too much engrossed by the recitals of Rossa and Ardal to return home.

"I would not have done it," she sobbed, her head pillowed on Ita's shoulder, "if I had only had a few hours to think about it. I never dreamed of his affronting my parents by such a public announcement. I would have sought my father and confessed to him, if I had had the slightest warning of what was going to happen."

"Then thou wouldst never have seen Bishop Fergus again," remarked Ita, quietly. "Thy father would have taken pains to hush it up, for he would have considered the marriage invalid. Fergus would never have shown his face in Ardmore again."

"Thinkest thou that they will disown me?" asked Mòr. "It was not because I loved them not, and I am their only child. Would that I could see my father for ten minutes!"

"I think not that he will be unapproachable," said Maidoc, gently; "yet I doubt the propriety of thy accosting him while the wound is sore."

Maidoc rose, and stepped heavily out of the cottage.

The good bishop was scarcely to be recognised as the same man that he had been in the morning. His figure seemed to have grown unwieldy, and the brightness of his face was dimmed by a murky cloud of care—his very skin seemed to have become darker. His feet moved, however, to a definite goal ; they carried him leisurely to the abbot's cell. "Enter," said a voice, in response to his knock, a key being at the same time turned from within.

Maidoc lifted the latch very timidly. The cell was much handsomer than any in Ardmore. It had a higher roof, and its wooden walls were adorned with devices of quaint colour. The furniture too, though plain, was of polished oak.

The abbot sat in his usual chair, his grief-stricken face, resting on one hand, was bowed over a couple of thick volumes which lay on his desk. Uailsi sat near the window, looking a picture of helpless misery.

Maidoc thought that he discerned traces of tears on the abbot's check. He stood for a moment as if lacking breath to speak.

"Thou seest us in heavy affliction, brother," said Erc. "If a father's joys have been denied thee, thou hast at least been spared his sorrows."

Maidoc sat down, and laid his arm also on the desk.

"Thou hast been wronged," he said, in his usual mild voice ; "but from the depths of our troubles our heavenly Father sometimes raises us to yet higher joys."

"It may be so," said the abbot, "but not in this case. I shrink not from saying it to thee, for I feel that thou art our friend. When a man has set his whole heart on another being, when he has showered on her all the benefits he can think of, when he has lived for years in the belief that she returned him the grateful affection which was all the recompense he craved, then all of a sudden she tears the mask from her face and proclaims herself a hypocrite, what can he think ? Why, that there is nothing on this earth worth living for !"

"Nothing," said Maidoc, "to one who is an ambassador for God ? "

"True," replied the abbot. "I slight not my sacred calling.

It may be that I have made an idol of the girl. This may be sent to wean my affections from earth, yet the process is a very painful one."

"Yea, verily," replied Maidoc. "We can only measure the depth of our own ingratitude to our Creator when we experience something of the same kind ourselves. But I have reason to know that things are not quite so bad as thou hast painted them. Thy child at this moment suffers even more severely than thou doest."

"I am glad of it," exclaimed Uailsi, rising from her seat at the window. "It is a relief to us, Bishop Maidoc, that we can give expression to our feelings. Mòr deserves to suffer."

The lady's lips were tightly pressed together; there was a hardness in her glassy eyes.

"She hath defied us at Declan's shrine," continued Uailsi, "in the presence of our whole subject community, surprising her father in the very exercise of his office. She hath affronted us by her low tastes, giving a hand which was fashioned for princes to an adventurous crafty churl. She hath distrusted her own mother, for the secret must have been hidden in her breast for months. O Maidoc, return thanks to heaven that thou hast no daughter!"

The good bishop was quite scared by this outburst. He sat contemplating her with wide open eyes.

"That is its worst feature," said the abbot. "It has been a deeply-laid scheme, carried out with cool persistence. Mòr is not an impulsive character."

"No," replied Maidoc, "but she is capable of hiding deep feeling. She is as a rock in which wounds remain for ever, not as a tree, where they are obliterated by the process of growth."

"She takes that from me," said Uailsi. "And she hath given me a wound which will not heal to-morrow; no, nor next year: I shall carry it with me to my grave, for I will never, never forgive her."

"That is scarcely Christian," said her husband, looking up at her beseechingly. "Thou canst hardly offer up the Lord's Prayer when thou diest."

"It matters not," cried Uailsi, fiercely. "I shall not hurt her, but she is no longer a child of mine."

"If thou wert a little calmer," said Maidoc, "I would try to make thee see that she hath been led iuto this error without her consent."

"I would fain hear no more of her," said Uailsi, as she opened the door and passed out of it.

Maidoc, shutting it softly, turned to the abbot.

"Thou hast spoken," he said, "of the Lord's Prayer. Hast thou forgotten the young man who went into a far country?"

"I know what thou wouldst urge," replied the abbot. "But that young man was less base than my daughter. He had made no profession of piety, or of a wish to do his duty to his father; therefore when repentance came, there was some ground for believing it to be genuine."

"Thy daughter hath made a full confession to me, or rather to my wife," said Maidoc. "Fergus and she have been secretly betrothed for a year; and she hath been most unhappy, for she thought herself bound to obey him."

"And how," said the abbot, "could a girl instructed as she has been take so false a view of her duty?"

"I believe there was a partial threat used," replied Maidoc. "Fergus seemed determined to give her up if she did not show by her actions that she trusted him: thou, who hast spent so much time in the study of the human heart, knowest what a tyrant love is."

"Yet how," persisted the abbot, "could this bring her to the length of affronting her father?"

"She dreamt not of that," replied Maidoc. "She was married before sunrise this morning, but she knew not what was to be till a few minutes before the ceremony, and she would not join in it except under the condition of remaining under thy roof till thou hadst been made aware of the change in her state. She imagined that the disclosure would be made privately. She was as much startled and distressed as her mother at the time it was done."

"Then she has been wronged!" cried the abbot, starting to his feet. "My instinct was a right one. Not on the ground of his birth, whereon Uailsi builds so many objections, but on that of his character. Fergus has a brazen boldness that is the very reverse of manliness."

"Wouldst thou have given thy daughter to him if he had come forward frankly?" asked Maidoc.

"I cannot tell what I should have done," replied the abbot. "Perchance I would, if I had found that her affections were so much engaged; for I must say I once thought well of him."

"He has, then, gained nothing by his policy of concealment?" said Maidoc.

"On the contrary," replied the abbot; "he has lost my esteem, though that may be worth little in his eyes. Yea, he would have attained his object, after some struggles, perchance, had he followed the straight path. As far as I am capable of examining myself, I think not that it is in my nature to be a cruel parent. I am stung by an adder which I have cherished in my bosom."

"Thou speakest now of Fergus," said Maidoc, gently. "I must confess that I also have been deceived. I cannot imagine why any one should take such a strange road to an honourable goal."

"I wish not, in this matter, to be guided only by my feelings," said the abbot. "I pity my daughter for having made herself the wife of such a man. I need lift no finger to punish her. She is in danger of suffering even more than she deserves. But, if I interest myself in her now, will not my doing so have the appearance of sanctioning undutiful conduct?"

"I read in the Old Testament," said Maidoc, "that if we wish for light and health, one of the first things required of us is that we hide not our face from our own flesh and blood."

"Then will I see her," said the abbot, rising. "How comes it, though, that we missed thy face in our solemn council, held as it was within the sacred cell apportioned to thee for thy studies?"

"I feared," replied Maidoc, "lest the place being strait, thou wouldst not have had honourable space for thy royal visitors."

"Thou art ever in the rear," said the abbot, smiling. "The O'Faolain hath had but sorry hospitality. He hath left with black Care as a fellow-rider, for ere dawn shall his heralds call the men of the Desies to arms. The princely boys were grieved indeed that they were not permitted to partake of the marriage feast; but the O'Faolain thought that his duty to their father constrained him to bid them return to Lismore."

"Many marvel at their coming," said Maidoc. "It cannot have been with the hearty approval of Bishop Christianus."

"I trow not," replied the abbot, shrugging his shoulders. "The O'Faolain's influence hath doubtless wrought on their father thus to honour his brother. But we regretted thy absence, for Bishop Christian's letter hath at length come to hand, and though we are addressed in it as vassals, it nevertheless gives us a faithful account of the English force before Wexford."

"Thou must answer the epistle cautiously," said Maidoc. "Doth the O'Faolain think that there is might in Munster to resist them?"

"None can doubt it," replied the abbot. "But what cuts us to the heart is to learn that they have come at the invitation of the Leinster king, Dermod Mac Murrough. Thus is Erin wounded by her own children."

"He filleth the cup of his evil deeds," said Maidoc. "He who honoureth not women cannot honour his fatherland. Hath not Dermod profaned the sanctuary of Bridget, taking her co-arb to be the wife of his vassal? And hath he not emulated the exploit of the Trojan Paris, by stealing the fair Devorgilla?"

"True," replied the abbot; "but he is in honour with those who bow to the authority of Rome; for hath he not covered the country with monastic foundations?"

"He will need all the prayers of their inmates," said Maidoc, "if haply the crimson stains of his sins may be removed. But what more saith Christian's letter?"

"That we have no mean foe," replied the abbot. "The leaders, Fitz-Gerald and Fitz-Stephen, have set fire to their fleet, that their followers may look for nought but victory."

"Would that we had a spark of the like courage," exclaimed Maidoc. "I am almost tempted to wish that the decision of Fothadh na Canoine * might be rescinded, and that our younger bishops might gird on spear and buckler."

"They can work more usefully," replied the abbot, "in seeking to shield the helpless of both sexes, by moving the hearts of rude warriors. That cause must be sacred which brings the glow of martial pride to thy cheek."

Maidoc blushed. "I have spoken foolishly," he said. "Farewell, I must needs go to partake of the marriage banquet."

Passing into the sunshine, he found that a large company had already gathered round several tables which had been spread in the open air. These were crowned with a goodly array of flowers of silver cups, and gem-studded drinking horns; with snowy wooden platters and spoons of a bronze-like metal, whose composition has defied the scrutiny of modern experts. Two lordly dishes, bearing the salmon, food

* Appendix.

of nobles and princes, were flanked by small piles of wheaten loaves, kneaded with honey.

The arrangements were, however, sadly spoiled by the defection of the royal guests, as well as of those who ought to have taken the lead in promoting the flow of merriment. The seat of honour reserved for the abbot now stood empty, and, as Maidoc had been from the first invisible, a look of dismay gathered over the faces of Sorcha's relatives as the banquet commenced.

" Who will be the governor of our feast ? " asked Amada.

"It were vain to hope for the abbot's presence," replied Grainné. "Maidoc and Ita comfort the other bride. What sayest thou to my husband ? "

" Nay,"replied Amada ; " the guests might murmur, seeing that he is of another family, and is not akin by blood to the bride."

"If thou, Grainné, wouldst do us a favour," suggested Ardal, " thou wouldst thyself be our queen."

"I ! " exclaimed the matron.

" Yea," replied the bridegroom. " We need to be ruled by a skilful hand. Thou wilt fill the chair better than the O'Faolain himself would have done, and thou wilt do the abbot's family a kindness by withdrawing attention from them."

Grainné was not slow to comply with the suggestion. It may be questioned if the company, postponing for a few hours all further meditations on the dangers of their fatherland, were the less merry for lack of the absentees.

There was one guest, however, whose presence was felt by Sorcha as of evil omen. Whilst his young bride wept in Maidoc's cottage, whilst all tongues were ready to discuss the motives and effects of his conduct, Fergus O'Flannahan sat at the snowy board, trying to charm all ears by his forced wit.

Loud were the shouts as each guest, dipping his sprig of rosemary in the pink foam of a silver tankard, drank long life and health to the newly-married pair. Sorcha retired into the cottage as an embroidered bag for the gathering of her tinal, or marriage collection, was handed round. She was followed by her grandmother.

"Alas, child!" said Amada, "thou must be content with my old hands in default of the fairer ones that should have decked thee. Couldst thou have dreamt that the owner of them would herself be a bride this morning?"

"Thou speakest as if that were pleasant," replied Sorcha. "It hath made her parents most unhappy."

"Have they not deserved it?" said Amada. "Could they expect aught but that the girl would rebel some day, having been reared, as it were, apart from her species?"

"Yea," replied Sorcha; "but in family wars both combatants are wounded. Mòr's victory cannot bring her much good. She looked as crushed and stunned as her mother did; thou seest that she could not feast with us. I fear that Fergus hath not dealt quite fairly by her."

"Thou wert never charitable to him," said Amada, "and it ill becomes thee to be otherwise. I always feel for those who have been kept down. I cannot grieve at the Lady Uailsi getting a humbling, though it be only herself who considers it one. She might be proud to have such a son-in-law. But I shall not quarrel with thee at the last moment."

"Nay," said Sorcha, kissing her. "I purpose making Ardal wait. Tell him, when he comes, that I have gone to Maidoc's house. I must have a word with Mòr."

Darting behind the screen of trees which overshadowed some of the cottages, she paused at the well-known door. Ita opened in response to her knock.

Mòr, lifting her tear-stained face, gave a scream of surprise. In a moment Sorcha's soft arms were round her neck.

The contrast was very striking. The one bride, radiant, beautiful, self-possessed, though with a pitiful quiver on her drooping eye-lid; the other, pale, trembling, and woe-begone.

Sorcha kissed her friend with a vigour which seemed determined to infuse some of her own warmth into the pale cheeks.

"Thou art an angel," said Mòr, sobbing. "Oh, Sorcha!
how often have I been ready to tell thee of this, but I had
promised secrecy."

"That was a pity," said Sorcha; "women were never
meant to bear such burdens alone."

"Would that I had thought of its ending thus!" continued
Mòr. "I had no presentiment that he would announce it as
he did. Thinkest thou that my parents will be for ever
angry? It were hard if I could never speak with my mother
again."

"I know not their hearts," replied Sorcha, quietly; "but
if thou shouldst lack a home, come to me. I speak as one of
the foolish women, for I am sure that Fergus will make up
to thee for this. But at least neither Ardal nor I can
forget thee."

"Else thou wouldst not have sought me now," said Mòr.
"And how may I thank Grainné for giving me the bride's
crown of honour? But for her I should have stood with
braided locks by the altar. But go, my beloved one, thy
bridegroom waiteth for thee."

The door was now opened softly. Maidoc entered. He
was followed by another dark-robed figure. Ita smiled, but
Sorcha and Mòr both started back as they recognised the
thought-seamed face of the abbot.

A ray of light appeared to dart from his eyes on beholding
Sorcha. Bending her head, she slipped quietly beneath his
outstretched arm and darted away with the swiftness of a
hare. She was followed more slowly by Maidoc and Ita,
who gladly seized this opportunity of witnessing her
departure.

Throwing herself on her father's breast, Mòr made a full
and frank confession. Bitter repentance mingled with her
sorrow when she heard him say that he would not have pre-

vented her marriage had he seen that she was in earnest about it.

"I am punished for it all now," said Mòr. "I am beginning my married life very differently from Sorcha. It is as if I had stumbled on the threshold of my new home."

"Let, then, this false step be thy last," replied her father, kissing her. "I could not but forgive thee, for I should have been too wretched had I done otherwise; but I cannot hold out the least hope of thy mother following my example. She feels what has happened as a personal affront."

"I cannot wonder," said Mòr. "The thought of it makes me miserable. If I had been left to my own impulses——" But here she checked herself.

"I know, I know," said the abbot, gently. "Thou must bend thy whole energies to the task of being a good and obedient wife, and I trust thou will find it no task."

"Thou wilt make Fergus regret it," said Mòr, drying her tears, "if thou art so kind to him. How much more honourable would it have been had he received me from thy hand!"

"Yea, verily," replied her father; "but we cannot help the past. Thou hast been the chief sufferer, after all is told. I purpose asking him to remain with thee here for a few days, till we know that the country about Waterford is quiet."

"But we must not trespass on thy hospitality long," said Mòr. "Fergus's place is with his flock in their hour of danger. Had it not been for me, he would have left with the O'Faolain. But thinkest thou that we are in peril?"

"If the Munstermen stand by each other, no," replied her father. "We have no lack of heroic blood, but it hath been too much spilt by the swords of brethren. The real difficulty lies in disunion, and I confess that it is an evil story about the Pope's gift to the English monarch."

"He must expect some service in return for it," said Mòr.

"Yea, truly," replied the abbot. "But one hath already been paid by Henry when he, with the French king Louis, held the pontiff's bridle at Courcy-le-roi."

"'Tis sad to think that we should be held as the price of such a mummery," said Mòr. "There will be one good for me in our remaining here for two days—it may give my mother time to relent. If she is not disposed to do so, I can bear her anger more easily at a distance. I would sooner brave Fitz-Stephen's archers."

"Hush," said her father; "thou knowest not well the drift of thine own words."

The abbot left Maidoc's cottage with a lighter heart. He had, however, traversed only some twenty feet of the greensward when he beheld the mis-shapen form of Phelim.

"Ha!" what doest thou here?" he exclaimed.

Phelim was leaning against a tree, his long beard nearly touching his knees, and his forked finger-nails clasping one of its branches.

"Have I not seen it?" he cried, in a shrill voice. "From the bosom of the forest pond hath arisen a mist; it hath gathered itself to the form of a wraith to whom our fame is hateful. Such spirits ride the winds when invasion cometh from the sea."

"Thou shouldst speak less with them, my son," said the abbot, calmly.

"And shall I not speak with the Virgin of the Curragh!" shrieked Phelim. "For the holy Bridget hath bared her glittering right arm to avenge on the men of Erin the violence of Dermod; for the foot of man hath broken through her hedge when the rude king carried off her daughter. The fire of Kildare burneth low; it shall be quenched in the blood of the children of Erin."

The abbot was a naturally calm man, yet he trembled at these words. There was a strange quiver in his voice as he gave to Ardal and Sorcha their parting benediction.

The newly-wedded pair departed shortly before sunset. Mounted in a two-wheeled chariot of basket-work, they were escorted by a troop of young men on horseback. They drove rapidly through the forest to the banks of the brimming Blackwater, where a small skiff was in waiting to convey them to Youghal.

The cloud which loomed on the political horizon soon passed away. After a few anxious weeks, the abbot received intelligence that the citizens of Waterford and Wexford had come to terms with their besiegers; and that the latter had settled down on land allotted to them by King Dermod, whose authority the men of southern Leinster agreed to acknowledge.

Fergus received an ample dowry with his bride, although he had to confess his inability to pay the customary price for her. He took her to Waterford, not quite at ease respecting his own achievement. He had felt something like a sensation of defeat at the very moment of triumph. It was not Uailsi's persistent disapproval, humbling as that was. He had shown his own power, yet its exhibition seemed to have placed him on a lower scale of the social ladder. Nor was he without apprehension lest the very good he had so much coveted might be made the instrument for checkmating him in his ambitious schemes. He would have been tempted to quarrel with that good, had Mòr given him the least opportunity. She was so submissive to his slightest wish, so active, so even-tempered, it seemed impossible for the most critical eye to find fault with her conduct. Her very excellences fretted Fergus; they made him feel his own meanness. How came it that the kind-hearted young bishop was half ashamed of his high-born and accomplished wife?

The little cloud had melted away, but it might be the harbinger of the tempest. At present there were no signs of such a catastrophe, but Fergus was in the position of a very ambitious man who knows not on which of two ladders to set his feet. The one on which he had the firmest hold might be planted on the smooth verdure of a bog. He had felt the ground vibrate beneath it on the very day of his marriage. The ladder had, it is true, become steadier, and would probably last till after his climbing days were ended ; but he had quite enough dread of its fall to make him wish that he had not ventured quite so far on it.

CHAPTER XXVII.

It was the beginning of September. The first faint streaks of yellow lay on the drooping foliage of the beech trees that clustered about the small but massively built church of Youghal, the centre of a fishing village that, sheltering itself against one of the grassy hills overlooking the broad bay at the mouth of the Blackwater, had become a harbour of refuge for storm-tossed mariners, as well as an emporium of the merchandise destined to supply the wants of Lismore.

Under the beech trees was the bishop's cottage, a hexagonal hut with two smaller ones attached to it, covered with creeping ivy. The ground on each side of it had been well planted with beds of leeks, onions, parsnips, and carrots, amongst which a number of flowering rose-bushes gave sustenance to the bees that swarmed, not only in a few yellow hives, but in the trunks of two old trees, and in several holes, half veiled by the creeping shamrock. From the summit of the hill above the church there was a fine view of the promontory of Ardmore, though not of the Round Tower, and of the sea rippling against the rim of white sand that separated it from the tilled fields. On the inland side the eye might wander over the forest country that extended round the estuary, and mark where the flowing river, bursting through its embankment of cliffs, expanded at once almost into a small lake.

Fourteen months had passed since Sorcha's wedding. They had been months of unbroken happiness. Her mind

had found abundant scope for its energies in quiet ministrations amongst her husband's flock, as well as in lightening
the burdens which increasing age brought to her grandmother. Another image, too, had come to nestle in her
heart; and as she stood at her cottage door in the light of
evening, she glanced down at the little bead-like eyes of her
infant, and thought of them as of two new stars kindled to
cheer her earthly pilgrimage.

Sorcha looked happy, as she had always done. The early
roses that had faded from the hedgerows seemed to have left
her their tints, both on lip and cheek. There was nought to
trouble her, save her grandmother's plaints, and even these
could be turned into smiles of gratitude. Amada's face, too,
often glowed with more than its wonted brightness. Grainné
had fulfilled her promise by contriving that all her grandchildren should visit her during the summer.

But a slight shade now gathered over the fair young brow.
"Why tarrieth Ardal?" thought Sorcha. "He hath gone on
a preaching tour for two weeks, and hath sent me word that
he might be constrained to remain away for a few days longer.
It seems strange that he hath given me no reason for this."

A little ragged boy now darted forth from behind a cluster
of hazel bushes.

"Our bishop approaches," he said, "bringing a lady and a
child on horseback."

Sorcha threw on her dark tartan-fringed mantle, clasping
it on her breast with a massive silver-knobbed buckle. Laying her baby on Amada's knee, she ran swiftly along the
well-trodden turfy road.

At about a mile's distance she perceived her husband,
leading a horse by its bridle, whilst in the other hand he
carried a light episcopal crosier. A muffled figure sat on the
horse, and two men walked on its other side.

Ardal stopped as Sorcha approached. The muffled figure
dropped its veil; in an instant she recognised Mòr.

But how changed!   The smooth, comely cheeks were sunken; the face, though no paler than when it left Ardmore, was streaked with premature wrinkles, and the clear eyes had a weird, haggard look about them.   On her arm there lay a round bundle, which Sorcha's instinct at once divined to be a living thing.   She took the thin hand, which closed tightly over hers.

"I am very tired," said Mòr.   "Thy husband is good enough to remember what thou didst once promise for him."

"Yea," replied Sorcha.   "We shall entertain angels, though not quite unawares.   But what has brought thee into such a plight?"

"I shudder to tell thee," said Ardal.   "It is another invasion.   An English army has again landed on our shores, stronger and more determined than the last was.   It is led by the Earl of Pembroke himself, and it has massacred half the people of Waterford."

Sorcha turned deadly pale.   "How horrible!" she gasped.   "Is Fergus safe, and the O'Faolain?"

"I believe so," replied Ardal, moving forward with the horse.   "I knew of it a few days ago, and was unwilling to return home or let thee hear of it before I had learned fresh details.   The O'Faolain hath proved himself a hero.   These two poor men have seen their wives and children mercilessly butchered before their eyes."

Sorcha gazed sadly at the stalwart forms of those whose sorrow seemed too deep for words.

"Are the English, then, beaten back?" she asked.

"Nay, verily," replied Ardal.   "The fair city lieth at their mercy.   It was but last Tuesday that they and their waving banners appeared before its walls.   The citizens repulsed them twice, led by the O'Faolain."

Sorcha's cheek flushed.   "Our prince is worthy," she said.   "How, then, could the English conquer?   Waterford hath good ramparts."

"There was a yellow-haired nephew of Fitz-Stephen's," replied Ardal; "a man of large body and quick grey eye, named Raymond Fitz-William. He had marched with a troop of the new settlers against Waterford just before the Earl of Pembroke arrived, and had built a wooden fort outside its walls. The O'Faolain lost no time in collecting his forces and attacking it. But the men of Munster were unused to the English arrows; they were shamefully routed, and seventy of the prisoners were thrown with broken limbs from a rock into the sea."

Sorcha shuddered. "But these are ruffians," she exclaimed. "Come they in the name of the Bishop of Rome and of King Henry?"

"Yea, verily," replied Ardal. "It is the first chastisement which the true Church inflicts on her erring sons. Men say that Raymond, surnamed the Grosse, had no hand in this massacre; nay, that he pleaded for mercy, but his fellow-captain, Henry, of Mount Maurice, executed the vile deed in spite of him. Thou mayest judge if this would not spur the men of Waterford to a desperate resistance. They shut their gates, determined to perish by the sword and by hunger sooner than surrender. The O'Faolain had strong hopes of holding out until my royal brother could march to his aid; but, unhappily, Raymond's keen eye spied out Fergus's house, which, built of timber, rested on posts, and was half within and half without the wall. He called his men, and by night they hewed down the posts on which the house stood. It fell, and a piece of the wall with it. The English soldiers rushed through the opening, and killed the people in the streets. They gave no quarter; but left the mangled bodies of their victims lying in great heaps."

"And where wert thou?" asked Sorcha, looking at Mòr.

"I was not in our dwelling," replied her friend. "I had sought refuge in the Danish church. Yet have I seen the ruthless dagger plunged into the heart of tender women; I have seen blood flowing like water, and suffering that will haunt me to my dying day. The English soldiers have been fiends in human shape; but they have only repeated the horrors which their forefathers inflicted on the holy men of Bangor. Earl Strongbow affirms loudly that he hath come to execute the commission given to his sovereign by the Roman bishop."

"And where is the O'Faolain?" asked Sorcha.

"He was captured in Reynold's Tower," replied Ardal. "He would have been slain but for the intervention of some Irishmen in King Dermod's service."

"Ah!" exclaimed Sorcha. "Is *he* with the invaders?"

"He hath plotted long with them," replied Ardal. "In fulfilment of an old covenant he hath given his daughter Eva in marriage to the Earl Strongbow."

"Yea," said Mòr, "and the bridal procession passed through the streets over the bodies of the slain. They have since gone with flying banners to Dublin."

"And where is Fergus?" asked Sorcha.

"He remains," replied Ardal, "to assist the Danish Tostius in making peace betwixt victor and vanquished. He hath some favour with the Earl of Pembroke; and his efforts, as well as those of the other clergy, have had some effect in staying the effusion of blood. For men become drunk with slaughter as with wine, and lose the control of their senses."

"I can well believe it of men," said Sorcha, "when a woman could suffer herself to be whirled to the altar over bleeding corpses."

All colour had now fled from Sorcha's face. Her brown eyes seemed more lustrous than ever.

"I found refuge in the Danish church," said Mòr, "because the foe respected not the sanctuary of ours; and I was an eye-witness of the princess's marriage. The trappings of her pomp seemed a vile insult to our misery."

"Are we safe here?" asked Sorcha.

"I fear not," replied Ardal. "The church of Youghal is ancient; and men say that the English warriors yearn to raze all the monuments of Irish piety. To scatter a Culdee family and to give the wives and children of bishops to the sword would be to fulfil the Pope's commission. Their zeal burns against you even as if you were Saracens."

"I doubt it not," said Sorcha. "Were it not well to warn our friends at Ardmore?"

"They know it," replied Ardal. "I have travelled towards Lismore, to learn all I could before alarming thee; for I knew that I must counsel thee to flight. It was thus that, hearing of Mòr's journey, I went forth to meet her."

"Whither may we flee?" asked Sorcha.

"My counsel is," replied Ardal, "that when the storm breaks, it should find us together. There may be negotiations for the safety of the defenceless; and these will be best carried out by our making them assemble in the religious sanctuaries. And should resistance be necessary, we have a fortress at Ardmore."

"My poor grandmother!" exclaimed Sorcha.

"She will be rudely shaken," said Ardal. "But yet she has a spirit that may rise with danger. The thought of suffering in a good cause may strengthen her feeble heart. I know that she will try to be brave for thy sake."

"Let me hasten homewards," said Sorcha; "and do ye slacken your pace, lest she be startled by too sudden a sight of Mòr."

Ten minutes later Sorcha knelt by Amada.

"Grandmother," she said, "hast thou read of the early martyrs?"

"Yea, child," replied Amada, smiling down on little Rossa. "There is no better reading. We had none of them in Erin, unless we count Clemons, who was burnt for saying that images and celibacy and the supremacy of the Roman bishop were corruptions of Christ's doctrine. But it was not the heathen that killed him—oh no! I like reading about the martyrs ; there's nothing better, hardly even in the Gospels."

"Couldst thou have borne to be one of them?" asked Sorcha.

"If God had given me grace," replied Amada. "I doubt not that He would have done it. But, child! why art thou so pale?"

"It cometh, grandmother," replied Sorcha, in a half-choking voice ; "already is the Norman heel on our necks."

"Hath aught befallen Ardal or Grainné?" cried Amada, starting back in terror.

Rossa now began to scream.

"Not them," replied Sorcha, snatching up her infant. "Grandmother, we are in God's hands, as this little creature is in ours. But Waterford hath been taken and sacked. The Earl of Pembroke, with an English army, hath landed in Erin ; and his captains may march any day on Ardmore."

"Then, say I, fight him!" exclaimed Amada, starting up ; her face aglow with the heroism of her race. "Would that I were a man!" she sighed, sinking back exhausted in her chair.

The step of a horse was now heard on the outside turf. "It is Mòr Ni-Flannahan," said Sorcha, rising, and setting the door wide open, whilst her husband assisted their guest to dismount.

Amada at first failed to recognise the proud daughter of the Cinel Conaill in the shrunken form before her. She gazed with speechless bewilderment on the wan cheek and clear blue eyes, which had in them such strange memories of the past.

But the pale lips only needed to utter a word, ere the fair head was pillowed on Amada's neck.

"Thank God that thou art safe!" she exclaimed. "Where is thy husband?"

" He is well," replied Mòr, disengaging herself. " Amada, I have done thee much wrong in the past; I am here to seek thy forgiveness."

" Thou speakest in riddles," replied Amada; " thou never didst me a wrong."

" Yea, but I did," persisted Mòr. " I little thought who were my true friends."

" I am confident that thou hast never shown me ill-will, whatever thou mayest have felt," replied Amada. " Thou art faint and weary; thou knowest not what thou sayest. If we must all needs ask pardon of each other for our thoughts we should soon lack time to do aught else."

CHAPTER XXVIII.

THERE was little rest for any one that night. Ardal, after taking some hasty refreshment, went forth to warn those of his flock whom an invasion was likely to bring into danger. Sorcha insisted on her grandmother's retiring to rest in the small chamber which was allotted her; approached, as was then the custom, only by an outside door. Mòr, however, resisted all efforts to make her retire.

"I slept even whilst I was riding," she said. "I was conscious only of keeping a firm grasp of little Erc. It is wonderful how an infant can make thee forget everything but itself; his least little movement was more to me than if I had overheard the English soldiers planning the manner of my death."

"It is of God's mercy that thou hast escaped from them," said Sorcha. "But thou must do thy utmost to reach Ardmore; sleep would nerve thee for it."

"That may be," said Mòr; "yet have I so much to tell thee, that the load on my mind is heavier than that on my body. Thou canst not think what an exquisite comfort it is to sit peacefully in a chair, and gaze at this bright fire, after being tossed about in the storm. Thou canst not sleep thyself; then why not listen to me?"

"If that be thy feeling, I am ready," replied Sorcha. "Thou hast witnessed terrible scenes."

Mòr was seated with her hands clasped over her knees, her large clear eyes fixed mournfully on Sorcha's.

" Yea," she answered, slowly; " but it is not these which
wear down the body. There are gnawing troubles which we
must hide in our hearts."

" Hast thou had such ? " asked Sorcha, gazing tenderly at
her.

" I will tell thee," replied Mòr. " I have no reason to
murmur against Providence, if thy days should prove to be
longer and happier than mine. The maiden who gives not
honour to her parents must expect to receive little from her
husband."

" Hath Fergus been unkind to thee ? " asked Sorcha,
starting.

" Not positively so," replied Mòr. " Yet are there things
which I dare not breathe in my father's ear. If thou and
Bishop Ardal should think it right for him to know them,
I must pray of your charity, that you will yourselves make
the disclosure."

" We will help you in every way we can," replied Sorcha.

" Fergus is often kind," continued Mòr, " in a certain
tender way, when I am alone with him ; but he has never
given me the place that his wife ought to have. I fear his
heart has never really been in the Irish Church. He
inclines to the Anglo-Romans, and is ashamed of being
married."

Sorcha looked horror-struck.

" Olrud was right," she said; " albeit he seemed to us so
uncharitable. What, then, impelled him to seek thee ? "

" That feeling I speak of," said Mòr, " appeared not when
I first married him. I was his queen, his angel, for a month
or two ; my very steps were like the notes of a song. Then
one of his sisters came to dwell with us." —

" Was she jealous of thee ? " asked Sorcha.

" Nay," replied Mòr; " yet hath she accustomed him to a
kind of flattery that benumbs his virtues. She was quite
scandalised when I made bold to contradict him, even in

trifles. It was nothing that she said—her looks were unutterable."

"She would deem it impious," said Sorcha; "he being thy husband and a bishop."

"Yea," replied Mòr. "Before that time Fergus never thought it strange in me to be frank. And I have learnt how well he can flatter, by seeing how he practises it on those members of his flock who are enriched by what cometh over the waves."

"Thinkest thou that it hath all been hollow?" asked Sorcha, trembling in spite of herself. She had a glimpse into the abyss from which Ardal's hand had plucked her.

"I know not," replied Mòr. "We differed about church ritual. Fergus hath adapted the old Irish forms to those of Rome as far as is possible. It matters not to me that he hath the 'Kyrie Eleison,' or even the 'Pange Lingua;' yet I cannot approve their being in dead tongues."

"Will Fergus not be grieved," asked Sorcha, "if his beautiful church should be destroyed?"

"He will find means to protect it," replied Mòr, with a strange ring in her voice. "I fear lest these changes should have been made less with a desire to improve our services, than to accustom men by degrees to those of foreigners."

"Thy voice is as the echo of Olrud's," said Sorcha. "Hast thou further ground for believing that Fergus's heart is with the aliens?"

"I have but too much," replied Mòr. "He is on the best of terms with the prelates of the Danish and of the new English colony. One of them, thou knowest, is that same Tostius who was at Ardmore two years ago."

"He would recollect thee," observed Sorcha.

Mòr looked inexpressibly sad. "It is surprising," she said, "how sensitive I was to what did not really hurt me. I had been accustomed when at Ardmore to receive more consideration than was perhaps my due, so it is possible that I was over quick to detect the want of it. When Fergus introduced me to the members of his flock I fancied that there was a suppressed complacency in the tone with which he uttered my name. But one evening Bishop Tostius spent a few hours beneath our roof. Enda was present, and Fergus merely said, ' My sister,' glancing at both of us."

"Wert thou not angry ?" inquired Sorcha.

" Yea," replied Mòr; " I felt my cheek tingle, and I resolved to enlighten our old friend by speaking boldly of my husband; but I soon found myself oppressed with an unconquerable timidity. Whether it were Enda's presence, or the fear of offending Fergus, I know not, but I felt my heart flutter in such a way that I could not get the words out—it was positive pain to try. I knew that Fergus was in the habit of visiting Bishop Tostius, yet I was startled when I observed on what a confidential footing the two stood. Some days afterwards my husband informed us that he wished to entertain some English priests. He would be grateful, he said, if I would take pains to provide them with a suitable banquet. But as they had some important questions to discuss, he thought the presence of women would be an embarrassment. I acquiesced, and so, I fancied, did Enda. I have rarely found an afternoon pass more slowly than that one did. The sand seemed as if it would never run down. Enda was suffering from a headache, and had shut herself up in her chamber. Thou mayest think, then, what was my surprise when my servant told me that she had slipped out, and, entering by the front door, had presided at the table !

" I taxed her with it in Fergus's presence. She and her brother turned it into a jest, saying that she had played a clever trick in thus asserting our feminine privileges. But I felt that I was being wronged; that my husband sought to hide from his new friends the fact of his being married. I know that I said something petulant, and I shed abundance of tears. Then Fergus and Enda talked together, ignoring my presence. It was more than I could endure. I was weak enough to rise from my chair and ask his forgiveness. Canst thou imagine my being brought so low as that?"

"Nay, verily," replied Sorcha, her brown eyes flashing indignantly.

"I cannot live without love," continued Mòr. "I suppose I have somewhat of the nature of a dog in me; at least I felt a strong sympathy with that animal.

"I never dreamt that Bishop Tostius had been amongst the guests. But one day I met him in the street.

"He was coming out of a house, whither he had carried the Host. On seeing me he started, gave the sacred elements to an attendant priest, and stepped forward with fatherly frankness. Knowest thou, Sorcha, I was so desolate at that moment, I almost felt as if I could fly to him for comfort.

"'What hath brought thee here?' he asked. 'Thy father must not be in Waterford without honouring my poor roof with his presence.'

"'My father is at Ardmore,' I replied. 'I have been wedded for more than six months. My husband is Bishop Fergus O'Flannahan.'

"The prelate looked startled; his brows knitted themselves in anger. Then he said in a compassionate tone—

"'It is not possible that Fergus O'Flannahan should be thy husband.'

"'Wherefore not?' I asked.

"'Because, my daughter,' he replied, 'Fergus O'Flannahan is an ordained priest.'

"It was as if he had thrust a dagger into my heart. By a great effort I kept myself from fainting.

"'When became he so?' I asked.

"The kind prelate held my arm firmly. Indeed, had it not been in the street, I doubt not that he would have supported me further. He drew me into an outbuilding of the house he had just quitted, shutting the door on the curious faces that had gathered outside, and placing me so as to shelter me from the gaze of a wench who was within.

"'Fergus was received into our communion whilst at Clugny,' he said, in a very low voice. 'I became aware of this only a few days ago. His consecration presupposed his having taken the vow of celibacy.'"

Sorcha's face had become as pale as Mòr's.

"What aileth thee?" asked the latter.

"Nothing," replied Sorcha; but her hand was trembling.

"Let me give thee some water," said Mòr. "I marvel not at it frightening thee."

"Go on," murmured Sorcha.

"Thou mayest wonder that the good bishop had not heard of Fergus's marriage," continued Mòr. "But the bitterness of the feud between our countrymen and the Danes had helped Fergus to conceal it from his Romish friends. The two parties make no effort even to become acquainted with each other's tongue, save for the purpose of barter.

"He counselled me to return to Ardmore. 'Thy stay under Fergus's roof is sacrilege,' he said. 'Come with me and I will arrange for thee a safe escort. Or, if thou dislikest a scandal, I could arrange for thy spending a little time with my sister, the new Abbess of Kilcheehan.'

"'I will consider of it and let thee know this evening,' I replied. 'I see thou art my friend, but I feel too much stunned to decide on anything at this moment.'

"'I understand thee,' he said. 'But remember that if thou art in trouble thou mayest count on my doing my utmost to get thee out of it.'

"I thanked him warmly, and then hastened away.

"Enda and Fergus were both at home when I reached our dwelling. My husband looked brighter than usual when I entered.

"'Fergus,' I said, 'is it true that thou art a Romish priest?'

"His whole countenance fell, and became suffused with crimson. I had never seen him look thus before.

"Enda burst out laughing.

"'Thou lovest a jest,' she said.

"Fergus at once recovered his self-possession. 'I confess to having gone through some ceremony when I was abroad,' he said, shrugging his shoulders, 'just to try what it was like. They have so many mummeries there that one more could not signify much.'

"'I would fain that thou hadst told me of it,' I said, 'before I agreed to be thy wife.'

"'Sit thee down, thou sunbeam of my heart,' said Fergus, in his tenderest voice. 'I would have told thee of it had it been done in earnest. I but hoodwinked the good people for the sake of being allowed to see things which must otherwise have remained strange to me. It cannot possibly hurt me, for my countrymen know well that I am a true son of the Irish Church. What sayest thou, O sister, more beloved than the light?'

"'I say,' replied Enda, 'that you had both best consult your own true interests by keeping it as secret as possible. You are husband and wedded wife by the laws of your own country, and you have no wish to live in exile.'

"Thou seest, Sorcha, that they treated it as a jest. Yet had I my doubts. My pride kept me from writing to consult my father; the image of my mother's scornful face rose before me; and I dreaded Fergus's wrath more than anything in this world. For the welfare of another was bound up with our living in peace." Mòr turned her head in the direction of her sleeping child.

"I was full of gloomy forebodings. Fergus became kinder to me than ever; and when he was again visited by an Anglo-Roman priest, I refrained from showing myself. Then came the invasion, the siege, and the horrible massacre. Bishop Tostius never knew that I had found shelter in his church; I was received there through the kindness of a priest with whom Fergus had become intimate. As I told thee, I beheld the Princess Eva's marriage. Fergus did not desert me; on the contrary, he visited me often during these dreadful hours, when our lives were hanging, as it were, on a thread. Yet an indefinable something bade me refrain from calling him husband; it was either the dread of making him dislike me, or it was that voice in the breast whose sound is unheard by any ear save our own. It was Fergus who procured me an escort hither. I thought that he had arranged for Enda's accompanying me; but she hung back at the last minute, and I had an impression, as I bade them farewell, that I was doing so for the last time."

"Thinkest thou that they would fain be rid of thee?" asked Sorcha.

"Yea," replied Mòr. "I have mused about it during my journey, and I see clearly that if the invasion succeeds, Fergus will have the strongest possible interest in repudiating me. His ambition is almost equal to his vanity. If things had remained as they were, I might have been a stepping-stone to distinction for him, but since Earl Strongbow's arrival I fear he will become Roman altogether."

"He hath never loved thee truly," said Sorcha.

"I cannot believe him wholly a hypocrite," replied Mòr. "He is romantic, and more changeable than the wind. Some men have a sort of affection for women, but it is not of the self-sacrificing kind. They love themselves first and best of all; in fact, they know not their own hearts."

"Yea," said Sorcha, "and most unhappily for us, they feel very warmly when the image of one of us is on their minds, and are more impetuous in showing it than their more sober and constant rivals."

"Ardal is a good husband," said Mòr.

"Yea," replied Sorcha; "I can truly say that he is. Not that he cannot be authoritative when he likes. I have

much less of my own way than I seem to have. But somehow or other, the sacrifice of my self-will seems to bring me
happiness—to differ from him would be just the same as to
differ from myself."

"I used to think," said Mòr, "that getting my own way
would make many crooked things straight."

"So did I," said Sorcha. "Yet I believe it is better as it
is. The exercise of our own wills often leads us into misery,
for we find that the things we sought after are no real good
after all. We are relieved of some responsibility when another
undertakes to judge for us."

"That may be pleasant enough," said Mòr, "to those
who have something firm to rely on. But hath not Fergus's
conduct to me been base ?"

"Most people would call it so," replied Sorcha; "but he
cannot hurt thee beyond a certain point. As my grandmother says, our worst enemies cannot go beyond the length
of the ropes to which they are fastened like the cattle. For
to the influence of men hath Providence placed a bound, as
well as to the sweep of the mighty waves."

"True," replied Mòr. "Fergus may humble me in the
eyes of others as he hath done in my own, but he cannot
change my mind nor my character; he cannot rob me of the
glorious prospects that are before every Christian. Perhaps
I needed this discipline. I was very proud and very dis-
contented."

Sorcha rose and kissed her:

"My best counsel is," she said, "to devote thy whole
mind to the task which Providence hath set thee. Who
knoweth what possibilities lie in that little cradle ?"

Mòr smiled very sadly. "I have been tempted," she said,
to wish that I had no such gift; for his father's conduct
throweth a stain upon him."

"Nay," exclaimed Sorcha, " there was a far deeper slur on
the holy Bridget's birth. And it can never be hidden that

our native Church sanctioned the marriage of her bishops. Why should not thy Erc follow in the steps of other priests' sons—of Patrick, for example ? "

Mòr smiled more brightly. " That would be a compensation," she said. " I have heard Bishop Muidoc say that our greatest pleasures come oft from our greatest pains. I may be the better able to train him because of my sufferings."

" Yea," replied Sorcha ; " and may he not perchance be inspired by his remembrance of thee to do great things after the hands with which thou hast held him are crumbled into dust ? It may be thine to kindle a spark which shall blaze for ages like Bridget's fire at Kildare."

The object of these bright hopes now stirred uneasily. A cry issued from his soft lips, and Mòr became engrossed in the task of quieting him.

CHAPTER XXIX.

Tidings of the conflict at Waterford had already reached Ardmore. Ardal had lost no time in despatching to the abbot a letter announcing his intention of seeking for Amada, Sorcha, and Mòr a safe shelter near the sanctuary of Declan.

It was a bleak morning when they left Youghal. Sorcha's heart swelled almost to bursting as, seated in a tiny coracle of hides and wicker-work, she looked back on the little stone church with its square bell tower, embosomed in the yellowing beech trees. The wind had a touch of winter in it, and rippled the surface of the corn that clothed the sides of the hills overlooking the estuary, into waves of gold. Sorcha stepped on to the opposite bank with a feeling that she had for the last time beheld the scene of her wedded happiness.

They journeyed on horseback through the forest, and on reaching Ardmore they found that a pleasant surprise had been prepared for them. Maidoc and Ita, who had for the last year occupied Mael-Patrick's cottage, had lost no time in vacating it, and returning into their old dwelling.

"We thought that Amada would like it," explained Ita. "It would seem so strange and cold for her to be at Ardmore under any other roof. You are more than welcome when you come to live under Declan's bell."

Ardal hastened, almost before sunrise, to acquaint Mòr's parents with the fact of her presence.

"Fergus hath been disposed to slight her," he said.

" His heart is with the aliens, and he will in all likelihood become a priest at their altar. Thy daughter, indeed, hath been informed that he hath accepted consecration at their hands."

" Vile hypocrite!" exclaimed the abbot, scornfully. "I wonder not that thou tremblest to speak of such villainy. He hath been faithless to his spiritual mother, even to the Church which hath nourished him. Can we, then, marvel at his being a bad husband?"

Uailsi had sat quite impassive whilst her husband spoke. Now, looking up from her embroidery, she asked:

" In what way does it interest us?"

Ardal recovered from his agitation in a moment. He had, indeed, been on the point of confessing his own errors. He responded to Uailsi's question by a look as stern as her own.

" I thought, lady," he replied, " that the blood of the Cinel Conaill and the Ua-Breasail could not well be changed into a commoner fluid. A diamond retaineth its lustre even after it hath been trampled in the dust. Mòr Ni-Flannahan is still thy daughter."

" Yea," replied Uailsi; " but I seek not to stay the course of Divine justice. She hath chosen her own path; let her keep to it."

" Uailsi," said the abbot, " she is my child as well as thine. I have not insisted on thy pardoning her whilst we thought she was happy; but now that she is in a manner cast off, I would fain have her dwell with us."

" Arrange thy plans," said Uailsi, rising; " but on the day that Mòr entereth thy house, I leave it."

" Stay," exclaimed Ardal, laying his hand on the proud woman's arm. " I would have thee bethink thee what thou doest. We walk on no Tyrian carpets. Sleepless nights and anxious days are now our portion. For the din of battle draweth near, and we may count, not the weeks only, but the hours, ere it hemmeth us round with its horrible music."

"Seekest thou to terrify me?" replied Uailsi. "I tell thee that, though Ardmore Tower were razed to its foundations, though every stone of Declan's shrine were cast into the waves, I have in mine own breast a fortress which fear cannot penetrate."

"Nor pity?" said Ardal. "Would thine eye behold but for a moment the outcast one, reft from all that she hath been wont to hold dear; pale, worn, and afflicted; bearing in her arms the image of what she once was in thine, but all too weak to protect it from the coming storm, thou wouldst find the gates of thy fortress opening. Mòr cometh not to thee claiming her natural rights, she cometh as a suppliant."

"She hath the less need of aught from me that she hath so eloquent a friend," replied Uailsi, bowing haughtily as she passed out of the cottage door.

"It were vain for us to force a reconciliation," said the abbot, when his wife had disappeared. "It would only make life unbearable to us all. Before I speak with Mòr, however, I would fain have thy counsel. Thinkest thou that I should take any steps towards making Fergus acknowledge her more openly?"

"I confess," replied Ardal, "that I like not the prospect of her waiting here in suspense till she learns his pleasure. Thou mightest well despatch a messenger with a letter to him, and challenge him to answer plainly whether he holdeth himself bound by his Roman consecration or purposeth to retain what I must consider the higher title of an Irish bishop. There is no time for trimming between the two parties now. It will be a life and death struggle betwixt us and the English. We shall have to fight for our religious freedom, if we would not tamely submit both soul and body to an alien rule."

"But is there any likelihood," asked the abbot, "of the

Anglo-Roman authorities punishing Fergus for the breach of his vow?"

Ardal shrugged his shoulders. "I cannot tell," he replied. "I have studied their politics carefully of late, and I suspect that they are trying to gain over the native pastors to make the English conquest easier. Once let us acknowledge the Pope's supremacy, and Henry becomes our lawful sovereign. For which reason I am inclined to think that a born orator of Fergus' stamp will be valuable in their eyes, and that they will therefore be disposed to overlook some of his inconsistencies."

"Yea, verily," said the abbot, "he may atone for them partly by penance, and partly by renewed zeal in the service of his new masters. He will be eager to wipe out the blot on his reputation. Oh, Ardal! we have sunk low indeed, for lack of our ancient manliness, both at Rathbresail and at Kells! My daughter's fate is but a type of what awaiteth both our nation and our Church!"

"Hast thou taken any measures for our defence?" asked Ardal.

"Yes," replied the abbot. "I have instructed our Erenach to store grain and water, in the Round Tower. All our parchments are removed thither. I would not have them buried in the ground, lest perchance the memory of them might perish; yet they fill a space that can ill be spared."

"I would not have it otherwise," said Ardal. "What availeth provender for the body, if that which should furnish the food of our minds—nay, of our immortal souls—be allowed to perish? There is not a woman nor child in Ardmore who would not sooner die than see our books given to the hand of the spoiler."

"Yea," replied the abbot, "thou speakest like a son of the great Brian. But are not the ways of Providence inscrutable? So hard is it for the struggling light of the spirit to force its way upwards amidst surrounding darkness; yet the waves of barbarism are allowed to swell up and put it out. Athens resisted the power of the Persians; yet she, too, hath been trampled in the dust, and most of her treasures, borne to a foreign shore, were destroyed by the ignorant Goth. So will it be with our colleges."

Ardal smiled. "Thou speakest well," he replied, "if it be only of human learning. Yet methinks that amongst our treasures there is one that hath more than the ægis of Athena to guard it. Its leaves may be torn, and scattered before the wild blast of the hills; they may light the fires of Strongbow's troopers; they may be ground down to fine dust; but yet from them ariseth a fragrance that shall pass into the very structure of the world; for He who cannot lie hath said it. Let Plato and Herodotus perish; let the very names of Ilion and of Hellas be blotted from the memory of man—that book shall live! and though it be buried, it shall rise again."

"Thou speakest truly, my son," said the abbot, laying his fatherly hand on Ardal's shoulder. "I often feel as if the burden were too much for me, and tremble lest I be called to account for the charge of such treasures. But since the Almighty's own Word is amongst them, He will surely watch over it, and perhaps even for its sake spare Homer and Sophocles."

"Yea, verily," replied Ardal, "how should we know into what kind of world the revelation came if it were not for these old histories? And the poets are prized by us, not merely for their own beauties, but because they illustrate the forms of ancient speech, and place beyond cavil the meaning of terms employed in the Sacred Word."

"Thou speakest truly," said the abbot. "As all human flesh became sanctified by the touch of our Incarnate Lord, so will the Grecian tongue ever seem to us bathed in a supernatural lustre."

"Hast thou called any warriors to our aid?" asked Ardal.

"Nay," replied the abbot. "We can dream of no lengthened siege with these women and children; the issue of this dire conflict must be decided elsewhere. Our tower will hold but scant provision; it will only enable us to parley for a short time. I have, however, sent messengers to learn the intentions of the neighbouring chieftains. One and all of them seem inclined to follow the advice which hath been given them from Lismore; which is, to swear allegiance to Henry."

"Have they, then, forgotten the ties of blood?" said Ardal, bitterly. "Thinkest thou that any word of mine might rouse them to succour the O'Faolain?"

"Thy face might do it," said the abbot; "for thou bearest the very features of the heroic Brian. Only let the locks hang over thy forehead, and they will think that he still liveth."

"That spell is broken," said Ardal. "The united powers of Anjou, Aquitaine, Normandy, and England could not crush us. But a spirit of darkness hovereth in the air. It is this which hath weakened our right arm."

"Yea, truly," replied the abbot; "the false teaching creepeth everywhere. It hath polluted the well of Carthagh, and we cannot keep it from trickling into that of Declan."

"Thou speakest no mysteries," said Ardal; "for the new prelates have shown the first example of submission. Our Irish ones think, I doubt not, that they kiss a soft glove; they will find an iron one beneath it."

"I think that thou wilt approve my counsel," said the abbot. "Methinks that the chiefs of the Deisi will fight; but if they shrink from doing so, it is not for us to grasp carnal weapons."

"The men of the Deisi have been but too ready for pettier contests," said Ardal, "when it was but a question of stolen cattle. But I blame them not. The blood of our country be on these foreign priests' heads. Yet what is before us but the extinction of our ancient foundation ? "

" Or its transformation into a community of Roman monks," replied the abbot. " It will but share the fate of Iona. We can no more drive back the cloud that gathereth above the ocean than attempt to avert this."

" Not so ! " exclaimed Ardal, with flashing eyes. " It shall never be said that Erin died tamely. Thou, as a spiritual ruler, art perhaps wise to counsel moderation; but I have royal blood in my veins! I will go forth to these coward chieftains ! I will urge them forward to the battle ! "

" Do so, if thou wilt," said the abbot. " Yet bethink thee of thy wife and child."

" Sorcha would despise me were I to act otherwise," replied Ardal; " so would Amada. I must leave them under thy protection for the present. I forget aught else but that I am an Irishman."

The abbot gazed at him fondly. " Would that Fergus had been like thee ! " he murmured to himself. " Go, my son," he said, aloud. " The God of thy fathers bless thee ! "

Ardal hastened towards the cottage to make known his resolve. But as he walked close to the turfy wall of the rath, he was startled by a serpent-like hiss.

Turning back, he saw two glittering eyes peering at him from the top of the wall. The face of Phelim O'Bric, with his chin planted on the edge of the parapet, loomed down at him with portentous solemnity.

" Seekest thou a sword ? " asked a grating voice. " There is one in thy family which never resteth. It hath drunk the blood of thy brothers, and the drops on it are not to be washed out by the floods of Shannon. Woe ! woe to the house of Brian ! The glory of the Milesian Eber hath vanished; it will be buried in the dust of ages. Woe ! woe to the fane of Declan ! The wind bloweth from the east; it bringeth the sparks with it, and the flame of that burning shall be as a beacon to future times."

Ardal's blood ran cold. There was more than a grain of truth in what this half-witted man had said about his kinsmen's sword. And for months the wind had blown from the east with astonishing persistence. The voice continued:

" Bring an oblation of peace offerings. The steel must be bright that would chase away the devil's brood of Anjou. The flame cometh, yea, it waxeth strong; it thirsteth to lick up the tarnished glory. Ardmore shall be but as a brand to feed it."

Ardal stayed to hear no more. With beating heart and flushed cheek he sought the cottage, there to pour into loving ears the tale of his new resolve.

But it was with much misgiving that he spoke. Amada bent forward to catch his every word, whilst Sorcha stood with averted face at the little window, holding her infant on her left arm.

As Ardal finished his recital, she turned slowly round. It was a moment of extreme suspense. The strong man felt that a word from her could overthrow all his heroic aspirations. Her eyes were downcast, her lip quivering.

" I am no Andromache," she said, " to bid thee place thy care for me and for our child before thy country's welfare. Go, for we are safe in the arms of the Everlasting One."

Ardal kissed away her fast-falling tears. " I knew that thou wouldst say so," he said; " yet the welfare of Erin is not more dear to me than thine. Thou wilt miss me sorely in the hour of danger, yet, methinks, I can do yet more for my country. We have no right to ask the help of Providence if we obey not His calls."

Sorcha nerved herself to prepare her husband's travelling wallet. Amada sat with folded hands watching her every movement, and from time to time pouring forth unconsciously some word of prayer. At length all was ready.

Mounted on a silver-bridled horse, clad partly in clerical dress, partly in the chequered trews and fine linen of a chieftain, Ardal paused on the border of the forest to speak his last farewells.

He had parted from his most loved ones within the cottage. A tress of Sorcha's hair, bound about his wrist, seemed to clasp him like a living thing. His eye fell on many sorrowing faces.

"What will thy return be?" said Maidoc, solemnly. "Will thine eyes behold this fair pile as it is? The gloomy prophet, Phelim, would have us believe that it is soon to perish. He hath circled about it like an ill-omened bird since we learnt of the fall of Waterford."

"Hath Cacht no spell to conjure him?" asked Ardal. "I dread not what he saith, but his words distil fear into the minds of those who hearken to him. To thee, Maidoc, and to thee, our revered abbot, I commit the charge of my beloved wife."

The two men answered by a silent pressure of the hand. They then walked sadly homewards, whilst Ardal disappeared into the wood. The path which he followed was thickly planted with memories. There was the pond from which Phelim's uncouth form had arisen to trouble the bliss of his spousal day. There was the shining river, in whose depths he could almost picture the mirrored image of Sorcha's face, when her ruby lips first uttered the words which revealed to him that he was free to woo her. There was the village, the very faces of the women who had been as the background to a most lovely picture, and how was he fulfilling the vows that had then seemed so easy?

Ardal tried to banish these thoughts. Sorcha's heart was with him, the curl of brown hair seemed to tell him that he was doing her no wrong. He could not bear to think of her weeping in loneliness; yet surely, for her sake, it were better to fulfil well the mission which he had undertaken. He was strong in the purity of his purposes; for it was no vain ambition that had led him to gird a golden-hilted sword to his side as the insignia of his royal rank. And his heart beat high at the thought that his might be the voice which would rouse the men of Erin to resist the invader.

Yet he was conscious of a sudden misgiving. From the clustering foliage before him issued a dark-plumaged raven. "It bringeth good fortune if it go with me," thought Ardal. But the bird, instead of flying in a straight course, darted towards the left, and, seating itself on a lofty branch, croaked down at him.

"I am no coward, false bird," said Ardal aloud. But he felt a strange sinking. The raven, spreading its dusky wings, glided rapidly away in the direction from which he had come.

The words of Phelim now haunted him; for a sword had been oft unsheathed in his father's house. Ardal despised superstition; yet in vain reason told him that any augury from the behaviour of a bird would be as much a fable as the story of those sable-clad hags who pursued Orestes. Yet was there some foundation for a curse in both cases; for the evil deeds of Ardal's father on his own kinsmen had been done in spite of sanctuary given by all the bishops of Munster; and the blood of his cousins, shed with the help of Prince Malachy O'Faolain, was even yet scarcely dry upon the ground.

"These are the sins for which we suffer," groaned Ardal to himself; "yet why are they marked only against us? The royal house with which we would fain match ourselves is not stained with the bloodshedding of kindred; yet hath it become famous for the mutual hatred betwixt father and son. Though our swords have been drawn against our own flesh, they drip not so much with the blood of the innocent alien.

Yet feel I as if I were unworthy to help in protecting the ark of our freedom."

"This is but a nightmare," he said at last, giving the reins to his horse. And as he sped through the forest there came back to him that vigour of mind which was so necessary for the success of his mission.

CHAPTER XXX.

THERE were months of waiting for the family of Ardmore. Weary months they were, when the sound of the wind in the leafless boughs sent tremors into many a heart; when the beams of the morning sun brought no gladness, and the whole of nature wore a look as melancholy as that of an unfrozen pond in the midst of snow. Few days passed without some messenger coming to tell of fresh submissions, and rumours were rife of these submissions having sometimes failed to protect the helpless natives from rapine and massacre.

Then tidings arrived of the fall of Dublin, and of the slaughter of many of its inhabitants. The English were, however, scarcely as yet numerous enough to do more than seize some of the chief towns in the eastern half of the island.

And Ardal's efforts were by no means fruitless. He indeed failed in persuading his brother Domnall, who had married a daughter of King Dermod, to turn the arms which he had disloyally taken up to attack the ard-righ Roderick, against the invader; but he had succeeded in rousing MacCarthy of Desmond to attempt the recapture of Waterford. The arrival of King Henry, however, put an end to his most sanguine hopes.

No sooner had the English monarch set foot on the banks of the Suir than crowds of the newly-nominated prelates flocked to do him homage. Every archbishop and bishop of the Romish persuasion bestowed on him a charter in the form of a letter with seal attached, confirming the kingdom of Ireland to him and to his heirs for ever.* Many chieftains followed their example, some because they had been persuaded by the representations of their new spiritual advisers; others because they saw that resistance had become quite hopeless. It was one thing to fight against Strongbow and his formidable horde of freebooters; it was quite another to withstand a sovereign who held in his hand the might of England, with that of half the empire of Charlemagne.

And Roderick himself submitted. Only, however, as the acknowledged sovereign of a country might in those days pay nominal homage to a suzerain. He was allured by the hope of being permitted to reign in peace over a people made more loyal by the taste which they had had of foreign rule. Nor was there aught but honour in yielding allegiance to the most powerful monarch in Europe.

But all plans for the simultaneous prosperity of wolves and lambs must prove unavailing. Henry, indeed, had come with a professed desire to further the interests of religion and morality; but his barons, like himself, were more given to hunting than to holiness. The simple truth was, that most of those who had accompanied him to Ireland were landless; some of them being younger or illegitimate sons, and the Saxon preserves being already well occupied by their fortunate elders, they had crossed the waves in quest of fresh game. Excuses were soon forthcoming for possessing themselves of Irish land, and those native chieftains who had been most zealous in the service of the English were the first to be despoiled. The Church lands offered a most tempting prey. Safe as they had been since the days of Brian Borumha from the ravages of war, they were the finest and best cultivated soil in the island. And as the Pope had given to these freebooters a wide commission for destroying all nurseries of vice, they might well hope to benefit their own souls

* Appendix.

whilst uprooting religious institutions so long famed for their opposition to catholic doctrine and unity.

The twelve fathers of Ardmore had thus but a choice between two evils. By sending in their submission to Christian of Lismore, they would lose two-thirds of their revenues, and be reduced to the rank of vicars-choral, whilst the bishops of the villages under their jurisdiction might be honoured with the strange title of chor-episcopi.

Such a proceeding would, however, be violating the sacred trust of antiquity. They felt as if the spirit of Declan might revisit his shrine, to call down a curse on those who had so far departed from his teachings. On the other hand, nought was to be expected but ruin, desolation, and slaughter. Were the stones of their beloved founder's church to be overturned? were the bodies of his spiritual children to lie bleeding in its dust? or were they to be saved by the sacrifice of his doctrine?

The good fathers were not long in deciding.

"The Almighty can raise other churches," said Maidoc. "He can call forth other saints to wax valiant for the truth. Had the martyrs of the Colosseum judged otherwise, where would now be the faith which we hold? These men were firm against the assaults of paganism, say some, whereas we are only asked to change one form of Christianity for another. But I say that our adversaries have sucked up the very essence of that paganism which they profess to abhor. For is not the worship of the Virgin, are not the prayers for the dead, but a continuation of the homage offered by a Themistocles at the altar of Minerva, and of the libations poured by pious Roman and Athenian sons over the ashes of their parents, in the fond hope of enhancing the welfare of their beloved ones in the world of spirits? Therefore, I say, let us resist, strong in faith, and leave the issue to Him whose altar we serve. Let those who fear greatly depart from amongst us. We will remain to perish, if need be, with our wives and little ones, to guard at least the library of Declan until it can be deposited in worthy hands."

Maidoc but gave voice to the feelings of his brethren. His scholars had now departed to their respective homes. The place was, however, crowded with the wives and families of village bishops, seeking shelter under the silver bell of the saint. The routine of college life was broken up, and men gave themselves with undivided hearts to prayer and to the study of the Scriptures.

Sorcha and Mòr resumed somewhat of their old life, devoting themselves with hearty zeal to their transcriptions, as well as to the work of compounding medicines. They were now sisters in affliction; for whilst the husband of the one was daily exposed to capture and the danger of an ignominious death, the other winced under the shame of repudiation —for though the abbot's letter to Fergus remained unanswered, all accounts from Waterford confirmed the fact that the latter was officiating as a priest of Rome.

"How is it, Sorcha," asked Mòr, one day, as they sat together bending over their faultlessly inscribed parchments— "how is it that we have ever found room for jealousy here? My cheeks burn when I think of it. Well do I recollect hòw mortified I once felt when my mother told me that thou hadst finished off thy smaller capitals with these little golden balls; and that thy page was more brilliant than mine, though the first letter of our Lord's name extended down the whole side of it?"

"These ornaments seem to me almost vain," replied Sorcha; "though perchance they may make the holy books a welcome gift to princes. Yet why should I speak slightly of them? God hath clothed His other works with material beauty; and if our childhood loves the flowers but for their colour, our riper age almost worships them because of the wonderful secrets of their being."

"Yea," replied Mòr; "yet in this time of trouble my

hand would rather form the letters of these living words than spend its strength in that ornament which suiteth better with our hours of gladness."

It had been a bitter grief to the abbot that he could not receive his daughter under his roof. Mòr shrank from Uailsi's presence. They worshipped, indeed, in the same church; but, whilst the mother entered by a side door into the inner sanctuary, the daughter occupied a place near the entrance of the outer one. No persuasions could induce Mòr to seat herself beyond the separating arch.

"I love not to have such heart-wounds," she said. "For when my father and I have wandered together at nightfall round the rath, and my mother hath come forth with a letter to meet him, she hath cast on me a glance as if she marked me not. I have slipped from his side, and rushed into the darkness to wish almost for death. Oh, Sorcha! I could bear scorn from any one but her!"

Sorcha could only look her pity. "Thou wouldst feel even more," she replied, "were thy little Erc to wound thee in like manner. He hath a soft medicinal touch, wilt thou not try it?"

At length news came that a band of English plunderers, commanded by a son of Strongbow, had marched out of Waterford. Their faces were towards the south-west, and their mules were getting loaded with the plunder of churches.

Nearer and nearer came the dread thunder-cloud. The abbot made haste to stow all the parchments on the shelves of the Round Tower, and to fill its floors with sacks of meal. He commanded that on the first alarm all women and children should repair thither.

As he passed out of the church, after having given these directions, he beheld the buxom figure of Cacht, her blooming cheeks pale with fear.

"May I have a word with thee?" she said.

"Speak, my daughter," replied the abbot.

"It liketh me not for Phelim," she stammered; "the man will starve when the foe is upon us."

"True," replied the abbot. "Canst thou not devise some means to save him from perishing? He hath little wit to help himself, and his life is precious in our sight. Thinkest thou that he might be coaxed into dwelling with us in the tower?"

"I doubt it," replied Cacht; "but he knoweth nought of the danger. Thy daughter hath penned him a letter which he threw into the sea. And who is there that can reach him?"

"Wouldst thou venture down thyself?" asked the abbot.

"Yea, if I had thy approbation," replied the girl.

"Then speak with thy friends," said the abbot, "that they may help thee to accomplish the task in safety. But make haste, for there are but few steps betwixt us and danger."

Cacht returned to seek help in the cottage. She found Amada locked in the arms of her daughter Grainné.

"Olrud advised me to go to Inisfallen," said the matron; "but as my sons remain at Lismore, I would fain share whatever fate may be in store for thee and Sorcha. The dames of our college like us not, and my being here will save us from being anxious about each other."

Cacht told of her proposed expedition.

"If it were not that thou hast the abbot's sanction," said Sorcha, "I would fain counsel thee against it. For the cliff is steep, and none would dare to be hung over it but thyself."

Cacht's face fell.

"I marvel not at thy wish," said Grainné; "the man is truly a strange being, yet hath Providence linked his fate to thine in some manner. I will do my best to help thee. But let not many know of it; for there are some, perchance, who would dislike his presence with us in one of yonder strait chambers."

"Or who would say," suggested Mòr, "that it were a distrusting of Providence to force sustenance on one who hath been nourished like the beasts and the ravens. I doubt," she whispered to Sorcha, " whether the man be more worth saving than they; yet hath he an immortal soul, and the blood of his curious body may be required at our hands."

The image of the hermit had, indeed, become more impressed on Cacht's mind than she had ever permitted any one to perceive. Through all the disfigurements which neglect and ascetic practices had inflicted upon it, her keen eye could still detect the form of the pale, well-shapen youth in whose dark eyes she had for a passing moment read the tale of his love for herself. There was something in him which had captivated her fancy; an appeal to her vanity, perhaps, in having thus attracted the notice of one who was her superior in education and in worldly position. It had led her to withstand the persistent addresses of much worthier men, amongst others of the stalwart smith, whose hammer rang so incessantly on the forge just within the great gate. Nor had she during all these years been without a hope that some day, suitably clothed and in his right mind, he might be drawn to forsake his cave, and spend his old age with her in some pretty leaf-embowered cottage.

By the early morning light a group of dark-robed, white-veiled women stood near the edge of the cliff which had been pierced by some freak of nature into a rude shelter for the outcast man.

Sorcha and Grainné held a large washerwoman's basket in their hands. Placing it on the rocks they fastened to its handles four twisted broom ropes.

"Doth thy heart misgive thee, Cacht?" asked Mòr. "Look at the waves that leap into foam against the rough stones beneath us. Wilt thou not rather that we fill this basket with a good measure of barley?"

"Nay, haste ye," replied Cacht, shuddering in spite of herself. "I shall close my eyes as I go down."

Two men now came forward, having been engaged by Sorcha to assist in lowering the basket. Cacht, being at length seated on a goodly lining of straw, was heaved bodily over the cliff.

The first lurch of her rude chariot, as she hung suspended betwixt earth and sky, nearly made her repent of her purpose. Her head was swimming, her heart throbbing as she alighted at the entrance of the cave.

A growl from within revealed the presence of the hermit. Cacht, supporting herself as best she could against the rocky doorway, found that her eyes were becoming accustomed to the scanty light, and the sights which it disclosed made her flesh creep. Death's heads were everywhere staring at her from their eyeless sockets, and grinning with their white jaws. Grotesque forms of lizards and other loathsome animals lay upon the ground, amongst heaps of small bones mingled with the half-burnt paws of black cats. The steam which issued from the place was heavy with charcoal fumes, and had a more decided odour of sulphur than of sanctity in it.

The death's heads began to move. Cacht shrieked, lost her footing, and fell backwards. But the hermit's strong arm was thrown round her. Half insensible, she was pulled back into the cave, and had time to collect her senses as she crouched upon its slimy floor. Then she became aware that a pair of fierce eyes were glaring at her.

"What doest thou here?" asked a grating voice. "Dost thou long to be dashed into these seething waters?"

"I come to serve thee," replied Cacht, shuddering all over. "I am bidden to tell thee that the foe is about to compass us round, and that if thou wouldst fain have sustenance, it can only be by joining thy fellows."

"Thinkest thou that I know it not?" replied Phelim, pointing with his bony claw to a small black caldron which simmered over a few bright embers. Cacht, straining her eyes, perceived the shrivelled form of a scorched and shrivelled animal suspended over it. Two greenish balls starting out from what had been its face gave token that Phelim had just performed the unholy rite of roasting a living cat.

"Seest thou nothing?" shrieked the hermit, withdrawing into the darkest corner of the cave.

"No," replied Cacht, making the sign of the cross.

Phelim took up a small pebble from the ground. He threw it into the caldron. A sound of hissing and spluttering followed. Cacht's face became as white as the bones which hung around her; yet she felt as if she could dare all the powers of hell could she but succeed in saving Phelim.

Then a blue smoke ascended to the roof.

"It cometh," exclaimed the hermit; "it leapeth on the fire. Hearest thou nothing?"

Cacht gazed in speechless horror. She had heard many a tale of the Taigheirm, that rite by which her heathen ancestors had been permitted to hold converse with the spirits of darkness. To her excited imagination it seemed as if the air were now filled with the howlings of the lately tortured cats; and the form of one, ferocious in mien and unlike to anything earthly, now appeared above the fire.

"It is the ghost of Merlin," said Phelim. "I will tell thee what he saith."

As the hermit spoke, his head and beard became alive with flashes of pale fire. His words were distinctly heard.

"A light hath come into this island; and all its birds shall flock to see the splendour of it. Then shall the greater birds be taken captive, and their wings shall be burned. No more shall their haughty beaks peck each other. A strange king cometh; he bringeth peace, yea, peace. His peace shall be so great that the pastures shall yield no cattle; the fields, no corn; the air, no birds; the seas, though full of fish, yet to the sons of Erin yielding nothing. The curse of God shall be on the green-valleyed land, and no home-born thing shall thrive in it save the wolves and foxes."

"I have warned thee of thine own fate," said Cacht, trembling violently. "For the love of Christ I beg thee either to come with me or to let me depart."

"Come with thee!" exclaimed Phelim, coming close to her. "Nay, the devil hath lost his hold on me. I fear him not in the creeping darkness, for his ministers are my servants. Thy feet bring no blessing with them. Thou art, as the holy Chrysostom saith, but a mischief of nature overlaid with glittering varnish. I counsel thee to be gone."

Cacht glanced at the fire. The caldron no longer steamed, the apparition had vanished; but something smote her on the arms with a violence which went through her whole frame. It was like nothing she had ever before felt, and was followed by a painful tingling. She fainted.

Cacht could never tell how she re-entered the basket; nor did she retain enough of self-possession to repeat more than half of the strange things which she had witnessed in the gloomy cavern.

"Leave Phelim to his fate," said Grainne. "Thou hast done what many a brave warrior dare not have attempted. They who hold converse with the spirits of darkness should look to them for help in trouble. As for the hermit's sanctity, I never believed in it; for hath not godliness promise of this life in the first instance? He would have been as much of a saint had he dwelt with thee as he will ever be in a whole graveyard of skulls."

Before cock-crowing next morning fell the first thunderbolt upon Ardmore. The silver bell pealed violently, and the blast of a trumpet summoned all to betake themselves to the Round Tower.

CHAPTER XXXI.

It was a wild bleak November morning. Winter had set in
early, with storms of such violence, that the sandhills of the
Welsh coast had been washed back into the sea, leaving bare
the blackened trunks of the old trees which they had covered
up in past ages. The great yew on Ardmore hill had been
uprooted by the wind; and the waves, thundering against
the cliffs by Declan's well, broke into the midnight slumbers
of the clerical community with their terrible music. Nature
seemed to partake of the violent spirit which swayed the mind
of man.

Amada's ascent into the tower was most painful to behold.
A rude ladder had been placed against the narrow entrance
door, some thirteen feet from the ground. Supported by
Maidoc, who held her firmly by means of a sheet passed
round her waist, she dragged her aged limbs up the steep
ascent. She was followed by her daughter, with Mòr, Sorcha,
and Cacht, their pale faces telling of anxious vigils. With
incredible toil she managed to reach an upper chamber,
where, worn and exhausted, she sank heavily down on one of
the corn-sacks which were piled on the floor.

"Thou wilt have less trouble here, mother," said Grainné,
"for in a lower chamber thou wouldst have been forced to
move whenever any one wished to pass thee. We shall also
have word sooner from those who keep a look-out above us."

"I shall mount as far as the bell," said Mòr, "leaving my
little Erc with Grainné. Has my mother entered?"

"Yea," replied Cacht; "I have seen her beneath."

"Even at this hour!" exclaimed Mòr, "will she give me no token of forgiveness?"

"I fear not," replied Grainné; "but should she be near me, I shall scruple not to show her thy child."

It was most touching to behold the crowd of pale faces in that dark, narrow, circular chamber. The massive stone walls were whitewashed in the interior, and supported some ten feet from the ground a strong circular wooden shelf, resting on corbels whose grotesque heads remain to the present day. The scanty sunbeams which entered through the narrow window revealed a strange confusion of meal-bags and human forms; piled up so as to bring the heads of the latter to a level with the row of caskets and leathern bags which, stored on the shelf, contained treasures dearer to some of their possessors than life itself. A long ladder passed through the midst, communicating with the chambers above and below.

Mòr stood beside the bell, peering anxiously through one of the four large windows. A loud blast of trumpets was soon heard.

"They come!" she exclaimed, looking down the ladder hole. "Men on horseback issue from the wood; and the foremost beareth the banner of St. George!"

Amada and Sorcha bent their heads in silent prayer.

"They come still!" exclaimed Mòr. "They swarm! A bishop hath gone out to speak with them at the gate. O merciful Heaven!"

"What is it?" asked Sorcha, terrified by her friend's shriek.

"They have stabbed him," replied Mòr; "they hew him to pieces. My father, and they that followed him, flee hither. The wild men rush towards the church; they break into our houses. Oh, pray that my father may be able to mount!"

All held their breath in intense anxiety. Sorcha pressed her child closely to her arms.

"He is safe now!" cried Mòr, at length; "they have drawn the ladder up. These thick walls are the only barrier betwixt us and death."

"Nay!" exclaimed Maidoc, who, with Ita, was in the act of mounting from the chamber beneath. "He hath given his angels charge concerning us. There be more that fight with us than they that be against us."

"True," replied Mòr, in a calmer voice. "But a smoke ariseth from the cow-houses outside, the straw-ricks are on fire; the sheep, the swine rush wildly about; their blood is being shed like water."

"Thank God that it is not ours," said Ita. "We have but a short time to spend here; let us try to fix our thoughts on our better inheritance."

Each minute, as it passed, brought a fresh report of destruction accomplished. The pretty rustic cottages were all sacked; their furniture, hallowed to the owners by many precious memories, was dragged out to make bonfires for the roasting of the slaughtered beasts. Ardmore was soon blazing; volumes of black smoke, mingled with shooting red sparks, enveloped the tower on every side. Those within sat in total darkness, illumined only by flashes of flame. They groaned in the stifling heat.

Then the wind arose with violence. Fiercer and fiercer grew the flames, blacker and blacker rolled the smoke; a horrible crackling replied to the voice of the tempest. As Mòr peered with blanched face on the dreadful scene, a sudden gust drove away the smoke from the summit of the rath beneath her, revealing the weird figure of Phelim, his shaggy beard half burnt away. He shook his long, bony arm wildly on perceiving Mòr.

"Spake I not truly," he shrieked. "Woe to Erin! she hath broken the covenant of her God; she hath left the faith of Patrick. Her portion be with the guides she hath chosen. They make the path bright whereon they essay to lead her; yea, bright."

So saying, he leapt from the summit of the rath down into the roaring flame.

Mòr sank shuddering on the ground. "I can gaze no longer," she murmured. "I would fain go down to abide the event in darkness."

Amada had now dropped asleep. She looked as peaceful as little Rossa himself in his mother's arms. At length some wild howls intimated that the soldiers were bent on attacking the tower. Then a terrible thud shook the building to its foundations.

"They have brought a battering ram," said Ita, who had mounted to the summit.

A shower of arrows now struck against the wall; they failed, however, to reach the watchers at the high window. Amada still slept.

"Try smoke," said a hoarse voice. It was answered by a succession of wolf-like howls. Savage men rushed over the blackened turf, bringing boughs, bedding, and everything inflammable on which they could lay their hands.

"This is horrible," exclaimed Maidoc. "Let me mount to the bell-chamber. I will adjure them in the name of Christ. We men might offer ourselves as prisoners of war, on condition that the women go free."

"Thinkest thou that they would keep faith?" replied the abbot. "These men are drunken. This good tower hath survived the fury of the Danes; and if it but stand till morning, the worst of that crew will be asleep. I may then venture forth and try to parley with the leaders."

The sun had long since set. The smoke had subsided, leaving the walls of the roofless church looming ghost-like above a mass of glowing ashes. Neither moon nor stars were visible.

But all was darkness to the terrified company in the tower. To the pangs of fear were now added those of hunger. There was no space for cooking, and the provision of bread could not be reached for the heaped-up sacks. Many began to consume handfuls of corn.

A black vapour now penetrated through the narrow windows. It woke Amada; she seized her daughter's arm.

" What is it ?" she gasped, faintly.

" They are trying to suffocate us," replied Grainné, trembling. " Let me place an arm round thee, and trust in Him who was with the three children in the furnace."

" Help me up," said Amada.

Grainné did so; but her mother withdrew from the gentle support she offered. Grainné was surprised to notice how the colour was returning to the aged face, and how the eyes were sparkling with a touch of their old gaiety.

Then Amada looked up. Her lips opened, and from her aged lips issued a quavering sound like the first accents of the Te Deum.

Two young bishops who were standing near comprehended what she meant. One sonorous voice after another took up the triumphal hymn bequeated by Ambrose to the Church Catholic.

Something now made the drunken assailants slacken their efforts; more than one face amongst them turned white. One by one they shrank back, disappearing into the darkness. Soon, nought but a smell of burning and a few wreaths of thin smoke remained to tell of the attempt which they had made.

De Clare, the English captain, was roused from his sleep. He had, like his father, a tall and stately form, a ruddy and somewhat feminine face.

He summoned his chief lieutenant, a young man named Myles Fitz-David, son of the Roman Catholic Bishop of St. David's.

"Is there a breach in the wall?" he asked.

"No," replied Fitz-David, crossing himself. "There hath been a miracle."

"A miracle, thou fool!" exclaimed the son of Strongbow, with an angry gesture.

"Yea," persisted his lieutenant, doggedly. "The yeoman Cedric proposed to smoke the unbelievers out."

"He hath a spark of sense," replied De Clare. "Methinks the work should be done by this time. Thinkest thou that we shall take them breathing?"

"Nay, but thou must hear," said Fitz-David, "that when the fires were kindled, and the smoke was rising in black clouds, a choir of angels burst out singing in the sky; the holy Virgin came down to protect those whom she would gather into the true fold."

"Thou shouldst have stayed by thy paternal altar," said the young chief, in a scornful, though musical voice. "Thy sword will be ever blunted by such mild fancies. But I must see to this."

Stepping forth he shook one sleeper after another.

"Besotted fools!" he exclaimed; "they would need my father's hand to rule them."

But all who had been engaged in the conflict shrank from renewing it. "The Virgin," they said, "had visibly interposed. They had distinctly seen her form, sitting crowned with stars on a white cloud above the tower." The young captain, therefore, saw himself obliged to relinquish all active measures until a few sober hours should dissipate the spell which had paralysed the energies of his troops.

To the weary, haggard prisoners in the tower this delay brought little comfort. They could not interpret the silence which now reigned around them.

"Why tarry the wheels of His chariot?" asked Amada.

"The foe contriveth something more effectual," responded Maidoc. "We witness the lull before the hurricane."

Some of the younger men employed this time of respite in discovering and distributing a small store of bread. Amada was with difficulty persuaded to partake of it.

"Methinks," she said, "that my one foot is already in heaven. What need to seek after what will keep me longer out of it."

"Remember that thy body is the Lord's," replied Maidoc; "it is His workmanship. Thou wert wont to cherish those bright pages which Sorcha transcribed for the sake of her whose hand had wrought on them, no less than for their own beauty; and wilt thou feel less kindly towards a creation of the Almighty Artist?"

"For my part," said Mòr, "I find it most strange to look at my hands with the consciousness that they will soon be but a mass of useless clay. Where should I now be but for the hope of immortality?"

"Yea, verily," replied Maidoc; "let us, then, give thanks over our last meal, as over the emblems of our Lord's death. Soon, very soon, shall we drink the new wine in His kingdom."

There were two of the company, however, who had other thoughts mingling with this ecstatic expectation. Mòr felt herself scarcely ready. It seemed to her most sad, most unnatural, to wait for an entrance into glory whilst estranged from her beloved mother. Yet how could she attempt to speak words of reconciliation? How expose herself to the pain of a repulse amongst such a crowd of witnesses? Yet the voice of conscience commanded it. She planted her foot on the ladder with the intention of descending, but exhausted nature gave way; fear and hunger and weakness were proving too much for her. Sinking down on a sack, she covered her face and wept bitterly.

Sorcha, too, felt that she could not depart in peace. Not for her own fate did she grieve. She had tasted a cup of earthly happiness, full, overflowing. If Ardal's strong arm had been around her at that moment, she would have welcomed·the last enemy. But a sword seemed to pierce her as she thought what *his* grief would be. Alas! no bird of the air would ever tell him how she had died.

The abbot, meanwhile, had exposed himself in the narrow doorway, and had contrived to parley with young Fitz-David.

"We would beg of thy charity," he said, "that thou wouldest tell us thy leader's terms of surrender. We have a firm trust that he will not stain the escutcheon of his house by breaking his plighted word. We have here twoscore of helpless women. I would fain commend them to thy honour as a knight."

"Is there aught else which thou holdest dear?" asked the bishop's son, somewhat scornfully. "We have found few of what are called the treasures of Declan."

"The gold and silver cups are here," replied the abbot; "also the rich bindings of many books. But for what is betwixt these bindings we would fain have thy captain's oath to bestow them on some learned university. There are copies of Greek poets which at Oxford would be weighed against gold. We have a few of Menander's plays, besides most of the works of Tacitus."

"Is that all?" exclaimed Fitz-David, contemptuously.

The abbot's hollow cheek flushed. "Nay, we have more," he cried; "we have two hundred copies of that living Word which was never conceived by mortal man. A draught of the pure waters which flow from it might moderate thy thirst for gold."

The young man turned aside to hold conference with his captain. In a few minutes the latter stood beneath the door. His doing so was an unconscious expression of confidence in the loyalty of the Irish bishops whom he was persecuting, for he presented a fair mark for an arrow. Yet was his womanish face disfigured by a most hateful expression.

Scorn, malice, bloodthirstiness, were all strongly marked on it.

"Ye ask for my terms," he said, in a voice whose naturally soft tones seemed ill-fitted to carry such words. "Know, then, that I summon you, in the name of our most gracious lord, King Henry, to surrender this tower."

"We stand ready to do so," replied the abbot, "on thy simple promise of a safe conduct for the women and children; also, that thou wilt spare our parchments."

"Of these I reck not," replied De Clare. "Yes, I may grant thy prayer. Know, however, that there are two whom I must exclude from it. No safe conduct will be granted to the wife of the arch rebel, Ardal O'Brien, nor the kin of a certain Olrud MacCarthy, who are branded as traitors, having stirred up his Highness's loyal subjects to disaffection."

A thrill of horror ran through every Irish heart. All felt that they would rather die than accept of a pardon from which the lovely and gifted daughter of Mael-Patrick should be excluded. The abbot withdrew from the doorway.

"Think not of us," said Grainné; "neither Sorcha nor I count our lives dear. We have already in spirit surrendered them through every minute of this night. Why, then, make their preservation for a few hours an obstacle to the safety of thy whole family?"

"It were unmanly of us to do otherwise," replied the abbot. "Our own lives would be degraded and worthless if ransomed at such a price. Hast thou looked on the countenance of yonder captain, Sorcha?"

"Yea, verily," replied the young matron, shuddering. "Yet methinks it were base in us to shrink from the cruel death which he perchance prepareth, when the lives of so many friends will be so uselessly sacrificed. Had I the least warrant in God's Word for doing so, I would end the matter by throwing myself from the summit of the tower."

"I will speak again with the cruel man," replied the abbot; "it may be that when he seeth we are resolved to protect thee, he may shrink from the sin of causing so many to perish."

But as he placed to his lips the small horn which he had used as the signal of conference, the shrill notes of a trumpet spoke of a fresh arrival.

CHAPTER XXXII.

ALL turned their eyes towards the forest. Few minutes
passed ere several figures on horseback emerged from it.
They drew up in front of the ruined arch which had spanned
the gateway of the rath.

One of them was enveloped in a purple cloak. The Earl's
son, advancing to meet him, knelt humbly on the ground.
The Danish Bishop of Waterford, for he it was, stretched
forth his arm.

"God bless thee, my son," he said; "is thy work complete? Where be thy prisoners?"

"We have them in plenty," replied the young captain,
rising and holding the prelate's bridle; "but the abbot and
the dwellers in this place are shut up in yonder tower."

"Have they fought with thee?" asked Tostius, dis-
mounting.

"No, reverend father," replied De Clare; "yet have we
failed to make them surrender. These drunken idiots, my
troopers, declare that they have seen the saints protecting
them."

The prelate smiled. "I rejoice if there has been no blood
shed," he remarked. "The Church is merciful, even when
most just. Canst thou speak with those in the tower?"

"Yea," replied the chieftain. "We may approach them
without fear. They are willing to surrender the treasures
of Declan, which I fear may prove of baser metal than we
recked of. But they are solicitous about some mouldering

parchments, fit only to light camp fires with. Also they hesitate because I expressly excluded from my safe conduct any women claiming kin with Ardal O'Brien and Olrud MacCarthy."

A cloud gathered over Tostius' face. "Is it much to thee that they yield about these women ?" he asked.

"Nay, verily," replied the captain, shrugging his shoulders. "But the tale of our vengeance will be worth something. These arch traitors must be made to suffer. Their movements have given my father many a sleepless night."

"Yet have they wrought thee good," said the prelate; "for without the sedition which they foment thou wouldst lack wit to lay thy hands on many a spoil. I have, however, a particular interest in what befalls Ardal O'Brien's wife. Thou must grant me this favour, and let her fate be in my hands."

"Willingly," replied De Clare. "Thou mayst have them both, an thou list. Shall we announce this ? My arm aches with this unwonted idleness."

Fitz-David, approaching the tower, now blew a few soft notes on a trumpet. The heads of the abbot and Maidoc appeared in the narrow doorway.

"We give you greeting," said the young soldier, "from our most reverend father, the Bishop of Waterford. He summoneth you to yield in the name of our Holy Mother Church. He is grieved that your lives have been imperilled, and he promises to every one of you, both men and women, a safe conduct from this place. Only the wives of Ardal O'Brien and of Olrud MacCarthy must remain his own prisoners. He biddeth me say, however, that he meaneth this in nought but friendship; and that he is willing to pledge his word that not a hair of their heads shall be hurt."

The voice was most distinct. Its accents penetrated through every window and corner of the narrow, round fortress.

"God be thanked!" exclaimed Mòr, throwing herself on Grainné's breast. "Surely He hath sent His own angel to let us out of this prison-house."

The abbot and Maidoc, having closed the door, now ascended to consult with the two women whose welfare was most at stake.

"I fear not to trust myself to Bishop Tostius," said Sorcha. "He hath eaten of our bread; he can surely mean us no ill."

"Thou dost not consider," said Ita, "whether or not it be possible for a Roman priest to betray his trust. Did not some of our bishops own the Pope's supremacy at Rathbresail? and hath he not used their compliance to hand this island over to the foreigner?"

"It is you women who are most concerned," said the abbot; "so we will abide by your decision. Were ye not here, I should prefer to fight and die, or else suffer the worst they could inflict."

"Oh, yield, yield!" sighed Uailsi.

"What sayest thou, Sorcha?" asked the abbot.

"Had we been warriors," replied Sorcha, "I should have said nay. But something in Bishop Tostius' face reassures me. And I cannot forget that my husband thought well of him. We know that resistance is hopeless. I am willing to become his prisoner."

"And I say the same," said Grainné.

Half an hour later the little door was opened. One by one the sad company walked down the steep ladder. The chill wind pinched their blue lips, but it was nothing to the cold despair that had taken possession of their souls. Their glorious and beautiful home was almost laid level with the dust. The double church still remained, but it looked like the ghost of its former self; its roof would never be rebuilt for the celebration of the old simple worship. The rath was half demolished, but Declan's little stone cell remained untouched. Heaps of charred wood marked the site of the college buildings, and of the pretty leaf-embowered cottages. The devastation was more complete than Danish pirates could have made it. The glory of Ardmore was for ever gone.

"Whither shall we go?" cried Uailsi, wringing her hands.

"Let us seek a home in the wilderness," replied her husband, "or on one of the lonely islands of our western coast. There we may live by the good-will of the rude inhabitants."

"Nay," exclaimed Uailsi; "I will seek an entrance into Kildare. There my birth entitles me to a home."

The abbot looked at her sternly. "Thou biddest me a lifelong farewell," he said.

"I have no other choice," replied Uailsi. "Thou canst not expect that I should live by the work of my hands; yet what else hast thou to offer me? Moreover," she continued, in a softer voice, "I deem myself bound to make a sacrifice for thee. Thou hast reputation enough to gain admittance into the monasteries of Ratisbon or St. Gallen, where I should be an encumbrance to thee."

"So be it, then," said the abbot, sighing. "I deny not that thy absence would be better for me. But what of Mòr? Wilt thou not take her with thee?"

Uailsi's pale cheek flushed. "Nay," she exclaimed, angrily. "She is doubly dishonoured; she can expect to share in none of the privileges of the Ua-Breasail."

"Then I ask them not for her," said the abbot; "but thou wilt never see her again on this side of the grave. It would be a sweeter memory for thee to carry about, wert thou to give her but one kind look."

"Urge me no further," replied Uailsi. "The Ua-Breasail have ever been men and women of their word."

The abbot turned hastily away. For the first time in his life he forbore to stifle a regret that he had ever won her.

Bishop Tostius had in the meantime advanced towards Sorcha and Mòr, who stood under the shelter of the church wall, holding their infants in the folds of their thick mantles.

"My daughters," he said, kindly, "you have been the guardian angels of this community. It was the thought of what might befall you that quickened my steps hither."

"We shall be grateful for thy counsel," replied Sorcha. "Mòr hath told me of thy goodness to her at Waterford."

The prelate gazed at Mòr's pale face. "Why didst thou not seek my help?" he asked, taking her hand.

"Because," replied Mòr, fixing her clear eyes on him, "I was unwilling to leave my husband while he would have me. Fergus made a jest of his Roman ordination."

"A jest!" exclaimed the prelate, frowning. "His mirth hath been the other way when in the house of my friends. Far better would it have been to have sought shelter with me ere thou hadst witnessed this. Thou canst think no more of Fergus without committing deadly sin."

"Whither may I look for shelter?" exclaimed Mòr. "My mother and my husband alike disown me."

"I will send you both to my sister, the Abbess of Kilchechan," replied Tostius. "You shall have a safe escort thither. Nothing else remains for you."

"I would ask of thy charity," said Sorcha, "that thou wouldst permit my grandmother and my mother's sister to accompany us. The one is very aged, and hath but few years to spend on earth; the other is in deadly peril, being the wife of Olrud MacCarthy, to whom we are assured that no quarter will be given."

"For thy grandmother thy petition is most fitting," replied the prelate; "but in regard to MacCarthy's wife—— "

"Say me not nay!" cried Sorcha, seizing his arm convulsively. Her eyes were irresistible in their eager entreaty.

"It shall be as thou listest," replied Tostius, in a softer

voice. "But I stretch my influence with these rude men to accomplish this."

"I have yet another favour," pleaded Sorcha. "Wilt thou not devise some means for me to communicate with Ardal ? I am loth to enter within the convent walls without his knowledge."

The prelate's frown grew darker. He looked at Sorcha inquiringly.

"Canst thou submit to renounce him ?" he asked.

Sorcha's cheek flushed. "Never !" she exclaimed, passionately, "whilst we are both above ground. I yield to no human will if opposed to his."

"Alas, my child !" said Tostius, laying his hand on her head; "vows of obedience are not binding when he to whom thou hast made them is forsworn. Be warned by what has befallen thy friend. Ardal will be only too glad to forsake thee. He hath transgressed a sacred canon in wedding thee. He, too, is an ordained priest."

Mòr gave a sudden scream. Sorcha became very pale.

"He may be so," she replied, bravely; "but he took no vow of celibacy."

"It is unusual for priests to do so formally at their consecration," replied the prelate. "The deacon's orders which they have already taken imply their submission in this respect. Thy husband's conscience must tell him that he is forsworn. He bowed to the authority of our Holy Church when she received him into her bosom. But the tale seemeth not strange to thee. Didst thou know this before thou didst wed him ?"

"Yea," replied Sorcha, the tears gathering in her eyes. "It was an act that Ardal hath bitterly regretted. He hath never held himself bound by it. He accepted consecration only on the distinct understanding that he was to be left free to obey the canons of the Church founded by Patrick. I understand that the royal Archbishop Henry gave him some dispensation to that effect."

"The Church accepts no half-homage," replied Tostius. "Ardal must have been fully aware that he was deceiving thee."

Sorcha's eyes flashed. "Nay," she exclaimed, "it is he who hath been betrayed. Ardal is incapable of practising on the innocence of a weak maiden."

The prelate shook his head. "Thou art too noble to speak otherwise," he replied. "Yet will I do what thou desirest. I will undertake to have a letter conveyed to him. In the meantime thou hadst better go to Kilcheechan. Ardal's hands are too full, from what I hear, to provide for thy safety."

A piercing shriek now issued from the tower. Grainné appeared in the narrow doorway with pain and terror written on her beautiful face. Her cheeks were bloodless, her hair dishevelled, her large brown eyes dilated.

"Oh, my mother!" she exclaimed, in a voice of heartrending grief.

"What is it?" gasped Sorcha, trembling violently. "I thought thou hadst remained there to bring her gently down."

"So I did," replied Grainné, half frantically. "Come, look!"

Sorcha bounded up the steep ladder, followed by Tostius, Mòr, Maidoc, and Ita. She paused not an iustant for breath, but continued mounting, preceded by Grainné, with almost superhuman agility. They paused on reaching the third chamber. There lay the lifeless form of Amada, weltering in blood; the fair locks half veiling her placid features.

Sorcha turned giddy, and leaned heavily on the prelate for support.

"Who hath wrought this vile deed?" asked Bishop Tostius.

"The English soldiers," replied Grainné. "They were

rushing up the ladder as we came slowly down. They ordered us with dreadful oaths to remount, in order that they might not be detained. My mother was unable to move without the greatest difficulty. I tried to quicken her steps, when one of the soldiers knocked her down; she fell in a senseless heap on the floor. I shrieked with grief and indignation. Then both soldiers, laughing coarsely, drew their daggers and stabbed her to the heart."

"I will have them punished," said the prelate. "Canst thou raise her with me?"

Grainné's arms were full, she having taken little Rossa from his mother. Tostius and Sorcha, therefore, lifted the poor body reverently, and conveyed it downwards with much difficulty.

But Amada's spirit had for ever left that scene of woe. The vindictive steel which had pierced her heart had perhaps been directed by angelic hands to open up for her an entrance into the glory she had so much longed after.

They laid her gently on the scorched and trampled grass. Sorrowing faces bent over her; but yet on some was the yearning look of those who would have wished to share her fate.

"Desire thy chief to speak with me," said the prelate, turning to young Fitz-David. "I would have him behold how his plighted word to me hath been kept."

A few minutes later and the Earl's son stood beside them. His brow grew dark as he beheld the blood-stained figure on the ground.

"Seest thou this?" said Tostius. "This aged woman was within my sanctuary, from which she hath, in spirit, been dragged and slain. The majesty of our Holy Church hath been insulted in her person. What offering will ye make to atone for this?"

"The blood of the slayer," answered De Clare, promptly. "Let him be put to death at her feet."

"Nay," exclaimed Grainné; "if it be thy Church which calls for satisfaction, she would surely have more glory in the man's life; and such honour to my mother's memory we value not. There is only one poor boon that we crave, and that is to be allowed to bury her within Ardmore church, offering over her remains the service of thanksgiving which her spirit would not willingly lack."

"Thanksgiving!" exclaimed Tostius. "Thou canst surely make this no matter for rejoicing. Methinks that thou speakest of something like a mass for the repose of her soul."

"The peace on her face might tell thee that she needeth it not," replied Grainné. "But it is with purpose that I speak of rejoicing. For is not this her birthday, the fairest hour in which she hath looked upon God's universe? Mistake me not. Our faces are not darkened with grief because of her departure; but we mourn the rather that any human soul could be so destitute of all that makes life precious as to stain itself with her blood. There was surely something in my mother which might have protected her from such a cruel assault."

Grainné looked touchingly beautiful in this triumph over her sorrow. The prelate could not but feel that there was here a power of faith which he could not measure.

"Thy wishes shall be fulfilled to the letter," he said. "Your funeral customs differ widely from ours, yet will we give you leisure to conform to them."

Amada's body was therefore borne into Declan's cell, that being the only place which could now afford it shelter. It was covered, not with the customary flowers, but with a few pine branches brought from the forest. Her friends, however, resolved to curtail the period of her wake from three nights to one, the earl's son, as well as Tostius, having announced his intention of departing on the morrow. The prelate proposed returning to Waterford, whilst the English soldiers were already discussing which ecclesiastical settlement might offer the best chance of more booty.

It was a night never to be forgotten. The wind blew with boisterous fury, howling round the walls of the dismantled church, and making the poor houseless ones cower against the roofless walls for shelter. Some there were who started at once on their painful journey to distant regions; whilst others betook themselves to the beach, dragging up some light fishing-boats to serve as a protection until the wind should become moderate enough to allow of their setting sail for the shores of Kerry.

Amada's personal friends were crowded into Declan's cell. A few slept; but most of them joined in raising the ceaseless psalm, or in echoing the prayers which the abbot and Maidoc offered up by turns. The sweet tones of Sorcha's harp sounded strange amidst so much trouble.

Yet these pale mourners were trying to turn their thoughts away from themselves. As they beheld each other's faces in the flickering torch-light, they could scarcely prevent anxiety for their own distress mingling with the grateful consideration which they were striving to bestow on the character and past life of the departed one.

"If thy mother hath less honour," remarked the abbot to Grainné, "in having so short a wake; if the fine linen and flowers be lacking, she is yet embalmed in much tender love. There are few indeed for whom we could pause to make melody amidst so much personal affliction."

"I feel it deeply," replied Grainné. "But methinks there is a brother who ought to have lain beside her: I speak of him who was slaughtered in the gateway."

"We sought for him," replied the abbot, "but the fire hath destroyed even the traces of his ashes. Yet methinks it were well to make mention of him and of Phelim in our song."

With the first streak of daylight all issued out of the cell.

They bore Amada's body, and laid it beneath the church floor, beside the remains of the saint whose name will for ever cling to Ardmore.

Then many gave way to bitter grief. There was no tone from the silver bell to summon them to the rude repast which they felt was the last they should all share together. Uailsi had departed during the night, having been furnished by Tostius with a fitting escort to Lismore, where she hoped to find some of her kindred.

Most affecting was Sorcha's farewell to Maidoc and Ita.

" We are all wrecks of our former selves," said the latter, drawing her dark mantle round her shivering frame ; " yet is the wrath of our God not unmixed with mercy. We have a firm trust that thou and Mòr will find fitting shelter, and it is little we ourselves want. We go to the Scattery Islands. The kind pity of our fellow-countrymen will provide a crust by the way."

" And meseems," said Maidoc, " that our heavier griefs have eaten up our lesser ones. Had it been foretold that I should see this desolation—Erin trampled beneath the feet of the alien, Declan's college consumed by the flame, the candle of my beloved Ardmore removed out of its place—should not I have gone wild with grief ? Yet the pain of it is deadened by my parting with thee."

" We shall meet again," said Sorcha, pressing his hand warmly. " What of thy beloved parchments ?"

" Alas ! " said Maidoc, " my eyes have not witnessed how roughly they have been handled. The abbot tells me, however, that they are loaded in sacks on the backs of mules, but with little regard to their relative worth ; that he had picked up most valuable leaves of Tacitus which had been dropped out of the loosely-tied bundles."

" That is grievous," said Sorcha ; " yet have I often marvelled to think, were the whole literary treasures here and at Lismore destroyed, the world would not miss them so much as it would the writing on the small parchment that I carry about with me."

"Nay, verily," replied Maidoc. "It hath supplied the first spark which made the glory and power of this place. Other beacons shall be kindled from it, which will perchance give a steadier light : it shall be in His own good time. But fare thee well, my child, mayst thou have a speedy meeting with thy husband ! "

Nor was the parting between Mòr and her father less melancholy. "Would that thou couldst have gone with me ! " said the latter. "I know that a safe shelter awaiteth me ; for within the walls of Ratisbon dwell brethren who will honour the Culdee Abbot. But they are celibates, and they have exchanged the rule of their Scottish founder for that of Benedict. I shall miss no intellectual pleasure, but some of the deeper needs of my heart must remain unsatisfied."

"Thou hast the Saviour," suggested Mòr.

"True," replied the father ; "yet the effulgence of His love hath never excluded the sweet flicker of those lights which He hath given to cheer our earthly pilgrimage. Every true spark of love hath been originally kindled at His altar, and my crushing anxiety is, that I leave thee with no protector. I would remain, could I but see how to benefit thee by doing so."

Mòr raised her tear-filled eyes. "Thou canst not help me," she said. "The shelter which Providence offers to each of us would be forfeited by our remaining together. Bishop Tostius hath a kind heart, and will let me stay beside his sister until peace return to Erin ; then hath Sorcha promised that I may dwell with her. Thy blessing, father, will make me strong to bear patiently."

The abbot's lip quivered. In broken accents he commended his daughter and her son to the care of the everlasting Father. Then, sinking down on the blackened stump of the yew-tree, he covered his face with his hands.

CHAPTER XXXIII.

Four months had passed since the night of Amada's burial. The bright spring sun had begun to pencil the hills and valleys of Ireland with fresh tints of green, and to weave into a robe of beauty the desolations of a stormy winter. And of all the spots which felt his magic touch, none responded to them more readily than did the softly-wooded banks of the river Suir.

They enclosed a broad, rushing stream of crystal water, undiminished as yet in volume by the clearance of forests from the hills that cradled it, untainted by aught more hurtful than the resin of the light keels that ploughed its sparkling surface.

And of all the picturesque groups of dwellings that clung to its shores, the most stately and beautiful was certainly the town of Waterford, or Port Lairge.

It was, in truth, the door of Ireland. Founded by the Danes in the seventh century, its wonderful position had attracted to it all the commerce which then passed across the Verginian* and Spanish seas. It stood on a plain on the south bank, enclosed within a triangular wall, strengthened at its corners by three towers, bearing the respective names of Colbeck, Turgesius, and Reginald. The streets were narrow, and the houses for the most part of wood; yet a few handsome buildings gave a character to the place. These were : the small Danish cathedral ; the Irish church of Bishop Fergus

* Verginian Sea—southern part of the Irish Channel.

O'Flannahan ; and a palace built for the Danish governor, now occupied by King Henry's lieutenant, Robert Fitz-Bernard.

On the north bank, opposite Reginald's Tower, stood a small church of stone, with a handsome wooden convent attached to it. This was Kilcheechan, called the Nunnery de Bello Portu, founded a few years previously by King Dermod of Leinster, as a dependency of his new convent of St. Mary de Hoggis, near Dublin.

Few pleasanter spots could well have been selected for a religious foundation. Secluded from the busy town by a broad watery barrier, it was yet near enough to be within the protection of the garrison in case of a civil war. Embowered in spreading oak trees, and surrounded with a blooming garden, it commanded a most enchanting view of the hills both up and down the river.

At a small casement window, guarded by iron bars, sat the stately form of Grainné, little changed from what we have known her, save for the expression of weariness that had gathered round her dark eyes. She was busily engaged in repairing a coarse woollen garment, pausing whilst she replenished her needle to gaze at the pale faces of Sorcha and Mòr, both intent on their old work of transcription.

Mòr's cheeks had regained some of their fulness. Sorcha looked as strong and beautiful, though much less blooming, than of yore. Suddenly pausing, she placed her hand to her ear.

" Hear ye nothing ? " she asked.

Mòr listened anxiously for a few moments.

" All is silent," she replied.

" It cometh to me in my dreams," said Sorcha. " In the midst of the night I start at the sound. Thinkest thou that he is really dead ? "

" I am sure of it," replied Grainné, looking compassionately at her. " I dressed his little body."

"He might have died in our keeping," said Mòr. "But it was cruel in them to take our children. No doubt the little darlings have been treated kindly ; but how can unmarried women handle a baby so well as its own mother ? "

"They say that thy Erc thrives," remarked Sorcha.

"Yea," replied Mòr ; "I believe that the sisters have some wise enough rules for his up-bringing ; but theories which succeed with one child need to be varied to suit another. Poor Rossa would not make his wants conform as he ought to have done. He caught cold when there was no reason for it."

"He is gathered home," said Sorcha, sighing deeply. "I would rather know of his being there than live in uncertainty about his future. Thinkest thou that they will make Erc a priest ? "

"I doubt it not," replied Mòr. "Bishop Tostius said that our stay here was to be only temporary. But every time when we have expressed a wish to shorten it, we have found our liberty curtailed."

"Yea," said Sorcha. "Yet they are kind to us withal. Sisters Anna and Mary could not speak more gently than they do. It is strange how such good women see not how they have trampled on our holiest affections."

"Thinkest thou that Ardal hath got thy letter ? " asked Grainné.

"I doubt it not," replied Sorcha. "He imagines me safe. Methinks it would be difficult for a messenger of his to penetrate here."

"Yet it is a comfort," said Grainné, "that Sister Mary can tell us so much. Her uncle keeps her well informed of thy husband's doings. The good Tostius hath not forgotten thee. Thou knowest not half the value of such a friend. It is quite impossible for me to have news of Olrud or of my boys."

"I marvel that they will not permit thee to join him,"

remarked Sorcha. " Yet they hold that thou art lawfully wedded. Thou art on a different footing from what we are."

" I cannot imagine the reason," replied Grainné. " It makes me suspect that Olrud is a very active foe of the new government. No doubt, like Ardal, he is a spring of the resistance which they still encounter."

" Yea," said Sorcha ; " yet it is hard for me to learn so little about Ardal. Fergus, it seems, wears the Roman tonsure. He is fully acknowledged as a priest."

" He is in his right place," said Mòr. " But comfort thyself ; I am as confident as thou canst be that Ardal will never stoop to repudiate thee."

Sorcha's eyes glistened. " I thank thee," she said, pressing Mòr's hand.

" I am thoroughly weary of this work," sighed Grainné. " I never had so much darning, even when my boys were little."

" If thou wouldst but take to thy pen," said Sorcha, " the hours would fly much faster."

" That is a sweet consolation to me," remarked Mòr. " When we are buried below that turf, this work of our hands will live. It may, perhaps, be a seed from which the true greatness of Erin may yet spring."

" Or something better," replied Sorcha. " It will assuredly be a seed for the kingdom of heaven. How we shall rejoice to welcome those who have benefited by our labours ! But methinks I hear the bell for our evening meal."

All laid down their work, Sorcha and Mòr consigning the parchments to a small oaken chest.

Groping their way along a dark passage, they descended a ladder, and found themselves in the large refectory, where a number of white-robed Augustinian nuns and young children were already seated.

The aged abbess motioned to the three to take their places at the board beside her. She had been a comely woman, yet there was a look of great weariness on her wrinkled face, her grey locks being effectually concealed by snowy bands. Her dark eyes had a dimness in them, very different from what had been the sparkle in Amada's.

Her two nieces sat beside her. They were tall, active women, with fresh faces and mild grey eyes, from which all lustre seemed to have died away. There was something touchingly gentle in their manner towards their three guests. Yet no syllable passed their lips after the abbess's clear tones had been heard in a Latin benediction. All sat with downcast eyes whilst partaking of some rye bread moistened with milk. One young sister, having been guilty of late attendance at matins, had her portion served out on the floor.

Then in a low, monotonous voice began the reading of the Scriptures. These, however, being in a tongue unknown to most of the fair recluses, failed to bring any expression of sympathetic assent to any eyes save those of their guests.

As they at length rose after the concluding benediction, Sister Anna laid her hand gently on Mòr's arm. They passed out into the garden together, followed by Grainné, Sorcha, and Sister Mary.

"I rejoice to tell thee," said the nun, speaking a little above her breath, "that thine Erc hath been good. He is most submissive to his teachers and companions."

"I thank thee," replied Mòr, observing the kindly twinkle in Sister Mary's eye.

"I love to have you in the garden," continued Anna. "My primroses grow well; I would fain have thee see them. Six of them have opened out since yesterday."

"We have done some work to-day," remarked Sorcha. "We have transcribed two chapters of the Epistle to the Thessalonians."

"I rejoice to hear it," replied Sister Mary. "It is the one thing by which you redeem yourselves from the charge of heresy."

" Yes," replied Sorcha, looking round to see that none of the other nuns were following. "Doth it never seem strange to you that we should be better instructed in the Word of God than you are, though you hold us to be no members of the true Church ? "

" You have more knowledge in every way," replied Mary; " yet methinks the great end of all education is not to cultivate the head, but the heart."

" And doth the one preclude the other ? " asked Grainné. " Shall we love our Creator less the more we know about Him ? "

" Nay," replied Mary, crossing herself; " but instruction hath danger in it when it placeth reason before a simple faith."

" I blush not to say," said Sorcha, " that I am a Christian in the first place because my reason is convinced."

" Thou art, then, happy," replied Mary; " though not more so by any means than we are. But reason hath misled the greatest thinker of France. Dost thou hope to have more wit than Abelard ? "

"It is like God's other gifts," said Grainné. "I might hurt myself very much, for instance, were I to consume a large honeycomb."

" The comparison is but specious," replied Sister Mary. "We make a willing sacrifice of our reason to the authorities whom God hath appointed to use it for us. It is this faculty which gives us the power of sinning."

" Eve had faith in the serpent," remarked Mòr.

" Thou speakest in ignorance," replied the nun. " If thou didst but once taste the intense happiness of belonging to the true Church, thou wouldst know what faith is."

Sorcha's eyes swam with tears. " Thou hast a love for me," she replied, " else thou wouldst not be so earnest to make me like thyself."

"I pray night and day," replied the nun, "that thou mayest

become a partaker of the joy that is sometimes vouchsafed to me. Often after I have partaken of the Holy Eucharist do I feel as if I were almost in heaven ; it is a wondrous privilege to come so near to *Him*."

Sorcha pressed her arm affectionately. "It is strange," she said, "though I cannot hope to make thee believe it, that I have felt exactly the same when breaking bread after our rite. I have had fellowship with the Son of God ; He has been very near me, though I think not that the bread hath been changed into His substance."

"Is that true ?" exclaimed Mary, looking surprised. "Didst thou scarcely know that thou wert treading our earth, for the very joy of thinking about Him ? "

"Yea, yea," replied Sorcha, with a sunny smile. "These are tokens that we are both in Christ, though we worship Him under very different forms."

"I love thee more than ever," said Mary. "I believe that thou wilt be saved, though thou hast fallen into error. God beareth much with His own."

"He doth so verily," exclaimed Sorcha, "else we should both be castaways. My friendship for thee, Mary, hath made me see more than ever that the true Church is not a visible one. Thou thinkest that thou attainest to such happy states because thou hast received grace through appointed human channels ; yet hast thou only received it, like me, by the power of the Spirit, and thou doest Him grievous wrong by attributing it so much to the ministrations of a priest."

"I am not learned enough to discuss these themes," replied Mary, "and would rather let them alone. My chief care is to make my own salvation sure."

"I could say much about that," said Sorcha, smiling, "but I fear it would not profit thee. Still this talk hath done me good. Thou mightest have had more hope of me if thou hadst not taken little Rossa away."

There was something unutterably sorrowful in the look

which the young mother cast on the nun. Mary felt it. She pressed Sorcha's hand warmly; perchance she suppressed a slight feeling of rebellion against the rigidness of the rule which had made her willingly carry out the decrees of others.

"It is the hour for meditation," she exclaimed, hearing the tinkle of a bell. " Wilt thou not join in that and in our even-song ? "

" I thank thee," replied Sorcha. " I find my thoughts flow more freely towards Divine things when I kneel not of set purpose in the presence of others. These hours of silent yet common devotion seem to me as if one should set lighted brands on a hearth in such manner that their flames may not approach each other, and then wonder at their smouldering out."

It had taken some time for Grainné and her young friends to discover their true position. They had been treated with every consideration and respect consistent with the loss of liberty. The abbess's manner to them had been such as a kind mother might have used towards returning prodigals. The first thing that had opened their eyes had been the removal of their children.

Tears and protestations had all been in vain. " In seek-ing our protection," the abbess had said, " you have virtually bound yourselves to refrain from disturbing our conventional arrangements. Your children will be reared by the sisters who are set apart for that purpose."

Sorcha and Mòr were not at all disposed to submit to this. But Grainné represented to them that their stay at Kilcheechan was only temporary, that the children were too small for any erroneous ideas to take root in their minds, that the hands to which they were being entrusted were experienced ones, and that the hour of their departure would be the hour of their re-union with the boys."

" But when will that be ? " asked Mòr. " There is no home left for me on earth."

"Say not so," exclaimed Sorcha. "Ardal and Olrud are both too energetic not to devise some plan for our future welfare. Our roof will be narrow indeed, if there be not a corner under it for thee."

Then came Sorcha's crushing sorrow. Erc throve, but Rossa pined and sickened with his new nurses. Only a few weeks passed ere she raised a very low psalm of thanksgiving over his tiny bier.

"I fancy," she said bitterly, when she found herself alone with her fellow-captives, "that the nuns' wish to keep him in life has been but slight. They have looked on our children with a kind of horror, being in their eyes the offspring of sacrilege. I say not that Rossa hath been starved, far from it; but what may not be neglect for one child, may be something very like it for another."

"Yea," replied Mòr. "There are troubles that only a mother's eye seeth in their beginnings. Had it been my Erc, I should not have been so much tempted to murmur. Thou wouldst have had a home for Rossa, whilst I shall often have to blush for my little darling."

"Thou hast no need to do so," said Graimné. "Even if public opinion hold him to be illegitimate, what, I ask, was Bridget, or Kentigern, or David? They certainly outlived any stigma of the kind."

"True," replied Mòr; "yet it hurteth me much to see that these sisters think him so. My mother would have said that it is the blood of the Ua-Breasail, which makes me dislike to be pitied."

"Thou must not heed them," said Sorcha. "I know that they cherish the same feeling towards me. It matters more what our Creator thinks of us. Still, I would fain that Ardal had not been so weak when he was at Clairvaux; yet I am more ready to excuse him since I have known these sisters. If they had not taken our children from us, I might not have found it so easy to shake off the spells they weave."

" Is it not wondrous," said Grainné, " the power which the faith of other men hath over us ? It is worth a boat's load of arguments ; and there is something very attractive in the idea of the truth having been handed down through an unbroken line of bishops. We have to grope in the dark for much amidst conflicting theories. It is little wonder, then, if we are ready to welcome a steady beacon."

" Were it but clear as it is steady," replied Sorcha, " there would be little more to wish for."

" It hath at least guided its followers to victory," said Mòr. " Wherever one turns one hears only of fresh submissions to Rome and to England."

" Because our native bishops have had so little firmness," said Sorcha. " Our Church committed the worst of errors when she allowed worldly motives to have so much influence on the entrance of candidates into her ministry. Men whose hearts are not in their work, will welcome a system such as the Roman one is."

" Yet the invasion began not yesterday," remarked Grainné ; " it hath been going on for half a century. Since Malachy O'Morgair displaced the co-arbs of Patrick at Armagh, and since the Synod of Rathbresail sanctioned the establishment of prelatic chairs, every tree of the Lord's planting in this island hath been tinged with the yellow hue of the coming change."

" Thou mayest go back yet further," said Sorcha, " and say that when Patrick's hereditary successors claimed supremacy over other bishops, they were but treading down a path for the lordly foot of him who should displace them."

" And Rossa told me," said Grainné, " what heart-burnings there have been at Lismore on account of some tampering with our ancient records. Some who have the charge of copying them, being trained in the Romish communion, understand not the terms that have been in use amongst us. They make a practice of substituting the word mass for religious service, and priest for a simple bishop. It may be that we women who have married ecclesiastics, when we slumber in our graves, will actually be considered to have had no existence."

CHAPTER XXXIV

The summer went past in unbroken monotony, Sorcha and her fellow-prisoners receiving no tidings whatever from the outer. world They felt morally convinced that everything there could not be so quiet as it seemed; yet of King Henry's departure for England, of the meeting of a great Synod at Cashel, of the frequent conflicts between the new-comers and the native Irish, they heard absolutely nothing.

Nor was the least sign given from Ardal nor from Olrud. Sorcha began, indeed, to doubt if they knew where their wives were.

"My husband would have found some means of sending me a message," she said, "if my letters had been indeed delivered to him. I fear that Bishop Tostius doth not keep strict faith with us."

"Thou hast surely forgotten," remarked Grainné, "that thy Ardal is looked upon as an outlaw. Any man, woman, or child who should carry a letter from him to thee would pay for it with his life."

"That may be," replied Sorcha; "yet are we now dwelling in the midst of his mother's kin. Few of the fishermen whom we see plying their craft down these waters are without a tinge of the blood of the O'Faolains; and it hath ever been in the Gaelic nature to serve their chiefs to the death."

"Thou speakest truth," said Grainné; "yet Ardal, perchance, may be loth to risk a poor man's life in such service ere his plans be ripe for our release. He would not willingly have us hunted about the country with himself. Olrud and he are probably content to know of our safety, and do not dream of what a crushing anxiety weighs upon our hearts."

The three had now no feeling that they were living on charity, Sister Mary having given them to understand that the convent was realising a little money by the sale of their transcriptions.

The feast of the Assumption drew near. It was to be celebrated with unusual pomp in all the churches of Waterford. There was to be a special service in that of Kilcheechan.

"I should much regret thy not seeing it," said the abbess to Grainné. "There is a croft in the western wall with a window which overlooks the church. Thou and thy two friends might sit there without being observed."

Grainné, Sorcha, and Mòr found themselves accordingly behind a wooden lattice, the perforations of which permitted them to enjoy an uninterrupted view over the assembled congregation. They looked down on the rows of hooded nuns and on the rosy faces of the little ones who were under their care; Mòr straining her eyes eagerly to catch a glimpse of her own boy. As the glorious roll of the Gregorian chant arose from the pealing voices of the choristers, a gorgeous procession entered though the chief door opposite to that which led from the convent. It marched up the centre of the nave.

But what face surmounted the violet robes of a tonsured priest who walked on the bishop's right hand ? Mòr grasped Sorcha's arm convulsively, for she recognised the blue eyes and mobile features of Fergus.

Sorcha, too, trembled. He was there, beneath the same roof; he who had dared to trample on the most sacred vows, under the shallow pretence of pleasing Heaven. He was coming, perhaps knowingly, into the presence of her whose life he had blasted. And he marched with unabashed front, moving amongst the servants of God towards the very steps of the altar.

Grainné herself shuddered. The anthem at length ended, the clouds of incense began to dissolve away, and the bishop stood ready to bless the Eucharistic elements.

An undefinable dread came over Sorcha. She had become sufficiently intimate with sincere Catholics to understand the awful meaning attached by them to this their highest act of faith. She tried to suppose for an instant that this faith was well grounded; and that the sacrifice on Calvary was about to be repeated. Would not Bishop Tostius be seized with such a tremulous awe that he would become unable to offer it?

"He can hardly realise the greatness of Him whose substance he touches," thought Sorcha, "else would he shrink back confounded at his own presumption."

But no! the elements were raised, whilst the tinkle of a bell warned the worshippers that the sacrifice was being offered. Few of those who knelt before it were so overpowered by the thought of it as the three captives. Even the presence of Fergus was, for the moment, forgotten by them.

The ceremony was at length over; the congregation dispersed. Some, however, lingered either for confession or to hear additional masses at the smaller altars.

Fergus was at length seen to emerge from the sacristy and walk up the steps of one of these. Mòr again grasped Sorcha's arm.

"Ah!" she exclaimed, in a tone of apprehensive horror, "he is never going to—— "

Sorcha's eyes were dilated. Her lips parted in a very bitter smile.

"It loseth nothing of its efficacy," she whispered, "by reason of the priest's unworthiness."

Mòr rose. "Let us hasten away," she exclaimed; "there are some things which might make the very devils blush. Either Fergus believes in what he is going to do, or he does not. In the one case he insults his fellow-worshippers, in the other he has accepted a doctrine which insults his Creator."

They reached their little room. Mòr threw open its casement.

"The air is freer here," she said. "I would rather have my body in a cage then my mind so bound with the chains of falsehood. Thinkest thou not, Sorcha, had it been the real ark of God which Fergus was touching, his hand would have been withered?"

"The Almighty, methinks, is more forbearing now than He was of old," replied Sorcha, trembling violently.

Mòr gazed at her in some amazement. "Thou seemest as much disturbed by my husband's presence as I am," she said.

Sorcha's cheeks were crimson. "I had a narrow escape from wedding Fergus myself," she said, softly.

"How could that be?" exclaimed Mòr. "Thou wert surely too young to be sought after when he finished his studies at Ardmore?"

"Yea verily," replied Sorcha, colouring. "It was after his return from abroad. On the very morning of the day that Ardal received my promise, I was hesitating whether or not I should accept Fergus."

A spasm of pain shot over Mòr's face. She fixed her clear eyes steadily on the speaker.

"Had he held to thee the language of love?" she asked.

"Yea," replied Sorcha; "I was his queen, his empress, the star without whose radiance life would be dark to him."

Mòr covered her face with her hands. "The very expressions he used to me," she said, "and it must have been at the very same time. Yes," she continued, clenching her hand, "I have been bitterly, cruelly deceived."

Sorcha kissed her affectionately. "Thou hast no need to be ashamed of it," she said. "I was almost tempted to believe in him, though I doubted whether or not his words might be the ravings of a poet. Yet have I only escaped by what seemed to me a miracle."

"Human affection is a holy thing," said Mòr. "They who play with it, who treat it but as an amusement, will have much to answer for."

"It is like sporting with fire," replied Sorcha. "Yet the man or woman who does it is not the one who is scorched."

"That seems wofully unjust," said Mòr. "But I doubt if it be so; for they have their recompence. Though their consciences may be dead, the blood of their victims' hearts will surely cry out against them. The absence of feeling which such conduct presupposes and confirms is in itself no slight punishment."

"I sometimes tremble lest I should have been guilty of it myself," said Sorcha. "For the knowledge of Ardal's love came upon me with an impulse so irresistible that I was as a vessel carried away from its moorings, and I seemed to have no leisure for reflection as to whether I had acted justly or not to my first wooer; but I now feel myself absolved. It was a true instinct which made me suspect Fergus' sincerity."

On the evening of the same day Sorcha wandered into the garden. She remained there for some time after all the nuns had re-entered for their half-hour of silent meditation. It was a close, warm night, the moon was riding high in the heavens, casting a weird radiance over the ramparts in front of the city on the opposite shore, and making Reginald's Tower stand forth in unwonted stateliness. The trees, heavy with dew, cast fitful shadows over the smooth turf. Sorcha was revolving in her mind the impressive though startling scene she had that day witnessed.

Suddenly she heard her name pronounced in an accent which thrilled through her very being.

" Sorcha ! "

Was she dreaming? Had the events of the morning un-settled her brain? It could not be—no, it could not ! It was the whisper of some disembodied spirit.

" Sorcha ! "

She started. The tone was more distinct. She trembled to hear it repeated.

" Sorcha ! "

It seemed to come the third time from a clump of thorn bushes close to the wall which skirted the river. Sorcha flew noiselessly thither. Her breath was hurried, her heart beating wildly. She discerned in the faint light, beneath the bushes, the tall figure of a man. Sorcha was intensely imaginative. No form of flesh, she judged, could have leapt over that garden wall without attracting the notice of the porter. This must be some messenger from the world of darkness.

Sorcha turned to flee; but a firm hand laid hold of her mantle. She tried to free herself. Then a quick sense of something came over her. She bent forward and was locked in the man's strong arms. It was only for a moment. Gasping, trembling, she laid her soft hand on his.

" Fly ! fly ! " she exclaimed.

" Not for worlds," replied a deep voice. " I could trust no other messenger. Take this, it will teach thee what to do."

Another embrace, a pressure of lips that seemed to be the contact of souls, and the beloved form had disappeared.

Sorcha stood bewildered for an instant, gazing intently into the thorn bushes. Nothing stirred. It was a still, calm night, the very gnats seemed to hover on lazy wings. Nothing was heard but a low ripple of water.

Sorcha walked leisurely towards the convent door. She was trying to regain her composure, but her cheeks were flushed and her eyes bright. She encountered Sister Mary.

" Thou doest ill to be out so late," remarked the nun. " Methinks thou hast caught cold."

There was a burning spot in Sorcha's bosom, caused by the pressure of a wax tablet.

"Shall I warm for thee some barley ptisane?" asked Mary.

"Nay, but I thank thee," replied Sorcha. "I am accustomed to be out after sunset."

She hastened to her chamber. Grainné and Mòr were both there. Sorcha bolted the door. Her friends stared at her in surprise.

"Hath anything happened?" asked Grainne.

"Yea," whispered Sorcha, making a sign first to her own ear, then towards the walls. She examined every corner about the three little straw-covered beds; then drew forth the wax tablet from her bosom.

She held it to the light; Grainné and Mòr looking over her shoulder. The writing ran thus:

"MY OWN LOVE,—To-morrow night, at the ninth hour, will Olrud and I come with a boat below the wall under whose shadow I spoke to thee. Bid Grainné and Mòr be ready. Come with the two boys if possible. A few hours will place us beyond the reach of pursuit."

The three captives clasped their hands, looking upwards in silent ecstasy. Placing the point of a small stylus in the flame of a rushlight, Sorcha kissed the writing, and then erased it.

None of the three closed an eye. Each nursed a joyful excitement which was the more powerful because of its enforced suppression. Grainné thought of freedom and of her children. Of her husband too. Now it could be hers to prove that she loved him; in real poverty and in exile he seemed for the first time to be noble.

Mòr was disturbed by a painful struggle. Should she leave Erc? With the first streak of light she wrote this question on a tablet, placing it before Grainné's eyes.

Her friend replied in the same manner. "Thou wilt never see him again by staying here."

Mòr shook her head sadly.

Never was day longer than the following one. Their few preparations were easily made. After evensong they sallied out.

But they had only gone a few steps across the greensward, when Mòr paused, hesitated for an instant, then turning, fled back towards the convent door. Sorcha tried to rush after her.

"Art thou mad?" asked Grainné, seizing her arm with some violence. "The mother's heart speaketh too strongly; let her remain. Thou riskest other lives than ours by delay."

Sorcha sighed heavily, then glided to the spot where she had spoken with Ardal. The night was dark, the moon struggling with heavy clouds. They discerned, close to the wall, the tall figures of two nuns.

One of these raised a long, powerful arm, pointing to two ropes which hung over the wall. Sorcha and Grainné both recognised their husbands.

Grasping the ends of the ropes, Ardal made them fast to Grainné's girdle. She was swung upwards. Olrud, who had already mounted, untied the knots, and fastened to her the ends of other ropes. He then deftly dropped her down on the outer side. There she fell rather roughly. She untied herself quickly, and the rope was drawn up.

Sorcha followed in the same way. Olrud and Ardal soon stood beside them.

" Where is Mòr?" asked the latter.

"Heed her not," replied Grainné; " she, indeed, set forth with us, but hath returned, in the fond wish to dwell under the same roof with her child."

"Let us run," said Olrud.

The four fled swiftly towards the river. Ardal paused for a moment; he seized Sorcha's arm.

"Where is Rossa?" he asked.

"Our child is dead," replied Sorcha.

The strong man groaned beneath his feminine dress. They reached the rapidly flowing water.

A boat floated on its bosom. Ardal, throwing off his long mantle, seized a rope, and brought it safely to the bank.

Olrud and he both leapt in; but they were startled by a piercing scream. Turning round, they saw their wives struggling in the rough grasp of two soldiers. The triumphant faces of several others stood around.

"Fly! fly!" cried Sorcha, waving her arm; "ye may live to save us."

The two bishops stood with drawn swords and flashing eyes.

"Fly!" shrieked Grainné; "they will not hurt us much. We have friends; ye but hasten our death by fighting where ye cannot prevail."

Several soldiers had approached the boat with their spears. There was something so terrible in Ardal's face, however, that they were loth to begin the conflict.

"She speaketh truth," exclaimed Olrud, seizing an oar.

In a few minutes the boat shot rapidly away. A shower of spears followed it.

The soldiers relaxed their rude hold on the shuddering women; a sweet voice had fallen on their ears. It was that of Sister Mary.

"Our abbess bids you hail," she said; "and thanks you for your diligence. If the hest of your captain allow it, she would fain have these erring ones return."

"It may not be, lady," said a voice, which Sorcha remembered to have once heard. It was that of young Fitz-David.

"We will bestow them in safe keeping till we learn the pleasure of Fitz-Bernard. They are guilty of holding converse with His Highness's enemies."

"There should be three of them," remarked a soldier. "Of this were we advised."

"But the third hath not sinned," said Mary, the tears gathering in her eyes.

"I know not that," replied Fitz-David. "My commands are to possess myself of the persons of three Irishwomen, and of two arch traitors. They will be lodged this night in the Reginald's Tower."

Mary drew a cross from her bosom. "If it must be, then," she said gently, "wilt thou take this as a sign of our favour? And by it we adjure thee to use no more harshness towards thy prisoners than may be necessary for carrying out thy instructions. By so doing thou wilt have a claim on our prayers."

The young captain accepted the proferred token. He kissed it reverently, then, hanging it round his neck, commanded two of his men to fetch Mòr.

Mary fixed her mild eyes upon Sorcha. "Thou hast been much misguided," she said, "in seeking to leave our peaceful roof for the allurements of the world. Perhaps thou wilt now see from what we have protected thee."

"I am not ungrateful," replied Sorcha, in a tone of utter despondency; "but farewell," she continued, stretching out her hand; "my heart tells me that we must resign ourselves to an ignominious death. Know, however, that we are proud to suffer for the sake of our husbands."

"I will do what I can to serve you," said Mary, weeping; "so I am sure will our reverend mother. But I cannot bid you hope. Our bishop hath been oft reproached for the favour he hath shown you."

"Of that we were quite unaware," said Grainné, with calm dignity; "yet is it to us a token of the worth of our beloved ones. Had they not been active in a cause which we think noble, you would find little difficulty in protecting us."

The blanched face of Mòr now appeared amongst them. Sorcha threw herself on her friend's neck.

"It is I who have brought thee to this," she exclaimed, bitterly.

" And is it not more welcome," said Mòr, " than the dreary state that I had fallen into? I could never hope to see my child again. In a few hours it will be all over."

" And perchance," said Grainné, " our memory may awaken a vengeance strong enough to free this land from a double curse. There have been rivers of blood already shed; yet may the sword of our cruel foe now lay open a spring which shall let loose the flood that may overwhelm him —for the sons of Erin will believe in their own enslavement when they hear of this."

Fitz-David now hurried them off. A few minutes later they found themselves lodged in the deep recess of a small window, let into one of the circular chambers which then, as now, formed one of the partitions of Reginald's Tower.

CHAPTER XXXV.

Waiting for death! waiting not in the comfort of a home surrounded by all the appliances which love can suggest for the sustenance of the fainting body; waiting, not on the bosom of the heaving waters, where every wave that tosses its foamy crest may be a gentle messenger to lull us to our last sleep: but waiting in a narrow chamber, separated by some thin planks from the bivouac of a rude and drunken soldiery, whose hands were but too eager to drag them to the place of execution—such was the condition of Sorcha, Grainné, and Mòr on that terrible night in August.

"Would that it were over!" sighed the elder matron, sinking exhausted on a small heap of dirty straw. "Would that we had all perished at Ardmore!"

"Nay, Grainné," replied Sorcha; "horrible as this is, it must yet work for some good. Perpetua and Felicitas did not choose the manner of their own death."

"Yea," said Mòr, "and methinks that as we have still breath within us we should recollect what Maidoc once said to Amada about our bodies. Let us not, by giving way to despair, lessen the control which our spirits have over them. Whilst two of us seek refreshment in sleep let the third watch until daybreak. So may we have grace given us to witness a good confession."

"Thou speakest well," replied Grainné. "Mine be the first vigil."

" Nay, but that is the privilege of the youngest," persisted Sorcha.

It was arranged accordingly. As her companions stretched their tender frames on the rough floor, the bride of an Irish prince pressed her throbbing brow against the cold stone beneath the window.

It was a fearful situation. Nothing but their dread of Bishop Tostius's anger, Sorcha well knew, kept the rude men whose words of blasphemy fell upon her ears from breaking through the thin wall and perchance dashing her headlong from the parapet. The air was hot, heavy, full of the steam of their unhallowed potations. It was a place where many a one might have been tempted to think that the eye of the Creator never came.

To a woman reared as Sorcha had been the sounds she heard were more painful to her than bodily torture. They outraged all the fine chords of a heart which had been wont to vibrate to the faintest breath of whatever was pure and beautiful. It was as if the slime of some loathsome serpent were being dropped over the delicate flowers of the meadow.

But the night passed away. Sorcha never recollected when she fell asleep. Mòr's vigil was not so terrible. The soldiers were then wrapped in heavy slumber, and the wind blew cold through the unglazed aperture. One faint starbeam penetrated the darkness; it seemed like the step of a herald from the celestial city.

Morning at length dawned. The hours grew apace whilst Grainné watched for the harbinger of death. Drawing a small parchment from her bosom, she sought comfort in the promises of the changeless One.

Their breakfast was passed through a loosened plank. Whilst they partook of it they were startled by the sight of a familiar face. It was that of Cacht. Her person was as stout, but her cheeks less blooming than they had been at Ardmore. She was, in truth, very pale.

Sorcha dropped an untasted morsel. "Art thou also captive?" she asked.

"Nay," replied Cacht. "I have taken service with the priest, Fergus O'Flannahan, who dwelleth in this town of Waterford. He was wont of old to speak me fair, and when I saw the Ardmore family scattered I bethought me of a promise which I had once made to him—that should anything befall Amada or thee, I would seek none but him for a master. I knew not well where my own kin were; so I thought I would run the risk of his having a bad memory. He has been better to me than to his wife," she continued in a half whisper, glancing at Mòr. "Yet must I work hard for a scanty sustenance."

"Art thou here with his approval?" asked Grainné.

Cacht shook her head. "Nay," she replied; "but one of the troopers here hath a kindness towards me."

Cacht's voice dropped. She made an expressive gesture, then held something towards Sorcha wrapped in a dirty rag.

"I must leave you," she said, "for my master hath not yet broken his fast. Yet I weep to see you in such straits."

She disappeared from the narrow chamber, leaving the three captives somewhat bewildered. Sorcha, stepping to the window, unfolded the bit of saffron-coloured wool.

Next moment she stood motionless, gasping as if struggling to suppress a scream. Her eyes shone with unearthly splendour as she held out a wax tablet.

Grainné and Mòr both started as they beheld the writing It was that of Ardal.

"We will again deliver you," it said, "if ye have aught to weave into a strong twist. If not, devise with the bearer of this how best she may furnish you with straw or with twigs."

Mòr's lips formed themselves as if to pronounce the word

"straw."   She glanced at the dirty floor.   Sorcha continued,

"The signal will be this night, a light waxing and waning in the little creek ten yards further down the river-bank. It may be at any hour; but when ye see it, descend."

The three clasped each other's hands. A rush of colour overspread their faces; but no sound could they utter. It was like the first fall of rain after severe drought.

Then Grainné, seating herself in a corner, began to plait the straw.

Mòr's eyes fell, however, on a small bundle. Opening it, she unrolled several coils of twisted heather.

"Cacht must have dropped this," she said. "Her hands and feet are verily those of an angel."

Sorcha laid her finger to her lips.

The hours went slowly past.   No glass had they to measure time.   The large chamber from the centre of which they were boarded off was less frequented in the daylight; only occasionally did the bluff face of a soldier intrude itself behind the partition, as if to make sure of their safety.

The sun at length began to go down. Looking through the narrow slit which was their one remaining hope of freedom, they perceived the hills becoming tinted with his parting radiance. They could see the sweep of the mighty river pouring the full tide of its waters a few yards from the base of the tower, and they could measure the breadth of the marsh dotted with clumps of yellow furze, which on that side stretched behind the city wall and the hills.

Then the inner room began to fill. Again was heard the sound of revelry, again the drunken shout and the shameless oath. Nor were these unmingled with coarse allusions to the fate of the fair captives.

"Why are they not in the common prison?" asked a voice.

"Because," replied another, "our governor feareth to offend that shaven priest. Were I a baron, not one of his crew should meddle with the working of the laws. But our rulers are frightened now, since the king hath done such a wondrous penance."

"What! for the blood of St. Thomas!" cried the first speaker, "methinks we should make our peace with heaven all the quicker were we to rid ourselves of such hypocrites."

There was silence for a few minutes. Some of these rude men were crossing themselves.

"Thou art rash," said a third voice. "But these women block out some of our light, and I pray that our masters would soon remove them, for cumbersome trash as they are."

But the night grew darker. The sounds of revelry at length died away; nought was heard but heavy snoring.

Grainné sat at the window, straining her eyes after a glimpse of the promised signal.

At length appeared a little flickering light, quite low near the water's edge.

There was not a moment to lose; yet the matron's fingers trembled as she bound the end of a heathery coil to Sorcha's girdle.

She conquered her agitation, however, by a determined effort. Then Sorcha forced her slender frame through the narrow window.

There was a drop of some twenty feet to the ground; yet all three reached it safely, finding themselves half-embedded in wet moss. Then they ran. As they neared the river, two dark forms arose out of the furze. Silently Olrud and Ardal conducted them into the boat.

It was a tiny coracle of rude wickerwork, covered both within and without with the skins of oxen; having for a keel, however, a good solid piece of oak. In such a vessel the fugitives well knew some of their countrymen had not shrunk from encountering the storms of ocean, when bearing to the shores of Caledonia and of Iceland the imperishable seed of a living faith.

Olrud and Ardal were both habited in the brown leather kilts of fishermen, with cloaks of saffron-coloured wool, fastened on the shoulder by an iron pin. Their oars soon dipped softly in the water.

Grainné gazed at the sky. Her whole soul seemed to expand in the delight of new-felt freedom.

"For once," she said, "we may speak our thoughts."

Mòr was crouching in the bottom of the boat; her chin supported on her thin hands, and her blue eyes fixed wistfully on the white church and dark convent of Kilcheechan. Her pent-up feelings soon found expression in a low wail.

Sorcha, kneeling at her side, passed an arm round her slender form. Ardal rested for a moment on his oar.

"Might we not return?" he suggested. "The women are strong enough to row down stream. I could linger about until I succeeded in stealing the little fellow."

"That is madness!" exclaimed Olrud. ".There will be a cry after us when morning breaks. Thou wilt lose thine own life, and thy country will miss thee. As for the women rowing, thou knowest that we must soon meet the in-flow of the Barrow, and if we cannot dart swiftly through its eddies, we must infallibly be carried downwards, to be borne in daylight past the new English settlement on the Pill."

"And methinks," suggested Grainné, "that we shall hardly be out of danger when we reach land. Hath Olrud strength to guide us to a place of safety?"

"You must go on," said Mòr. "Much as I grieve for Erc, I will never consent to thy seeking him. No life but mine should be endangered on his account."

"Perchance," said Sorcha, "when thou hast grown a little stronger, thou mayst be able to devise some plan for getting possession of him."

The two men now bent eagerly to their work. The foam

flew in shining wreaths from their oars, and the low gurgle of water around the prow gave token that they were speeding.

"Whither are ye taking us ?" asked Grainné.

"We go up the Barrow to-night," replied Ardal. "We shall linger for some days in a forest by its shores. Then we must proceed on fast for many a mile. We hope to find shelter on an island in the mouth of the great river. There a missionary foundation hath existed since the days of Patrick."

"But will the Saxon be long in reaching it?" asked Grainné.

"Surely not," replied her husband; "yet are there other isles along the western coast where hermits have dwelt. They are barren enough to be safe from the spoiler. Maidoo and Ita have gone thither, and we may have a little home, whence Ardal and I can issue forth to break the bread of life to our countrymen on the mainland."

"But seas are rough," suggested Sorcha. "The great ocean rages round these isles with resistless fury."

"The God of Columba and of Cormac will be with us," replied Ardal. "And He who bade Peter come to Him on the water, will not leave Peter's true successors to sink while bearing His message."

The shores had now risen into stately wood-covered hills. They had turned southward, into a channel running betwixt the southern bank and a large island.

"What have you done since you left Ardmore and Killagve ?" asked Grainné.

"Ardal has become famous," replied Olrud. "There is a heavy price on his head."

Sorcha shuddered. "We know that well," she replied; "we were told of it when Ardmore was in flames."

"Yet are we fighting in a lost cause," said Olrud. "Erin will soon be thoroughly Roman. Had this English invasion come two hundred years ago, when our bishops were still generally beloved, she might have made a firmer stand against the foe."

" 'Tis passing strange," observed Ardal, " that she should be so lightly won.   For the pretensions of the Roman Church were of yore associated with Saxon triumphs ; but the native Britons have been so constantly defeated and driven back on their mountain strongholds, that men have at length got a superstitious feeling as if victory must remain with those who obey orders from Rome.   It is quite possible that we are being punished for our national sins ; yet will I never allow that it is for the one of schism."

"And Irishmen cannot perceive the issues at stake," said Olrud. "They have ever been content to seek for present good, without looking to the future.   The principle of Divine authority being committed to men is most dangerous.   For hath it not been already misused, even in the very gift of ourselves to the foreigner ?   This new system openeth out to the clergy prospects of wealth and power, and it suiteth those of our chieftains whose pride could hardly be brought to bend before the ministrations of humble bishops like ourselves.   There is also a hankering in human nature for some visible sign of acceptance from heaven.   This the Roman Church has abundant means of satisfying."

They had now fairly rounded the island, and were proceeding rapidly down the full channel.

"It may be that we belong to a forlorn hope," said Ardal; "but this remnant of the Celtic Church must not die without a struggle. We have too often forgotten our first love ; yet is our faith purer by far than the one which threatens to take its place."

"The water ripples loudly," remarked Sorcha. "Doth the darkness make sounds more vivid ? "

"Perchance it doth," replied Grainné. " I am wretchedly cold."

Mòr shivered.

"Put your fair hands to the oars," suggested Ardal. "You will make less progress, but we shall pull all the more strongly afterwards."

"And we are now fairly in the Barrow," said Olrud. "We are going up stream."

Grainné and Sorcha changed places with their husbands. The boat in their hands made slow progress.

"I would that you had brought four oars," said Mòr.

"It would have made but little difference," replied Ardal. "We are now far on our way; and, as we must needs hide in a thicket during daylight, we may as well arrive at our landing place an hour later."

"I never heard a boat ripple like this one," observed Mòr. "Every sound that it makes seems to be repeated in the distance."

"You have told us little of the foreigner's doings," said Grainné.

"The first changes which he hath made," replied Olrud, "have been in Church matters. The English king, with hands stained in the blood of his own archbishop, summoned a Synod to Cashel. Christian of Lismore presided over it, and it regulated the payment of tithes, besides ordaining that all offices of Divine service should be performed according to the ritual of the Church of England. * It hath also decreed that prayers be offered for the dead."

"There is much in the very solemnity of these services to deaden men's consciences," said Ardal. "For when they perchance hear some great man spoken of as if his benefactions to the Church would shorten his period of probation in another world, they are not discouraged from imitating his vices."

"'Tis getting very cold," said Grainné. "The moonlight waxeth faint, and the clouds are black."

Some drops now fell heavily.

* Appendix.

"Let us take the oars," said Ardal. "A storm cometh. In a few hours we shall be in safety."

Sorcha seated herself again in the stern. Her cheek was flushed, her brown eyes glowing with happiness.

"I know not how it is," she said, "but I feel more joy this day than even in the hour when I became a spouse."

"But not more than on the day of our wedding?" asked Ardal, gazing proudly and fondly at her.

"Thou knowest how that day was marred," replied Sorcha, more gravely. "But danger hath its own delight when it is shared with thee!"

"And I confess very candidly," said Grainné, bestowing on her husband a look of deep affection, "that the joy of our marriage-day was nothing to this."

"Would that thou couldst experience the like!" exclaimed Ardal, glancing at Mòr. "But Erc is better where he is. This journey is not for him."

The young mother shook her head. "Nay," she replied. "It is not only because I may not see him that I grieve; it is because I know that he will be taught to think of me as of a reprobate. Not only so, but he may become a priest. His life may be spent in teaching error."

"Leave him in God's hands," said Sorcha. "Our sojourn in the convent hath taught thee that errors do not always prevent the presence of saving faith. I cannot believe that men will be condemned on account of their opinions, unless these are the result of wilful blindness."

"Yea, verily," replied Ardal. "Therein methinks the creed of the Romans is much too harsh. The only theology which our forefathers knew was that of the Apostle Paul. Now, the man is esteemed worthy of most praise who shall state in precise terms the exact relationship subsisting between the Persons of the glorious Trinity, and bring down to the level of created minds mysteries which are hid from the inhabitants of heaven."

A whizzing sound now fell on their ears. The air become alive with it.

"The foe is upon us," exclaimed Olrud, writhing with pain : an arrow had transfixed his arm.

The frail craft swerved suddenly from the movements of the terrified creatures within it. The water was nearly up to their knees.

"It is over !" exclaimed Ardal, as Sorcha threw herself on his breast. Another moment and they were struggling in the water.

Mòr, ere her eyes closed for ever, caught sight of two boats and of men in them. Only one face could she discern in the red glow of a lamp which had now been uncovered. There was a look of apprehension mingled with triumph in its blue eyes.

Some hands were stretched out to seize her. "Not that woman !" exclaimed Fergus. "Save, save the other !"

But Sorcha had already sunk. Clinging to Ardal, she had been unable to swim. Together they had entered into that joy whose first faint foreshadowings had been so inexpressibly sweet.

Olrud alone, after a fruitless attempt to save Grainné, and favoured by the discussion betwixt his pursuers, struck out for the shore. As he landed he caught sight of something in the middle of the river, borne rapidly along by the current. It was a woman's face, exquisitely beautiful in its last sleep, surrounded by a wealth of blonde hair, and wearing an expression of affectionate tenderness. The remembrance of it imparted a gentler tone to his voice for the remainder of his life.

Alas ! they had not known how well the water would carry the sound of their conversation. Every word as they uttered it had been distinctly heard by the occupants of a small flotilla following it at a short distance.

But few hours had elapsed ere the absence of the prisoners

was discovered in the tower. Fitz-David at once fell in with Fergus' suggestion that their flight was probably for the second time being attempted by water. The chase was speedily urged forward, all engaged in it being nerved to unwonted effort by the hope of earning distinction through the capture of the rebel ringleaders. The pursuing boats had been carried on men's shoulders along the short and shallow channel to the north of the island, and had thus been enabled speedily to overtake the fugitives.

Olrud carried the news of his companion's fate to the Scattery Isles. There he, Maidoc, and Ita dwelt for many years, carrying on their ministrations amongst the mountains of Connaught. As they kept aloof from politics, they were too obscure to attract notice from the invader.

Erc, as well as Grainné's four boys, became priests. Amada's family, therefore, soon died out. It was a pity, for they were a fine stock.

And a cloud settled over the green island, such a cloud as Egypt knew not in the days of Moses. So thick and heavy hath become the mental vision of those born under it, that in the very spots where Columba and his contemporaries had their spiritual senses quickened to see every oak-leaf crowded full with heaven's angels, the natives, forgetting their own ancient and beautiful melodies, have now no music save of an earthly kind wherewith to entertain the passing stranger, treating verily of no higher theme than of their love for the little " cruiskeen lawn."

And no longer is wisdom the one commodity which Irishmen have to offer in the markets of Europe.*

The glory of Ardmore is gone for ever. Yet do men say that the sweet tones of its silver bell may yet be heard, sounding forth a wail from the depths of the rivulet which floweth at the base of its tower.

* Appendix.

APPENDIX.

1. "It was by him (Patrick) that bishops, priests, and persons of every dignity were ordained; seven hundred bishops, and three hundred priests was their number."—*Annals of Four Masters*, A.D. 493.

Nennius, who lived in the ninth century, says, " Sanctus Patricius . . . ordinavit episcopos tricentos sexaginta quinque aut eo amplius in quibus Spiritus Dei erat."

It is evident that such bishops could not have ruled over dioceses, and it is therefore probable that in Ireland, as in Brittany, the title was given to every ordained pastor.

St. Bernard mentions this fact in his Life of Malachy O'Morgair, first Roman Catholic Abbot of Armagh.   He says:

" Num (quod inauditum est ab ipso Christianitatis initio) sine ordine, sine ratione mutabantur et multiplicabantur episcopi, pro libiter metropolitani; ita ut unus episcopatus uno non esset contentus, sed singulae pene ecclesiae singulos habent episcopos."—*Vita S. Malachiae*, caput x.   Migne clxxxii.

That this was so in still earlier times is established by Phil. i. 1., as well as by the oft-quoted testimony of Jerome:

" Sed nostram esse sententiam, episcopum et presbyterum unum esse, et aliud aetatis, aliud esse nomen officii. . . . Sed quia eosdem episcopos illo tempore quos et presbyteros appellabant, propterea de episcopis quasi de presbyteris est locutus."—*Commentary on Titus*.

Chapter I.

1. *Who preferred to live in holy wedlock* (page 2).—For the non-existence of celibacy in Culdee monasteries we have the confession of

a Roman Catholic writer, Ozanam. Whilst contending for the theory of the Western Church having been always submissive to the Holy See, he says :

"Un seul point reste acquis à nos adversaires, cest que l'Eglise Romaine toléra quelque temps chez les Bretons et les Irlandais l'ordination des hommes mariés, comme elle la tolère encore chez les catholiques des rites orientaux."—*La Predication des Irlandais Note.*

In a synod held in Ireland A.D. 456, there is the following remarkable canon :

" Quicunque clericus ab hostiario usque ad sacerdotem sine tunica visus fuit . . . et uxor ejus si non velato capita ambulaverit, pariter a laicis contemnentur, et ab ecclesia separentur."—Wilkins' *Concilia*, vol. i. p. 2 ; *Synodus Patricii Auxilii et Isserini.*

The Senchus Mòr, or great Book of Irish laws, compiled in the fifth century, makes a special mention of married priests.

The Northumbrian priests had a law :

" Si presbyter ' cwenan' ('wife,' *Johnson* original of queen) deserat et aliam accipiat, anathema sit."—Wilkins' *Concilia*, vol. i. p. 219, can. 85.

We have, moreover, the testimony of the Romanist prelate Giraldus Cambrensis, who visited Ireland about the time of the conquest :

" Verumtamen viri qui ecclesiastica gaudent immunitate, et quos viros ecclesiasticos vocant, quanquam laici et uxorati, comis quoque perlongis trans humerum diffusis, solum armis renuntiantes, in signum protectionis pontificale impositioue amplas in capite coronas habent."—*Top. Hib.* dis. iii. cap. xxvi.

He thus speaks of their character :

" Est autem terrae istius clerus satis religione commendabilis." —Cap. xxvii.

2. *It was still independent of foreign control* (page 6.)—Pope Alex. III., in a letter addressed to Henry II. dated September, 1172, speaks of the Holy See's relation to Ireland in these terms, " ubi nullum jus habet."

That the ecclesiastics of England had no inter-communion with those of Ireland previous to the conquest, we learn from Giraldus Cambrensis. Writing to Stephen Langton, Archbishop of Canterbury, he says :

"Item et juxta apostoli doctrina nemini cito manum imponat. . . . Et sic episcoporum Walliae, Hiberniae, et Scotiae, qui reprobatos in Anglia et pro indignis habitos et ubique recusatos, passim et absque delectu, non autem absque delicto, cunctos ordinare praesumunt, opprobrium vitet."—*De Jure et Statu*, dist. xii.

Giraldus was born A.D. 1147. Died A.D. 1220.

His words are in keeping with the decree of the Council of Celcyth A.D. 816.

Cap. v. "Quinto interdictum est: ut nullus permittatur de genere Scotorum in alicujus diocesi sacrum sibi ministerium usurpare, neque ei consentire liceat ex sacro ordine aliquod attingere, vel ab eis accipere in baptismo aut in celebratione missarum, vel etiam eucharistiam populo praebere, quia incertum est nobis, unde, et an ab aliquo ordinentur. Scimus quomodo in canonibus praecipitur, ut nullus episcoporum (vel) presbyterorum invadere tentaverit alius parochiam, nisi cum consensu proprii episcopi. Tanto magis respuendum est ab alienis nationibus sacra ministeria percipere, cum quibus nullus ordo metropolitanis, nec honor aliquis habeatur." —Wilkins' *Concilia*, vol. i. p. 170.

CHAPTER II.

1. Page 11., Four Masters. A.D. 1151.

2. *The Celtic Church not having yet discovered that vows of perpetual celibacy were pleasing to the Creator* (page 20).—There were doubtless monastic institutions in Ireland from the days of Patrick and Bridget; yet the constitution of these must have differed considerably from the continental models. The Senchus Mòr has a special decree for "a young nun who has not renounced her veil."

St. Bernard also, writing to Malachy O'Morgair, says:

"Et quoniam multa adhuc opus est vigilantia, tanquam in loco novo, et *in terra tam insueta, imo et inesperta monasticae religionis,* obsecramus in Domino, ne retrahatis manum vestram, sed quod bene incœpistis, optime perficiatis."—Migne clxxxii., epistola 357.

CHAPTER V.

A heritage which his family had enjoyed for fifteen generations (page 43).—A full account of the succession to the abbacy of Armagh will be found in King's Memoir Introductory to the Early

History of the Primacy of Armagh. The state of affairs there roused St. Bernard's indignation. He informs us in his Life of St. Malachy:

"Contigit infirmari archiepiscopum Celsum, et ipse est qui Malachiam in diaconem, presbyterum, episcopumque ordinavit, et cognoscens quia moreretur, fecit quasi testamentum, quatenus Malachias deberet succedere sibi . . . . Verum mos pessimus inoleverat quorumdam diabolica ambitione potentum sedem sanctum obtentum iri haereditaria successione. Nec enim patiebantur episcopari; nisi qui essent de tribu et familia sua. Nec parum processerat exsecranda successio, decursis jam in hac malitia quasi generationibus quindecim. Denique jam veto extiterant ante Celsum, viri uxorati, et absque ordinibus, literati tamen."—*Vita S. Malachiae, S. Bernardi Abbatis Clarae Vallensis*, caput x. Migne clxxxii.

By "absque ordinibus," St. Bernard probably meant without consecration from his Church. We are surprised, however, to find that Malachy, though a Roman Catholic bishop, should have been ordained by Celsus, a married man. The wife of Celsus appeared to Malachy in a vision. For, says St. Barnard, *Vita.* cap. x. :

" Nempe jam aegrotante Celso, apparuit Malachiae . . . . mulier procerae staturae et reverendi vultus. Percontati quaenam esset, responsum est esse uxorem Celsi."

That the Irish did not relish Malachy's installation is evident from the bloodshed to which it gave rise.

Chapter VII.

1. *And had not Palladius come?* (Page 59.)

" Palladius was sent by Pope Celestine, with a gospel *for Patrick* to preach to the Irish."—*Leabhar Brac.*

This statement is confirmed by Saint Prosper of Aquitaine, who lived from A.D. 387 till A.D. 455. He says :

" Ad Scotos iu Christum credentes ordinatus à Papa Caelestino Palladius primus Episcopus mittitur."—*Chronicon*, A.D. 431.

Dr. Killen has shown, by a comparison of dates, that Patrick had been about a quarter of a century in Ireland before the arrival of Palladius. The subject is so important that I make no apology for quoting his words :

" Marcus, an Irish bishop who flourished in the beginning of the ninth century, informs us that Patrick came to Ireland A.D. 405; and Nennius, a Briton who lived about the same period, repeats this statement. Other circumstances lead us to infer that this is the true date of the commencement of his mission. According to the best authorities, he was born about A.D. 378; and a late most acute and learned Roman Catholic historian (Dr. Lanigan) has adduced good evidence to prove that he died A.D. 465."

"Traditions of the highest antiquity attest that he spent sixty years in Ireland (as the Hymn of Fiech)."—*Old Catholic Church,* p. 311.

St. Patrick is said to have died on a Wednesday, the 17th of March.

Lanigan, after assigning other arguments, says: "I find it clearly laid down in a copy of the Annals of Inisfallen. This copy assigns the death of St. Patrick to the 432nd year after the passion of our Lord—a date which exactly corresponds to A.D. 465. And the 17th of March fell in that year on a Wednesday."—*Ecclesiastical History,* vol. i. p. 362.

"Benignus, Patrick's successor in the see of Armagh, died A.D. 468."—*Ecclesiastical History,* vol. i. p. 357.

Pope Celestine died on the 6th of April, A.D. 432, before he could have heard of the non-success of Palladius's mission. It is therefore impossible for us to give credit to the statement that he afterwards sent Patrick to Ireland.

Palladius, disappointed with his reception in Ireland, sailed to Scotland. We have notices of his doings there in Fordun's Chronicle. He seems there to have met with Christians who, though more amenable to his teachings, were yet of the same type as those of Ireland. For, says John of Fordun:

"Anno Domini ccccxxx. papa Celestinus primum episcopum in Scocia misit sanctum Palladium, de quo Scotis convenit, quia suam, id est, Scotorum gentem longe quamvis in Christum ante credentem, fidem orthodoxam verbo sollicite perdocuit, et exemplo festa simul et memoriae ecclesiasticae diligenter celebrare. Ante cujus adventum habebant Scoti fidei doctores, ac sacramentorum ministratores, presbiteros solum modo vel monachos, ritum sequentes ecclesiae primitivae." The MS. in Trin. Coll., Camb., omits "vel monachos"—magna cleri.—*Scoto-chronicon Liber Tertius,* cap. viii. (*Skene's Edition.*)

2. *By the overpowering influence of the Saxon Queen Margaret.* (page 60).—The wife of Malcolm Canmore, sister of Edgar Atheling, did much, in her zeal for religion, to establish the power of the Roman See in Scotland. It is a significant fact that no Episcopal See in Scotland can date its foundation earlier than the twelfth century, nor was any at first occupied by a native Scot. That the Christians, previous to this time, followed other usages than that of Rome, we may gather from more than one ancient chronicle. Thus Turgot, in his Life of Queen Margaret, says :

" Cum enim contra rectae fidei regulam et sanctam universalis ecclesiae consuetudinem, multa in gente illa fieri perspexisset, crebra Concilia statuit."—Pinkerton, *Vitae Antiquae Sanctorum*, p. 339.

" Praeterea in aliquibus locis Scottorum quidam fuerant, qui contra totius Ecclesiae consuetudinem, nescio quo ritu barbaro, Missas celebrare consueverant." — *Idem*, p. 341. The word " Missa " was originally applied to any religious service.

" Multo quoque alia, quae contra fidei regulam et ecclesiasticarum observationum instituta inoleverant, ipsa in eodem Concilio damnare, et de Regni sui finibus curavit proturbare."

The Life of Queen Margaret, attributed to St. Adelredue, also says :

" Cum autem in gente illa Scotorum, contra universalis Ecclesiae sanctam consuetudinem multa illicita fieri videret, multa adhibuit consilia."—Pinkerton's *Collection*, p. 376.

" Multa quoque alia contra morem Ecclesiae inoleverant, quae in eodem Concilio damnans de regni finibus extirpavit." —*Idem*, p. 378.

Jocelin, a monk of Furness, in Lancashire, writing to Jocelin, who was Bishop of Glasgow from A.D. 1174 to A.D. 1179, concerning the Life of St. Kentigern, which he was about to write, says :

" Circuivi enim per plateas et vicos civitatis, juxta mandatum vestrum, querens vitam Sancti Kentigerni descriptam, quem diligat anima vestra, cujus cathedrae filiorum adoptione. . . Quesivi igitur diligenter, vitam, si forte inveniretur, quem majori auctoritati, et evidentiori veritate, sulciri (fulciri ?) et stilo certiori videretur exarari, quam illa, quem vestra frequentat ecclesia ; quia illam, est pluribus videtur, tractata per totum declarat inculta oratio, obnubilat stilus incompositus, et quod prae his omnibus sane sapiens magis abhorret, in ipso narrationis frontispitio quoddam *sanae doctrinae, et catholicae fidei adversum evidentius apparet.*"

Kentigern lived about A.D. 580.

Jocelin about A.D. 1180.

CHAPTER VIII.

The University of Lismore (page 62).—" Ireland," says O'Halloran, " was now the only country in Europe in which arts and sciences blazed in their full lustre ; it became not only the common asylum of learned men from all parts, but such as chose to excel in letters flocked here from distant countries to become the pupils of our regents and doctors." In the Life of Sulgentius the Briton we are told :

> " Exemplo patrum commotus amore legendi
> Ivit ad Hibernos, sophiâ mirabilè claros."

The following lines are taken from the Life of St. Cataldus, first Bishop of Tarentum in Italy. They are written by Bonaventura Moronus, a Tarentine born :

> " Undique conveniunt proceres, quos dolce trahebat
> Discendi studium. . . .
> . . . Celeres vastissima Rheni
> Jam vada Teutonici, jam deservère Sicambri ;
> Mittit ab extremo gelidos aquilone Boiemos
> Albi et Averni coëunt, Batavique frequentes
> Et quicunque colunt altâ sub rupe Gebenas ;
> Non omnes prospectat Arar Rhodanique fluenta
> Helvetios : multos desiderat ultima Thule.
> Certatim hi properant diverso tramite, ad urbem
> Lismoriam, juvenis primos ubi transigit annos."

When a man of learning in Britain, or on the Continent, was missing, the common adage was, " Amandatus est ad disciplinam in Hiberniâ."

CHAPTER X.

Confession was not practised in the ancient Church of Ireland (page 98).—For this we have the testimony of St. Bernard:

"Deinde usum saluberrimum Confessionis, sacramentum Confirmationis . . . quae omnia aut ignorabant, aut negligebant, Malachias de novo instituat."—*Vita S. Malachiae*, cap. iii. Migne, clxxxii.

He thus describes the Irish :

"Cristiani nomine, re pagani. Non decimus, non primitias dare, non legitima more (Romauo ?), inire conjugia ; non facere confessiones ; poenitentias nec qui peteret ; nec qui daret, penitus invenire."—*Idem*, cap. viii.

CHAPTER XI.

The Book of Armagh (page 107).—For a description of this singular compilation, and of the influence which it exercised on the Irish Church, we would refer the reader to the pages of Dr. Killen, *Ecclesiastical History*, vol. i. p. 115.

CHAPTER XII.

1. *The decree of King Nectan* (page 121).—This fact is recorded in the Annals of Ulster. It occurred in A.D. 716. In the same year the priest Egbert went from Northumbria to Iona and persuaded some of the monks to submit to Roman usages. As, however, "the family" are said to have been banished, we may infer that the majority were thus punished for their adherence to the traditions they had received from Columba.

2. *A sovereign, himself the descendant of pious bishops* (page 121).—Malcolm Canmore, whose first name signifies servant of Colmkill, or Columba, was the son of the Duncan killed by Macbeth. Duncan's father was Cronan, Abbot of Dunkeld, who had for wife the daughter of Malcolm II. (Burton's *History of Scotland*.)

3. *In England the disastrous change has gone further* (page 122). —Some writers assert that the only differences between the Roman Catholic Church, as represented by Augustine, and that of the Scoto-Britons, as represented by Dinooth and Aidan, were those of the tonsure and the time of keeping Easter. Enough, however, may be gathered from the pages of Bede to show how superficial is this view. For he states :

"Et *alia plurima* unitati ecclesiasticae contraria faciebant." —*Hist. Eccl.* lib. ii. cap. 2.

Dicebat autem" (Augustine to the monks of Bangor), "eis,

Quia *in multis* quidem nostrae consuetudini imo universalis ecclesiae, contraria geritis."—*Idem.*

A.D. 661. " Defuncto autem Finano, qui post illum (Ædanum) fuit, cum Colmanus in episcopatum succederet, et ipse missus a Scottia, gravior de observatione paschae, *et de aliis* ecclesiasticae vitae disciplinis controversia nata est."

A.D. 664. " Venerat eo tempore Agilberctus, etc. ad provinciam Nordanhymbrarum. . . . . Mota ergo ibi quaestione de pascha, vel tonsura, vel aliis rebus ecclesiasticis," etc.

The root of the question was evidently the supremacy of the Roman bishop. Had the Britons admitted this, they could not have held out so long on the question of Easter. Bede relates that Augustine experienced a determined opposition :

" Longa disputatione habitu, neque precibus, neque hortamentis, neque increpationibus Augustini ac sociorum ejus assensum praebere voluissent, sed suas potius traditiones universis, quae per orbem sibi in Christo concordant, ecclesiis praeferrent."

" At illi nil horum se facturos, neque illum pro archiepiscopo habituros esse respondebant."

Giraldus Cambrensis bears the same testimony :

" Audiens Augustinus in occidentali insulae parte Christianos esse, accedens ad fines illos, convocatis septem episcopis Britonum, cum de termino Paschali, quem non more ecclesiae Romanae colere videbantur, et *aliis quibusdam* corrigendis, diutius disputatum esset. . . . Si ergo Augustini renuerunt esse socii, multo minus sibi vel successoribus suis vellent esse subjecti." — *De Invectionibus*, lib. ii. cap. 1.

We have also the reply of Dinooth, Abbot of Bangor, to Augustine :

" Be it known without doubt unto you, that we all are and every one of us obedient and subject to the Church of God, and to the Pope of Rome, and to every true Christian, and godly to love every one in his degree in perfect charity, and to help every one of them in word and deed to be the children of God ; and other obedience than this I do not know due to him, whom you name to be Pope, nor to be the father of fathers."—Wilkins' *Concilia*, vol. i. p. 26.

4. *The married bishops* (page 122).—The native clergy of Brittany and of Wales were in the twelfth century heads of families. This grieved the soul of Giraldus Cambrensis. He says :

"Successiones in clero, radicatis olim in Armorica Galliae, Britannica, necdum eradicatis, similiter scribit in quadam epistola sua Hildebertus Cenomannensis episcopus, dicens se concilio interfuisse cum clero Britanniae ob has enormitates gentis illius extirpandas convocato. Ex quibus constare potest utrumque vitium toti huic genti Britannicae tam transmarinae scilicet quam cismarinae, ab antiquo commune fuisse."—Gir. Camb., *De Jure et Statu Menevensis Ecclesiae*, dis. i.

"Successio quoque, et post patres, filii ecclesias obtinent, non elective, hereditate possidentes, et polluentes sanctuarium Dei."—Gir. Camb., *Descriptio Kambriae*, lib. ii. cap. 6.

5. *No Swedish or Danish priest doubted his own right to marry before the Council of Rheims, in* A.D. *1120 (page 124).*

These facts are recorded by Munter, Bishop of Zealand, in his *Zeitschrift für die historische Theologie.*

6. *Milan and Florence have seen their altars deserted for want of ministers (page 124).*

This is recorded by Milman.

7. *The rule of our Columbanus, travestied as it hath been (page 126).*

Columbanus was an Irish missionary to the continent of Europe, contemporary with Columba of Iona. He was the founder of Luxueil, Bobbio, and other monasteries.

He instituted a monastic rule which at length came into conflict with that of Benedict. This rule is erroneously supposed to have been very harsh.

But in judging of anything connected with the ancient British Church, we must bear in mind that all notices of it have come down to us through the hands of its enemies; most of the proofs of its existence being derived from their incidental statements. The argument on behalf of Columbanus' rule is very ably stated by Ebrard. There are, in fact, two versions of it. The first breathes a spirit of Christian mildness and fatherly exhortation; the second enjoins the application of the scourge *ad nauseam*. A comparison between the two raises doubts as to whether they are the work of the same hand.

The manuscripts of this rule, which Ebrard supposes to be genuine, contain only the mild chapters. They are the two oldest ones, those of the cod. St. Gallensis, and cod. Bobiensis; Bobbio having been founded by Columbanus, and St. Gallen by his disciple, Gallus. The spurious ones are those of a Benedictine abbey in Ochsenshausen, and of a Benedictine cloister in Augsburg.

A Liber Poenitentialis was found at Bobbio with the name of Columbanus attached to it. But a similar one exists at St. Gallen, and professes itself to be the work of "Scti Cumeani Abbatis in Scotia."

Ebrard supposes that the two spurious rules and the Liber Poenitentialis were the work of Benedictine monks, who tried to make them more acceptable to their brethren by prefixing to them the name of Columbanus. Cummean himself was an apostate from the Irish Church to that of Rome.

Columbanus was the writer of a remarkable letter to Pope Boniface IV. He fully acknowledged that the Bishop of Rome had a right to take precedence of all other bishops, save him of Jerusalem, for he says :

"Roma orbis terrarum caput est ecclesiarum, salva loci dominicae resurrectionis singulari prerogativa."

But he was very far from conceding to him infallibility when he wrote:

"Jam vestra culpa est, si vos deviastis de vera fiducia, et primam fidem irritam fecistis (1 Tim. v. 12), merito vestri juniores vobis resistunt et merito vobis non communicant."

For the Irish he claimed that,

"Nos . . . toti Heberi, ultimi habitatores mundi, nihil extra evangelicam et apostolicam doctrinam recipientis."

CHAPTER XIII.

1. *The Bishop of Rome hath made a gift of the whole island to the English king* (page 131).

Some writers have tried to throw doubts on the genuineness of Adrian's Bull. It is not in the *Bullarium Romanum*, the editors of which, suggests Dr. Lanigan, "were ashamed of it." But it is confirmed in a letter of Pope Alexander III. to King Henry II. in A.D. 1172. And in the *Bullarium Romanum* there is a Brief of Pope John XXII. to King Edward II., which refers to it. Pope John says :

"Quod cum felicis recordationis Adrianus praedecessor noster, sub certis modo et forma distinctis apertius in apostolicis literis inde factis, clarae memoriae Henrico regi Angliae, progenitori tno, dominium Hiberniae concessisset, ipse rex ac successores ipsius, reges Angliae."—Wilkins' *Concilia*, vol. ii. p. 491.

"There is no doubt of the authenticity of this document," says the Roman Catholic historian, Miss Cusack. (*Students' Manual of Irish History*, p. 170.)

The text of it will be found in Rymer's *Faedera*, tom. i.

The object which the Pope had in granting it is clearly enough stated. It was "pro dilatandis Ecclesiae terminis . . . insulam illam ingrediaris."

2. *Queen Devorgilla* (page 140).—Devorgilla, wife of Tiernan O'Rourke, Lord of Breffny, eloped with the infamous Dermod Mac Murrough, King of Leinster. She was compelled by Turlough O'Connor to return to her family, and Dermod, unable to hold his own against the host of enemies which this deed had raised against him, fled to seek help from the English king.

CHAPTER XIV.

Nor was there danger, even in that rude age, for a lovely girl (page 141).—This will not seem surprising to those who reflect that in the preceding century a young lady performed the exploit immortalised by Moore in the song beginning "Rich and Rare:"

> " On she went, and her maiden smile
>   In safety lighted her round the green isle;
> And blest for ever was she who relied
>   Upon Erin's honour and Erin's pride."

CHAPTER XV.

The original of this will be found in Ussher's Works: *Religion Professed by the Ancient Irish*, chap. x. (page 153).

CHAPTER XXI.

That a simple presbyter should have rule over bishops (page 215). Iona and Durrow set the example in this. So Bede tells us :

" Ex quo utroque monasterio (Iona and Durrow) plurima exinde

monasteria per discipulos ejus (Columbae) et in Brittania et in
Hibernia propagata sunt. Habere autem solet ipsa insula recto-
rem semper abbatem presbyterum, cujus juri et omnis provincia et
ipsi etiam episcopi, ordine inusitato, debeant esse subjecti, juxta
exemplum primi doctoris illius, qui non episcopus, sed presbyter,
exstitit et monachus."

CHAPTER XXIII.

1. *As Sedulius and Duns Scotus have shown* (page 239).—Two
distinguished Irishmen bore the name of Sedulius—one, a poet of
the fifth century; the other, supposed to have been Abbot of Kildare
in the ninth. Both express views on the Eucharist which are in
agreement with those of Calvin. The latter is the author of a commentary on St. Paul's epistles, which, if translated into English,
might be mistaken for the work of some Low Church divine. We
give his explanation of 1 Cor. xi. 24 :

"Hoc facite in meam commemorationem. Suam memoriam
nobis reliquit, quemadmodum si quis peregre profisciens, aliquod
pignus ei quem diligit derelinquat, ut quotiescunque illud viderit,
possit ejus beneficia et amicitiam recordari, quoniam ille si perfecte
dilexit, sine ingenti desiderio et fletu illud non potest videre."
—*Scoti Sedulii.* Migne, ciii.

2. *The fire of Kildare* (page 241).—The Druidesses kept a fire
perpetually burning at Kildare. Like the unquenchable fire of
Athena on the Acropolis of Athens, and that of the Vestal Virgins at
Rome, it was supposed to have been kindled from Heaven. To the
Druidesses succeeded Bridget's nuns. Their fire was surrounded
by an osier hedge, which no male person might pass through. The
fire was extinguished by Henri, Archbishop of Dublin, early in the
thirteenth century. It was re-lighted, and continued to burn until
the suppression of monasteries at the Reformation.

CHAPTER XXV.

His queen the Amazon Crusader (page 268).—Eleanora, in her
own right Duchess of Aquitaine, was for fifteen years married to
Louis VII. of France. Having placed herself at the head of a troop
of Amazons, she accompanied her husband in the second crusade.
Her foolish conduct in presence of the Saracens brought ruin on

the whole expedition. Divorced on account of her intrigues, she was immediately espoused by Henry II. The reader of her story and of that of Rosamond in Miss Strickland's pages cannot fail to be of opinion that neither she nor Henry were morally free to unite in wedlock. The strangest part of her story is, however, the fact that some of her children by Henry were married to the children of Louis VII. by his second marriage. Henry, in his eagerness to secure the " great Provençal dower," trampled underfoot some of the holiest of social laws, and was more deserving of papal excommunication than of being entrusted with the task of reclaiming the Irish from their errors.

CHAPTER XXVI.

That the decision of Fothadh-na-Canoine might be rescinded (page 276).—The decree of Fothadh-na-Canoine in A.D. 804, by which Irish ecclesiastics were exempted from taking part in war. (*Annals of Four Masters.*)

CHAPTER XXX.

Every archbishop and bishop of the Romish persuasion bestowed on him a charter in the form of a letter with seal attached, confirming the kingdom of Ireland to him and to his heirs for ever (page 314).

"Et inde recepit ab unoquoque archiepiscopo et episcopo litteras suas in modum cartae extra sigillum pendentes, et confirmantes ei et haeredibus suum regnum Hiberniae, et testimonium perhibentes ipsos eum et haeredes suos sibi in reges et dominos constituisse in perpetuum."—BENEDICT OF PETERBOROUGH, *Gesta Regis Henrici Secundi*, p. 26. London, 1867.

CHAPTER XXXV.

1. *Besides ordaining that all offices of Divine service should be performed according to the ritual of the Church of England* (page 375).

"Rex . . . . totius cleri Hiberniae concilium apud Cassiliam convocavit. Ubi . . . . ecclesiae illius statum ad Anglicanae ecclesiae formam redigere modis omnibus elaborando." A. D. 1172. Gir. Camb., *Ex. Hib.*, lib. i. cap. 34.

2. *No longer is wisdom,* etc. (page 378).—We are indebted to a monk of St. Gall for the following story. " In the days of Charlemagne, when literature was almost forgotten, there came with some British merchants to the shores of France, two Scots of Ireland. They produced no merchandize for sale, but used to cry to the crowds in the market-place: ' If any man wants wisdom, let him come to us, for we have it to sell.' So often did they repeat this cry, that an account of it came to the ears of King Charles, who, desirous to attain wisdom, had the strangers brought in haste before him. When he asked the price of their wares, they replied that they asked for nought but accommodation, food, and raiment. Charles was filled with joy, and kept them beside himself." This led to the great monarch opening up communication with other Irish scholars. It is possible that he was encouraged by them in his opposition to the use of images in worship.